"This isn't writing. It is magic. . . . Updike's asperities on age reflect back on himself, but not in the way we might expect. At seventy-six, he still wrings more from a sentence than almost anyone else. His sorcery is startlingly fresh, page upon page."

—*The New York Times Book Review*

"If wit is a form of witchcraft, igniting sparks from airy nothing-ness, concocting a peppery brew of words, then John Updike's powers are undiminished. . . . In wickedly glinting sentences, Updike explores the distinctly unmagical humiliations of ad-vancing age, and the prickly temptations of sin."

—*O: The Oprah Magazine*

"*The Widows of Eastwick* might just be [Updike's] best novel since 1990's Pulitzer Prize–winning *Rabbit at Rest.*"

—*The Kansas City Star*

"There's no one quite like John Updike for a trip to New En-gland. History, theology, period-detailed houses and frequent sex whiz by in a blur of inimitable writing. . . . As with New England autumns, we witness a maturing of these women's natures—a last, hot-red, end-of-season change as rendered by this literary sorcerer." —*Town & Country*

"Its seamless blending of dexterously plotted narrative with pen-etrating characterizations . . . evoke with nearly Tolstoyan poignancy the weary, resigned clairvoyance of old age."

—*Kirkus Reviews*

"*The Widows of Eastwick* is by turns funny, philosophical, sus-penseful, and sad. Updike remains America's greatest writer, invoking his distinctive brand of magical realism in an elegantly written, occasionally crabby, often moving meditation on orig-inal sin, aging, and atonement. . . . [He] provides in *Widows* a penetrating and poignant portrait of the domestic lives of women, married and single, so many of whom feel disempow-ered or warped." —*The Jerusalem Post*

Also by John Updike

POEMS

The Carpentered Hen (1958) · Telephone Poles (1963) · Midpoint
(1969) · Tossing and Turning (1977) · Facing Nature (1985) · Collected
Poems 1953–1993 (1993) · Americana (2001)

NOVELS

The Poorhouse Fair (1959) · Rabbit, Run (1960) · The Centaur (1963) · Of
the Farm (1965) · Couples (1968) · Rabbit Redux (1971) · A Month of Sundays (1975) · Marry Me (1976) · The Coup (1978) · Rabbit Is Rich
(1981) · The Witches of Eastwick (1984) · Roger's Version (1986) · S.
(1988) · Rabbit at Rest (1990) · Memories of the Ford Administration
(1992) · Brazil (1994) · In the Beauty of the Lilies (1996) · Toward the End
of Time (1997) · Gertrude and Claudius (2000) · Seek My Face
(2002) · Villages (2004) · Terrorist (2006)

SHORT STORIES

The Same Door (1959) · Pigeon Feathers (1962) · Olinger Stories (a
selection, 1964) · The Music School (1966) · Bech: A Book (1970) · Museums and Women (1972) · Problems and Other Stories (1979) · Too Far to Go
(a selection, 1979) · Bech Is Back (1982) · Trust Me (1987) · The Afterlife
(1994) · Bech at Bay (1998) · Licks of Love (2000) · The Complete Henry
Bech (2001) · The Early Stories: 1953–1975 (2003)

ESSAYS AND CRITICISM

Assorted Prose (1965) · Picked-Up Pieces (1975) · Hugging the Shore
(1983) · Just Looking (1989) · Odd Jobs (1991) · Golf Dreams: Writings
on Golf (1996) · More Matter (1999) · Still Looking (2005) · Due Consid-
erations (2007)

PLAY

Buchanan Dying (1974)

MEMOIRS

Self-Consciousness (1989)

CHILDREN'S BOOKS

The Magic Flute (1962) · The Ring (1964) · A Child's Calendar
(1965) · Bottom's Dream (1969) · A Helpful Alphabet of Friendly Objects
(1996)

THE WIDOWS
OF EASTWICK

John Updike

THE WIDOWS
OF EASTWICK

Ballantine Books

NEW YORK

2009 Ballantine Books Trade Paperback Edition

Copyright © 2008 by John Updike

Published in the United States by Ballantine Books,
an imprint of The Random House Publishing Group,
a division of Random House, Inc., New York.

BALLANTINE and colophon are registered
trademarks of Random House, Inc.

Originally published in hardcover in the
United States by Alfred A. Knopf,
a division of Random House, Inc., in 2008.

LIBRARY OF CONGRESS CATALOGING-IN-PUBLICATION DATA
Updike, John.
The widows of Eastwick / by John Updike.
p. cm.
A sequel to: The witches of Eastwick.
ISBN 978-0-345-50697-9
1. Widows—Fiction. 2. Witches—Fiction. 3. Women—
Rhode Island—Fiction. 4. Rhode Island—Fiction.
I. Title.
PS3571.P4W48 1996
813'.54—dc22   2008018513

Printed in the United States of America
www.ballantinebooks.com

2 4 6 8 9 7 5 3 1

And then (they say) no Spirit can walke abroad,
The nights are wholsome, then no Planets strike,
No Faiery talkes, nor Witch hath power to Charme:
So hallow'd, and so gracious is the time.

—*Hamlet*, ACT I, SCENE I

Chapters

i.   The Coven Reconstituted   3

ii. Maleficia Revisited   101

iii. Guilt Assuaged   207

THE WIDOWS
OF EASTWICK

i. *The Coven Reconstituted*

THOSE OF US acquainted with their sordid and scandalous story were not surprised to hear, by way of rumors from the various localities where the sorceresses had settled after fleeing our pleasant town of Eastwick, Rhode Island, that the husbands whom the three Godforsaken women had by their dark arts concocted for themselves did not prove durable. Wicked methods make weak products. Satan counterfeits Creation, yes, but with inferior goods.

Alexandra, the oldest in age, the broadest in body, and the nearest in character to normal, generous-spirited humanity, was the first to become a widow. Her instinct, as with so many a wife suddenly liberated into solitude, was to travel — as if the world at large, by way of flimsy boarding cards and tedious airport delays and the faint but undeniable risk of flight in a time of rising fuel costs, airline bankruptcy, suicidal terrorists, and accumulating metal fatigue, could be compelled to yield the fruitful aggravation of having a mate. Jim Farlander, the husband she had conjured for herself from a hollowed pumpkin, a cowboy hat, and a pinch of Western soil scraped from inside the back fender of a pickup truck with Colorado plates that she had seen parked, looking eerily out of place, on Oak Street in the early 1970s, had, as their marriage settled and hardened, proved difficult to budge from his ceramics studio and little-frequented pottery shop on a side street in Taos, New Mexico.

Jim's idea of a trip had been the hour's drive south to Santa Fe; his idea of a holiday was spending a day in one of the Indian reservations—Navajo, Zuni, Apache, Acoma, Isleta Pueblo—spying out what the Native American potters were offering in the reservation souvenir shops, and hoping to pick up cheap in some dusty Indian Bureau commissary an authentic old black-and-white geometric Pueblo jar or a red-on-buff Hohokam storage jar, with its spiral-and-maze pattern, which he could peddle for a small fortune to a newly endowed museum in one of the burgeoning resort cities of the Southwest. Jim liked where he was, and Alexandra liked that in him, since she as his wife was part of where he was. She liked his lean build (a flat stomach to the day he died, and never performed a sit-up in his life) and the saddle smell of his sweat and the scent of clay that clung, like a sepia aura, to his strong and knowing hands. They had met, on the natural plane, when she, for some time divorced, had taken a course at the Rhode Island School of Design, where he had been enlisted as a fill-in instructor. The four stepchildren—Marcy, Ben, Linda, Eric—that she saddled him with couldn't have asked for a calmer, more soothingly taciturn father-substitute. He was easier for her children—half out of the nest in any case, Marcy being all of eighteen—to relate to than their own father, Oswald Spofford, a small manufacturer of kitchen fixtures from Norwich, Connecticut. Poor Ozzie had become so earnestly involved in Little League baseball and company bowling that no one, not even his children, could take him seriously.

People had taken Jim Farlander seriously, women and children especially, giving him back his own poised silence. His level gray eyes had the glint of a gun from within the shade of his wide-brimmed hat, its crown darkened where his thumb and fingers pinched it. When he was at the pottery wheel he tied a faded blue bandana around his head to keep his long hair—gray but still streaked with its original sun-bleached auburn and gathered behind into an eight-inch ponytail—out of the clay, wet and spinning on the foot-powered wheel. A fall in his teens from a horse had left him with a limp, and the wheel, which he refused to electrify, limped with him, while out of the spinning his masculine hands shaped blobs upward into graceful vessels with slender waists and swelling bottoms.

It was in bed she first felt his death coming. His erections began to wilt just as she might have come if he had held on; instead, in his body upon hers, there was a palpable loosening in the knit of his sinews. There had been a challenging nicety in the taut way Jim dressed himself—pointy vanilla colored boots, butt-hugging jeans with rivet-bordered pockets, and crisp checked shirts double-buttoned at the cuff. Once a dandy of his type, he began to wear the same shirt two and even three days in a row. His jaw showed shadows of white whisker underneath, from careless shaving or troubled eyesight. When the ominous blood counts began to arrive from the hospital, and the shadows in the X-rays were visible to even her untrained eyes, he greeted the news with stoic lassitude; Alexandra had to fight to get him out of his crusty work clothes into something decent. They had joined the legion of elderly couples who fill hospital waiting rooms, as quiet with nervousness as parents and children before a recital. She felt the other couples idly pawing at them with their eyes, trying to guess which of the two was the sick one, the doomed one; she didn't want it to be obvious. She wanted to present Jim as a mother presents a child going to school for the first time: as a credit to her. They had lived, these thirty-plus years since she had lived in Eastwick, by their own rules, up in Taos; there the free spirits of the Lawrences and Mabel Dodge Luhan still cast a sheltering cachet over the remnant tribe of artistic wannabes, a hard-drinking, New Age–superstitious, artsy-craftsy crowd who aimed their artifacts, in their shop-window displays, more and more plaintively at scrimping, low-brow tourists rather than the well-heeled local collectors of Southwestern art. Alexandra for a time had revived her manufacture of little ceramic "bubbies"—faceless, footless little female figures, pleasant to hold in the hand and roughly painted in clothes worn as close to the skin as tattoos—but Jim, jealous and dictatorial in his art as true artists are, had been less than gracious about sharing his kiln. In any case, the miniature women, their vulval cleft boldly dented into the clay with a toothpick or nail file held sideways, belonged to an uncomfortable prior period of her life, when she had practiced, with two other Rhode Island divorcées, a half-baked suburban variety of witchcraft.

Jim's illness drove her and Jim down from safe, arty Taos into the wider society, the valleys of the ailing, a vast herd moving like stampeded bison toward the killing cliff. The socialization forced upon her—interviews with doctors, most of them unsettlingly young; encounters with nurses, demanding merciful attentions the hospitalized patient was too manly and depressed to ask for himself; commiseration with others in her condition, soon-to-be widows and widowers she would have shunned on the street but now,

in these antiseptic hallways, embraced with shared tears—
prepared her for travel in the company of strangers.

She could not believe it—how totally Jim was gone, his
morning absence as vivid as a rooster's wake-up crow, his
evening non-appearance a refusal bound, she felt, to be can-
celled, any moment, by the scuffling sound of his boots
limping across the entry hall or the squeak, two rooms away,
of his potter's wheel. Three months after his death, she
signed up for a ten-day tour of the Canadian Rockies. Her
old, married, cosseted self, a bohemian snob proud of her
careless, mannish clothes and high-desert privacy, would
have sneered at the feigned camaraderie of an organized
group tour. She foresaw the daily duty to rise and gorge on
cafeteria-style hotel breakfasts en route to the day's marvel,
and the resisted but irresistible naps in the swaying bus in
clammy proximity to an alien body, usually that of another
plucky widow, overweight and remorselessly talkative. Then
there would be the sleepless hours, amid worrisome small
noises and mysterious tiny red lights, in a king-size bed built
for a couple. Hotel pillows were always too stuffed, too full,
and lifted her head too high, so she would wake, groggily
dumfounded to have slept at all, with a stiff neck. The pillow
next to hers would be undented. It would dawn on her that
she would never be one of a couple again.

But, born in Colorado, she thought it an amusing idea to
follow the Rockies north into another country, where a dra-
matic landscape did not flatter the rapacious vanity of the
United States. And Canada, she discovered, did have its
good points: airports not bribed to install television sets
pouring forth an inescapable babble, and voices whose
familiar North American accent was braced by a few leftover
Scots vowels, and a gray imperial gravity of public architecture. This national identity had been created by the sensible

spirit of business enterprise, linking the provinces like great beads on an iron railroad line, rather than by any evangelical preachment of a Manifest Destiny—manifest only to its Anglo perpetrators—that had hurled the agglutinated United States westwards and then outwards, across all the oceans, where its boy soldiers lost limbs and died. The daily death-tolls from Iraq were worth escaping.

On the other hand, Canadian hotel restaurants seemed to think Frank Sinatra and Nat "King" Cole were the latest thing in background music, and the giant cruise ships docked in Vancouver were headed off to dreary cold Alaska. Canada, its tundra and icefields and miles of forest pressing its population down tight against the forty-ninth parallel, had in self-defense embraced Green-ness, trying to make a pet of it, mining for tourist dollars the nostalgia and righteousness inherent in its cause. Bring Back Nature—who could object to that? But for Alexandra, totem poles and moose had a basic boringness. She felt, up here, trapped in an attic full of stuffed animals. Nature had been her ally in witchcraft, but still she distrusted it, as a conscienceless killer, spendthrift and blind.

After a day in Vancouver, and another in determinedly quaint Victoria, the tour—forty travellers, none of them young and eight of them Australian—boarded a sleeper train and were dragged northwards through the dark. They woke amid mountains dazzling with the yellow of turning aspens. The tour had reserved a viewing car for their party, and Alexandra, hesitantly entering, after a heavy breakfast fetched by lurching waiters in the dining car, was greeted with hesitant smiles from the already seated couples. She took one of the few seats left and was conscious of the vacancy at her side, as if of a monstrous wen throwing her face out of symmetry.

But, then, she could never have talked Jim into coming on such an adventure. He hated foreign countries, even the Virgin Islands, where, a few times early in their marriage, she had persuaded him to take her, as a break from the long Taos winter and the ski-season traffic jams along Route 522. They had arrived in St. Thomas, as it turned out, in the late afternoon, and were caught, in their rented Volkswagen Beetle, in the evening rush hour, Jim trying to drive for the first time in his life on the wrong side of the road. More unfortunately still, they were surrounded by black drivers who took a racist pleasure in tailgating them and in rebuking every sign of automotive uncertainty with prolonged, indignant honking. Though eventually they found the resort, at the end of a poorly marked road, Jim got sunburned the first day, having scorned her repeated offer of sunscreen, and then got deadly sick on some conch salad. Whenever, ever after, he felt bested in an exchange of accusations, he would remind her, in detail, of that week that almost—twenty-five years before he really died—killed him.

Now, in Canada, there was not a road or car in sight, just the tracks and tunnels ahead as the train bored upward through mountains splashed with quaking golden leaves. "There's Mount Robson!" a woman behind Alexandra excitedly told her husband.

An Australian across the aisle, in an attempt at friendliness, said to Alexandra, "Mount Robson ahead," as if she were deaf as well as alone.

From behind this speaker, another voice—not Australian, less peppy, with a tinge of the American South—explained to her, everybody around her suddenly solicitous, as if of a defective in their midst, "The tallest peak in the Canadian Rockies."

"Really? Already?" Alexandra asked, knowing she sounded

stupid and covering herself with "I mean, shouldn't they have saved it for later in the tour?"

Nobody laughed, perhaps not hearing, or understanding, her little joke. The train was taking a long curve, and the gleaming mountain-tip sank from view behind the aspens; the peak had been oddly regular, like a pyramid in a set of child's blocks, but white. "How high is it?" she asked aloud, determined to combat her sense of non-existence.

Again, she had struck a silencing note. "Nearly four thousand meters," an Australian voice volunteered.

She had trouble translating out of the metric system, and, borrowing a bit of her late husband's xenophobia, refused to try. The slightly Southern voice understood, and explained, "Nearly thirteen thousand feet, ma'am."

"My goodness!" Alexandra said, beginning to enjoy her own inanity. She turned her head to look at her informant. He was lanky, like Jim, and lean-faced, with deep creases and a mustache just long enough to droop. His costume, too—faded tight blue jeans and a long-sleeved red-checked shirt—reminded her of Jim. "*Thank* you," she said, with more warmth than she had strictly intended. Perhaps this man with his air of dignified sorrow was a widower. Or was waiting for some slow-moving wife to join him here in the viewing car.

"Mount Robson isn't on the tour," the wife behind Alexandra was saying in her ear, in a penetrating, slightly vexed voice. "It's in a separate national park from Jasper."

"I really haven't done my homework," Alexandra apologized, backwards, experiencing a flash of hatred—the old impatient, witchy, bug-zapping kind of hate she thought she had long outgrown. Why should this woman, common and shrewish from the sound of her voice, have a live husband, when she, Alexandra, did not, sitting here exposed on all sides to these well-meant interventions from strangers?

"That's my style, too," a male Australian reassured her. "Learn as you go. It's my wife reads the books ahead."

"And sees to the tickets and passports, you lazy sod," the wife said, in the humorous tone of a practiced complaint.

The train, smoother-running than American trains, on Canadian National Railway tracks welded and upheld by the government, continued to nose skyward. Mount Robson again appeared above the trees, its whiteness marked now by black striations—by snow-striped patches, faceted as if the peak had been carved to a point like a flint weapon. The hard cobalt of a picture-postcard sky pressed on these concave contours until the peak disappeared again behind the waves of yellow leaves. "It says here," the Australian wife loudly announced, holding a guidebook, "it was first climbed in 1913, by an Austrian bloke named Kain. K-A-I-N. It says the Canadian mountain men didn't like it when foreigners were the first to climb their mountains to the top. Got their ruddy noses out of joint."

Alexandra sighed and closed her lids, excusing herself from hearing any more. She wanted to relieve them all of having to pay her any further attention. Being a big woman, tall and somewhat broad, her full head of chestnut-brown hair still only half white, had given her a presence when she was younger but now that she was old and mateless made her conspicuous, an embarrassment to herself. *Kain, Cain,* she thought. The first man to do a truly wicked deed, worse even than eating the apple of knowledge. Slew his brother, Abel. Thirty years ago Alexandra had slain a sister witch: she and Sukie Rougemont and Jane Smart had killed little Jenny Gabriel, though the death certificate blamed metastasized malignancy of the ovaries. The curse of it was always there, inside Alexandra, even when she didn't close her eyes, a sour gnawing. As negligible as a worm in the earth during the daylight hours, at night in her dreams the curse grew large and threatened to eat her alive. Again and again her dreams returned her to that hectic period, when Darryl Van Horne had taken as wife not one of the three of them but a younger woman, fair and ivory-skinned, with innocent, ice-blue eyes—too damned innocent, the older witches had felt. Had Jenny been less innocent, had she been as corrupt as they were, they would have accepted her besting them as part of a game among equals, marrying a man who after all hadn't cared for women, it turned out, and was not even rich, as they had been led to believe. They had imagined him, conjured him out of their own needs.

In her dreams Alexandra often searched, in a thicket of brambles—swampy tufty earth yielding and treacherous beneath her cold feet—for something deadly, a tinfoil egg of death, whose discovery would reverse Jenny's death. She had never found it, though sometimes she dreamed of discovering a golf ball stained half-brown by Nature's chemicals, and sometimes a tiny skeleton, that of a human infant, dead of starvation and the cold. She woke then with a start, recalled to her children, remembering how casually she had treated them, neglected them, though all four were still alive, living far away, in four different states, with children of their own and middle-aged complaints. They were beyond any help or harm from her, far from whatever imperfect nurture she could extend to them. Her sins kept her awake. Jim used to be there, warm and long-limbed beside her, his tobacco-roughened breath rasping in the dark, his musty male smell tinting the square space of the bedroom, where moonlight blanched the rectangular window shades. The homey reality of him would anchor her senses after the fluid nonsensical terror of her dream, her younger self battered by guilt as if by water pouring into a sealed ship cabin, the circumstances of that time jumbled but unmistakable, her frantic wish to *undo* denied, her soul forever suspended, like a staring fetus in formaldehyde, in guilt.

As her pupils dilated to take in the patches of light in the room, she would realize that those circumstances had been long shed. Jenny Gabriel was dead—a little skeleton, as in the dream—and the man gently snoring beside her was her man, her husband, who in his abstracted fashion loved her, with what love he had left over from his precious pots and vases, their soft-lipped mouths and pliant waists. No man can love like a woman can, they don't have the internal organs for it. Rescued from Eastwick, she had resolved to be a good wife, better than she had ever been for poor Ozzie. When Jim in those first years of their marriage, not broken to it yet, would come back from Eagle Nest or Tres Piedras radiating the smell of liquor and showing a cockiness in the face of her questions that betrayed an encounter with another woman, she suppressed her feelings, having had prior experience of what a poison possessive jealousy can be. And his evenings away from her slowly grew fewer in number; he knew she had made the effort, difficult for her, of forgiving, and grudgingly granted her in turn more respect and tamer behavior.

Now the dreams of Eastwick still recurred, but Jim's leathery long body was not there when they ended, and reality was a hotel room where an elderly woman had hung up her old-fashioned XL underwear to dry on the bathroom cord. Red lights like little dragon eyes blinked at her from the corners, meaning she didn't know what. Fire protection, she guessed. Or a run-down battery. Or an unexplained emergency. She felt shapeless in her nightie, a pale cloud in the mirror. Her body in its gown gave off that sweetish stale smell, like cooking cauliflower or the underside of oilcloth, which she remembered from standing close to her grand-mother with a child's sensitive nose. *Ruddy noses out of joint*, that Australian bitch had said.

As the tour moved south, by bus, from Jasper to Calgary, through a series of huge old resort hotels thrown up by Canadian ambition and painstaking Scots craftsmen, Alex-andra kept her eye on the lanky mustached man with the Southern accent. The group's sole loners, they could not help winding up walking side by side to scenic vistas and thunderous gorges, and sharing a table at some meals, though always in the company of others. A short Asian cou-ple, he a Taiwanese and she a Malay, both of them eagerly conversational but hard to understand, were easy to join at a table—easier than the other Americans, who sensed some-thing occult and off-putting about Alexandra and whose smugly mundane mind-set and demotic lingo did rouse, as they suspected, her snobbish distaste, and easier than the eight Australians, handsome and prosperous and bump-tiously happy to have escaped, if only for some weeks, Down Under. Once the Australians had eaten and drunk their way through the Rockies, they were going on to devour Texas, its steak and rodeos, and then to New England, its lobsters and leaves. "But," Alexandra pointed out to one couple—a bloke and his sheila, gendered aspects of a single rugged Australian identity—"the prime leaf season may be by."

"A bit or two's bound to be left," the male said cheerfully. "We'll extrapolate."

"Our guidebook," the wife said, "says it lasts to the mid-dle of November. It's the lovely village greens with their white Puritan churches we're dying to see."

"A lot of them have burned down, over the years," Alexandra told the couple, with a vehemence that surprised her, too, "and they get replaced by hideous cut-rate glass-and-steel bubbles, or by pre-fab A-frames. Or are not rebuilt at all. New England isn't as religious as the rest of the country."

The two faces glazed over, trying to picture these disappointments, and penitently Alexandra assured them, as they turned their backs, "You'll have a *won*derful time. Be sure to try fried clams."

The Asian couple, too, impressed her with their appetites. Little and trim as they were, they heaped up sausages, pancakes, and unnamable Oriental delicacies (Canada catered to Asia, its Pacific near-neighbor) from the breakfast buffet on their plates, their smiling lips bright with oily intake. They ran through roll after roll of film, and never missed an optional mountain hike or an arranged opportunity to shop. At Jasper, bravely embarking to walk by herself around the little lake the hotel faced, Alexandra took a turning that led her onto a golf course, groomed for play but without a player on it. It was eerie; but then she saw the Asian couple, small in the tapering green distance, coming merrily toward her, crying a mysterious word that sounded like "Rost! Rost!"

As they drew close, the Malay woman, who had the better English, explained: "We made same mistake. Very tricky turn back there. We met worker. He told us, not very poritely, this private golf course. He said go back to dirt road to go around rake."

"You rost, too!" her husband summed up, his grin triumphant.

Alexandra found herself, unaccountably, blushing, feeling herself stupidly torpid as she loomed above this bustling, undiscourageable pair. Together the three of them strolled back up the deserted fairway, past a green still pale with the morning's dew, and deep sand bunkers without a footprint, and a fresh-mowed tee whose markers were water-smoothed stones taken from the lake shore and painted different colors for different abilities. Banished from this artificial paradise, they came back to the unmarked dirt road; Alexandra turned right, and the couple hurried to the left, to return to the lodge in time to take a bus to a tram to some celebrated outlook miles away. Alone again, she reflected upon the appetite for life, and wondered if her own relative lack of it, and the stab of nausea she now and then felt in the midst of the ordinary, were symptoms of disease. She had always dreaded cancer, and had given her cells more than seventy years in which to scramble their code and percolate through her veins with a deranged passion to multiply.

The road became a path in woods—white spruce, Douglas fir, paper birch, quivering aspen, a froth of nameless undergrowth, and, in a passage of sunlight, a thick stand of lodgepole pines, straight and slender and some of them, suffocated by their own shade, fallen into the lake, littering the edge where small waves cast nets of refracted sunlight across a shallow bottom of rounded stones. Huffing plump girl joggers and a couple on the tour, gnarled Québecois even more elderly than she, passed her coming the other way, counterclockwise. For stretches she was quite alone. If you meet a grizzly bear, their group had been advised by their tour guide, hold utterly still; if it's a brown bear—smaller, without a hump—fight like hell. Alexandra listened for wildlife and heard nothing, not even a bird. But the lake shimmered companionably, reflecting as in a lightly corrugated mirror the aspens' trembling gold. Beyond the trees across the lake, the Rockies bared themselves; they were a pleasing dove-gray, a giant geological sample of Canadian understatement.

The mountains were made of limestone, laid down by unthinkably many small aquatic creatures armored in delicate shells. Their tour guide, Heidi, an ebullient former airline stewardess, had explained that a billion and a half years ago this part of the globe was just off the western shore of what is now North America, on the sloping edge of the continental plate. Sediments transported by vanished Mesozoic rivers accumulated and were compressed, and a change of direction in plate drift about two hundred million years ago crumpled and folded the great sheets of solidified sediment, thrust them upward, and piled them into the tilted layers and sharp peaks, honed and whittled by wind and abrasive glaciers, of the apparently motionless mountains around her. It was all—the continental drift reversing direction, the folding of rocks like ribbon pasta in the earth's warm ovens—as challenging to belief as the most fantastic dogmas of religion, but accepted by everybody sane in the modern world. The weight of evidence accumulated all the time, like all those protective shells contributed by tiny creatures as keen to live, as self-important and ultimately insignificant as she. Alexandra's relation to Nature had always puzzled her; she leaned on Nature, she learned from it, she *was* it, and yet there was something in her, something *else*, that feared and hated it.

At an exceptionally lonely section of the road, another presence, large, strode toward her. As quickly as her heart skipped, her mind hoped it was a grizzly and not a brown bear, and all she had to do was remain still. She was too old and feeble to fight like hell. The presence metamorphosed into a tall, erect-striding man, the melancholy-mustached semi-Southerner, wearing a blue-checked long-sleeved shirt. His name was Willard McHugh, and he came from the

Nashville area: he had told her this much about himself. But now, intent on keeping his pace, he merely nodded, in a formally friendly way, and kept striding.

She, too, had not been tempted to stop. They were too much out in Nature, it would have felt indecent. He was shy, and so was she. Nature had burned them, somehow. Heidi had explained how lodgepole pines need fire, to crack open their resin-sealed cones. It was horrifying, really, how complacently Nature accommodates violence; Nature loves it and needs it to such an extent that the wardens of Canada's national parks, in the absence, these last seventy years, of enough natural forest fires, had taken to setting them, to initiate regeneration and encourage biodiversity. Diversity—why do we all assume it's so good, when it is uniformity that makes us comfortable?

Thinking of such basic things, and of how uncannily fate had presented her on this trip with Jim's physical doppelgänger, Alexandra missed the short cut back to the lodge through a parking lot. She worked up such a sweat of annoyance and panic, walking the long way around the serpentine shore, with its picnic tables and trash barrels unctuously urging her not to pollute—to be kind to Nature instead—that she had to take her second shower of the morning just to make herself presentable for lunch.

The next morning, at around eleven, she was standing with cold feet on the Athabasca Glacier, confronting Nature again. The bus, heading south toward Lake Louise, had made a planned stop. The Columbia Icefields, trapped in a bowl of peaks along the Continental Divide, pushed outwards through the mountain passes broad glacial arms, of which the Athabasca was the handiest to the highway.

Fat-wheeled big vehicles, driven by youngsters and called Snocoaches, took tourists down a precipice—"the steepest grade drivable," the boy's miked voice claimed—onto the ice. Alexandra and her fellow-tourists dutifully extracted their bulks from their seats and clambered down, expecting something wondrous. She was prepared for a world of inhuman purity, but the glacier was as grimy as a city street, only harder to stand on. It was dirty, and pitted, and hollowed. It gurgled beneath its slick skin. Though summer was over, melting was still in progress, and made footing treacherous. She didn't know much about being an old lady—just think, every second you live, you have never been this old before—but knew that she shouldn't break a hip. Years ago she had seen a male taxi dancer interviewed on television and he had said, of his customers, "Once they fall and break a hip, they come back to the dance hall all right, for the company, for the memories; but the dears don't ever dance again." Not that she had done much dancing with Jim—just a weekend square dance now and then, when they were new to their marriage and game for most anything. She had liked the patterning, the weaving in and out and the flickering quick touch of other hands as in a sabbat orgy, but the New Mexico women with their bouffant hairdos and twirling, ballooning skirts and the men in their two-tone boots and bolo ties threaded through jade or turquoise slides, frowning in their concentration on the voice of the caller twanging above the fiddles, came to disgust her. They were bankers and feed merchants disguised as cowhands; they exuded the glossy falsity of the bourgeoisie at play. And Jim's game leg would complain for days afterwards. So they gave up square dances. Giving things up agreed with Alexandra—appealed to her inner witch. There was so much unnecessary and superfluous clutter connected with living. Living itself, all that eating and propagating, was a study in superfluity. A cancer.

The boy driving the bus had been given an ingratiating patter to recite: "Folks, these special glacier buses, called Snocoaches, cost a hundred thousand dollars each. Relax— we calculate that more than half of them return intact, with many of their passengers still aboard." There was unanimous nervous laughter. Down the precipice they plunged, and then coasted on the level ice to a stop beside some other Snocoaches. The driver recited into his mike, "One of the commonest questions we get is 'Why is the ice so dirty?' Well, glacier ice is made of snow, meters of it compressed to a centimeter or two of ice. As you may already know, every snowflake and raindrop has to form around a tiny piece of dirt in the air. The snow melts, but the dirt stays there."

Had Alexandra known that? That snowflakes and raindrops each need a germ of dirt? Does the sky hold enough dirt to supply them all? Suppose the heavenly dirt runs out? And this Canadian theme of compression—was that what kept pressing on her chest at night? If everything—snow, sediment, rock—keeps compressing, why doesn't the world get heavier and smaller, until it becomes a black hole? This was the kind of question she used to ask Jim, who never laughed at her, and always tried to give an answer, out of his practical knowledge. Men for all their hidden rage did have that—a plain sense of cause and effect, a practical desire to be reasonable. Women love them for that.

She looked around for the lanky, morose man from Nashville, but their tour had been scrambled up with several others, and everybody around her looked strange, silhouetted against the glare like those space creatures emerging from the light in *Close Encounters of the Third Kind*. The glacier sloped upward, and in the distance she could see a ridge, a murky wall, a long frozen waterfall. The herd instinct of the apparitions on the glacier was to shuffle toward it, fish moving blindly upstream, until they met a row of red traffic cones and a sign prohibiting further progress. Thus confined, the tourists milled about, treading cautiously, dark blots on the ice like restless aggregates of dirt. Groups of Japanese on other tours coagulated to have their photographs taken.

A familiar couple, the short Asians, came up smiling to Alexandra and offered to take her picture. "The grare is terrible," the woman said, pointing her camera experimentally.

"Code feet!" her husband cried, pointing downward and grinning.

Alexandra posed with first one of the couple, and then the other. Holding these compact bodies, with their low centers of gravity, under her arm eased her sensation of tippiness, of endangered balance. To their left, a long crevasse held a running stream of meltwater that had carved its channel down and down, into perilous curved spaces tinted a luminous lime-green. If she were in a mad moment to walk a few paces and let herself slide and slip into this purling crevasse, no one nearby would have the wit or strength to fish her out. That was why people don't travel alone: to be protected from their own craziness. Companions however incidental keep us focused on the fretful nag of living. We all are swaying on the makeshift rope bridge that society suspends above the crevasse.

Back on the special bus with its giant balloon tires, the dutiful tourists and their fear of death were teased by the boy driver: "O.K., now, folks, we are going to endeavor to steer this device back up this impossible grade. Like I said before, the odds are close to fifty-fifty. You can all help me by holding your breath. Think light, *light*." Idiotically, they all,

Alexandra included, inhaled with a loud gasp and didn't breathe again until the bus had swooped up the slope and swung into the pebbly, muddy parking lot. "Folks, we made it," the boy announced in his almost-American accent. "Upon disembarking, look to your right across the Icefields Parkway to a small stone cairn in the considerable distance. That marks the spot the Athabasca Glacier had reached by 1870. Since then it has retreated by one-point-six kilometers. For our good friends from south of the border, where they haven't yet managed to sign on to the metric system, that's pretty much all of a mile. Come back in another hundred thirty years, ladies and gentlemen, you'll be lucky to find a snowball here."

Alexandra entertained a vision of a world without glaciers: all mountain slopes stony, and a ruinous leaking and weeping in the valleys, and all coastal cities drowned by risen sea levels, and wheat flourishing in northern Canada's tundra, and the American Midwest a desert lightly etched, from the air, with its old farm roads.

In the lobby of the hotel at Lake Louise hung framed photographs of the region as it had looked around 1900, when the Canadian Pacific had replaced the first log chalets with a timbered château, Victorian Tudor in style, housing hundreds of guests. The view as then photographed from the front terrace across the lake showed a sprawling glacier on Mount Victoria, of which the present glacier was a nibbled remnant. Alexandra discovered she could not walk around the lake as she had in Jasper; here, after a mile's stroll along the shoreline, she met a dead end of rocks and fallen timber and could have followed an upward path to "a cosy tea-house" and "tiny and picturesque Mirror Lake" or else turned back toward the immense château. She turned back, keeping an eye out for advertised beavers, which she did not see. The walk was crowded with the hotel guests, including children and people in wheelchairs. It did not unduly startle her when, in the gloaming, the man from Nashville crept up behind her and shortened his stride to fall in with hers. *Here it comes*, she thought, without quite knowing what "it" was. She knew that people being noticed always notice it. Auras in a state of matched vibration compel the bodies to collide.

His voice in her ear was sugary with Southern courtesy, the mournful music of losers. "Isn't the blue of the lake remarkable," Willard asked, "even in this dying light?"

"It is," she responded cautiously. "Except all the glacier lakes are this color, more or less. Heidi explained why in the bus, but I didn't understand it." Heidi was always twittering away into her little bud microphone, as if she were still soothing passengers in an airplane.

"Rock flour," Willard stated, "scraped from the mountains by the glaciers as they rub along. Minute mineral particles." He drew the word out: "mine-*ute*."

His pedantic possessiveness made her restive; she felt obliged to quarrel. "It's not a process I find easy to picture," she told him. "I mean, why would rock flour make water bluer? And that glacier we saw yesterday, it didn't look like it was rubbing anything. It looked stuck."

He silently pondered, as if chastised. "The flow is slow," he at last pointed out.

"I know," she conceded. She had adapted her own forward motion to his stride. Then she startled them both with a sudden exclamation: she had thought she spotted a beaver. But it was only a detached piece of brown turf, jutting out in silhouette against the lake's unreal, glacier-enriched blue.

"Is anything the matter?" he asked, gently alarmed.

"No. Sorry. I thought I saw a beaver. The guidebook said they were here. It promised. In abundance, it said."

"In certain seasons, I believe." His smooth, deferential tone was irritating her. Perhaps sensing this, he asked, "Of all we have seen, Alexandra, what has impressed you the most so far?"

It was a tough question. Throughout this trip she had been most conscious of all the isolating space around her. Jim's absence formed a transparent shield over what she was seeing, like the sneeze guard at a salad bar. "I think, Willard," she said, matching his cautious deliberation, "the antlers on the bull elk beside the highway yesterday, right after the stop at the Athabasca Falls. I had no idea how big they could be—the rack, Heidi called it. The rack seemed to stretch all the way down his back, and tipped his head way back, as if it might break his neck." *Ack—ack—ack—eck—* her tongue was playing tricks. Perhaps this doppelganger was a wizard. He said nothing, so she added, prattling the way men's silence forces women to do, "Imagine, carrying all that just so you can fend off other bulls and keep your harem. What did Heidi say—up to a *hun*dred does?"

How much fucking does Nature need? The topic had excited Heidi, making her dimple; the shadows in her cheeks were visible from the middle of the bus, where Alexandra sat with another widow. Heidi had gone on, in her soothing stewardess manner, to describe how all that fighting and "servicing their ladies" wore the old bulls out and left them to face the winter exhausted and half-starved. They died, letting the young bachelor elks skulking on the edge of the harem move in. They died of Nature's furious will to propagate.

The train of Alexandra's thoughts, expressed and unexpressed, had led her companion into a parallel intimacy, for out of the blue Willard McHugh pronounced, "Alexandra, I was truly moved to hear of your recent sorrow." So: he knew her name, and now her sorrow. He had been gossiping, in his solemn way, his long head cocked as if to favor a good ear.

"My sorrow?"

"Your husband's recent passing. One of your lady friends confided that to me."

Lady friends? Alexandra tried to remember whom she had talked to, among the boring, overfed human does herded onto this tour. She had tried to avoid conversations, and the other women sensed in her an electric aloofness—a negative charge of potential social disruption, a witch's scorn of normal, tame order. "Whoever she was, she was right. Jim died three months ago."

"I'm very sorry, Alexandra."

"Thank you, Willard."

But he had more to say. With a widow's clumsiness, her thanks had interrupted him. He went on, in his sugary, melancholy voice, to tell her, "I know what you're suffering. My partner passed last year. We'd been together for thirty-seven years."

Partner. One of the new code words, usefully bland. Willard was one of those. She'd been fooled before. She felt some relief and some resentment. This fag had been wasting her time. But, then, what was her time worth? Less and less: she was an old lady, post-menopausal, on Nature's trash-heap, having outlasted her Biblical span of seventy years. "That's a long time," Alexandra said. She did not add, *for a pair of fairies*. Who notoriously flit around, breaking each other's hearts with their infidelities, their unchecked attraction to younger fairies.

"He was a beautiful person," this intruder into her solitude solemnly avowed. He would have gone on, detailing the beauty, had not Alexandra curtly said, "I don't doubt it. Thank you for your company, Willard. Don't the hotel lights look cozy, now that it's dark?"

"Shall we share a drink, inside the château?"

So, with his orientation out in the open, he felt free to be socially aggressive. "Thank you, Willard," she said. "You're kind. But I think I'd better go lie down before dinner. I've not been sleeping very well on this trip. It's more work than I expected. The altitude, I suppose, and all the packing and unpacking. And so much Nature!" Hoping that whatever wound her refusal had given him was stanched by this wad of hurried words, she added more: "And it never lets up! Tomorrow, Heidi tells us, we must get up before dawn, to see the sunrise on Mount Victoria. They must think we're all spring chickens! I might just skip it."

But, betraying him, she asked the desk to call her room at five-thirty. The shrill ring shattered a dream she was having, about Eastwick—a misty morning, sea fog beaded in the window screens, the children off at school, she trying to do housework but tensely expecting Joe Marino to come calling. In the dream he had brought her a present of a chicken, a live chicken but wrapped, in stiff pink-striped wrapping paper. She had to thank him but was secretly appalled; what could she do with a chicken? Even if she could bear to wring its neck she didn't know how to pluck its feathers. What was dear Joe thinking of? His ridiculous middle-class guilt lay behind this. Why can't men just fuck you and not bother with useless presents? The bird's angry eye, above its collar of wrapping paper, transfixed her. A scraping, terrible noise came from its throat: the telephone shrilling with her wake-up call. This was her chance, *the day that has been given thee.* Alexandra would never see Lake Louise again.

She threw on clothes and went out, unshowered and

sleepy, into the dark, to join the tourist throngs already present on the paved tiers and hedged paths between the hotel and the lake. It was like a square in some European city, where the tourist, inconveniently awake early, is startled by the numbers of people hurrying diagonally to work, revealing the secret life of labor behind the stage scenery of palaces and cathedrals, museums and overpriced restaurants that have beguiled the days of vacation. The Asian couple was there, and the eight Australians, all taking one another's pictures with the lake and mountain in the background, and jollily including Alexandra in shot after shot, which they promised to send her. Already a mood of farewell had infiltrated the tour, though two days in Banff and a day in Calgary remained.

Inch by inch, a rosy tinge on the snowbound upper edge of Mount Victoria enlarged, expanding down the surface of the peak. Its horizontal strata, underlying the snow, calibrated the descent. The rosy tinge slowly broadened and turned golden; daylight came to reign over the glassy surface of the uncannily blue lake, where the burning apparition of the dawn-struck peak hung suspended, upside down, like a chunk of gold in a New World's cerulean Rhine.

The little male Asian, taking a stance beside her, asked with his unquenchable grin, "Worth earry gerring up?"

"The sunrise? Oh yes—beautiful." *A beautiful person.* Though, against her own advice to herself, she glanced through the sunrise crowd for Willard, alert to spot his violet aura and coolly snub him. But he was evidently not a morning person. She felt, after all, rejected, which was unreasonable, since she, with Nature's concurrence, had rejected him. More than thirty years ago, in Eastwick, she had been sucked into the orbit of a homosexual man, seduced by his love of fun and art—he made her laugh, he fed her pot, he loosened her up. He gave her, in his ridiculous mansion, a setting that flattered her fantasies of her own glamour. Then he had betrayed her, and Sukie and Jane as well. They had extracted a revenge. The memory of it all was shameful but invigorating, reviving a younger self with a healthy, anarchic appetite and arcane powers. Arriving, after a short bus trip, in Banff, she felt renewed.

Jasper had been an upland settlement, with lonely wide streets and a single business block; whereas Banff was a city, with an art museum and a First People museum and many coffee shops and a downtown bustle and hot springs and a conference center and, spreading downhill from the Banff Springs Hotel, curving neighborhoods of expensive homes. She walked into the town, cruised the local watercolors and old photographs at the Whyte Museum, and had lunch in a coffee nook where the Australians were eating. They invited her to join them, at their two tables pushed together, but she declined and ate her turkey roll-up staring at a blank wall. The time had come, its blankness told her, to take stock, to gather herself for this last life stage, a sprint to the grave in widow's weeds.

The tour had scheduled a gondola ride up Sulphur Mountain at two o'clock. The bus took them to the base, and then the gondola ascended. At the top, there were souvenirs and snacks and warm air inside and, outside, cold air and viewing telescopes that accepted Canadian dollar coins, called "loonies" for the waterfowl on them, on the side opposite from the profile of an aging queen. Two-dollar coins were called "toonies." Alexandra wondered why the United States couldn't come up with a dollar coin that people would use. The Canadians made it look so easy, such fun. American men hated to have heavy pockets, she supposed; they're afraid of being dragged down. They love freedom.

Hundreds of meters down, two rivers met and a golf course had been fitted alongside one of them. Banff was a bent grid between a mountain and two lakes. A flight of wooden stairs descended from the viewing porch, and a boardwalk headed off toward another, slightly higher peak. Other tourists were coming back along this reverberating boardwalk, including some Australian couples.

"How was it?" Alexandra asked them.

"Wonderful, love. Worth the trek."

Still she hesitated, dawdling in the gift shop, wondering which of her seven grandchildren might like a toy moose. But give to one, they all should get something of equal value, age-appropriate. Their ages varied from sixteen to one. It was too hard to calculate. In the corner of her eye she sensed a tall man approaching, a tall man with a mustache, and rather than cope with Willard any more she went out into the high cold and down the wooden steps.

The planks levelled and then, upheld above gray rocks on thick posts, they climbed to fit the ridge, several steps at a time. Other people were moving back and forth around her, yet Alexandra felt more and more alone as the walk beneath her feet changed direction and then again levelled into a straightaway. Treetops fell away around her, and all but a few rock outcroppings. She didn't usually like heights but was determined to experience this. She felt she was treading air, as in all directions gray mountains, range upon range, slate and ash and dove in color, streaked with avalanches and littered with scraps of snow, opened under her. Alexandra was flying. She was above and among endless gentle mountains; they were her friends, a grand Other holding her in Its hand. Nature was within her and around her and infinite.

The boardwalk with its solid steps turned, and turned again, narrowing its purchase on Sanson Peak, and brought her up to a shack, a sturdy shack with a glass window through which she could see a desk and papers but no human being, no weatherman, for that is what this had been, a weather station to which—an explanatory signboard explained—Norman Sanson had climbed more than a thousand times, in the course of his life, to record weather observations. Having looked in and seen the shack as empty of Norman Sanson as her bed was of Jim Farlander, and feeling dizzy and fragile among the pushy young hikers, Japanese and Caucasian, crowding around to peer with her into this Canadian holy site, Alexandra retraced her steps, down and around, and down some more, and then on the echoing straight stretch, hurrying in a panic, fearing that the tour would leave her behind, in all those glorious, impassive gray mountains. But Willard McHugh was there, at the head of the last set of stairs, lanky and trim in a green-checked shirt. His studied lumberjack costumes seemed, in retrospect, faggy. "The others have pretty much gone down already," he drawled.

His lugubrious, proprietary manner made her glad, for a second, that she had no husband. She turned to Heidi, their bright-eyed, frizzy-haired tour mother, who stood a few feet away. It was to her that Alexandra said, "I'm *so* sorry. Was I keeping everybody waiting?"

"Not at all," Heidi said. Her smile was a stewardess's; no jolt, no ominous rumble, no sudden drop in an air pocket could shake it. "How was the view up there?"

"Stupendous. Breathtaking," Alexandra gasped, her heart still thumping from the last panicky stretch of boardwalk.

Heidi's smile broadened, deepening her dimples. "I can see it was. Now, you get your breath back, Lexa, and we'll all get on the bus together."

Once they had abandoned the venerable coastal town where they had done their vile mischief, the three witches had hardly kept in touch, geographically scattered as they were, and busy concocting their new married lives. Dirty hands shouldn't fold fresh linen. Early in the post-Eastwick years they did sometimes meet again, Sukie in Connecticut and Jane in Massachusetts managing more visits between them than Alexandra in far-off New Mexico. But conversation would run dry with their husbands sitting restlessly in the same room, and without the coven of all three there was no cone of power to lend them a strength beyond their own. In each awkward silence the prickings of conscience would trouble them and thicken their tongues. So the contacts were slowly reduced to telephone calls and then token notes of remembrance at Christmastime. The December of the year after her fall trip to the Canadian Rockies, Alexandra received a religiously neutral—pine cones, an elfin squirrel in red hat with white trim—holiday card from New England, the anodyne *Season's Greetings* printed inside wreathed in a scrawled note that rather frantically spilled, sideways and even upside down, into available spaces. Jane Smart's handwriting had always been vehement, gouging the paper, driving itself into slanting lines whose closeness caused loops to entwine and overlap.

Lexa darling—
You will be sorry to hear that my dear Nat died, after years of suffering, in and out of Mass. General—all these treatments—chemo, radiation, laser burns, platelet infusions, a hundred expensive drugs—what did they do but prolong everybody's agony? Better to sit in the inglenook

THE WIDOWS OF EASTWICK

and waste away with an ague [a word that took Alexandra minutes to decipher] the way our ancestors did. Mass. General tormented him to give the residents practical experience and fatten up the Medicare payment. He was so docile, too, the sweet old thing, believing everything these white-coated con men with their beauty-parlor haircuts told him. The look on his face when the nurses found him dead in the bed finally was pure astonishment—he couldn't believe they would let this happen to him. Death, I mean. Me, I'd rather be burned at the stake when the time comes and go out at least with a flare. I've read in one of the old books that the way to cope, which all the savvy so-called heretics used, was to inhale the smoke—it knocked you right out. Sorry to be so grim, on a Christmas card yet. He "passed," as the ridiculous undertakers say now—as if life is a game of bridge—last month, and it's been a lot of hours with the lawyers to settle that his mother—she's still alive, at over a hundred, isn't that pathetic?—will let me stay on in the house, this enormous brick ark they claim is by H. H. Richardson but was only by a younger partner, an imitator—"from the school of," as they say in art museums, labelling their fakes. Everybody in Brookline is from the school of. Tweed skirts, square-toed shoes, and thinned bloodlines. Sorry you never knew Nat—the enclosed clipping tells you the meager basics but not how he talked, ate, slept, fucked, etc. Will we ever meet again? Call me, far beauty, sometime.

Yours ever, Jane

The enclosed obituary from the *Boston Globe*—**Nathaniel Tinker III, 79, antiquarian, benefactor**—was only four or five inches long and, even so, groped for things to say. His profession was given as investment adviser, which was a way, Alexandra surmised, of saying that he dabbled with his own money and that of some trusting friends. His memberships were many: the Somerset Club, the Country Club, the Harvard Club of Boston, the New England Historical Society, societies for the preservation of this and that, and boards of the New England Conservatory, the Museum of Fine Arts, Mount Auburn Hospital, McLean Hospital, the New England Home for Little Wanderers, and the Pine Street Inn shelter. He had done everything right, everything his social and geographic circumstances dictated, and then, in his mid-forties, married Jane Pain, as Lexa and Sukie used to call her when she especially annoyed them. They had known her as Jane Smart, the divorced wife of Sam Smart, who had been hung up to dry in the basement of her ranch house in Eastwick and occasionally sprinkled into a magic philter, for piquancy. Jane had seemed emotionally attached to only two things—her cello, which she played with a frenzied concentration that was frightening to behold, a vortex that might suck you in, and her young Doberman pinscher, a hideous orange-spotted black drooler and rung-chewer named Randolph. The smallest and lightest of the three witches, and the only one to have mastered the art of flight, Jane had taken with some verve to the elevated life that Nat's birth and wealth opened to her, the upper circles of Brookline and Boston and Cambridge. Her acid accent, her sharp-nosed profile, and her angry eyes the bright brown of tortoiseshell blended into these polite circles like the vein of brandy in a rich, sluggish gravy; and then there was, for piquancy as it were, her unseen underside, the darkness she sat on, the heat and dirtiness that roused dear androgynous Nat Tinker out of his mother-smothered torpor to marry a divorcée with children whose number local gossip lost track of, they were so quickly bundled off to proper boarding schools.

When Sukie, at first once or twice a year and then less and less, had visited Jane in the brick-and-exposed-timber ark on Clyde Street, she had been awed out of her usual sauciness by the height of the ceilings, the Gothic spikiness and wax-glazed redolence of the glass-fronted bookcases and near-churchly furniture, and the breadth of the dark stairs that led up—their flight accompanied, stair by stair, by murky small framed prints that ascended on the wall opposite the banister—to landings and bedrooms of a privacy so intense that trying to imagine it left her short of breath. Sukie, whose descriptive gifts had been developed by her stint as a reporter with the Eastwick *Word*, had amusingly planted, over the telephone, these images in Alexandra's mind years ago, before this pair of friends, too, fell out of touch. When, accepting Jane's invitation, Alexandra dialed the number alphabetized under "S" for "Smart" in her address book—a decades-old red booklet falling apart with its burden of undeleted dead, moved, and forgotten—the distant ring was like a glow of embers in an abandoned cave.

It was not Jane who answered the ring. "Tinker residence," a pretentious voice, young and male, responded.

"Hello!" Alexandra exclaimed, taken aback. "Could I speak with"—"Jane" seemed too familiar, and "the lady of the house" could mean the mother as well as the widow—"Jane Tinker?"

The frosty voice answered her question with another: "And whom shall I say is calling?"

"Tell her Alexandra." She added needlessly, "We're very old friends." What business was it of this snotty boy's?

"I will see if Mrs. Tinker is available." As if being in the house and being available were two different things. Alexandra tried to picture Jane at the head of those broad dark stairs, sequestered in her grief, protected by thicknesses of old money. She had risen a long way from that little ill-kept ranch house on a damp quarter-acre of the Cove region, its bleak Fifties modernism overlaid with a dilapidating coat of faux-Puritan cabinets, mock cobbler's benches, and light switches carved like pump handles by the previous owner, an unemployed mechanical engineer. It was in that kitchen, with her dirty-faced children coming in and out, that the three of them had put the fatal spell on Jenny Gabriel.

Though those days seemed forever away, Jane's voice, when she came to the telephone, was little changed—it still had that old accusatory sting, delivered with a bit more of a whiskey rasp. "Lexa! Can it be really you?"

"Dearie, who else? You told me on your card to call you. I was sorry to hear your sad news. Nat must have been a lovely man; I'm sorry I never met him." She had prepared this much to say.

"But I wrote you two months ago," Jane accused.

"We Westerners move slow. I wasn't sure you meant it."

"Of course I meant it. There hasn't been a day in thirty years you haven't walked through my mind, lightly clad and quite majestic."

"How nice, Jane. You haven't seen me lately. My face is crackled like an old squaw's with too much sun, and I've gained weight."

"Listen, doll: we're ancient. It's the inner woman that matters now."

"Well, I'm an inner woman wrapped in too much outer. I have twinges all over my body."

"That sounds rather *sss*eductive," Jane said. Her "s"s still hissed. "Come east. I know a wonderful spa, and an acupuncturist who takes off years. The more the needles hurt going in, the better you feel lying there. I fall asleep right on the table, bristling like a porcupine."

How like Jane Pain, Alexandra thought, smiling into the

receiver. She told her old friend, "I'm a widow now, too. It'll be two years this July. Jim, his name was. I think you met him a few times, back in Eastwick."

"Ye*ss*. I did, toward the end, after Darryl's pathetic charade had fallen apart. Jim *Ss*omething. I hated him, because he was taking you away from *usss*. As to my 'lovely man,' well, yes, you could say that. It was a deal. He did nice things for me, and I did nice things for him. He gave me money, I gave him ass. He needed a lot of special attention. Only certain things turned him on. Weird things." The husky acid voice hovered close to something—indignation, or tears. "Well, shit, *sss*weetie," she said, closing the door on that closet. "It all worked out."

Alexandra tried to picture the working out—the implied intimate details beyond the dark head of those broad stairs. "It worked out for us, too," she offered. "I loved Jim." She waited for Jane Tinker to echo this conventional sentiment, but in vain. So she added, defiantly, "And I think he loved me. You know, as much as a man can. Loving makes them feel helpless."

At this Jane, with one of her alarming shifts of direction, plunged into suggestive and possibly sardonic flattery. "Lexa, *no*body could help loving you. You're so *open*. You're a force of Nature."

"I'm not sure I like Nature any more. She's too cruel. As to not loving me, I think my children are managing that." She thinks of the impervious Mr. McHugh, on last year's Canadian trip, but doesn't mention him. Such confiding with Jane would take physical proximity, and drinks and snacks on a little table between their knees. "How are yours?" Alexandra asked instead.

"Oh, they're *ss*urviving somewhere," Jane said. "All four, here and there; I keep losing track of exactly where, along with the grandchildren's birthdays. I never believed they could, somehow—*sss*urvive. I couldn't picture them handling jobs, and houses, and marriages to strangers, and getting raises and catching the right airplanes, but they do, amazingly. I never could fathom *how* until I realized that it wasn't *our* world they had to survive in, competing with the people of *our* generation, but *their* world, competing against the *sss*ame little people they went to kindergarten with. And growing up with the same idiotic technology. That's where you feel old, I find. The technology. I can't do computers and *hate* dialing ten digits. At my grandfather's big old place in Maine the phone was one of the first in the region and the number was two digits—two! I still remember them: one, eight. Only seventeen phones ahead of ours on the island. And I hate talking to these sugary automated voices that only when you make a mistake act like machines, repeating themselves absurdly. Though Nat made me carry a cell phone for my own protection, so he said, I never think to turn it on and can't believe anyway my voice is getting through, with this little grid thing you talk into halfway up to your ear. Now you see these self-important kids just out of business school wearing them clipped to their heads and talking out loud as if in a trance. And the things take photos and videos, too, as well as being cell phones. I can't *ssstand* it, all these tiny circuits crammed in there making everything digital, it's worse than our brains, which are bad enough. They liked coming to this house, though," she continued, lurching back to the subject of her children, "hanging out and filling the third floor with the smell of hashish or whatever the controlled substance of the week was, until they all got houses and children of their own—amazingly, as I said. They liked Nat. They thought he was cool; they used the word 'cool' of this utterly uncool little stuffed shirt. That did hurt, I confes*ss*. And he *loved* having them around, having been too infantile to get married before and have any children of his own."

"Mine, too!" Alexandra had to interject. She'd forgotten how insistent Jane could be, how possessed she could be by her own harsh tongue, her complaints against the world. "My children were crazy about Jim, and he seemed to enjoy them until they got weird or went off to college. Somehow their not being his helped. Did you ever think, Jane, the men we had children by, that that was all they were good for? A kind of specialized function, like parasites and sea anemones have? And then we *really* married, the second time."

"A specialized fuck*tion*," Jane said. That was another of her deficits, a weakness for puns, dragging them out in the middle of anybody else's thought. And yet, talking to Jane, Alexandra felt warmed as by no other female intercourse in the thirty years since the three divorcées went their separate ways. "Oh, Jane!" she exclaimed in a spurt of irrational gratitude. "We must get together now, now that we're widows."

"You come here, darling. The house is huge, and my mother-in-law keeps to her room, surrounded day and night with nurses giving her breast milk and mushed-up monkey glands or whatever. I've hardly seen her since Nat's memorial service. She's over a hundred, it's monstrous—like having a two-headed mother-in-law; people laugh at me. I'd like to say she hated my guts and made life here next to impossible for me, but in fact she was secretly relieved that I took Nat off her hands; he was one of those men with so little *ss*ubstance to him that he needed not just one but *two* strong women behind him. He was her only child, and I think to *her* generation having children was rather unnatural and very *odd*, something you felt obliged to do only because your parents and their parents before them had obviously done it; otherwise there wouldn't be ancestors. Before she became quite so batty she used to say these uncanny things that made me laugh. In fact"—Jane's voice lowered into a virtual rustle; Alexandra strained to hear it—"I used to wonder if she wasn't another—" The word stopped her tongue.

"Witch?" Alexandra asked.

Jane didn't answer, saying, "I used to avoid seeing her undressed, for fear I'd spot a false teat."

"Jane!" Alexandra had to exclaim, shocked and thrilled. "You still believe all that horrible, medieval nonsense!"

"I believe in what *is*," came the answer, in a voice still low, but sizzling at its sibilant edges, "and if that's horrible, so be it. But *sser*iously—*do* come see me, *sss*weetheart."

A dark old house, a dark old friend. "It's so far," Alexandra fended. "It's so sunny where I am. You have more money— why not come see *me*? We have wonderful Indian reservations, and Georgia O'Keeffe's home in Abiquiu, and the Continental Divide. Santa Fe hosts spectacular opera in the summer."

"Yes, I have some money now, but it's New England money. It hates being *ss*pent, except for educational purposes. Nat was always giving to Harvard, which doesn't need it, and Roxbury Community College, which does, I suppose, though the politicians will never let it go under. I made him give to Berklee and the Conservatory, despite *S*symphony not agreeing with him. He would get quite rigid in his seat listening to it, especially after intermission, so I'd take his hand to see if he still had a pulse. It would be icy cold, especially during Brahms and Mahler. With Mozart and Bach he hovered nearer room temperature; you would even see his fingers twitch when the beat picked up."

"You sound quite fond of him," Alexandra told her, trying to infect the other woman with her own generous-spirited humanity.

Jane's response was testy, betraying after all the fury of bereavement. "What if I were—what good would it do now?"

"What would he *want* you to do? Not stay in his house with a moribund mother, I bet."

"Sweetie, I don't want to come to New Mexico, I'm sorry. It's all too American, everything from the Hudson west, like something you'd switch off if it were television. But you *can't*, it's too *big* to flip off, growing all that boring wheat and corn and cattle, full of fat religious people flying flags on their pickup trucks with their shotgun racks. It's frightening to me, Lexa, like a foreign country, only worse, because you can understand the language."

In this spiky, inviting discourse Alexandra glimpsed a possibility of breaking out of her widow's monotonous life: pushing through her book club's monthly choice of "literary fiction," having drinks and Dutch-treat dinners with her Taos "girlfriends," leaving querulous messages on the telephones of her evasive children, fighting her weight with cheek-stinging hikes in the high ranch country north toward Wheeler Peak, her only companion the arthritic old black Lab she and Jim had raised from a puppy they had called Cinder because of his ash-gray fuzziness, his eyes the wonder-struck white glass of a husky's. In Eastwick her Lab had been called Coal. Cinder and she tugged each other along through the tall tan fescue, united by a leash meant less to protect the small game from the dog than to protect him from the coyotes. She carried Jim's Colt .45 in case a pack attacked. But suburban tracts were climbing higher into the hills, and an old woman in jeans and leather jacket with a half-gray head of hair and a decrepit dog and a holstered .45 was viewed by these tract-dwelling strangers as strange herself, and suspect. You live, she saw, surrounded by more and more strangers, to whom you are a disposable apparition cluttering the view. Only someone like Jane who knew her when she was in her handsome, questing prime could forgive her now for becoming ancient. She grasped at this straw of connection. "We could travel to a real foreign country," she suggested to Jane. "Together."

"Widows on the road. Widows on the world," Jane said, punning as only a very heartless person would on the name of a well-patronized restaurant on the top floor of a Manhattan skyscraper infamously felled not many years before.

"I went to Canada the year Jim died," Alexandra pursued, sounding craven in her own ears.

"Canada," Jane rasped dismissively. "What a *s*stupid country to go to."

"Their Rockies are quite beautiful," Alexandra weakly protested. "The other people on the trip were nice enough to me, especially the Australians, but I felt queasy being alone. Queasy and timid. Two of us might be braver, and could share a room. Couldn't we at least think about it?"

Ensconced in her posh dark house, Jane resisted being coaxed. "I don't want to go to any place as dreary as Canada."

"Of course not."

"The whole North American continent is dreary."

"Even Mexico?"

"People get the runs. And now there's social breakdown. An American isn't safe in the middle of Mexico City. In fact, Americans aren't safe anywhere. The world hates us, face it. They're jealous and they hate us and blame us for their own stupidity and corruption and misery."

"Oh, surely not the hotel concierges. And the people who run tour buses. I can't believe there isn't *any*where you want to go. Did you and Nat ever go to the Nile and see the Pyramids? Or to China and see the Wall? Don't you want to see the world, before we leave it? Once we break a hip and can't walk, we can't travel."

"I don't intend to break a hip."

"Nobody intends to. But it happens. They just snap. As you just said, horrible things happen."

"Did I say that? I don't think so."

"That was your sense. About the world not being safe any more for Americans." Alexandra surprised herself, being so aggressive. Just having Jane back in her life to push against got her blood flowing. She heard herself pleading, "You don't have to decide now. We're in touch again, and I love it. Think about a trip together, and call me. I'll go anywhere you want to go, if I can afford it. Not the South Pole or North Korea."

"Nat always said the Communist countries were the safest in the world. The state had all the guns, and kept a good tight lid on things. Not that he ever went. He got as far as England, which was *sss*ocialist enough."

If they talked any more about travel, the subject might grow stale in their mouths. Alexandra, her wrist aching from holding the phone against her ear, changed the subject. "Tinker," she said. "Tell me about the name. Were there Tinkers on the *Mayflower*?"

"They *greeted* the *Mayflower*. The Tinkers had come over years before, rowing a dinghy."

"Oh, Jane. It's so good to hear you joke. The people my age I know down here are all so solemn, talking about nothing but their medications and real estate and the sad state of government support for the arts."

But when Jane called her back, enough time had passed that Alexandra didn't recognize the menacing voice. Sounding like a man's, it pronounced one word: "Egypt."

Alexandra was so taken aback that she stammered: "B-beg your pardon?"

"Egypt is where we ought to go, you *ss*illy thing," the voice explained, with a twist of impatience that made it clear Jane Smart was speaking. Alexandra had trouble thinking of her as Jane Tinker.

"But, Jane, isn't it dangerous? Aren't all the Arab countries dangerous for American tourists?"

"For one thing, Lexa, the Egyptians aren't Arabs. They think of Arabs as scary crazy people just as much as we do. They are Muslims, most of them, it's true, though the upper classes are agnostics just like ours, and there are still some Coptic Christians."

"But wasn't Mohamed Atta an Egyptian? And haven't there been massacres of tourists?"

"I asked about that at the travel agency," Jane said in her stoniest, steadiest voice. "They gave me a pamphlet. I have it right here. There have been 'incidents'—*ss*eventeen Greek tourists at a Cairo hotel in 1996, nine Germans at the main museum in 1997. Later that year, the worst of all— fifty-eight foreign tourists, including thirty-five *Ss*wis*ss*, plus four Egyptians killed outside some ancient queen's quite lovely temple in Luxor. But there don't seem to have been any Americans, and the Egyptian police acted very efficiently, killing all six of the terrorists quite quickly. If tourists stay away, Lexa, then you're letting the terrorists win. The Egyptian economy will suffer, which is what the Islamic Jihad or whatever *wants*. It wants poverty, ignorance, and desperation, because they make people more religious. What it doesn't want is the peaceful operation of the global marketplace and its modernizing influence. What it *very much* doesn't want is the education of women, which is the key to everything good and progressive happening in the world, from lowering the birthrate to combatting AIDS. I can't believe that you are *against* these things, darling, you and Osama bin Laden and Mullah Omar."

"Oh, Jane, of course I'm not against the *idea* of going to Egypt; in fact, I think I mentioned it to you originally. It's just the *fact* of going there, right at this unsettled time, that's worrisome."

"Things will never *not* be unsettled, not for a long time," Jane said, with a certain relish, bred of malice and fatalism.

As she listened to this far-off voice from a distant, sinister house, a hissing harsh voice from the past, Alexandra's eyes rested on the straight-edged splashes of Southwestern sun on her glass-topped coffee table, its shiny stack of art books, and the stripes—black, red, green, and tan—of the tough wool Navajo rug underneath it, with a fringe throwing tiny fuzzy shadows on the earth-colored floor tiles. Her heart resisted the idea of leaving this safe island of known satisfactions. Jim's pots, delicate in tint and silhouette, sat on shelves and sills in the sunny large room, and each fabric and piece of solid, sensible furniture had been chosen by her, after thought and discussion with Jim and leisurely shopping. Back east, the furniture had just grown around her, like a fungus, inherited and cast-off and stop-gap all jumbled together; her home had been a way-station like the stages of the children's growth, needing to be supplied with new clothes, toys, equipment, and lessons only to demand at the next stage totally different equipment. Here, in high, dry, precious Taos, she had settled for good, until nothing needed to be changed. But then Jim had died, leaving her with the need to keep reinventing the motions of living. "Jane," she said, fending for time in which to frame a refusal that would not irrevocably break this link with her old self, when she was less afraid of fresh possibilities, "you're sweeping me off my feet."

"That's how you always were, Alexandra. Always. You hated to take any initiative. Look how long you let that ridiculous fat Italian plumber *sss*crew you. I forget his name, he always wore that hat with the stupid little brim, as if to say he wasn't really a plumber but a country *ss*quire."

"Joe Marino," Alexandra reminded her, and the very name warmed her with the memory of his body, the butterfly shape of dark hair on his back, the salty-sweet taste, like nougat, of his abundant sweat. She pictured his fleshy face when he would furtively arrive and then when, sated but still furtive, he would leave—though what was wrong, in the eyes of the town, with his plumber's truck parked in front of her old house on Orchard Road, with all its decrepit pipes and fixtures? His face had the hook nose and debauched eyes of a Renaissance prince but wore a slightly baffled look, whether he was plumbing the mysteries of an antique shut-off valve or trying to fit her, his bewitching mistress, into the web of family loyalties that dogged his Catholic conscience. She would tell him not to bother, just enjoy her: she was a gift, Nature was full of gifts, enjoying her took nothing away from Gina, his wife and the mother of five children; but he couldn't quite let go of the Christian baggage, the great No spoken to our conscienceless appetites. "I always thought the brim was cute," she said, defending Joe.

"You would. Let's face it, Gorgeous—you were a push-over. Not as bad as Sukie, but *ss*leeping around for her was a kind of news-gathering. For you, you put yourself on the line, and it kept breaking your heart. Darryl broke your heart, by never popping the question."

"I never expected him to."

"My heart, too. He never popped the question to me, either. Then it turned out he wasn't a popper gentleman."

"Ha. Just thinking about those days—aren't you glad all that's behind us? Sex, and all that lost sleep, all that hard-hearted scheming that went with it."

"Is it?" Jane asked ominously.

"Jane, we're *old*. Nobody wants us, except our grand-children for the first half-hour of a visit. It's very freeing, I find."

"We're *not* free. You're never free of wanting. Sam Smart used to tell me, the cunt is very sensitive, but not very smart. It doesn't know enough to quit."

"Oh, that Sam. Frankly—forgive me, Jane—I never could take to him. He was—"

"A *ss*marty-pants," Jane inserted.

"But Sukie—I'm so glad you mentioned her. How is she doing? You must see her now and then, Connecticut being so close."

"Not as close as you'd think. We have Rhode Island in between. She and I had *ss*ocial differences that were awk-ward. That clown from Stamford she married—he was in computers when they came in big boxes and nobody but the government could afford them, and then they got smaller and cheaper and he made a fortune in the early Eighties with one of the first word-processors, but then IBM moved in with dirt-cheap PC's and he was struggling again. Anyway, he was too nouveau and pushy for Nat, and the few times we got together as couples fizzled—upstairs at the Ritz on Arlington Street, when it still served upstairs, I remember as very stilted—and in New York City once when Nat had one of his pompous board meetings, eating up the stockholders' money with fancy meals and travel tickets. Lennie—that was his name—struck us as cocky and nouveau and I don't think bothers to be faithful to Sukie. As an escape for herself she's taken to writing these romances I just can't believe, they are beyond awful, pornography really, an utter embarrassment, though she keeps sending me copies. So we've let each other drop, ever so *sss*ubtly."

"Is her husband still alive?"

"Why wouldn't he be? He wasn't, frankly, classy enough to die."

This remark stung, implying that Jim's dying had been, like Nat's, a tactful withdrawal. Jane didn't want Alexandra to love anybody. Out of loyalty to Jim, then, and to Joe, she found courage to say bluntly, "Jane dear, I just can't see going to Egypt with you. It's too scary and, frankly, too expensive."

"Oh, but it's *not* expensive. Cruises on the Nile, they're almost giving them away to keep Westerners coming. Think of it, Lexa, floating through the Sahara when it's below zero in Boston and Taos is all noisy *ss*kiers and *ss*nowboarders. Snowboarders drove us right out of our ski lodge at Loon Mountain. Nat was doing one of his slow traverses when two boys made him the meat in a snowboard sandwich. He survived, but that was it for skiing at Loon. The ski patrol took him down in one of those toboggans, all swaddled like a baby or a mummy—it was the affront to his dignity that I think he couldn't get over. Oh, *please*, Lexa, be a pushover for *me*. You mustn't abandon me; I've been virtually living at the travel agency. They said if we sign up now we can get there in time for Ramadan. Egypt is most romantic during Ramadan. What with that terrorist nest exposed in Canada, or was it New Jersey, there've apparently been cancellations."

"I bet," Alexandra said. "Jane, what's there for us? Why don't we go to Italy and look at art and little hill towns for ten days?"

"Myssstery," Jane answered in a travelogue baritone. "The Sssphinx, and the meaning of the Pyramids. Don't they *fas-cinate* you—the biggest buildings ever built, right there at the beginning of civilization, and how and why?"

"I thought those weren't mysteries so much any more. Stone by stone dragged from quarries is how, and to get the pharaoh into the afterlife was why."

"Really, Lexa, you're such a *ss*coffer. The purpose was to preserve the dead person's body from damage or distur-bance, and to house all the supplies that he, or to be exact his *ka*, would need."

"His *what*?"

"His *ka*. His soul, you could say, although it's rather more practical and complicated than that. There's also a *ba*. If you're an ancient Egyptian, your *ka* is created at the same time you are, on a different potter's wheel, by the god Khnum—I think I'm pronouncing it right. It's not exactly the same as the *ba*, your spirit, which is pictured as a bird, a stork. The *ka* appears in the hieroglyphs as a bearded human figure wearing a crown consisting of two bent arms. Some-times it's represented simply as the two arms."

"It sounds very depressing, Jane. Other people's religions tend to be, don't you think? Other people's make even your own seem ridiculous."

"I'm just answering your question, not trying to con-vert you. You don't have to know or do *anything*, just sit on the boat and watch the scenery go by, getting off at vari-ous temples, one or two a day. The climate will be divine, and the food, if you absolutely don't eat *ss*alad or any raw vegetables and brush your teeth in only bottled water."

The more Jane said, the realer this un-asked-for trip became. Alexandra liked the idea of our being created on a potter's wheel, spinning wetly away in its brown juices. The pull of this other woman's need, when nobody else needed her as much—not even her enchanting little granddaughters, with their long lashes, bright eyes, amusingly expanding vocabularies, and powder-soft, silky warm cheeks—moved her to consider Jane's plea. The cruise part, sharing a cabin, only cost $795. Jim's dealings in more or less authentic Native American jars and bowls had generated more savings than she had realized while he was alive. He had tucked money away. He would want her to be comfortable—to have enough room in her widow's pinched life for a whim now and then.

So there Alexandra sat, she and Jane Tinker, having tea in a British-style hotel behind a large pane of glass in which loomed a huge triangular shadow, the Great Pyramid of Cheops. This august view was vertically sliced by vaguely Arabic strands of colored glass capturing the bright sun outside. Silverware and cups clattered around the two women as they tried to remember what they had just learned. Jane said, "Let's ssee. The greatest, and earliest, was by Cheops, and the slightly lesser, with its cap of surviving limestone facing, by Chephren, and the much lesser, begun in granite but finished in crude brick, by Mycerinus. What did the guide say?" Jane asked. "His was the smallest pyramid but he was the nicest pharaoh."

Alexandra responded, "Niceness wasn't I think paramount for the pharoahs. The guide said, if I heard him right, that the other two, Mycerinus's father and grandfather, were tyrants, but the gods had decreed that Egypt would have

THE WIDOWS OF EASTWICK

tyrannical rulers for a hundred fifty years, and the quota hadn't quite been reached, so an oracle told him he would only rule for six years. So they would feel like more to him, he spent them drinking and eating all night, every night. It makes you tired, doesn't it?" she went on. "All this superstition and oppression, and so long ago, when the world should have been still innocent."

For the Pyramids, the two women had learned, had been erected near the outset of Egyptian civilization, in the Fourth Dynasty, twenty-five hundred years before Christ. "I don't see why that would make you tired," Jane said, faithfully contrarian. "You could just as easily be cheered up by the fact that the Pyramids are still here. Think of it. What in the United States is going to still be there forty-five hundred years from now?"

The two women, jet-lagged, felt transparent and weary in their clothes. It was hot, with a gritty desert wind hard to breathe in. Yesterday, the Cairo airport, to their sleepless senses, had been a nightmare of haggling and shouting, and the tour representative who greeted them seemed suspect, his large dark eyes and sharp small smile darting everywhere but directly at their faces. Even when he had busily corralled a few others belonging to the tour, these were French speakers, boarded at Paris and full of unintelligible questions and complaints, and no comfort to the two American widows. Warned of chicanery in third-world airports, Alexandra and Jane exasperated their hurried escort by being reluctant to part with their passports and return tickets. They were slow to obey his command to follow him, as he threaded a devious path, marked by furtive donations of pastel paper currency, to the baggage belt and the bus waiting, engine noisomely racing, outside in a dusty jumble of traffic. The bus stopped and started, breaking the jammed streets into a sepia album of exotica, of biscuit-colored buildings either delapidated or unfinished.

In the hotel room, the pair of women discovered that they had different philosophies concerning jet lag: Alexandra longed to sleep, if only for an hour, in her bed, whereas Jane insisted that you should be ruthless with yourself, pretending that Egyptian time is now your body's time. Groggily Alexandra wandered with her on the streets outside. There was something delicious in the air of the foreign metropolis, scented with cooking odors and engine exhaust and a spicy tang like that of mesquite smoke, but she felt helplessly more conspicuous, large and foreign and female, than petite, quick, impervious Jane. Alexandra attracted stares, and felt them cling, where Jane crossly brushed them aside and plowed on. Thus far, Alexandra had been grateful for the other woman's company: Jane relieved her of the constant decisions and calculations incumbent upon a lone woman. Now she felt, instead, the fear of desertion and betrayal that linking yourself with another person brings. Jane was hard to keep up with as she pushed through the afternoon crowds, a bobbing mass in caftans and galabiyahs, burqas and veils out of which lively liquid eyes glared like the bright backs of captured beetles. The streets narrowed, more tightly lined with assorted wares—intricately worked copper pots and platters, dried herbs in glassine envelopes, miniature Sphinxes and Pyramids in lustrous lightweight metal and lurid plastic, scarabs carved from gray-green soapstone, and, in several successive stalls, in the full flat rainbow of tinted plastics, utilitarian household equipment such as tubs and buckets, dustpans and scrub brushes, scouring pads and wash baskets whose mold imitated the flattened weave of organic wicker. The humbleness of these domestic items, much as one would see gathering dust in a failing small-town hardware store in New Mexico, stirred in Alexandra a sense of common humanity but with it, too, a heightened sense of herself as a blundering, conspicuous alien. Out of these swathed and veiled multitudes around her a knife might flash, as it did years ago for that Nobel Prize-winner one of whose novels she had begun to read for her book club in Taos but never finished. Or a bomb planted to some obscure fanatic purpose might erupt, flattening and scattering all these packed and fragile stalls, her poor body, shredded by steel fragments, exploded with them.

But no Islamic violence disrupted their exploratory walk, which ended where the stalls thinned, and when the city lights dimmed to a few bluish streetlamps, not so much illuminating the pavement below as adding a lighter shadow, as it were, to a darkness of bricks and cobbles and crumbling stucco wherein a few sallow windows glowed with hints of occupancy and pedestrians in pale robes quickly and silently sidled past. The two American women found their way back to the hotel and, squandering one of the few, carefully contemplated "dressy" outfits they had packed, attended the tour's get-acquainted cocktail party and Western-style welcoming dinner. The other tourists, it turned out, were mostly European—French and German and Scandinavian, plus a cluster of Japanese. Some of the Germans with mannerly stiffness came forward to offer pleasantries in their very adequate English, and several English couples, occupying the same snug niche of insular jollity that the Australians had filled in Canada, did introduce themselves. But the few Americans present, Jane confided with a hiss, were all "assholes." Their compatriots' overheard conversation, full of barking, lewd laughter from both sexes, seemed to be mostly about their own crazy bravery in being here, in this hostile Muslim world, at all.

Safe in their own room, Jane and Alexandra agreed they were on their own and would ignore everybody else. Jane swiftly undressed and inserted herself in the bed away from the room's one window, and five minutes later Alexandra discovered something she had never known about her old friend, for all the hours, at parties and committee meetings and sabbats, over coffee and tea and cocktails, they had spent together in Eastwick: Jane snored. In Alexandra's experience, Ozzie Spofford, a seasonal hay-fever sufferer, had snuffled in his sleep, and Jim Farlander, especially when loaded for slumber with whiskey and beer, could descend into a snort so loud it would wake him before she resorted to an exasperated poke that would produce, within his cocoon of dreams, a muting change of position. Husbands you could poke; lovers left you before falling asleep. Jane, out of reach in her own twin bed, deep-breathed with an audible friction of inner membranes that knew no let-up. Each long intake arrived at a place of reverberation, a dip into nasal resonance at the exact same insistent pitch, it seemed to Alexandra, as her daytime conversation. Awake or asleep, Jane insisted, with a relentless, unforgiving will, on being heard; there had always been something unstoppable about her, whether she was playing the cello or making a pun or casting an evil spell. As Jane slept, she sucked the oxygen from the air in the inflexible rhythm of a mechanical pump, monotonous and insatiable, each breath attaining a kind of abrasive wall where it scraped and dipped before turning back in the shape of a hook, tugging Alexandra's brain another notch wider awake; she tried putting herself to sleep by counting these breaths, and then by focusing on the ceiling floating above her as it received, ever fewer, the flickering, wheeling traces of taxi lights on the streets below. But nothing distracted her enough from the sibilant insult of each emphatic snore as

Jane's body steadily rowed its way through the night, storing up energy for the coming day's strenuous, once-in-a-lifetime sights. Such unconscious self-assertion betrayed, it seemed to Alexandra, a ruthless animus; it came clear to her, in her woozy and infuriated state, that Jane had murdered her husband, by keeping him awake listening to her snore year after year. Remorselessly she had ground little Nat Tinker, with his carefully assembled antiques and memberships, into the dust of the grave.

At last, at an unknowable pitch-black hour, Jane's sheets rustled and her bare feet padded on the floor. Her elderly bladder had roused her to empty it of the night's cocktails and wine, and Alexandra, like a naughty child in the mere moment when the teacher is not looking her way, sneaked, as the toilet distantly flushed, into healing oblivion.

Nevertheless, it was not with a fully rested brain that she tried to confront the riddle of the Great Pyramid through the intervening glass and dust. She had already ridden around it. Their bus had parked, and the group had made its way across flat terrain, part stone and part sand, that reminded her of the alien surface of the Athabasca glacier. Boy peddlers kept snapping accordion-folded chains of postcards at her; blond camels in a weary finery of blankets and tassels were offered to her by hungry men in dirty gowns. Thinking in her daze to escape this inhospitable environment and perhaps relive her exalting stroll on the boardwalk to Sanson Peak, triumphantly treading the air above a vast spread of dove-gray mountains, she had opted, when pressed by an especially piteous camel-driver, to take, for a number of Egyptian pounds amounting to less than thirty American dollars, a camel ride around the Pyramid.

But sitting on a camel, in the crude carpeted wooden seat that did for a saddle, was nothing like striding along a broad boardwalk on her own two feet, and the four-footed creature beneath her felt a world removed from the thoroughly broken and tractable horses she had ridden as a girl in Colorado and then as a second wife in New Mexico. The camel's knobby knock-kneed legs lifted Alexandra up too high, with no reins to grip. She was pitched back and forth as if the beast wanted to throw her off, to snap her into space with his hump's catapult. This camel had too many joints, and his brain, like hers, was only half on the job. She felt mounted, while Jane's tiny white face far below mirrored her alarm, on pure, pungent, hairy turbulence — the rapids of evolution as it swung around a corner to cast up a quadruped that could cope with the desert. Yet out of politeness and pity toward the camel driver, whose missing teeth possibly made him look more pitiable than he really was, she held on unprotesting as the horizon pitched like an enraged sea, and sand got into her eyes, and the giant cubical stones of the Great Pyramid as they lunged closer seemed about to burst the bonds of gravity and tumble down upon her.

At last, the Pyramid circumnavigated, the driver with a few guttural commands and cursory gestures of his switch signalled the camel to kneel. Alexandra fought toppling forward and losing the last particles of her dignity; she stepped onto the stable earth with legs trembling as if they had been packed in ice. The camel, his segmented, velour-soft face suddenly next to hers, exposed long corn-yellow teeth and, batting his double eyelashes superciliously, produced the sound of flatulence with his absurdly flexible lips, as glad to be rid of her as she of him. The driver received his payment with a salaam so deep that she realized she had overtipped him. Groping for some international form of disclaimer, she murmured *"Pas de quoi"* and, feeling overheated and tousled, simpered like a maiden flirt; but the man was already looking beyond her, hungrily scanning the camel-shy other tourists for his next victim.

Jane did not flatter her courage or applaud her survival. She greeted her saying, "Don't you feel *filthy*? How many fleas and germy little things do you think live in a camel's coat?"

After her sleepless hours of torment by Jane's snore, Alexandra was in no mood for further insult. "No more than in most places, I would think. If you're going to be obsessed with germs, Jane, you shouldn't have come to Africa." To soften this scolding, she asked, "How did I look?"

"You didn't look like Lawrence of Arabia, if that's what you wanted."

"Did you get a picture of me?" Before entrusting herself to the camel, she had given Jane her camera, a little pre-digital Canon. "With the Pyramid in the background?"

"Yes, I think I did, though I *hate* other people's cameras. Things snapped and whirred inside. I'm not so sure about the Pyramid. The angle wasn't easy, and you never held *sss*till."

"Don't I know it? I do hope you didn't mess up, Jane. It would have made an amusing print to send my grandchildren. But without the Pyramid it could be in some zoo."

"Oh, grandchildren. They don't care about us, face it, dear. They find us boring and embarrassing. Only we care about us."

It was a desire to smooth away the negativity from Jane that had so soon entered their joint adventure that led her to ask the other, as they sat together over their tea looking out through glittering beads upon the Great Pyramid, "What do you think of it? What does it say to you?"

"It *ss*ays to me," Jane said, "what idiots people are and

always have been. Imagine all that labor and engineering so one man could imagine he was going to cheat his own death."

"But hasn't he? We know his name, all these years later. Cheops. Or Khufu. Jane, you must admit, the thing itself is stupendous. What did the guide in the bus say—over two *million* blocks, ranging from two to fifteen tons in weight? Archaeologists still don't know how they got the stones up there."

"Very simple. A ramp." When Alexandra became enthusiastic, Jane tended to sulk.

"But think of it—all the material a ramp would have used, where would they have put it afterwards? And the effect is so simple, so elegant—so *modest*, really. And the other one, by his son, nearly as big. And the little one, like Baby Bear, built by the grandson. I love them. I'm so glad we're here. I feel *wiser*. How can you not?"

"I don't know," Jane confessed. "I often fail to be moved by what moves other people. It frightens me. Like those people born with missing nerves, who chew up their own tongues because they feel no pain."

Alexandra was moved to touch the other woman, quickly, on the exposed skin of the back of her hand. They had been asked by the tour to cover their arms and wear long skirts; it was not yet necessary for female tourists to conceal the hair on the heads. A revived religious faith as monolithic as the Pyramids was still held at partial bay by the government's military. "Don't say that, dear," Alexandra urged. "You have all the nerves the rest of us do. You don't have to *like* the Great Pyramid, just try to *respect* it. It was your idea to come to Egypt, remember?"

Jane looked aged in the harsh desert light, shrunken. Blue

veins writhed on the backs of her hands. "There's this *s*stink to the past," she said, "of magic that stopped working. It never really did work, of course. Just gave the priests more power than was good for them."

"If they believed it worked, maybe it did. It made them less anxious. As I remember us in Eastwick, we used to believe that there was an old religion, before men came in and took it over just like they took over midwifing and *haute couture*. It was a nature religion that never died—women carried it on even when they were tortured and killed."

"What are you saying? That women built the Pyramids?"

"No, but they went along with it, the queens at least. There's something delicate and gentle about the ancient Egyptians. They loved Nature—look at the tomb paintings that are on all the postcards they keep trying to sell us, the reeds and flowers and food they wanted the dead to have. To them the afterlife was *this* life, going on forever. That's what the Pyramids say: Give us more life. More, more, *please*. They made them enormous so everybody could see them—could see that the Pharaoh had believed in another life, and would take them all with him into it."

"I don't think that was part of the bargain," Jane said dryly. "The Pharaoh was a special case. He sailed on alone."

"They were like our Presidents," Alexandra urged. "We won't elect people who don't believe in God, or pretend they do. They believe on behalf of everybody. They make us all feel better, the way even an awful Pope used to do."

Jane sighed and said, "I'll be all right, Lexa. Once we get on the river. Nat loved being on the water. I hated it, and discouraged his sailing. That's on my conscience, with everything else."

But before they caught the plane to Luxor, where they would board their sightseeing vessel, the *Horus*, another day in dismal vast decaying Cairo was scheduled; their bus carried them through the clogged streets to the bustling forecourt of the great museum of pharaonic antiquities. Their group of tourists, dwarfed, shuffled docilely through security gates and then room after room of colossal doorways, entablatures, sarcophagi. Pharaohs, broad-faced and bare-shouldered, with high cheekbones and slight feline smiles, were bodied forth in granite, some of it mottled pink and gray, some of it pure black, all quarried and carried and carved and painstakingly polished by men whose eyes and hands and even bones had long since evaporated in the cauldron of time. Life's airy spell, asking *more, more,* was silenced by the solemn ponderosity of death. The first floor had the highest ceilings and the biggest statues. A huge Ramses II stood near the entrance, a colossus with arms frozen at his sides, his gaze locked in the stark sky of his divinity. Elsewhere, a wide-hipped, long-faced Akhenaten bodied forth with a spectacular and repulsive androgeny a momentary lapse, in the rustling procession of pharaohs and dynasties and deities, into monotheism and sun-worship. His wide hips, sagging fat lips, and lack of male genitals made Alexandra ponder gender—sex's monstrous, ecstatic gene-swapping, now found to exist in even the bacteria. Nature's deep sweet secret, a dimming memory for her now. Upstairs, detached from the group, she yielded to the low temptation, as if to a country fair's freak show, of the well-guarded mummy room. Placards in English and Arabic urged respect for the dead. Little brown dried bodies, the hands and facial muscles forever snagged on their final contraction, were swaddled like babies, their tiny feet exposed—as stringy as beef jerky, as dark as if charred. Alexandra's eyes rested on the label of an especially shriveled, pathetic one, its lips pulled back in a snarl and its skull snapped back like a stargazer's. The label read RAMSES II. The great statue downstairs. The same person. The god-man couldn't save himself. History's depths, she saw, were as sickeningly precipitous as Nature's.

On the museum's upper floor the leg-weary, eye-weary tourists and their semi-intelligible, slightly crippled guide came to the treasures of the teen-aged king Tutankhamun, whose tomb, almost uniquely in the Valley of the Kings, escaped plunder until modern times. There were life-size ebony statues that stood guard in the king's burial chamber as well as the king's ostrich-feather fan and his gameboards and hunting equipment—boomerangs, staves, a buckler— and model hoes, baskets, and other amulets intended to give the boy, dead so young, all he needed in the afterlife.

"Don't you hate *stuff*?" Jane asked at Alexandra's side.

"You think you need it at the time," Alexandra whispered.

The limping guide explained in stiff, high-pitched English, "Tutankhamun's entombed priceless treasures were discovered by the Englishman Howard Carter in 1922. He found them in a jumbled state, left as if by tomb robbers whose crime was interrupted, or by priests fulfilling their duties in unseemly haste."

Room after airless room held young King Tut's possessions: ebony statues, plain and gilded; various thrones and stools, all beautifully designed, including the famous golden throne; alabaster vases; model boats containing mummified food and magical emblems; various beds, including a folding camp bed and two large beds used in the embalming, a process supervised by the modelled heads of the goddess Hathor's cow and the hippopotamus goddess, Tawaret. In yet another high-ceilinged chamber, the two American women paused at an alabaster canopic chest with its four cavities for the boy-king's embalmed viscera. Dusty cases held crumbling textiles; the numbed tourists viewed a realistic bust in wood and stucco of Tutankhamun, and an "Osiris bed" shaped like the pharaoh's profile and filled with earth, on a linen bed, sewn with grain and moistened so that it would germinate in his tomb, symbolizing resurrection. Late rooms sequestered the pharaoh's solid-gold sarcophagus and the famous and gorgeous gold mask that covered the mummy's head, and scarabs and red-gold buckles and earrings and rings and, invading from another, crueler, future world, a knife with a blade of iron. Final rooms held spells for the dead king's guidance from the *Book of the Dead* and depicted figures of various deities to be encountered in the Underworld. Like spectres viewing their own corpses, the women inspected the detritus of a magical system as elaborate as it was useless. "They believed," the guide explained, his voice growing thin and irritated, "each person had five selves: your name, your *ka*, your *ba*, your heart, and your shadow. At the gateway of the afterlife, your heart was weighed against a feather, the feather of truth and justice. If it failed to balance, it fell to the Devourer—part hippo, part crocodile."

"How are you doing, doll?" Alexandra solicitously asked Jane. Last night her snoring had been not so bad—less a succession of infuriating hooks than a steady, rasping background noise, and Alexandra was so exhausted, the nervous shocks of travel ebbing from her system and being gradually replaced by habituation and acceptance, that she accepted this flaw in the room's silence, reflecting that at least she was not troubled, as she had been in Canada, by small noises and red safety lights in the room. In Egypt, there seemed to be no safety lights.

Jane answered, "I'm numb. How much more crap can there be in this attic?"

"Jane, so much of it is so beautifully made. So tender. To them, death was a journey to the Field of Reeds."

"Ye*ss*? If so, why did they put the corpse in so many stone boxes within boxes? They didn't want him *ever* to get out."

"They were tucking him in," Alexandra fantasized. "They wanted his *ba* to be able to use his body. Or was it his *ka*?" She had become the one who cared about Egypt, who wanted to rescue these fragile ancients from themselves, though Egypt had been Jane's idea. But Alexandra had been a widow for over two years and Jane had only had ten months to adjust. She kept mentioning Nat Tinker, as if she could bring him back with incantation. But he, too, was encased in stone boxes within boxes.

Once they had flown, next day, to Luxor and transferred to the *Horus*, it was, as Nat could have predicted, bliss. Each night, as the boat prowled to the next docking, the next temple, the thrumming of the engine absorbed much of Jane's snore, though the beds were close together in the little cabin. By day, the banks of the Nile passed as if an endless scroll was being unrolled. Oxen plodding in circles and shadoofs lifting and falling like wooden oil rigs ministered to the green fields with irrigation, under a sky as smoothly blue as a painted dome, while on board the *Horus* the tourists, smiling and nodding at one another through the many language barriers, swam in the little pool, a square no more than two strokes across, and basked on deck chairs, drank alcoholic drinks, nibbled peanuts called *soudani*, and gradually turned brown in the strengthening sun.

"Why are Egyptians so happy?" Jane asked Alexandra from her adjacent deck chair.

"I don't know. Why?"

"They're in de-Nile."

"Ouch."

The cruise first took them south from Luxor, to Esna in its sunken site beside a market where unappetizing parts of butchered oxen like the roofs of their mouths were displayed. Their guide was now a woman, a chic, unveiled Muslim in flared black silk slacks and broad silver bracelets and necklaces that flattered her olive skin. "The great dam at Aswan," she explained, "has raised the water levels in the Nile valley. Esna's foundations have become a set of wet cookies." It was true, the ground beneath their feet was soft, almost mud. Next day, they disembarked at sunstruck Edfu on its precipice, the best preserved of all the Late Dynasty temples. "The three B's," the guide told them, her heavily ringed fingers flicking toward the delicate reliefs. "Butts, boobs, and belly buttons—that is how we recognize the Graeco-Roman style. The sculptors tried to follow the old conventions but their hands and eyes wouldn't let them. They rounded limbs, they showed knees and little toes. The older style, always seeking the ideal, put the same feet on both legs, with the big toe toward the viewer. The Graeco-Romans couldn't do that, it was too ridiculous. They showed one foot with the little toe toward the viewer, the way it is. Heresy!" She laughed with dazzling teeth, beneath her big sunglasses and the straw hat with its curled brim that sat strictly level on her head. The next day brought them to lovable Kom Ombo, a double temple to the crocodile god Sobek and the late Horus—Haroeris, the falcon-headed, out to kill his uncle Seth, who had slain his father, Osiris. The guide, with her gleaming wristlets and flexible silver collar, led them to a room whose ceiling held the image of the sky-goddess Nut stretched across the sky, one end of her giving birth to baby Horus, Harpakhrad. Next day, the good ship *Horus* came to the temple of Philae, moved stone by stone to an island out of the reach of the rising waters of Lake Nasser. "This," their Muslim guide told them, in the hushed halls of transplanted stone, "was the last place the old religion was practiced. It lasted until the sixth century A.D., for two hundred years after the Christian edict of Theodosius the First in 378 A.D. Then, it became a church. Here"—she pointed with her aubergine fingernails at a nearly illegible small carving—"Isis suckling Horus became the Virgin Mary suckling Jesus. The cult of Isis spread widely through the Roman empire. She was the perfect widow, collecting fourteen pieces of the fifteen of her husband's body which the evil Seth had hidden in sarcophagi sunk in the Nile. The fifteenth piece she never found. You ladies can guess what it was."

The Nile boat had floated them to Aswan, site of the great dam the Russians had built, and of the Aga Khan's tomb and Lord Kitchener's gardens, reached by picturesque felucca, its crude sail tilting, on its return, in the sunset's blood-red light. As the two widows sat on the *Horus*'s cooling deck, waiting for the chimed summons to dinner to sound, bats flickered through the darkening sky. Jane extended her arm toward them and pronounced in an even harsher, deeper voice than her usual one the lethal words "*Mortibus, mortibus, necesse est.* Tzabaoth, Elchim, Messiach, and Yod: *audite!*"

Against the sanguine blush of the western sky—the eastern sky was already black and sprinkled with emerging stars—Alexandra saw one of the tiny black shapes, flicking back and forth above the river harvesting insects, cease its darting motion and plummet like a small broken umbrella into the river's lingering sheen.

"Jane!" Alexandra exclaimed. "Why did you do that?"

"To see if I still could. All those phony spells on the temple walls pissed me off, a little."

"The poor innocent bat—it wasn't 'a little' to him."

"Don't be sentimental, Angel. You know what a heartless stew Nature is. Think of the dragonflies I just saved from being crunched by nasty sharp bat teeth."

"Oh, Jane. After what we did to poor Jenny, I can't bear to think there's anything to it. Hexes and curses and so on. I want to believe we didn't do *any*thing."

"She trespasssed," Jane decreed, with the same malevolent sibilance with which she had pronounced, *Necesse est.* "She went beyond her bounds."

"All she did was say yes when Darryl asked her to marry him. And the way he fell apart later should make us glad he didn't ask us."

"If he'd asked one of us, maybe he wouldn't have fallen apart."

"I say fallen apart, but really he never looked quite put together. He was a hoax," Alexandra concluded, a bit smugly.

"Darryl was, and Horus wasn't? Really, *s*sweetie, those old Egyptian priests must have laughed themselves silly, thinking of the nonsense they put over on everybody, not for a day or a week but for *millennia*! What did the guide at Edfu tell us? The Temple of Amun at Thebes was given fifteen hundred square kilometers by Ramses III alone? Ten percent of all the cultivatable land at the time? No wonder the Nubians and Hyksos and whoever kept pushing in. It was a very *s*sick situation."

The thought hung there, in air so still Alexandra imagined she could hear the wiry high peeping of the remaining bats, frantically working their sonar. Black-haired Jane had taken a deep tan these days on the Nile, and her face blended into the dark. Her smile, and a glint of jewelry at her neck, and a crescent gleam from her Daiquiri glass betrayed her presence in the shadows of the afterdeck. To break the silence, Alexandra said, "I wonder how the bartenders and waiters feel, feeding us alcoholic drinks all the time?"

"Disgusted," Jane agreed. "Yet they do it very well. My Daiquiri is excellent. How's your whiskey sour?"

"Fine, actually. It's interesting—there's a whole population, of Muslims catering to Westerners, that's going to be thrown out of work when Al Qaeda takes over. Or will they be executed, as hopelessly impure?"

"Al Qaeda won't take over. Who on earth would want what they have to offer?"

"Not you and me, but . . . the people? The poor and miserable and so on. They need religion, whatever it costs. That's why I wonder if you aren't hard on the old Egyptian priesthood."

"It makes *me* wonder about the Jews," Jane said, her tongue rambling as the rum took hold. "How did they ever get mixed up in religion? They're too smart, usually. Abraham about to *ss*lit his own *ss*son's throat because God told him to—what an idiot!"

Alexandra offered, placatingly, "I've read somewhere the whole Captivity and Exodus wasn't historical. There's no Egyptian record of it—Moses and the bulrushes and 'let my people go.' "

"I never believed it," Jane said. "Any of it. Even as a tiny child. Nat was a churchgoer—Episcopalian, high church like his ridiculous mother—but I never went with him except to weddings and funerals. The whole fraud made me furious. I want to be cremated and stuck in the ground and everybody else walk away glad it's not them. No mumbo-jumbo, Lexa. Promise."

"Jane," her friend said. "You're too hard on us. All of us."

Jane might have replied, but the dinner chime broadcast its pretty tune, which sounded like the first six notes of "Oh Come, All You Faithful" but probably wasn't.

That night, with a throttling of engines and churning of water that woke Alexandra in her bunk from her first solid sleep in ages, the boat undocked and turned around and headed back to Luxor and the pointed obelisks and rounded temple pillars of Karnak, from which the cult of the ithy-phallic Amun, "the great god," had extended tentacles throughout the Nile's fertile valley. The tourists on the *Horus* had already paid some homage to the outdoor wonders of the east bank. Alexandra had coiled in her little pre-digital Canon many images of the massive ruins, of the deep-carved hieroglyphs and royal cartouches that, however long bombarded by photons sent from the blank blue sky, held their knife-sharp relief and decisive shadows in the sere air. The tourists' turn had come to visit the opposite side of the Nile, the western side, death's side, the Valley of the Kings, the Valley of the Queens, the Colossi of Memnon, and the lovely memorial temple of Queen Hatshepsut, widow of her half brother Thutmose II; upon his death she became regent for her infant half nephew and stepson, Thutmose III, and reigned with full pharaonic authority, wearing in her monuments masculine attire even to the beard, though she was still labelled with the feminine gender in her inscriptions. After her death a reaction, led by her ungrateful nephew, set in; her cartouches were defaced and her monuments eclipsed, and her peaceful, intelligent reign was stricken from the official lists. "Poor old witch," said Jane.

Building pyramids lapsed from favor after the Old and Middle Kingdoms. Monarchs of the New, for four centuries, sought safety while their *ka*s journeyed to the Field of Reeds by digging their tombs into the limestone cliffs of the Theban hills, by the bay of Deir el-Bahri. Illumination into their depths had been provided by linseed-oil lamps and by mirrors held to ricochet sunlight into what had been solid limestone; the excavators chipped and tunnelled and carted away the rubble by this borrowed light. The artists who followed them painted processions—head and legs in profile, chest seen frontally—of servants carrying, to the immured, supplies of fruit and drink and fresh candles to sustain their journey through the netherworld. Scenes of banquets and harvests and fishing parties illustrated the life they had left behind and the similar life they would reach. These scenes have been likened to music scores that only the dead have the instruments to play. The first mural on the left, traditionally, depicted offerings to Amun in his aspect as Rē, the falcon-headed sun-god, who reappeared further along in both his aged and nascent form—ram and beetle—within the solar disc, circumscribed between two of his enemies, the serpent and the crocodile.

The tourists shuffled downward by the light not of mirrors but of wan electric bulbs strung from a ceiling of limestone bearing countless chisel marks, down at a gentle slant on boardwalks that took them over pits dug to entrap tomb robbers and sealed false portals meant to bewilder them, down corridors adorned with scenes of priests performing the mouth-opening ceremony before the pharaoh's statue, into the pillared hall that led to the burial chamber itself, where the sarcophagus was sunk in its rectangular recess. "Amusingly," their guide—a goateed man in a tattered dusty suit and wire-rimmed glasses, an archaeology scholar hunched and desiccated by a life spent in tombs—announced to them, "Merneptah's anthropoid granite sarcophagus evidently proved too massive to carry all the way into the burial chamber, so here it sits at an angle, cockeyed, abandoned for three thousand years!" He managed a dry chuckle, took off his glasses, wiped the dust from their lenses with a handkerchief, restored the handkerchief to his hip pocket and the spectacles (their curved earpieces sheathed in flesh-colored sleeves) nicely to his nose, and confided to his stifling little audience, "The gravediggers were not superhuman but human—lazy and corrupt and distractible. Look, here in this side chamber—the murals were sketched in gray ink, but never finished, never colored in! I think they are charming, unfinished. You can feel the painter's hand, you can see his impatient strokes, made millennia ago. Even with so much time before him, he was in a hurry. He didn't know we would come and critique his work!"

Alexandra was fighting for breath. As if in a misstep, in the gloomy tilted space, she deliberately brushed against Jane, to feel another warm, still-living body. *No escape*, everything around her proclaimed. *No escape*, however energetically and luxuriously religions make a show of rescuing us from death. There is no magic, the world is solid, clear through, like the depths of limestone above her.

After emerging from the tomb of Merneptah, the tour group, blind as bats in the oppressive sun, trooped to the tomb of Ramses VI, one of the biggest, and to that of Tutankhamun, one of the smallest, its entrance lost for three thousand years under the rubble created by the excavation of the former. "They are touching, are they not?" their guide asked. "These small bare chambers hastily devoted to the dead boy-king. They seem too small for a king. It is thought that they might have been created for his chief minister, Ay, who succeeded him as pharaoh and may have poisoned him. Adding insult to injury, as you English say, Ay then may have taken over for himself the tomb intended for Tutankhamun in the Western Valley, near that of his grandfather Amen-hotep III—who may have been, in fact, his father. This is said, but to the serious scholar it is merely gossip. It seems beyond dispute, however, that Tutankhamun was the instrument, if not the instigator, of the restoration of the cult of Amun, undoing the revolution of Amenhotep IV, who called himself Akhenaten. You have heard enough, from other guides no doubt, about Akhenaten, a religious radical, perhaps a crazy man, who wished to abolish the cult of Amun and many gods in favor of Aton, the solar disk. He transferred the capital of Egypt from Thebes to a city he built and called Akhetaton. Tutankhamun, his successor after his son-in-law Smenkhkare—Tutankhamun was also his son-in-law, having married Akhenaten's third daughter when both were children. Tutankhamun was a sad small boy of ten when he ascended the throne and nineteen when he died. He was originally called Tutankhaton, after the solar disk. But he then turned coattails—is that a phrase?—and restored the priesthood of Amun, whose name means 'the hidden god,' to its old domination. Had he not turned his coat, who knows? Egypt might have embraced monotheism before the invasion of Islam. I believe you have all seen the Tutankhamun treasures, the glory of the Cairo museum. Can you imagine them crammed and jumbled into these little chambers? It makes us sad, no? The little fellow was used by the priests to bring back Amun and then was bundled off to the afterlife, possibly poisoned. The ancient politics was no more edifying than politics now."

This earned him a polite, tired, mystified titter. If he was alluding to Mubarak, he was playing with fire. If he meant Bush and Sharon, it was a cheap shot. In any case, the entombed tourists were thirsty, and it was time to return to the boat, return to the bar for *soudani* and iced arrack, and fly back next morning to Cairo, to Paris, Frankfurt, Tokyo, New York. At Kennedy, that shabby old port on the ocean of the air, Jane and Alexandra, having been together without remission for twelve days, having shared bathrooms and the dark of the night, all talked out, rather sick of each other if truth be known, were ready to part—Alexandra to Fort Worth–Dallas and then Albuquerque, and Jane to La Guardia and a shuttle flight to Boston. "That was great fun," Jane purred in a voice that didn't seem greatly to mean it. "Such fun to be with you, Gorgeous."

"I loved every minute," Alexandra lied. "The Nile, the heat, the boat, the pyramids and tombs. The paintings on the walls of the brown people with straight hair and long eyes doing their daily things. Squatting, eating, carrying, gathering papyrus. Playing the harp, remember that one? They loved life. *Ankh*, isn't that the word?"

"It was. Let's do another trip soon."

"How soon? I'm not like you. I have to save up, and rest up."

"A year or two?"

"Wouldn't it be fun," Alexandra shyly wondered, "if Sukie could come along? You and I both tend to be depressive. One's up, the other's down. Not Sukie. She's steady. But she's still married," she reminded herself.

Jane gave a strange look, askance, from her bright-brown tortoiseshell eyes. "Is she, though?" she asked. She tucked the hint of a smile into her left cheek, and there, in the ramshackle international airport, the two wicked women, not quite kissing each other on the lips, embraced and parted.

Suzanne Mitchell, as she had become with her marriage to jaunty, sandy-haired Lennie Mitchell, was a writer of a lowly

sort—small-town journalism, paperback romance novels—
but a writer nevertheless, married furthermore to a fast-
talking computer salesman, so it was second nature to her
to sit down before a humming, glaring screen and type out
her thoughts as they darted through her brain. Alexandra
unfolded the several smooth, laser-printed pages and read:

Dear, dear Lexa:
  Jane, whom I've seen a fair amount of since the sad event
I will describe in a minute, has been after me to phone you,
but it's been so long since we've been in touch obviously I've
felt shy. The kind of closeness the three of us had in Eastwick depends really on being there every day, and bumping
into one another by accident on Dock Street where you
could spontaneously say "Let's duck into Nemo's for a cup
of coffee," and having children in the same local schools
with the same teachers to bitch to each other about, and all
experiencing the same wretched weather and the same
tedious cocktail parties, and hearing without even knowing
you're hearing it the same town fire siren go off at every
noon, cutting the day in two, and sharing the same sense of
cozy isolation, Boston and New York way over the horizon
in different directions and Providence though closer always
somehow, maybe because of the repulsive religious name, a
place you stayed away from.
  Connecticut turned out not to be like that. The towns are
closer together, though not crammed together so one runs
right into the next as in northern New Jersey—that is *really*
repulsive—and have a more monied look (I hate to write it,
it sounds so snobby), even the sections where the handymen
and babysitters live. There aren't any of those delicious lost
corners, marshy waste spaces with abandoned duck blinds
and rotting striped mattresses somebody dumped, that you
find in Rhode Island, small as it is. The dumps, speaking of
dumps, are *terribly* well organized for recycling—paper in
one Dumpster and glass in another and colored glass in a
third and cans in a fourth, all of it arranged so you just drive

up and drop your nicely sorted trash down from above—
and even the woods they set aside as natural Nature places
seem weeded, with the fallen timber taken away and the
underbrush cleared so they have that carpeted look of English beech woods in those movies about Robin Hood that
even we could see as credulous children were Hollywood
sets. The little downtowns all have uniform antique signage
(love that word, like "dotage") and the school grounds and
children's playgrounds are tended right to the edges. For
that wasteland look you have to go to Bridgeport, which
nobody does. As you may remember I came from upstate
New York where everything had the look of not belonging
to this century, by which I mean of course the century that's
dead and gone by now, the good old twentieth. Upstate was
all nineteenth. When Lennie Mitchell brought me down
here to live I couldn't believe how self-conscious everything
was, everybody facing New York City in their minds, even
in Stamford when it was just Greenwich's poor cousin,
before all the companies getting away from city taxes
opened branches here and put up one blue glass skyscraper
after another, almost as bad as Hartford. Our section, on the
edge closest to the Merritt, hasn't been too affected yet—
that "our" is a slip, Lennie's and mine, I must get a grip. I've
started to sniffle and get that raw-throat feeling, thinking
about him. But the thing about all these suburbs is that having such a big city, *the* big city as far as the U.S. is concerned, keeps us on our toes and at the same time is rather
demoralizing, because we don't *quite* live there, we just live
in its aura, so to speak. The restaurants and shops and
beauty parlors aren't quite up to Manhattan standards but
they *try*, and even all those who don't commute in and out,
the local tradesmen and so on, share a certain New York
attitude, chip on the shoulder and gritting it out and standing tall and so on, like I imagine the English when they had
an Empire and then the Blitz. But people don't *know* each
other the way they did in Eastwick; they come and go, moving to more upscale houses or towns, and everybody terri-

bly competitive underneath, measuring each other by the standards of New York. It was a lesson to me and I couldn't have had the success with my writing that I have had living anywhere else. My agent lives right next door in South Norwalk and without him I'd be still doing small-town gossip columns, except all those little local newspapers are dying off, killed by blogs and e-mails, and in a strange way there aren't any small towns any more, just malls and commercial strips and assisted-living developments between them, and there isn't even *gossip* any more, the way there was when everybody was more sexually repressed. I think repression was the key to the kind of energy people used to have, we weren't burnt-out the way people are in their twenties now, all this hooking up the young people do. Now don't I sound prudish? And you know I'm not.

My news, in case you're wondering why I'm writing after all these years, is that Lennie died two months ago, quite suddenly, and Jane thought you should know. She's come back into my life almost as if she foresaw it coming. But how could she have?—he was in lovely health, never fat, always active, and gave up smoking about the time I met him, while I stupidly puffed on, though mostly only at parties and when trying to write, so they tell me my lung function is less than fifty percent. He still liked to do the organized dancing when we went to Florida for January, and tennis, just doubles, and jogged on the town paths (the local town boards plan for *everything*) and played squash and paddleball all winter. He dropped over in a squash court after making what the other man in there with him said was a marvellous retrieve. Just dropped there, against this wall full of dirty ball marks, and even though the other man was a doctor he was a gynecologist and couldn't even do resuscitation properly. By the time the paramedics came Lennie was quite gone. After eight minutes, they told me, there's bound to be brain damage, and I wouldn't have wanted to live with that. I suppose so but I wish they had let me decide. I still didn't like hearing it from them after the fact and can't help resenting that Lennie's so-called friend, being an M.D. with a cell phone right on him, didn't get help sooner. The squash courts are in the sub-basement of a big brassy new corporate building and hard to find if you haven't been there before.

Jane and I have been back-and-forthing a bit lately—I drive up more to her house than she to mine. Her ancient mother-in-law is rather a dear, though Jane thinks the old lady ruined her marriage to Nat Tinker. She also thinks it would do me good in my grief if I took a trip with her. With the two of you, ideally, if the trip to Egypt with just Jane Pain didn't do you in. It sounds terribly dry and educational and brave with all those Muslims giving you dirty looks for not wearing a veil, but I don't see how you stood all that death the Egyptians dwelt on. Those long deep passageways, I doubt I could have stood it and don't know how you did, being such an outdoors person. Jane said you rode a camel and got a sunburn on the boat where she got a great tan. I don't know how many steps you had to climb but I can't do many with my emphysema. Steps were where I first noticed that I wasn't my girlish self any more. If we ever were to go anywhere together—and I'm not sure it's a good idea, maybe we all *had* our fun in life—I think it should be China. It seemed everybody we knew socially in Stamford had been to China but when I'd suggest it Lennie would say he'd rather go have a Chinese meal and pay for it and leave. He didn't like Communists even if we *had* won the Cold War, as if everybody didn't know that the Chinese are only Communists in name anymore. I picture it as a wide-open sort of place, with a big sky and huge open city squares and people eating noodles in the little alleys. The *hutongs*, aren't they called? I've had a romantic thing about China ever since seeing Ingrid Bergman in that movie about leading a pack of children to safety in some kind of an inn. Of the sixth happiness, it just came to me. Think about it, dearest. Jane will be in touch with you also. She seems to want to devour the whole world before she leaves it, or else she just wants to stay away from her mother-in-law, who ancient or not doesn't miss much. She has Jane's number, is my impression when we talk (the old lady and I) briefly.

About widowhood, what can I tell you? You've been through it. I still keep expecting Lennie to come home at night and when he doesn't it's like he's willfully refusing or up to some mischief and it makes me *mad*. I'm free of course of a lot of annoying male habits and laziness — the kitchen floor over by the toaster doesn't have English-muffin crumbs all over it, for instance — but what good is freedom if nobody's watching you have it? Lennie was a salesman and a wife can get tired of being sold things she doesn't want much. For instance, he had to have this ski place in southern Vermont though once the children began to rebel at being herded into the station wagon every weekend we hardly ever used it, and as the mountain lost cachet — they do, you know, just like restaurants — real-estate values went way down. For another instance, he bought me one of these fashionable new stoves with smooth black tops and the burners under it just barely visible, so I kept burning myself and setting vegetables in the wrong place where they stayed raw. As his computer business picked up again what with so many companies coming out from NYC to Stamford, he bought me a heavyweight navy-blue BMW because when he met me I was still driving that gray Corvair with the top you pulled down and locked by hand. I loved that car, remember? Like sitting in a bathtub going all over town with my hair streaming behind me and Hank (my beautiful Weimaraner, remember?) sitting up in the front seat beside me with his ears flattened pink inside out. Lennie thought the Corvair was tinny and unsafe for me to be driving. The BMW, which I still have, always feels to me like a man's fantasy car — it has this phallic stick shift on the floor I'm always jamming into the wrong gear, and it rides so you feel every bump on the road. That was manly right there. At first in Stamford — not exactly Stamford but a village on the northern edge called Rocky Ridge — I had a comfy old red

Taurus that I just loved, its trunk took a week's worth of groceries plus a golf bag. But Lennie had to buy me that expensive BMW, just to let people know we had money again. And he would make me buy flashy clothes—a "fun fur" that made me look like a stupid puffball, and backless party dresses that would give me a cold for weeks. The reason, it turned out, was that his girlfriend at the office, who kept getting younger of course, one after another, wore clothes like that. Once, we turned up at the same business party on his boss's lawn in Old Greenwich in the same exact clingy silk print, with a sash instead of a belt. We hugged each other at the end, it was so humiliating. He would sell me his affairs, too, after I discovered them, convincing me they were my fault. But that push of his, that salesman's constant aggravating engaging push—it's *gone*, dear Lexa. The way the dead vanish is almost enough to make you believe they go somewhere else. Going from room to room in our useless oversize house here I feel like that girl in the palace where the Beast never shows himself. That silence in the hour he used to pull into the driveway—do you ever get used to it? I'm so glad you met him that time in Manhattan at the Roosevelt Grill, in case I ever forget that he really existed or come to believe he was a perfect saint.

Now that I have a little distance on him I can see he was a lot like Monty—a spiffy dresser and a male chauvinist. Sexual attraction keeps making the same mistakes. But less sardonic—he never made me feel stupid the way Monty sometimes tried to do. But, then, I was so young, just twenty, when I married him (Monty). The children have taken his death (Lennie's) rather too much in stride, it seems to me. But why not, they're all middle-aged, even little Bob, our one joint product (Lennie and me), on top of the three I brought with me from Monty. To the children his death is just part of Nature's natural cycle, but to me it's the end of my life of being important to *anybody*.

Give me a call if you can't be bothered to write. I know it's more work for most people than it is for me. The trouble with these word processors is it's too easy to go and on, and once they've perfected voice recognition and transcription, won't that be a horror of sheer unhampered babble?— just the way the world used to be when it was all tribes and shamans and oral literature. I'd love to come visit you in sunny Taos but where I used to freckle charmingly I now get a hideous blotchy sun rash. O the joys of these sunset years! Does the sun ever shine in China? I hope not. You never see shadows in the scenes on their teapots and room-divider screens, I know that.

> *Mucho* love, long overdue,
> Sukie

So, the next September, Alexandra joined the two others in the San Francisco airport, and together they flew for eleven and a half hours to Narita Airport in Japan, suspended within the engines' giant hum. Flying in the same direction as the planet's rotation, they arrived three and a half hours later the next day. Their inner clocks thoroughly deranged, they rose from a few hours' attempted sleep in a transit hotel and were ushered onto an Air China flight to Beijing. After the hyper-modernity of the Narita facility, the Chinese airport seemed barny and crude, floored in uneven linoleum and echoing with the coarse, hooting laughter of the baggage handlers in their baggy clothes. China, the three exhausted women apprehended, was a jolly place, where the past was in the present tense and visitors who obeyed all the rules would come to no harm.

Sukie's being along greatly helped Alexandra's sense of well-being. She hadn't seen her, the youngest and most cheerful of their little coven, since before the millennium, back when Bill Clinton was President and wriggling pitifully in the grip of the Lewinsky scandal. Jim Farlander had

grudgingly consented to their last winter trip to the Caribbean, and the bargain flight came back through Kennedy, so
Alexandra had suggested they take two extra nights and visit
some museums, not just the Met and the Modern and the
Guggenheim but the Cooper-Hewitt with its fantastic collection of American ceramics. To cement her inspiration she
had called a number in Connecticut—it still rang!—and
invited her old friend from Eastwick to come into Manhattan for dinner. She and Jim couldn't get a reservation at
"21," where the famous ate, so they met the Mitchells at the
grill in the Roosevelt.

Lennie had seemed a bit preoccupied and jumpy at first
but on the second round of drinks began to reveal himself as
a blowhard, loud like the double-breasted Harris tweed suit
he had on. By the second bottle of wine with the meal, while
Jim waxed more and more silent, Lennie got confiding, as
though he had successfully sold them whatever it was he was
selling, fuller and fuller of little twinkles and winks as he told
a few stories illustrating what a lovable featherhead Sukie
was, churning out these little romance novels for frustrated
lamebrain women. He was that type of sandy-haired man,
with even teeth, small ears, and blue eyes, who early in life
got the idea, probably from his infatuated mother, that he
was irresistible. He kept putting his hand on Alexandra's
forearm when the punch line of a story was approaching,
and by the time they were into dessert and Irish coffee his
hand, dropping casually out of sight behind the table edge,
had migrated to her thigh, resting there like a heavier napkin. What she especially didn't like about Lennie Mitchell
was how mousy Sukie seemed in his presence, cowed even,
with a trace of a stammer and a defensive bluestocking
drabness. Her carrot-colored hair, that she used to grow
as long as a flower child's, was cut shorter and showing gray;

her plump lips nibbled at each other as if she were trying to remember something, or perhaps this was just her
nearsighted squint when she wasn't wearing contacts. Her
attempts to reinforce her husband and revive a conspiratorial gaiety with Alexandra seemed forced efforts, from a
stressed and washed-out version of the blithe oversexed
Sukie of old.

Afterwards, in their room at the Roosevelt, after the other
couple had rushed off to catch the ten-seventeen, in such a
flurry that they put up the feeblest token resistance to Jim's
gallant insistence on signing for the check, her husband
said to Alexandra, "That's some slick con man there. But
Suzanne's a little honey."

His words were still cut into his memorial chamber in her
mind: *Suzanne's a little honey.* She had replied, "I'm glad you
saw that. She was our beauty, back then. But she seemed a
ghost tonight."

Now, by a trick of lesser expectations or of fresh context,
Sukie seemed her old self, giddy and crisp and even shiny, to
match Chinese décor. Her hair was tinted its former color,
her lipstick was glossily applied. Her body, to Alexandra's
eye, was a few pounds leaner in her late sixties than the glim-
mering soft shape, lithe and freckled and firm-breasted, that
she presented in her thirties, filmed with droplets of con-
densed steam, in Darryl Van Horne's dark-panelled hot-tub
room. Alexandra had caressed this apparition with not only
fingertips but a thirsty mouth. Sukie's own lips, though now
less plump with natural collagen, still had a habit of remaining parted, in a wondering way, on her face, in a lingering
afterglow of astonishment.

Everything in China was more or less astonishing, beginning with their being here at all, on the other side of the
world, in a country the size of the United States, with four

times as many people. China within their memory-span had taken various forms: a fabled land of starving children, Pearl Buck peasants, dragon ladies, rickshaws, and comic-strip pirates; a friendly democracy ably led by Chiang Kai-shek and his glamorous Soong-sister wife; a suffering victim of the vicious Japanese and a staunch ally of President Roosevelt; a post-war, Cold War field of civil conflict wherein President Truman cannily declined to intervene and wherein the staunch Nationalists lost to the Communists; a tightly closed bastion of inimical political creed; a source of hordes of enemy "volunteers" pouring southward in Korea; a ponderous mass of robotized humanity that might swallow us if prodded at Quemoy or Matsu or Formosa; a mob of Mao-chanting Red Guards in a Cultural Revolution brutally parodying the West's Sixties counterculture; then, after Nixon's trip and gawky dinner toasts, an ally again, against the Soviet Union; after Mao's death and the Gang of Four's overthrow, a tender seedbed of budding free enterprise; after Deng Xiaoping's triumph of pragmatism, a voracious consumer of American jobs and receiver of American dollars; and now the twenty-first century's impending superpower, a billion three hundred million factory workers and consumers, a creditor of sagging American capitalism and competitor for the dwindling global supply of oil. There in the airport Sukie cried in her high, faintly breathless voice, "We're going to have such *fun!*"

Their baggage was still to emerge on the creaky belts. Other Americans, like frogs whose eyes and nostrils emerge from the muck rimming a shallow pond, began to be visible to them. Deeper into the turmoil of arrival, their tour escort, a sallow small New Zealander whose parents had been medical missionaries in Taiwan and who had taken in Mandarin, Cantonese, and Japanese with his daily rice, appeared beyond a certain gate, and, hurling scraps of language right and left to clear a path, led the group he had collected to a waiting bus. The three women inhaled the exciting, dim-lit air, the air of China, peppered with indecipherable aromas and unintelligible announcements, a vast underworld surfacing into tourism. The bus was almost too cozy, full of contented babble all too easily understood—those languid on-rolling American voices, the drawled flirtatious "kidding," the self-pleasing accent of the last century's superpower, its retirees complacently settling into their seats as if at the dark start of a long movie.

The road from the airport felt lightly trafficked; young trees lined it, miles of it, and flickering low lights, like stage footlights. The city gradually enclosed the bus with illumined alleyways and low buildings roofed in red tile. "*Hutongs*," Sukie pronounced, from the seat ahead.

Under a streetlight a man sat in a straight chair having a haircut, a sheet tucked around his chin just as if he were in a barbershop indoors. To Alexandra the sight, so calm and stark, seemed magical: the simplicity of using an alley as a room. The rent-free economy of it, your professional equipment pared down to a sheet and a pair of scissors.

It must have been after midnight. Jane, seated beside her, had fallen asleep, her breath rasping in a pale echo of her snores in Egypt, like a small caged animal that has given up any real hope of escape. Of the three of them, Jane, being the richest widow, had arranged for a single room, leaving the other two to share a second room. Jane's wish to be alone made Alexandra wonder if she also had snored; it was a disconcerting thought. Jim had never complained, but, then, he was often deaf to her, sitting at his singing wheel, thinking his monotonous masculine thoughts. What a curious test Nature sets us, surrendering consciousness every day, baring ourselves to who knows what oneiric assaults and embarrassments.

The hotel loomed above its neighborhood of dark low houses like a great ship showing rows of burning lights above sullen waves. In the towering atrium a pianist, late as the hour must be, was playing Broadway show tunes for a scattering of Asian bar customers: a meditative "Blue Moon," a bouncy "Mountain Greenery." "Oh, I do love this crazy place!" Sukie exclaimed. "Lexa, let's be *happy* here!" She had replaced Jane at Alexandra's side. Jane had drifted off and slumped into a bloated lobby chair, thus detaching herself at a moment that should have been shared three ways.

Sharing: that was what China let them do that was harder to do in their own country, with all its private property and enlightened self-interest. They ate lunch and dinner at round tables with plates of food on great lazy Susans laden with platters that bustling waitresses replaced by the armful. Twelve or fourteen Americans at each table had to attack mounds of noodles, vegetables, pieces of meat, dumplings (especially delicious and slippery, the dumplings), and even grains of rice with nothing more acquisitive than chopsticks. The morning's sightseeing, and then the afternoon's, with no snacking possible, left them hungry, and there was a spiritual gain in seizing, with acquired patience and deftness, a portion as the swiftly dwindling dishes rotated by. Alexandra shared with Sukie the hour or two of recapitulation, reading, and underwear-washing in the hotel room before sleep seized them as if they were innocent children who had played hard all day. Sukie's breathing, on her fifty percent of lung function, was not noisy; rather, it was so quiet that on the first nights Alexandra would climb out of bed and

THE WIDOWS OF EASTWICK

bend over and listen to make sure her friend was inhaling oxygen and expelling carbon dioxide. She resisted the temptation to caress the other woman's hair, or touch a gleaming piece of exposed shoulder, though she did sometimes adjust the covers where Sukie, cuddling herself, had tangled them. Any more contact than that, and Jane in the next room would sense it, and wax jealous, and their precious trinity would be broken. The flaw in a threesome is that two can gang up on one.

The Great Wall, which they had come all this way to see, was their first sight, the first day, when they were all still jet-lagged. The bus containing the three widows lurched and swayed on the small, twisting roads that led through the hills that climbed for an hour toward the Great Wall, nearer the capital than they had imagined. The tour was provided with not only the Taiwan-educated guide and two smiling though generally silent young Party escorts but with an American lecturer, who stood up front and fought for balance as he talked into his hand-held microphone. "Whenever there's a problem in China," he said, staggering sideways as the bus swung around a hairpin curve, "the government says, 'Let's throw a party!' " He went on to say, as best as Alexandra could hear him, "The first emperor of a unified China, spelled Q-I-N but pronounced 'Ch'in,' a man we're going to hear a lot about on this trip, conscripted an estimated one million people, about one-fifth of China's total workforce, to erect a continuous wall along the entire northern frontier of his newly assembled empire. Some walls already existed, built as long ago as the seventh century B.C. In the [she didn't catch the name] desert you can find sections dating back to the second century B.C. made of twigs, straw, rice, and sand. In most other sections, rammed earth was the preferred material. The substantial section you're going to see, of bricks and mortar, broad enough on the top for five horsemen to ride abreast, with garrisoned beacon towers equipped to set off smoke signals or fireworks in case of enemy attack, was built that way in the Ming Dynasty, four-teenth to seventeenth century, and restored to its excellent present condition twenty-five years ago by a team of Ger-man masons, engineers, archaeologists, and existentialists."

There was laughter in the bus, a few damp firecrackers of nervous, anxious-to-please laughter, and Alexandra won-dered if the word had truly been "existentialists." Her hear-ing was not improving with age. But the lecturer, learning to flex his knees to cushion the swerves of the bus, frowned and persisted in what she thought might be an existential, despairing style. He frowned and brought the little micro-phone closer to his lips. "The fact is, it never worked. Not for Ch'in, not for the Mings. The Manchus came right in over the wall, or right through the gaps, and formed the next dynasty. Ch'in threw an entire generation into the Wall— think of it as stuck together with blood, and broken backs, and long nights trying to sleep in the cold on a dirt floor. Nevertheless, his empire crumbled anyway. His son suc-ceeded him but couldn't hold it together for more than four years. Ch'in was like Cromwell, a one-man dynasty. He took the title 'First Emperor' when he was thirty-eight and died eleven years later. But he gave China its enduring shape. He standardized its script, its weights and measures, its coinage—that little square in the center of a coin was his— and the width of chariot axles. He organized the empire into administrative units and brought under his thumb the pow-erful families in the capital. He wasn't a Confucian or a Taoist but a legalist—he believed people were basically evil or at least stupid and had to be restrained by written laws, ruthlessly enforced. He was a totalitarian, not as a matter of contingency but of dogma, of doctrine. No individual counted, except himself. It was a beautiful absolutism, broken up, after his death, into warring states. We'll see the clay army he was buried with later in this tour. He was a murderous megalomaniac, but it wasn't enough to secure China's borders. As history makes clear, there is no keeping barbarians out. They always eventually win. Energy comes from below, from the excluded and oppressed, from those with nothing to lose. It's like water in a pot on a stove: the hottest, on the bottom, rises to the top."

"He means the Arabs," Jane muttered into Alexandra's ear. The Chinese bus driver, perhaps losing patience with this American's unintelligible, amplified voice, took a curve especially fast, without braking. The lecturer staggered and nearly fell down the steps where passengers boarded and disembarked. "We'll be there in half an hour," he announced into the microphone, and sat down in the front row.

The day had begun under a pearly overcast, but by the time the buses parked and the tourists trudged up the steep dirt slope, the sun had worked its way through and infected all things visible with dazzle. The path up to the Wall was lined on both sides by stalls selling silk scarves, cotton T-shirts lettered in Chinese characters or Roman characters, and trinkets—painted tops, toy acrobats, birds of plastic and wood that fluttered and chirped at the end of a stick, carved balls within balls, miniature pagodas, images of the Great Wall painted on porcelain ovals or stamped on round medallions—that glittered in the sun. Oppressively, the proprietors of each stall called out to the shuffling tourists, and a few intruded into the roadway, desperately thrusting some gaudy useless thing into a likely-looking

Western face. Alexandra kept moving, spurning importunities with a regretful half-smile. Jane didn't bother with a smile but kept making a sharp hand motion as if brushing away midges hovering in front of her face. Sukie smiled tentatively, with a round-eyed look of piqued curiosity, so the vendors congregated around her, shouting and upholding their wares. Her two companions thought it most politic to keep moving upward, to the Wall's top. When Sukie, puffing slightly, caught up with them, she was wearing a conical straw hat, tied beneath her chin with a soft red string. Further, she had two more such hats in her hand, and held them out for her friends to don.

"*Sss*uzanne Mitchell," Jane admonished her, emphasizing each syllable. "Think of all the germs and filth that have been breathed on it. You shouldn't touch it, let alone buy it. They still have tuberculosis here. People *ss*pit everywhere; I saw them doing it in the airport."

"Oh, Jane, don't be such a pain," Sukie said breezily. "How often are we going to be in China? Lexa, here, take yours. They were asking fifty each but gave me three for a hundred yuan. That's about twelve dollars. And they're so classic. Don't you like it on me?" She flirted her head this way and that, and tipped the hat back. Her long hair, pulled back over her tidy small ears, was a brassier imitation of its old orange color; her bangs flashed in the sun, on the edge of the shadow of the Great Wall.

"Very much, Sukie," Alexandra said. "But maybe it's you more than the hat." She set her own on her head—one size fit all—and tied the crimson cord beneath her chin. She felt safer in the hat's weightless shade. Floating motes of sunshine filtered through. Jane doubtfully followed suit, slightly out of step with her sisters in mischief.

Sukie told them, a little breathlessly, "Once I put it on, the other vendors stopped pestering me. It was magic." Alexandra saw her lips tense, to get more air, after that little climb. They stayed open, expelling breath, trying to clear her lungs for the next breath. Pity squeezed her friend's heart.

Alexandra said, "If you listened to the lecturer, the whole Wall is magic—a ten-thousand-mile charm against barbarian invaders." On its top, attained by stone steps, the view of it—a broad brown-brick dragon snaking its way along a ridge from one squat tower to the next—excited in Alexandra the same sensation of lightness, of being *on high*, that she had felt in Canada on the boardwalk to Sanson Peak. The Great Wall, she had once read as a child in *Ripley's Believe It or Not!*, is the only work of Man that could be seen by observers on the moon.

A little distance away, the Wall's broad top held a pay-telephone booth with a sign advertising in many languages and scripts that from here you could call anywhere in the world. Though the vicinity was thronged, the booth was empty. "We could call some of our children," Alexandra suggested.

"They wouldn't get the wonder of it," Sukie said. "They live in a world where when you dial the local airport for information you get somebody in India reading from a card in an accent you can't understand."

Jane told them, "My older son plays bridge on the Internet with a group that includes a man from Ulan Bator and a woman from Albania. They talk entirely in cards." Alexandra tried to recall Jane's children—there had been an obese boy and a scrawny girl and two others. The girl had a dirty face with food always stuck in her braces. They had, none of the three witches, been ideal mothers—not by the standards of today's obsessive parents, who never let their children out of their sight, even at a bus stop just across the street—but even by the laxer standards of their less careful era Jane had been scandalously neglectful.

"But we're not them," Sukie insisted, trying to keep their party spirits up. "We're pre-electronic, and *thrilled* to actually *be* here. To us the Earth is still enormous, right?" She took each companion by one hand and dragged them with her, walking and then racing, downhill, three abreast, on the top of the Wall, to the next tower, where the emperor's soldiers had kept watch and slept and cooked, leaving smoke stains that could still be seen, centuries later. Beyond that tower, the German restorers had lost interest, and the Wall was more loosely repaired, and in another hundred yards, they could see ahead, it turned upward into an untraversable rubble, guarded by barriers. Out of breath with running and giggling, having flown on pattering feet through the askance glances of other tourists and stony-faced guards, the widows took time to peer out through the Wall's battlements at the territory beyond, the terrain of the dreaded nomadic barbarians. Blue mountain ranges, each dimmer than the one before it, receded into the hazed sky without yielding a speck of visible habitation or a patch of cultivation. On the other side, the side to the east and south that they had come from, every slope had been terraced and flooded, every valley cupped a village, and a gaudy mess of shops and quick eateries spilled downhill from the Wall's foundations. This was China, teeming under Heaven's mandate.

Exhilarated by their romp along the edge of the civilized world, Sukie asked a plump American, a grotesque barbarian in Bermuda shorts, billed baseball cap, and running shoes, to take their photograph on her little digital Nikon, the newest thing, bought specially for this trip; he rapidly took several and showed them on the viewing screen what they looked like in China, their three coolie hats tipped back to show their gamely grinning elderly faces. Three magi, framed in preposterous oversize haloes of straw. "That will be our Christmas card," Sukie promised, laughing.

How quickly, Alexandra thought, they had slipped back into being a trio, a trinity coming together to form a cone of power. It was not that she liked the other two women better than her leathery, bohemian, long-haired, jeans-clad female friends in Taos—comparatively, Sukie and Jane had narrow, Northeastern horizons—but in their company she felt more powerful, more deeply appreciated, more positively enjoyed. They had known her at the height of her desirability, in a society that, isolated from urban narcissism and yet partaking of the sex-centered excitement of the times, had valued desirability above all else. Compared with Sukie she had not been promiscuous—rather, lazily loyal to her hopeless husband and her long-term lover, the would-be husbandly Joe Marino. Compared with Jane she had been motherly and conventionally observant of traditional decencies. Yet she somehow reigned over the others, as a broader conduit into the subterranean flow of Nature, that dark countercurrent to patriarchal tyranny which witchcraft drew upon. It was chemistry: without her as catalyst, the dangerous, empowering reaction did not occur.

The next day was allotted for a bus tour of Beijing. Cleansed by setting foot on the Wall and viewing from its parapets the unpeopled blue majesty of the barbarian realms, which no wall was able to exclude, and refreshed by a night of solid sleep (Sukie did not snore, drawing breath into her damaged lungs with the lightness of a kitten, a near-inaudible sound that merged with the Western-style hotel's fan-driven ministrations of thermal comfort; yet having another person in the room with her relaxed Alexandra, as if this other weak widow could protect her), the three tourists were led through the stately labyrinth of the Forbidden City. It was built, their lecturer told them in the lurching bus, by the third Ming emperor, to strengthen the always vulnerable northern frontier nearby. "Talk about giving a party!" he said into his microphone. "Two hundred thousand laborers slapped it up in just fourteen years, ending in 1420. It was first named the Purple Forbidden City. The North Star was called 'the purple palace' and thought to be the center of the universe. The emperor by association was meant to be a divine instrument of universal power. The emperors of two dynasties ruled from here until 1911, when the boy-emperor Pun-yi abdicated—poor little Pun-yi. No doubt a number of you have seen the movie, some of it filmed right here. The Forbidden City is quite a survivor. It has survived fire, war, civil war, and the Cultural Revolution, which not much else historical did. Mao thought China's past was a dead weight on the country and had been for ages. The Forbidden City was laid out on principles first devised in the Shang Dynasty, three millennia ago, at which time our own Caucasian ancestors were painting themselves blue and chipping away at flint arrowheads."

The bus driver, having failed, through many abrupt turns in the city streets, to throw the lecturer off his feet, braked to a stop next to Tiananmen Square. The tourists dismounted. The lecturer stood his ground in a flood of other tourist groups at the Tianan Gate, the Gate of Heavenly Peace, and shouted, "Everything is symmetrical, as you can see. All the courts and ceremonial halls are built on a north-south axis. The marble walkway is for only the emperor's sedan chair. Everybody else, no matter how important— ministers, scribes, concubines, the empress herself—walked through side passages and doorways. Now look at us— tourists, barbarians, *jengin*—standing in the dead middle, where only the emperor's sedan chair used to go! When Starbucks applied for a permit to build right next to the Gate of Heavenly Purity, Starbucks got it! Good-bye *feng shui*; hello, half-caf latté!"

Alexandra studied the lecturer: a short, soft-bellied, pasty man in rimless glasses, his thinning hair standing up in dry clumps, a dishevelled academic on semi-vacation, tieless and coatless and the cuffs of his white shirt rolled up in the late-summer heat, yet with something passionate and even defiant in his loud, insistently instructive voice and his beetling black eyebrows. She liked to look at men and ask herself if, when she was nubile, she would have been attracted enough to this one, that one, to go to bed with them. Sex had faded from her life years ago; even when Jim was still there it had ceased to make urgent claims; yet the reflexes, the frame of reference, remained.

Gates, courtyards, halls—of Supreme Harmony, of Preserving Harmony, of Mental Cultivation, of Complete Harmony, of Clocks and Watches—succeeded one another stupefyingly. Double eaves tiled in shiny imperial yellow curved up at the ends, against the sky. At the Gate of Heavenly Purity, even the emperor's most trusted ministers could not pass, but had to gather outside at dawn to deliver a report. Could he hear it? Could he act upon it? Who heard his edicts, read with ultimate pomp at the Gate of Heavenly Peace? Boxes within boxes, a paralysis of harmony. Life must have collected, Alexandra sensed, in little pockets, in murmurous furtive drifts. The little wooden rooms, almost cages, in which the concubines passed their lives, made her smile in a sort of recognition: captive women, bored, filling the interminable minutes with jealous quarrels and desperate spells, their small hearts trembling in fearful hope of the emperor's fickle favor alighting at last.

The long morning became afternoon. The lecturer led them back out, past the two-hundred-ton marble relief of nine dragons, past bronze cranes symbolizing longevity, sandalwood thrones cushioned in pale silk, and cloisonné screens, through musty treasuries of candleholders, wine vessels, tea sets, imperial seals, carved jade and coral, across floor after floor of golden tiles, and released them back at the Gate of Heavenly Peace, to the vastness of Tiananmen Square, the largest such public space in the world. The lecturer pointed out that the huge portrait of Mao hung above the gate was squarely on the imperial axis; even the Great Helmsman's asymmetrical facial mole had been realigned. Their trip's own helmsman, whose name was Mr. Muir, looked at his wristwatch, a big cheap one, and shouted out, "Be back at the bus in one hour. Don't do anything barbaric."

While Chinese children and peddlers of gimcrack souvenirs stared at them as if at exotic, human-size animals, Alexandra, Jane, and Sukie debated whether or not to get into line for Mao's Mausoleum, at the far end of the square. "Do they still adore him?" Alexandra asked. "I thought that other one, Deng somebody, had overthrown him."

"Not quite," Jane snapped. "Honeymooners come, and other people in from the country. The poor, yes, still adore him. Like *S*stalin in Russia—the losers under the new system *s*still adore him."

"Oh, we *must* do it!" Sukie said. "We'll never have the chance again. I want to see honeymooners!"

Young newlyweds, touchingly well dressed and discreetly touching hands, did indeed compose an element of the two long lines. But also there were children, one each per pair of parents, and elderly people in pajamas, and Taiwanese businessmen in sleek dark suits, joking and smoking among themselves. The lines, kept in order by uniformed guards, moved swiftly; before she could quite believe it, Alexandra was in the hushed hall, her eyes actually resting on the globally famous face, the implacable Other, absolute ruler for twenty-seven years of a quarter of the world's population, an emperor at last accessible to his people. The body lay in a crystal coffin, blanketed by a red flag. The face was smaller than she had expected it to be, and didn't look like him. For all his cult of personality, Mao looked impersonal, evenly coated with orange makeup not quite the color of living skin, his face deflated and generic: it could have been anybody, at least any stolid Chinese man immobilized by taxidermy, his hair combed straight back. As Alexandra stared at the orange profile, Mao's eye opened; its black iris seemingly slid sideways as if to see her, and then shut again, quick as a wink, the eyelid sealed like glued paper.

Her heart leaped in her chest; a soft high-pitched grunt escaped her, and the young couple behind her glanced at her resentfully, their sacred moment with the corpse marred by a female barbarian. *Don't do anything barbaric.* Visible on the other side of the crystal coffin, Sukie and Jane, in the other line, were already moving by, with set respectful expressions. The lines passed through the official souvenir shop and into the clamor outside, of vendors hawking obsolete Little Red Books and paperweights preserving Mao's image. Alexandra asked her two companions, "Did you do that?"

"Do what?"

"Make Mao wink at me. I nearly died of fright, right on the spot. If I'd fainted or screamed we all would have been clapped into jail for disturbing the peace."

Sukie laughed gaily. Jane seemed determined not to apologize. She said without smiling, "We couldn't *ssee* if it worked or not. Nothing happened on our *s*side of his profile."

Sukie tried to soften the trick, explaining, "It was just that we could see you wearing this look of fake solemnity, like an atheist taking mass, so we cooked up a little tease."

Alexandra protested: "I was just blending in. They can see I'm not Chinese, but maybe they can think I'm a fellow traveller."

"Lexa," said Sukie fondly, "you're such a darling goody-goody. And so conceited, really. Why would he wink at you, especially? He's been lying there for years, with millions going by."

Jane added, rather angrily, "They know why you're in line. *S*simple, *s*stupid curiosity. You don't give these people credit for being as sophisticated as they are. They have the Internet now—they know all about the West. They know how childlike we are, wanting to see Mao's body. They know how we used to have his picture up in all the college dorms, even though he'd promised to bury us."

"That was somebody else," Sukie said. "That funny bald Russian with all the consonants in his name. I loved him when he was in Hollywood, acting up. Remember?"

Alexandra continued to protest. "But he *did* wink," she said. "I wondered if the couple behind me saw it, but I didn't know how to ask them. They acted a little annoyed." She was jealous, in truth, that the other two women had ganged up on her, bewitching her, if only for a second.

And the other two sensed that they had trespassed, however playfully, against their trinity. With their reunion their powers were returning as prickings, foreshadowings, a girlish relish in malice, in *maleficia*. They agreed, over dizzying plum brandy in the hotel bar, that their next illusory projection—this faintest, flimsiest exercise, scarcely more supernatural than hypnosis and female intuition—would come from all three, united under their cone of power, against an outsider.

Next day, the tour flew in two hours to ancient Xian, the emperor Ch'in's capital city, site of matriarchal neolithic settlements dating back to 4500 B.C.: Xian, birthplace of Chinese pottery and, much later, of Chinese Communism. North and west of the city lay many imperial tombs, including Ch'in's, not yet excavated, though it held such rumored wonders as rivers of mercury. His buried army of terra-cotta warriors was discovered, a mile away, in 1974, when farmers digging a well unearthed some sculpture. Mr. Muir ("Not *D.* Muir," Jane punned), swaying and nearly toppling at the front of the bus, told them all this. Then he led them into the great shed, equipped with touch-screen computer displays and a 360-degree movie, erected over the pits containing ranks of terra-cotta soldiers, numbering in the thousands, though only a thousand or so had been completely pieced together by archaeologists. "Pit One," Mr. Muir told them, as they clustered tightly around to hear him above the noise of other tourists and other lecturers on the walkway around the pits, "consists of eleven parallel sunken corridors. They were originally roofed with wood covered in straw matting and clay. The roof collapsed over the years, and the soldiers were crushed. Their legs are solid, but their torsos are hollow. Hands and heads were added later, with features like ears and beards sculpted last. No two faces are said to be alike, but I doubt this. I think there were four or so basic types and the system was mix-and-match. A range of ethnic types is indicated—perhaps the emperor's boast of his empire's diversity. The infantrymen have no armor or helmets; it was more to the point militarily that they could move fast. Bowmen had chariots. Queen Elizabeth II, one of the few Westerners ever allowed to stand down there with the army, was given a replica of a chariot as a souvenir. Well, what else can I say? The attempt at individualization is interesting, isn't it, coming from a legalist tyrant? Compare it, those of you who have been, with the art on Egyptian tombs—everybody but the pharaoh and his queen is interchangeable, standardized. The thing about these soldiers, that makes them such a hit, is how natural they look. I've had women, widows, who tell me they'd like to take one home as a husband. He wouldn't snore, I promise you that."

Widows, snoring—Alexandra's scalp and the back of her neck tingled. It was as if Mr. Muir had invaded her head before they could invade his. They had settled upon him as their victim, if a prank was to be pulled. At this moment, obliging laughter from his circle of close listeners made him feel he should produce another joke; his face slightly bulged as he tried to think of one and failed. As if to push everybody away, Mr. Muir said loudly, "Walk around. Don't just hang here. Go to the back, where the soldiers are still being dug up. Bits and pieces, it's not easy. In Pit Two you can see excavations in progress—ant work, the way it's always been in China. You can take pictures now. Ten years ago, you couldn't; they'd snatch the camera right out of your hand. If you come to China as often as I do, you can feel the paranoia getting less, a little less every time. Soon we'll be more paranoid than they. Move around, look and learn. We'll meet at the chariot pavilion in forty minutes."

Though Mr. Muir—Eric, she had learned, was his first name—wanted to be alone, Alexandra and some others, including Sukie and Jane, stayed by his side, there at the railing, looking down upon the slightly irregular ranks of clay soldiers advancing toward them, in battle order, facing east,

whence the emperor Ch'in thought his enemies in the here-
after might come. The soldiers' impassive silence and stillness took on a tinge of menace. In Eric Muir's eyes, they
began to move—a particle of motion on the periphery of his
vision, a warp like a bubble in old glass. A distortion of trans-
parency, an elusive twitch. His eyes stung, as if with too
many hours of reading, and he removed his rimless glasses
and pinched the bridge of his nose to clear his brain.

Alexandra inhaled the smell of clay from the great pit;
with it came an odor from the chunky lecturer's body, from
his armpits and those hidden creases where sweat congeals.
Some men, even unbathed, are odorless, like her first husband, Oswald Spofford, and others strengthen their masculine presence with a tangy blend of leather and horse and
tobacco and whiskey and clay, like Jim Farlander. Mr. Muir
was one whose flesh, forgotten in his cerebral pursuits, had
about it the scent of stale secretions and midnight oil gone
rancid. It was a distasteful but a male smell, recalling her to
the lost demimonde of physical intimacy, of grateful shame-
lessness and interpenetration.

Eric Muir replaced his glasses and, there was no doubt,
the terra-cotta soldiers were moving, not swinging their
arms and legs and shouting out a marching song but advancing like oceanic waves that crested and fell forward and
sucked back without altering the underlying volume of cold,
submarine depths. Their weapons, bronze scythes whose
wooden handles had ages ago rotted away, shook as if being
brandished, and now he could hear their chant as they
marched toward slaughter, slaughtering others and being
slaughtered, rhythmic corrugations in the crowd noise
caught beneath the roof of the great modern shed erected
above the uncovered pits. The chant went: *Da, sha, xie, si.*
Fight, kill, blood, death. That was China, he perceived—

millennia of slaughter, war, famine, floods, torture, of being buried alive, being skinned alive, being worked to death, but there was never enough death to relieve the land of its burden of people. The army kept coming, advancing, epitomizing the atrocious history of mankind.

He wondered if he was going mad, by himself or in the grip of a group hallucination. He turned to the person who happened to be nearest him, the biggest and broadest of the three old gals, widows, who clung together with a somewhat sinister closeness. This one might have been a beauty once; there was something self-satisfied about her mouth, which was teased by a smile between her curiously cleft chin and the tip, more subtly cleft, of her nose. She appeared intent upon the sight of the army below, and her two friends, not far behind her, actually had their eyes shut, as if concentrating upon an inner vision.

Noticing his questioning stare, his air of agitation, the woman asked, "Is something the matter, Mr. Muir?"

He lied, "No," but croaked on the monosyllable.

She took pity. "Did you see them move? I did."

"You did?"

"I thought so, for a moment. They're quiet now. It must be something they're working on—you know, holograms."

"Oh, yes," he agreed, relieved. "The new Chinese. They love high-tech toys."

And the tour went on, to four days on the Yangtze, through picturesque gorges soon to be flooded by the people's inexorable progress, then to Chungking, where Vinegar Joe Stilwell's headquarters was eerily preserved in its honorable wartime drabness and modesty, and on to the River Li, where giant rock-faces seemed to hold in their wrinkles columns of ancient inscription and where emaciated fishermen squatting on their haunches poled their delicate boats skimmingly along, and finally to Shanghai and Hong Kong, congested soaring cities of the future, the future when the world shall be nothing but cities, cities and deserts making the air tremble and melting the glaciers and the poles in the devastating global warming.

China delighted the three women. Each day dawned with a new bauble, a fresh sight or two to see, in colors as fresh as wet paint. The vast land felt corrupted by time and suffering but—save for a few controlled churches left behind by centuries of spurned mission effort—innocent of Christianity, the Christianity that had persecuted witches with the fury of its own denied desires. Here, the air felt clear of that particular history, of those tyrannical ghosts preaching sin and salvation, and the Godforsaken women in their impudent tourism felt free.

ii. *Maleficia Revisited*

S ATAN'S MARK is upon our pleasures; else we would not be driven to repeat them, even when sated, until they devour us. China should have left the widows ready to knit up the loose ends of their formerly married lives and to prepare themselves with repentance for their graves and the judgment beyond, but, excited by whatever rediscovery of their powers the foreign excursion had provoked, and unwilling to let their seasoned accomplices in evildoing become again estranged and distant, the three remained in contact, by e-mail and letter but primarily by the quaint means they chiefly used when living in the same small town, the telephone. Thirty years had shrunk those solid Seventies instruments of Bakelite and soldered color-coded wires down to silver cell phones, with a ring that could be programmed to be a favorite tune or a silent vibration within an apron pocket. The steep long-distance rates that not long ago compelled AT&T customers closely to monitor the minutes of gab had shrivelled to negligible Verizon or

Sprint charges and even less, as free minutes became part of every cell-phone user's agreement. New Mexico had become as cheap to call, by punching in a string of numbers with a newly agile opposable thumb, as New York.

"Lexa?" Sukie's voice had a tentative lilt to it, as if she expected a refusal to a question she had not yet asked.

"Yes, sweetie, what is it?"

It was not as if Alexandra's life here in Taos were utterly empty. She had begun to use Jim's wheel, making pots of her own to replenish the shop's supply, which slowly but surely dwindled through the winter, as the Eastern and Midwestern snowbirds decorated their new homes in what they imagined was authentic Western fashion. She tried to capture Jim's style, but something female in her touch thinned the pots' walls of clay and subdued the painted stripes to softer colors than Jim had used. Also, her social life was picking up: she had been asked to join the advisory board of the Mabel Dodge Luhan House, and one of the other members, a ruddy-faced widower, Ward Linklater, a sculptor of big bronzes of Western wildlife, coyotes and jackrabbits and wild mustangs mostly, a large man with a white mustache and a dandified bit of cultivated stubble under his lower lip, had been giving her the eye. He had invited her out to dinner a few times, and she had liked it that they talked lovingly of their dead spouses deep into the red wine, and then went to their separate homes too tired to do anything else. Sex after seventy—she didn't even want to know if it existed. When she asked him, playfully, if the stubble under his lip had a name, he had blushed and said, "I think the young folks call it a 'love brush,' " but that had been the end of it.

Sukie said, "Jane and I were wondering, how would you feel about Machu Picchu?"

"Machu Picchu in the Andes?"

"Yes, since you seemed to like the Canadian Rockies so much. And it wouldn't be just the ruins—there's Lima, and Cusco, the tour takes in Bolivia and Ecuador as well. One charm of it, Jane wanted me to emphasize, was there's no jet lag—it's all right under our own time zones."

"Why doesn't Jane call me herself, if she's so keen on this?"

"She thinks you'll take it better from me. She thinks you're sore at her for something that happened in Egypt, she doesn't know what."

"How ridiculous. She was fine in Egypt, though she did snore. But I can't possibly go on another big excursion so soon after China. The Wall and the Pyramids are about it for me, as far as wonders of the world go. I can't afford another wonder, frankly. You and Jane were left very comfortable, it would seem, but Jim and I just scraped along, and now I'm doing the scraping by myself. I'm sorry, dearest."

"Don't be sorry. I figured you'd say something of the sort. I'm relieved, actually. I wasn't sure how my emphysema would do at that altitude, though the travel agent thought it would be no problem."

"Well, she would think that. No problem for *her*."

"Exactly." A pause, while they savored their rapport. "Still," Sukie went on wistfully, "it *would* be nice to go somewhere together, before we get *too* much older. Jane has some health problems, though she doesn't like to talk about them."

"What kind of problems?"

"Inside, somewhere. She won't talk about them. Could you afford Mexico?"

"Jim and I did Mexico. More than once. Now they say some of the highways we drove, with my poor children, still new to the marriage, hot and complaining in back, and then

just the two of us, on a second honeymoon, are full of ban-
dits who kidnap Americans for ransom. The world is a less
and less friendly place for us, isn't it?"

"How about Ireland? They're still friendly, though I hear
it's not as cheap as it used to be, before they got into the EU
and became the Celtic Tiger. The men in Rocky Ridge were
always running over to Ireland for a week of golf. Wouldn't
you love to see the Western Isles, and the Ring of Kerry?
The monks used to live in little stone beehives. Wasn't
Lennie kind of Irish?"

"Oh, Sukie. You're so young. Just thinking about getting
on an airplane makes me tired. Isn't it nice where you are? It
is where I am." Dry desert sun fell at a dusky five o'clock
slant on the glass-topped coffee table, and the shiny art
books about American pottery ancient and modern, and the
thick Navajo rug. The floor tiles were the same pale tint as
the sandy earth sustaining her cactus garden outside the
patio doors—comical mouse-eared prickly pear and wand-
like ocotillo, making the best of their deprivations.

"But," the remote voice—bounced into her ear, for all
Alexandra knew, off the belly of a satellite many miles above
the world and its wonders—persisted, "*you're* not where I
am. I feel so alone since Lennie passed."

"You mean 'died.' "

"Whatever. 'Passed' feels less final. He had his limitations,
but he was company. All our old friends try to stay still
friendly, but I can tell my presence pains them. I just don't
fit any more. Except for my books and the fan letters these
screwed-up, over-identifying people write me, I'm utterly
unimportant to everybody. I can see why the Indians—the
Asian ones, not ours—invented suttee."

"What about your children? And grandchildren? Surely
you're important to them." She heard herself getting sharp

with Sukie, like a harassed mother. She preferred to concentrate upon the fuzz on the miniature cactus in the square bowl, how incandescent it looked in the sun, a veritable halo. From there her mind wandered to why Ward, who had such a handsome genial mouth really, affected that silly little patch of bristle just under his lip. She was afraid, with enough red wine some evening, she would come out against it, and if he defied her and kept it or complied and shaved it off, it would push them either way into an intimacy she wasn't ready for. She didn't want to get into keeping score with a man again, the unspoken tussle of favors given or withheld, of largesse and revenge.

"Well, they're polite," Sukie said, of her children, "but they don't go overboard. There are all these things you think of you might have done better when they were little, things you regret and would love to undo, but they move on; they must. You try to apologize and they look at you with this blank stare: they've forgotten. I saw from Lennie's passing— excuse me, his *death*—how they'd take mine in stride. *Good old Mom*, they'd say. *Rest in peace*. If they'd say even that much. Don't you have one that stayed in Eastwick?"

This last turn of Sukie's stream of consciousness took Alexandra aback. "Marcy," she said. "The oldest. She didn't stay west with us when Jim and I married. She had a boyfriend in Eastwick High she was very involved with, and when she graduated said she wanted to go to Rizdee and become a *real* artist—real in contrast to me, I suppose. She was determined to get away from me. She earned her keep waitressing at the Bakery Coffee Nook and after dropping out of Rizdee—she didn't like being an artist after all, she said, it was too egocentric—she switched to waitressing at Nemo's, since she had gotten old enough to serve liquor. Eventually, after doing some sleeping around I suppose, she married a local, a man some years older—an electrician, would you believe, after her father had owned an entire fixture factory in Norwich."

"Nemo's," Sukie repeated in a betranced voice. "What a cozy place that was—those buttery johnnycakes. That roast beef on a bun. I used to eat lunch there every day when I was with the *Word*. Remember the *Word*?"

"Of course. In the beginning was the *Word*. Nemo's may be being sold, to Dunkin' Donuts, Marcy told me a while or so ago. She doesn't tell me much; I think we're semi-estranged. She doesn't want people to know she's my daughter; they still remember us a bit."

"How lovely. Being remembered," said Sukie dreamily.

"It can be, or not. Sweetie, there's somebody at the door. I'll think about places we could go together. Is the Caribbean too ordinary? I used to love St. Croix, even after those radicals shot that foursome on the golf course."

"The sun, darling. You've forgotten. I'm dreadfully allergic. I break out in blotches." As if offended, Sukie hung up without another utterance. Even she was getting cranky in old age.

Time enough went by for Alexandra to imagine that the two other witches had faded back into the past. She had had a good enough life without them, and was still having it. Her pots were improving, she thought. When a couple came into the shop it was often the woman whose curiosity had been piqued by the window display, and who made the purchase. Away from the wheel, Alexandra began to make again the little figurines, with legs and arms but not hands or feet, that when she made them in Eastwick she called her "bubbies." One woman who came into the shop looked them over and told her, "They're charming, but not especially Southwest, are they?" Alexandra agreed; but she liked shaping them with leftover clay, their blank faces turned on their small heads as if sunbathing, or confronting a surprise visitation, their heavy hips good to heft in her hand and to make a solid base on a shelf. Men were amused by them; women, something more—charmed, or touched, recognizing themselves.

Ward Linklater kept asking her to dinner now and then, but their moment to crest had somehow slid by, and he never made a sexual move, so the gracious rebuff she had framed in her mind stayed coiled within her. The summer sun beat mercilessly on the roof; the cacti cried out for a November thunderstorm that never came, though translucent sharp-edged clouds towered in the west, and the desert rats made nests in the dead prickly pears. She drove north into Colorado for a sentimental visit. The open country she had known as a girl was unrecognizable, unfenced grassy acres where she used to ride given over to tract houses and a nine-hole golf course sucking irrigation from an artificial lake. In December, the telephone rang, and it was Jane Smart Tinker, picking up on the conversation with Sukie as if it had been yesterday. "*Ss*aint Croix is a *sss*illy suggestion," she hissed. "The Caribbean is for Club Med types, who want to do drugs and fornicate by moonlight on a snow-white coral beach."

"That sounds not bad," Alexandra admitted.

"Lexa, you must grow up. That part, for us, is over. Even Sukie can see that for her it's over."

"So, Jane, what's left?"

"Being wise is left, darling. Seeing the world is left. Using your eyes and ears is left. Just think—you have consciousness, isn't that amazing, all those neurons? This fall I went on a garden tour of the Himalayas. *Ss*ikkim. Bhutan. We had to cancel some of Nepal, with the Maoist uprising. There are some lovely princely estates, still, and Kashmir really *is* paradise, once you get past the hopeless politics."

"So Paradise is left. Who did you go with? Whom." Expecting her to say that it had been with Sukie, Alexandra braced for a surge of jealousy.

But Jane said, "Nobody you know, dear. The Brookline and Dedham Garden Clubs. There were two or three husbands along—pathetic people, always in the way. I love women, it turns out. Did you know that about me?"

"Well, not exactly *know*. Jane, I think *all* women, more or less, are more comfortable with other women. With women you know what to expect, and don't expect too much. Is that what you called up to talk about? You're coming out of the closet? I understand your state permits homosexual marriage. Every other state is up in arms about it."

"You can stop trying to be funny. Sukie and I have a serious idea for you."

"Antarctica." Something menacingly purposeful in Jane's call made Alexandra want to fend her off with jokes.

Jane didn't take it as a joke. She said, "No—but people who *have* gone there *ss*wear by it, they say you can't believe the beauty. But no—Sukie says you're too poor to go anywhere pricey, so what about going back to Eastwick?"

"*East*wick? Now?"

"Next *ss*ummer, Lexa. For a month or two, depending on what rentals are available. Don't forget, we didn't notice because we were trying to live there, but it's a summer place. The beach, the Bay, the little shops selling kitschy watercolors and stained glass and candles on Dock Street. Surely you need to get away from all the bea*ss*stly heat in New Mexico."

"Usually it's not that bad—we're high, you know; we have snow on the ground right now—but last summer, I admit—"

"Well, then. And you know the summers are all going to be hotter from now on. Aren't you curious to see how the town has changed?"

"I know how it's changed. Or, rather, I know how little it's changed. Marcy and I still communicate, somewhat. It has a few more chi-chi restaurants, and art galleries that come and go. Those scrawny trees downtown are strung with white Christmas lights all year long—they have an improvement society and that's their idea of improvement."

Jane resisted being dragged under, with her inspiration, by Alexandra's depressive side. She said, her sibilants bristling, "How *ss*ad, but I don't believe it. Or I don't believe it's all there is. There's something there, there always was. The *sss*pirit of Anne Hutchinson, it could be. It was liberating, empowering. We came into our own. We never should have found husbands and left."

"Oh, Jane, how can you say that, after what we did?"

The other woman's hard voice pounced. "What did we do? What? We fucked a few of the local jerks, which was a great kindness. We played tennis with what's-his-name, Van Horne, and used his hot tub. We *played*."

"We killed Jenny Gabriel, that's what we did. After bewitching Clyde's wife so that he killed her with a poker and then hung himself."

"Dearie, this is all hearsay. It can't be proved. And so what in any case? That was over thirty years ago. Most everyone who would remember us is dead."

"I do not *want* to go *back*," Alexandra said, with such conviction that she was momentarily blind to the winter sunshine on the dusting of snow and, inside, the comforting

Southwestern artifacts, in their humble tans and browns and rusty reds borrowed from the earth by an indigenous people with no concept of sin, the eclipsing blackness of sin. The First People, they were called in Canada. The braves fought and tortured other braves, the women pounded corn into cornmeal. All was harsh and taciturn and innocent. "Marcy at first was always asking me to come visit her and I always ducked, so she stopped asking. She didn't press me. She was more than a child at the time it happened, you know. She was seventeen. She was aware of things. Of evil."

"Oh, you sweet tender-hearted thing, how you do go on. Evil, my goodness. Reality, I'd say. Doesn't life these days seem terribly flat to you, the way it never was in Eastwick?"

Can this be true? Alexandra shifts the terrain to the other woman's widowhood. "Why would you want to go there in the summer? Didn't Nat's family have a big place in Maine, near Bath or Bar Harbor?"

"The old lady sold it. She said the only reason she hung on to it was so Nat could do his sailing in August."

"She's able to do things like that? Buy and sell and so on, at a hundred and four?"

"Nat's funeral energized the old bat. She even goes to Friday-afternoon *Ss*ymphony again, with a big black chauffeur. For a while, while Nat was still here, she didn't know who she was or where she was, only that she didn't like the wallpaper she stared at all day and was sure the nurse was poisoning her. The upkeep on the Maine place had become monstrous. It was one of these huge shingled barns with a hundred dormers, and the thing about shingles is, they dry out and warp and fall off. I always hated it there. It was heated only by fireplaces, and the ocean was always too icy to swim in, even in August. The people who went to Maine for the summer were Puritan stock and wanted to be punished for being rich. So no, I'm happy to go to Rhode Island. Not Newport or Jamestown, though. They're overrun with gawkers in the summer. Just Easstwick. Nobody goes to Eastwick but oddballs."

"Oh, Jane, how can you? Sound so enthusiastic. I'm sure Sukie will agree with me, it's a horrible, horrible idea. Talk about the scene of a crime."

"I repeat, there was no crime. There was healthy exploration of our female potential. Sukie loves the idea. She gets all bright-eyed and pink in the face when we talk about it. Didn't you think, in China, she had gotten alarmingly pasty? Washed-out, with her pathetic dyed hair. I mean, the poor dear has only two half-lungs."

"You've been seeing her? Where do you meet?"

Jane's voice put up a shield of terseness. "She comes to Boston. Lennie had some interests here. Once we met at New Haven, where one of Nat's great-nephews goes to Yale. Do you mind, Lexa? It's not our fault you live so far away. You never invite us to visit you."

"I did, but you pooh-poohed it. You said the West was full of fat religious people." Still, Alexandra found herself reluctant to pollute the dry clarity of Taos with whiffs of her guilty, swampy past. She backtracked: "Why would Sukie want to go back to Eastwick?"

"Oh, you know her. Journalistic curiosity. Maybe she'll get something for her next ridiculous romance novel. Maybe she'll meet an old flame or make a fresh conquest. In Connecticut, apparently, the wives run a tight ship, and what loose men there are have those city skills at commitment-avoidance."

The phrase made Alexandra wonder if Ward Linklater didn't have those skills. It emerged over red wine that in his prior life sculpting had been a weekend hobby; his real work,

and the source of his comfortable wealth, had been as a con-
tractor, filling the helpless desert between Albuquerque and
Santa Fe with acres and acres of the kind of cut-rate retirement homes that Alexandra despised.

"Well, I have no such delusions," she told Jane. "I am *not*
going. Absolutely not. Eastwick was a phase, and one I'm
very glad I'm out of. Period, dear."

When, a few rankled days later, she called Sukie, the
younger woman was vague; it was like talking to somebody
at a party whose eyes keep darting over your shoulder.
"Sukie, I can't believe you want us to rent for the summer in
Eastwick."

"Do I? Jane seemed so keen on it, I could hardly argue. It
might be amusing, I don't know. Couldn't we all use a
change? Aren't you curious to see what would happen?
Either way, don't make it into such a big deal, Lexa. It's only
an idea, a way of us getting together."

"A very repugnant idea, if you ask me. To me, that town is
something I left behind. It's hexed."

"Well, who hexed it?" Sukie asked.

"It wasn't just us. There was Brenda Parsley and Marge
Perley and Greta Neff and Rose Hallybread and I guess
you'd have to include Felicia in that category." Superstitiously, her tongue hesitated to pronounce "Felicia," the
murdered wife of Clyde Gabriel—Clyde who went crazy
partly with drink and partly with love of Sukie. It was where
the *maleficia* had deepened to a depth they couldn't escape,
and she disliked pronouncing the name because Felicia was
dead. But, then, probably, so were all the others by now.

Sukie laughed; Alexandra felt that her laugh covered up
the start of a yawn. "She certainly frothed at the mouth,"

Sukie said, of the late Felicia, "when she'd go on and on about Vietnam." She sensed that the nostalgic tone wasn't meeting Alexandra's present need, and said more briskly, "Darling, you're so sweetly superstitious. Hexes don't last forever. That poisonous atmosphere had to do with the times, the Sixties decaying into the Seventies, and with us being young and still full of juice and stuck in the middle class."

"Well, these aren't exactly *Happy Days* on television right now," Alexandra claimed. "People are as unhappy about Bush as they were about Johnson and Nixon. It's another quagmire. And meanwhile the infrastructure and the public schools and the national parks are going to hell."

Sukie paused, as if she were weighing these assertions, and then, maddeningly, concluded, "Well, it doesn't sound to me as though you like the idea, and we just can't do it without you."

"Why not? You and Jane seem suddenly to be perfectly on the same wavelength on everything."

"Don't be jealous, darling, there's nothing to be jealous of. Jane is not an easy person. But as I say she's not entirely well, and I think she feels very lonely, in that big dark house, with not only Nat gone but the matriarch showing so much pep. As to me, I don't know, Lexa; I just feel so washed-out, so un*real*, with Lennie dead. I thought Eastwick might bring me back to reality. In China I kept thinking how delicious it was, as life begins to close in, to have old friends who knew you when, who can laugh at the same things and remember the same awful people. But maybe I was silly." She sighed, with her tender half-lungs. "Forget it, doll, let's just forget it."

"You're making me feel guilty, Sukie, but I still won't go. You can both come here if you want, and visit Indian reser-

: 113 :

vations. They're fascinating. They still have shamans that can do mind-boggling things. Really, I've seen it. You might even talk me into a cruise to Antarctica, to see these animated penguins."

Silence. No laugh. Then: "Lexa, I should get back to work before I forget what color the heroine's eyes are. I was in the middle of ripping her bodice. But *do* understand, Jane and I don't want to talk you into *any*thing. We just were offering you an oppor*tu*nity." Since they had once been, in the steamy black hot-tub room, lovers of a sort, Sukie knew how to communicate hurt; Alexandra hung up still rankled.

When, somewhat later in the winter, the phone rang again, with the caller-ID panel showing OUT OF AREA, Alexandra picked it up with a heart fluttering between the possibility of repairing her relations with the two other widows and the need to keep standing firm against them. But the female voice on the other end of the line belonged to neither. "Mother?" it said.

Of her two daughters, the younger, Linda, lived in Atlanta with her second husband, and had developed over the years a feathery touch of a Southern accent, and the high-pitched coziness of regionally inculcated femininity. This voice had no such pitch—it was a low, sexually neutral, aggressively flat voice, with the hardened "a"s and dropped "r"s of New England. "Marcy!" Alexandra exclaimed. "What a nice surprise!"

Neither daughter telephoned more than courtesy demanded, and Marcy a little less even than that. "I hear you may be coming here next summer," she said, in that lumpish factual tone of hers. Marcy had thickened, after that gracile teen-age moment of virgin womanhood, and had darkened, especially in her thick eyebrows and her sullen, deep-set eyes.

"Where would you ever hear that? It's not true, dear." Alexandra heard herself sounding, in the defensiveness her older daughter aroused in her, a shade like the younger daughter, feather-headed Linda. Her voice, strained with feigning, seemed to plead: "Jane and Sukie—you remember them, Jane Smart she used to be, and Sukie Rougemont— have been trying to talk me into coming back to Eastwick as a summer person. I keep telling them no. For one thing, you wouldn't like it, I tell them."

"Why would you say that? That's hurtful, Mother. It would give us some time to be together, in a way we've hardly had, and you could get to know Howie and the boys better."

Marcy had married the local electrician Howard Little-field at the point where it seemed she might stay a chunky spinster forever, and had borne him two sons as she approached forty—typical of her mulish, late-blooming generation, thought Alexandra, whose own generation had relegated childbearing to a post-teen interval, clearing the decks for an adult life unencumbered by hospital stays and around-the-clock nursing schedules. "The boys—are they still in high school?"

"Mother, it's so discouraging. You don't pay *any* attention. Roger is twelve and Howard Junior just turned nine. You sent him a computer game, remember?"

"Of course. I hope not one of the violent and obscene ones."

Alexandra disliked facing the fact that she had a daughter over fifty, with gray hair she did nothing to hide and a wart on the side of her nose she didn't bother to have removed. Marcy's brother Ben, the next-oldest child, was even worse—balder than Oz had been at his age and thoroughly pompous and conventional, living in Virginia and doing something in Washington that he couldn't discuss in detail. He actually was a Republican, like his father; but it seemed much worse in a son than in a husband. You expected it in a husband. To Alexandra there was something so bizarre about being the mother of males—their penises and testicles once packed inside you along with their genetic predispositions to messy rooms and televised sports—that she could relate to her sons more easily, their connection being at bottom a kind of joke, than to her daughters, whom she regarded with the same appraising eye with which she regarded herself.

"They're all like that," Marcy was saying. "It's more about hand-eye coördination than sociopathic content. Anyway, he loved it and uses it constantly. Did you get his thank-you note?"

"I did," Alexandra lied. "It was charming."

"What did it say?" Marcy mulishly pursued.

"The usual sweet boyish things. I'd still like to know who told you I was coming to Eastwick."

"Jane Tinker has been in touch with me. Isn't she amusing, by the way? A real game old gal, unlike—"

"Me, you're going to say."

"Unlike the mothers of a lot of my friends, I was going to say. You're not *un*game, Mother. You just keep your distance."

"Darling, I'm out here trying to survive, by selling pots. I've learned how to turn them on Jim's wheel. At the end of the day, I'm dizzy."

"She asked me to look around for rentals."

"Jane did? After I kept telling her no?"

"She said it might be for her and one or two other women."

"*One* or two. I can't believe the two of them would do that to me. Go behind my back that way."

"She was just asking for me to give her a feel for what's available. And I didn't find much, in fact. Eastwick never was a go-to kind of place; all those are on the island side of the Bay. There's the motel toward East Beach, past the shuttered-up pizza place—"

"Oh? It's closed? The pizzas used to be so good. Thin and crisp, instead of gross and cheesy."

"The man who made them retired ages ago and went to Florida. That's where we'd all go, if we could afford it. Howie and I already have our town picked out. Right on the water, on the Gulf side. We go there two weeks every winter. Around here, there are a few houses for rent, but for the full three summer months and usually to the same family, that keeps coming back. There's a Days Inn a few miles north, on Route One, but it wouldn't give you the small-town feeling."

"No," Alexandra said, and then regretted saying even this much; she was being drawn in.

"The only thing possible I could find — and this is why I'm calling you—is, do you have any negative feelings about the old Lenox mansion? The bank that had to take it over turned it into condo units, really rather charmingly."

"The Lenox mansion. Is that what they've gone back to calling it?" She and her daughter had moved into uncomfortable territory—the scandalous past—but there was no easy way out. "I guess it wasn't the Van Horne mansion very long. I do have negative feelings, yes."

"The tennis court is still there, but not the big bubble Mr. Van Horne put over it. It's been a struggle with the condos—tenants don't like the causeway being flooded once or twice a month—so some, on the side without a sea view, *are* available for short rentals. Three women, the manager told me, could take two adjacent suites on the second floor. They cut up the old hot-tub area—you remember it, with the retractable ceiling—and created a second floor in all that space. It's a little jerry-built, I guess—he showed me one of the rooms, and the ceiling *did* seem pretty low— but by leaning out the window there's a view of the cause- way, and unlike the middle of town it would be quiet at night."

"How can a condo be quiet? Suppose the neighbor on the other side of the wall watches television compulsively?"

"Mother, really. Don't be such a snob. It isn't as quiet as the New Mexico desert, no. In the real world almost every- body lives with somebody else's television set on the other side of the wall."

"Is that so, dear? I didn't know you knew so much about the real world. You wouldn't come with me and Jim to New Mexico because you had this boyfriend you were so hot for, and then you were dying to go to Rizdee and show me up as an artist, and then you dropped out after a year and became a greasy-spoon waitress right back where you were born. How much in your life have you ever been out of Rhode Island? Tiny, *tiny* Rhode Island."

"Whereas you've been all over the world lately, right? Mother, I love you dearly but you've always been spoiled. Your parents spoiled you and then poor Daddy and then Jim. You've never had to face real need or real loneliness."

"That's not true, darling. Just being human is having to face those things."

"Don't call me 'darling.' It's too late for 'darling.' I'm sorry; I don't mean to bitch. My mother just happened to be a May Queen, a nice big queen bee full of royal jelly, and I'm a plain worker bee, a wallflower."

"That's not true, dar—Marcy. You're very attractive. You were a perfect baby."

"That's just a way of saying it's all been downhill since. Well, life is all downhill, it turns out. Except that, believe it or not, Howie and I have our fun. Our modest fun. With the boys and without. And some day we're going to retire to Florida and buy a boat."

"A boat you fish from? That's lovely, dear."

"Just the way you say that—you're *such* a snob, *so* above it all. Where do you get it from? Everybody wants to serve you. Jane and this Sukie woman, *they* want to serve you, *I'm* trying to serve you, and you turn up your nose at the idea of a condo, for even a month or two."

Alexandra didn't mind this quarrel, now that it had settled into a certain tone. At least it was conversation; it was something happening, Marcy spilling out all this absurd resentment, as if her mother were God and had created the universe. In New Mexico, since Jim's death and even before, Alexandra had battled spells of depression. The dryness of her aging skin, the thinness of the desert vegetation upon the depth of rocks and minerals, the monotony of the sunny days, the mountain winds hollowing her out, Nature's grand desolation unsoftened: it all added up to a fearful weight to push through the day. In Eastwick, she had been many things—scared, ashamed, exhilarated, hopeful—but never depressed as best she could remember.

"You," she told Marcy levelly, "are the main reason I don't want to come. I thought I might be an embarrassment."

"Now? The time to worry about my embarrassment was when I was fifteen. The things the other kids at the high school said to me, having to look Eva Marino in the eye when we both knew you were fucking her father, all those nights when you'd be out till way past midnight—"

"I'm *so* sorry. But *I* had to have a life, too. A parent is a person, not just a function." *A fucktion*, Jane had punned. Oh, evil Jane, Jane Pain, her saw-edged truthful tongue. The three of them dancing, the night Darryl and Jenny announced their marriage: "*Har, har, diable, diable, saute ici, saute là, joue ici, joue là,*" linked hands smeared with wedding cake. And now this adult female child presuming to pass judgment on them, putting everything in the worst possible light. Alexandra went on, trying to keep her tone level and maternal, albeit chastising, "Have no fear, I won't be an embarrassment. I won't come. Tell your new friend Jane she won't need any condos as far as I'm concerned."

The child burst out, "Mother, anybody who ever cared about all that is *dead*. I thought you'd care enough about me to *want* to come. We could get to know each other b-better." She was crying.

"Oh, my goodness, Marcy," Alexandra hurried to say, guilty, panicky. "What a sweet idea! After that tirade of yours?"

Perhaps she had imagined the tears, for Marcy said, calmly enough, "It was good to let it out, I think. My feelings. But it wasn't the whole story. You could be a pretty good mother. You weren't priggish and scolding, at least. I loved it when you used to put up tomato sauce, and have us weed with you in the garden. You taught us about Nature."

"Did I, though? I used to think Nature was on my side. Now I doubt it."

Marcy wasn't listening, she was going on, "Howie and I have a little patch we eat from, mostly easy things—two rows of lettuce for salads, and some parsley, and Brussels sprouts. Isn't it amazing, how Brussels sprouts just keep coming, more and more, right into frost? I'd grow tomatoes except that Howie hates them. They're the only thing he

won't eat." And this little confession hoarsened her voice
and threatened to bring back the tears. How stable, really,
was Marcy?

"Yes, it is amazing," Alexandra agreed. Just hearing about
her mothering wearied her. Bowing to Nature's demands,
going forth and multiplying, *In sorrow thou shalt bring forth
children, and thy desire shall be to thy husband, and he shall
rule over thee*, the whole patriarchal bad rap. Not that Adam
had it much easier: *Cursed is the ground for thy sake; in sorrow shalt thou eat of it all the days of thy life; thorns also and
thistles shall it bring forth to thee. In the sweat of thy face shalt
thou eat bread, for dust thou art*. And onward to the next:
*Cain was a tiller of the ground, but unto Cain and to his offer-
ing He had not respect*. The thought of Marcy growing a few
vegetables in that stony, impoverished, acid Eastwick soil,
sprinkling with pinched fingers the lettuce seeds scarcely
bigger than grains of sand and sealing them hopefully into
their temporary grave, and bearing two sons by a terrible
stretch of her nether parts, and loving the boys even as they
turned out to be just two more excess male Americans avidly
consuming junk, lifts Alexandra to a dizzying height of
parental sorrow. "Dear, I feel a little faint. This is all so
unexpected. Let me rethink a bit, if you really do see our
renting next summer as having a positive aspect."

"Oh, I *do*," came the almost musical reply. "It would mean
so much to the boys."

News that the damnable trio were back in town perco-
lated from ear to ear like rainwater trickling through the
tunnels of an ant colony. Betsy Prinz, Herbie Prinz's granddaughter, heard it from Amy Arsenault in what used to be
the Armenians' hardware store but was now an under-

THE WIDOWS OF EASTWICK

stocked, demoralized True Value—no match for the Home
Depot over on Route 102 or the giant new Lowe's slapped
up overnight, it seemed, on Route One toward Warwick.
Betsy, too young at twenty-seven to have ever actually seen
any of the purported witches, passed the rumor on to Veronica Marino, with an innocent dim sense that there had been,
in the remote past, a scandalous connection with the Mari-
nos. Veronica, the youngest of Joe and Gina's five children,
still lived, at the age of thirty-nine, with her mother in her
parents' narrow clapboard house some blocks beyond Kazmierczak Square. Not only she but her husband, Mike
O'Brien, lived there; he was a shiftless drinker but at the age
she married, six years ago, she was lucky to catch a man at
all. They had no children and made do with two rooms and
a bathroom back from the street. Some took their childless-
ness to be the natural result of a mismatch between an Italian and an Irishman; others blamed the proximity of the
all-powerful mother—Joe had died of a heart attack the year
his youngest daughter married. When Veronica told her
mother that no less an authority than Harry Perley of Perley Realty had told Amy Arsenault that the three women
had rented two units for July and August in the Lenox Mansion Seaview Apartments, Gina, moving painfully on a hip
ripening to be replaced, scarcely glanced up from rins-
ing and trimming a bunch of the season's first local aspara-
gus for a microwave container. "Returning to their mess,"
she mumbled.

"What's that, Mother?" Veronica asked, a shade too
loudly, her eyes widened by something like alarm. Her
mother frightened her with her aura of the Old World—her
leaden deliberation and her mannish laced black shoes and
the fringe of dark hairs on her upper lip.

"An old saying. Too nasty for you to understand."

"Mother, I'm not a child," Veronica stated, with the sinking feeling that without a child of her own she was. "Mike says all sorts of things to me." She reddened, feeling more foolish still.

"Your father used to say, 'It's a free country.' I'd say to him, 'The way some people don't pay their bills, they think it's free all right.' That man who had the Lenox place way back was one of the worst. He owed your father a fortune, all the fancy plumbing work he had done over there. The police never did catch him."

"Tell me exactly what happened back then. All I ever hear is vague things. Amy was quite agog, whispering right there in the Armenians'."

"You don't want to hear," her mother said, clumping on her hurting hip to the refrigerator and placing the plastic container on a shelf, to be heated up for tonight's dinner. Because Joe had been a plumber their kitchen had always been smartly up-to-date. They were among the first homes in town to have a microwave oven, and a trash masher, a built-in sink Disposall, and faucets sealed not by rubber washers but with hard plastic ball valves not so different, Gina imagined, from the plastic ball and titanium socket with which they intended to replace her excruciating hip. In the meantime, she lived with it. Living with things can outlast them. Since Joe died the kitchen has stood still and even slid backwards; her own mother's old spatter-pattern blue enamel pots, brought from Napoli on the ship, have come up from the cellar to replace copper and stainless steel. Pasta cooked in copper and steel never tasted quite so good as it had in those blue enamel pots. Aware of her daughter still standing there awaiting illumination, Gina told her, "I never knew myself what all happened."

"Did Papa know?"

Gina was quick to answer. "He didn't bring home tales of those he worked for, he thought it wasn't good business." She added, stepping heavily around her daughter while drying her hands on a dish towel, "I don't think I'd know any of those women if I saw them on the street, we're all such old *streghe* by now."

But when she did, early in July, meet up with Alexandra, they knew each other instantly. The encounter occurred not downtown on Dock Street, but outside at the new Stop & Shop on the edge of town, a half mile past Alexandra's former house on Orchard Road. The midsummer sun made waves of heat rise trembling from the tar of the parking lot, and struck sparks of horizontal reflection off the wire grids of the shopping carts in the stall where people were supposed to park them after unloading the shopping bags into their cars. "I heard you were back in Eastwick," Gina admitted, with a grunt. Just pronouncing the town's name signalled her territorial possession. She felt that, as the permanent resident and (though she did not say so to her children) the wronged wife, she was behooved to speak first.

Both ample women, Gina in a dark dress and Alexandra in white jeans and a splashy cotton camise with three-quarter-length sleeves, were sweating in the sun. "Just as an experiment, Gina," Alexandra assured her old rival. "Through August, if we last. I live in New Mexico now, and though it gets hot I'm not used to this humidity."

"It's dull enough around here," Gina told her, "since you left."

"That's what we're hoping. We're all widows now, Jane and Sukie and I. Dullness is all we're up to. I'm sorry, may I say, about Joe. Six years ago, was it?"

"Yes," Gina said, her breath to say more snatched from her by this fat old harlot's boldness in mentioning his name.

"I know what it's like," Alexandra said, daring touch the other on her bare forearm. Gina flinched, superstitiously. The noontime slant of sun was such that the two women stood on the knife-edge between blazing sun and the shade of the Stop & Shop. Alexandra stepped backwards, having dared the touch, into the relative cool there, by the moistened trays of supermarket petunias and marigolds set out for sale. This retreat drew Gina after her, with a limping step. "He was a good man," Alexandra said, her voice lowered in the shadow.

Gina had regained enough breath to respond, "A good *family* man." Her black eyes flashed, boring into Alexandra's face as if daring her to contradict.

Alexandra agreed, in a voice still softer, laying claim to insider knowledge, "He loved you. And his children." It had been she, in her memory of the affair, who had always scoffed at Joe's offers to leave Gina and marry her.

"And his job," Gina continued the sequence, deflecting their exchange from these unacknowledged depths. "Your furnace go out at two in the morning, he'd get out of bed and be there. Now for a plumber you must phone to a slick company with its office over at the Coddington Junction Mall, and they never send the same man twice." She felt, to judge by the way her lips clamped together, a certain triumph in uttering a sentence so aggressively long. "Who can you trust?"

Poor soul, Alexandra thought, seeing how neither walking nor talking was easy for Gina. She herself was enjoying this encounter, in that it brought Joe back to her. The bulk and warmth of his body, the fur on his back and the glaze of sweat on his belly, the exciting strength his hands had gained from wrestling with many a corroded joint and frozen shutoff valve. She also had loved Joe's male sheepishness, sneaking in and out of her little yellow divorcée's house on Orchard Road a half mile from where she and Joe's widow stood now—his sheepishness at being driven by so base a need to betray his sacred vows, to risk his domestic peace, his brood of children, his in-laws, his significant portion of local prestige. "He was a good workman," she told Gina in docile agreement. Rapturous in lovemaking, he would call her his white cow, *mia vacca bianca*, taking her from behind. He held regions of fastidious shame— ashamed of his bald head, with its faint bony ripples, and of his imperious genitals, which had fathered five children and pounded away in guilt and impurity at the safe fortress of her womb, with its sterilizing IUD. For in that era enlightened women went to some trouble to make themselves always available for sex. She had relished that, the gift of sin and sacrilegious birth control with which she enriched Joe's dull, hard-working, stuck-valve life by crouching passively on her knees and elbows on her creaking bed and letting herself be battered and pumped full from behind.

Gina seemed to squint into her mind, closing one eye malevolently. The remaining eye glittered, boring in. "Remember Veronica?" she asked.

Fearing Gina had read her mind, seeing the obscene pictures in it, Alexandra blurted gratefully, "Of course. Your youngest." Joe had been dismayed and furious when Gina had announced this last pregnancy, at her age of forty-one, claiming that he had hardly touched the superstitious bitch. No IUD for pious Gina. Alexandra told her, "I understand she still lives with you."

"With her husband," Gina said, still keeping one eye closed. "They don't have children yet. After six years trying."

Alexandra concealed her surprise. For years she and this

woman had shared a man; perhaps the unspoken secret spurred Gina to share her intimate information. "I'm sorry, if a child is what she wants."

"She wants, who doesn't?" The question came so bluntly, out of this squinting, black-clad woman, that Alexandra felt menace in it and fell self-protectively silent. Gina kept on: "Can you do something about it?"

"Me? Gina, what could *I* do?"

Both eyes glittered open again. "You know what."

"I do? I don't even know Veronica." Except what Joe used to confide during their trysts on Orchard Road. Once the unwanted baby had been born, he doted on her—spunky as a boy, brighter than all her sisters.

Gina was irritated by the stupidity that forced her to spell things out. She explained, "Some say she can't because of— I don't know the English—*un fascino. Magia.*"

"Oh. You mean a spell?"

"Yes. Some say. When she is still a girl and you live here. Because of the jealousy."

The bright sunshine beating down on the parking lot mocked the shadowiness of this exchange, wherein the two women's tongues were locked on what lay between them. "Why would I be jealous of a tiny girl?"

Gina's mouth clamped tight rather than dignify such a prevaricating question with an answer. She backed a step into the sun; the black hairs on the old woman's upper lip were vivid in the raw light. Alexandra stumbled toward answering her own question: "You mean could I lift a spell because—? But I never could do the things people said I could. I was just a housewife. An unhappy one, until Ozzie and I got a divorce."

Gina resumed her squint against the glare; the lid of the closed eye began to tremble with the strain, but still she let the other woman, the bane of her marriage, do the talking. That was her revenge.

"I'll do what I can," Alexandra promised. "I have nothing against Veronica, or you. As I say, Joe loved you both."

And this may have been too much to say, too close to mutual exposure. As if fearing where further talk might take them, Gina turned her back and melted in her baggy dark short-sleeved dress into the furious sun, leaving Alexandra in her summery outfit to repress a shiver there in the Stop & Shop's flower-fragrant margin of shade.

When they all lived here, Sukie was the one who inhabited the downtown, working as a reporter for the Eastwick *Word*, eating lunch at Nemo's, sticking her head into Paul LaRue's barbershop with the chirpy query "What's up, guys?" (they could hardly wait to tell her), and walking with her lithe lean stride, in one of those tawny, tweedy outfits slightly too smart for Eastwick, past the display window of the Hungry Sheep, with its sensible cashmere sweaters and boxy wool skirts, and the Yapping Fox, which offered high-school girls somewhat trendier wear; past the wide-windowed dark hardware store run by Armenians, and the Bay Superette, staffed by acneous high-school boys and stocked with overpriced staples like milk and cranberry juice and puffed-up bags of deleterious nibbles; past the Bakery Coffee Nook and Christian Science Reading Room and the Eastwick branch of the Old Stone Bank and Perley Realty with its window of curling, bleaching snapshots of unsold homes. She would inhale the town, its salt air and tipping, cracked sidewalks and clapboarded shop fronts in need of fresh paint, gathering gossip and impressions for the weekly *Word*, whose editor, weary, worried, wiry Clyde Gabriel, was fatally to fall in love with her. Now, more than three decades later, she walked the same sidewalk savoring memories. Not the same sidewalk, in truth—its cracks had been filled, its squares levelled, its shade trees wrapped in all-year Christmas lights. Dock Street had been broadened and straightened, and high granite curbs had been installed where once the concrete pavement had blended into the asphalt with hardly a drop; bad boys used to hop their bicycle wheels from street to sidewalk and swerve back again, blithely terrorizing pedestrians. The blue marble horse trough where Dock met Oak Street at right angles was still there, but instead of brimming with seasonal flowers it was planted with juniper and a dwarf Alberta spruce that had grown so tall and bushy automobile drivers could not see around it.

But, then, the town, which dated back to the days when the colony was called, under the parliamentary patent of 1644, Providence Plantations, was full of occultations: graceful early-eighteenth-century houses were invisible from the road, all but swallowed by hemlocks whose droopy limbs had never been trimmed; in certain rambling Victorian mansions, steep staircases lurked behind library panels, and cellars opened onto tunnels of raw rock that led to moonlit water; rotting piers once used by bootleggers waited tucked out of sight on a pebbled beach hidden from the main harbor by craggy outcroppings. Rhode Island was settled, it was said in Massachusetts and Connecticut, as a haven for apostasy and piracy. Roger Williams welcomed Quakers, Jews, and antinomians because he believed not that salvation was extended to all but that there were not enough true believers to populate a community. Off Oak Street, as it wound beyond the village limits, long driveways sloped up to no visible domicile. It was oddly impossible to see, from the Eastwick downtown, the old Lenox mansion on its hill, though in aerial maps the distance between them did not appear great. Even the downtown shop fronts concealed: just behind them the waters of an estuary sparkled and purled their way to Narragansett Bay and thence to the sea. Scintillations flashed in the narrow spaces between the shingled mercantile buildings. Saltwater was in the air in a way it wasn't in sprawling, overpriced Stamford, and Sukie inhaled through her narrow nostrils, feeling a lusty old self seeping back.

"Mrs. Rougemont!" a voice called behind her.

She turned as if stabbed, wondering who would use a name long shed. A man she didn't seem to know came toward her, a beefy, bearded, barrel-chested man, middle-aged, his grizzled hair caught up in a dirty ponytail behind, his cheeks and nose burned red by a life of exposure to the elements. Seeing her puzzled and wary, he grinned, showing a missing upper tooth, quickening her repugnance. "Tom Gorton, ma'am. You interviewed me when I'd become the youngest ever harbormaster, remember?"

"Tommy! Of course." At the time he had struck her as pompous and immature, but that had not prevented her from sleeping with him later, the summer before she conjured up a husband for herself and left town, the last of the three enchantresses to leave. She carried a plastic bag holding a few staples from the Superette, so she had to switch hands to offer her right for a chaste handshake. "How *are* you?" she said perhaps too heartily, and bravely grinned, exposing her gums.

With a smile sadder than hers he took her right hand in his left. For a second she mistook this for a former lover's presumptuous gesture of tenderness, but then she saw that his right hand, held curled close to his chest, had been cruelly mangled, missing a finger and the rest crushed to a kind of knotted paw. He saw where her eyes had darted and explained, with a boyishly shy smile that gave her a pang of remembering him as he had been, too sure of himself and yet timid and abashed when she offered herself, "An accident. I was helping crew a trawler out on the cod banks in winter ice. Slipped in my borrowed boots, and the right hand got caught between the rope and pulley hauling in a full load. They thought to amputate but decided to leave me something. Not good for much, though." He brought it a few inches away from his chest, to show her.

"Oh, Tom!" she exclaimed, using the name he seemed to prefer now. "You poor thing. How can you work with that?"

"With difficulty, as they say." The shyness of his smile was yielding to another quality of his, which she had taken for arrogance at their initial interview, but which as they became lovers she felt as his proper appreciation of himself as a male beauty—a sensual self-regard that a boy of his social class would not have come to a generation or even a half-generation earlier. Permission for male sexual vanity needed the Sixties, flower-power and the Beatles and big-screen pornography. She had been thirty-three as the Sixties became the Seventies and her lovers had been older men— some of them, like Clyde Gabriel and Arthur Hallybread, distinctly older, rank in their creases and erratic in arousal— until she slept with Toby Bergman, the young new editor of the *Word*, replacing tragically dead Clyde. Toby soon left town, having broken his leg in another accident involving winter ice. But he had introduced her to the body of a young man and a new power relation to sex: she as the instigator, the admirer, the predator, the worshipper. She would crouch naked like a ravenous she-wolf over first Toby's and then Tommy's body, marvelling at the perfect skin, the clean scent, the fat-smoothed interlace of muscles, the beautiful, fresh-furred, unfailingly responsive genitals. They were so beautiful and monstrous, these glossy erect pricks—Toby's circumcised, Tommy's not—that she had to take them into her mouth. She would command these young men to lie utterly still and with a teasing, tormenting deliberation, amid flurries of her little kisses and murmurs, the left hand gripping the taut member at the root and the right hand rapidly brushing her long falling hair away from her lips, swallow their semen when, with a live throb in her hand like that of a captured bird, Toby or Tommy came, pumping out a viscid, ropey, semi-transparent white substance, the ambrosial, eggy-tasting food of a savage goddess, gobs of it, so that it embarrassed these boys to look at her smeared, dazed face as she crouched there, hungry for more.

Here on Dock Street she felt this memory of a younger self betrayed by a blush as Tommy Gorton's cracked lips, moving like pale worms within his beard, continued the oft-told tale of his misfortune: "They eased me out of harbormaster—it's hard to row a dinghy to a mooring one-handed—but they take me on as extra hand, so to speak, out to the Banks, for a half-share. It was harder when the kids were little—Jean couldn't let go of her job at the bank, though at the level they kept her at she wasn't earning anything like what she was worth. Now they're off our dole—two boys and a girl, all grown up and married on their own."

Was this some kind of a taunt, saying that despite her having been such a whore for him he had come through respectably? Sukie wondered, did Jean do for him what she used to, or just earn money at the bank? Sukie would bite Tommy's shoulder in orgasm sometimes, and he took to imitating her, and would bite to hurt, it seemed. She didn't totally mind: the marks went away in two or three days, and the pain sharpened her sensations. Looking at this overfed, wind-burned lout, ripe for cardiac trouble, Sukie marvelled at the contortions she had gone through in a few months of courting him, loving him, abasing herself before him. It happens: men get the benefit of a woman's madness, and conceitedly take it as their due. "That sounds like a happy ending, Tom," she said, intending to conclude. "I'm glad for you."

But he wasn't done with her; he had joined her in remembering, right there on Dock Street, in the sunshine. "*Happy* may not be the word," he told her. "What you and I had, that was happy."

"Crazy," she said, wondering if he would block the sidewalk if she tried to step around. "*Crazy*'s the word I would use."

"I used to think you were crazy. But after you left town I thought we should all be so crazy. Jean's a more practical sort. She loves numbers. She says they put limits on things."

"She sounds very intelligent." Sukie took a step to the right, his weak side.

He sidestepped, to remain in front of her. "What brings you back to these parts anyway?" Other people on the sidewalk were noticing.

"Summer vacation," she said curtly. "I'm here with two old friends, renting." She stopped herself from saying where.

"With those other two," he said. "I heard." His manner had ceased to be so friendly.

"So you remember them."

"Yeah, they're remembered."

"Kindly, I hope."

"They're remembered."

Sukie took a further step diagonally, so that to block her he would have sent her crashing into the display window of the Christian Science Reading Room, which held a sun-parched copy of the Bible, propped open to Matthew, chapter 8, with a little plastic arrow on the verse, *And Jesus put forth his hand, and touched him, saying, I will; be thou clean. And immediately his leprosy was cleansed.*

"What do you do all day?" Tommy asked. The question was belligerent; out of an old instinct of intimacy he had raised his hand to prevent her passing, but it was the bad, mutilated hand, and he let it drop.

"Much what we do all day at home. Shop. Eat. Go out for a drive. It was good to see you, Tommy."

"Maybe you'll see me again."

That hand, with no muscle in it, no grip: horrible. His heavy, hairy belly, his gnarly nest of a beard. She remembered his pubic hair as blondish, as if sun-bleached. It would tickle her nose. "I don't know how long we'll be staying," she told him. "It depends on the other two."

"Don't depend on those two," he presumed to warn her, backing off, moving heavily to one side. "You used to do your own thing, pretty much."

"Like we said, Tommy, I was crazy. Now I'm an old lady. It was good to see you. Be well."

She was glad to get away. But as she walked the rest of Dock Street, to the great purplish, ridiculously overplanted horse trough, with the old wooden dock and the gently heaving boat landing beyond it, intending to turn left onto Oak Street to retrieve from its parking space, in this L-shaped town bent to fit the shore of Narragansett Bay, the powerful navy-blue BMW her late husband had insisted on her having, Sukie was aware, joyfully, of the saltwater flashing in the narrow spaces between the commercial buildings, as if the reflected light tracked some flow bright within herself. Her old house, a tiny 1760 saltbox, on a curved little alley off Oak called Hemlock Lane, was not far from here; she had lived as well as worked downtown. In these streets and houses she had loved and been loved; she was known here as nowhere else, not in her birthplace—a dirty nail at the end of a Finger Lake in New York State, where she had been an invisible child—or in the tidy Connecticut satellite city where she had been a second wife and where thirty years had gone by like a game of Pretend.

"Did you remember cream cheese?" Jane asked her sharply when she returned, having steered the BMW down the beach road and across the causeway, puddled from last night's high tide, and up the sweep of driveway around Darryl Van Horne's old house, to whose side entrance she now had a little brass key. "With my *s*stomach the way it is, cream cheese on a toasted bagel is the only thing that gets my *s*saliva going. Everything else tastes like *sss*awdust," Jane complained.

"The Superette doesn't stock cream cheese," Sukie said. "Not the Philadelphia brand, which is the only good one. I got you some blueberry yogurt instead. I'm sorry, sweetnips, you don't feel better." The pet name was one Alexandra had given to Sukie back in the days of Darryl Van Hornc's hot tub, and had just sprung to her lips, warmed as they were by encountering Tommy. More sternly, she said to Jane, "You should get out and do your own shopping—it's a gorgeous day. Where's Lexa? I didn't see your car on the lot."

The three women had two cars between them—Sukie's BMW, and Jane's old Racing Green Jaguar. Nat Tinker had been very vain of that car—an antique classic, a 1963 XKE convertible with sleek low lines, spoked hubcaps, and a grille like a shark mouth open to gather in oxygen. Its color was a

Racing Green so dark that by night it looked black, and when Jane drove it with the top down her black hair whipped every which way behind her. The two Eastern women had easily driven their automobiles to Rhode Island but Alexandra could not be expected to bring her white Ford pickup, dented and dirty from its years of Jim's rough use, all the way from New Mexico. So they shared. They shared their four rented rooms, two small condos carved from the old hot-tub-and-hi-fi room, adapted in turn by Darryl Van Horne from the Lenox family's glass-walled conservatory, heated by encircling steampipes and stocked not only with orchids and forced bulbs but with tropical trees, great ferns and palms and ficus and a single fragrant lemon tree. The bank's construction crew, in remodelling the foreclosed property, had sliced the high space horizontally in two. The ceiling, which once was retractable, displaying the stars to the lulled gazers immersed in the hot tub, was eighteen feet high, which meant, losing space to the flooring and dropped ceilings, that the upper rooms had the cozy closeness of college dorms. Alexandra, the tallest, could reach up and touch the ceiling. It felt larky, at first—old girls on their own, making do—but as July's temperatures rose these small rooms were sweltering, especially at night, as the sea breeze caressed the other side of the building, not theirs.

The two youngest and relatively affluent widows agreed that Alexandra, as the oldest and poorest and farthest from home, should have the biggest bedroom, with its queen-size bed. Sukie took an adjacent chamber, with a fold-down wall bed and a round table she could set up her word processor on; she was strict about doing her hour or two of work, with coffee and a bowl of cocktail nibbles in place of the cigarettes she had finally, right after Lennie died, given up. Jane, the latest riser of the three, often was still asleep when Sukie had finished writing and was ready to tackle a boiled egg on toast. With the specious argument that it made up in privacy what it lacked in space and light, Jane had been assigned the narrow windowless bedroom on the far side of the so-called living room, where the three gathered and read and watched television and had their pre-dinner drinks whether they ate dinner out or in. They sometimes reminisced about how they used to erect the cone of power over cocktails, but the rite involved some formal preparation and belonged to vanished times, when they were younger and more engaged in the lives around them, more passionate and more jealous and more persuaded that they could move the material world with sympathetic magic. Their suite held two bathrooms—Sukie and Alexandra shared the larger—and various inadequate closets and built-in bureaus and a small but adequate kitchen fitted with cabinets and shelves and a microwave and a revolving rack for pots and pans and an under-the-sink dishwasher so small it could barely hold three place settings. Their windows overlooked the parking lot and, beyond it to the right, Darryl's little used tennis court minus the canvas bubble he used to keep inflated with hot air.

"She took my car to the beach," Jane answered, of Alexandra, "even though I warned her it would be crawling with people and she'd have to park it on the public lot. One of us *must* go up to Town Hall and prove we're renting so we can have a temporary sticker. I would have thought you'd have done it by now, you're the one so fond of townies."

"You forget, I can't stand the sun any more. I break out in a rash. I never was the beach rat you and Lexa were."

"I don't blame you for not doing it," Jane said, as if

she hadn't quite heard. "It's all gotten so much more sticky and bureaucratic since we lived here. The guys at the gate just knew you and waved you in. Eastwick's lost its messy charm."

"Hasn't the whole world?" Sukie asked idly, unpacking milk and orange juice and yogurt and ground coffee and cranberry juice and Jewish rye into the refrigerator. "There are more and more people to regulate. I had to park on Oak today, where there always used to be space on Dock. People adjust, is the frightening thing. They forget, generation by generation, what it ever was to be free."

"Free," Jane mused. "What does that mean? You *have* to be born, you *have* to die. You're never in control."

"Speaking of control, on another topic: I think we should organize, the three of us, and do more real shopping at the Stop and Shop. There's no fresh meat or vegetables at the Superette, and we're running out of places to eat out. And it's expensive," she added, a bit scoldingly. As the youngest of the three, she was feeling an obligation to organize her two older roommates. Both Alexandra and Jane were vaguer than she remembered them—deeper into the engulfing indifference that readies us for death.

"I thought Lexa went to the *Ss*top and Shop," Jane said.

"She did, but she hardly bought anything. She ran into Gina Marino and came back in a trance."

"Just the thought of eating," Jane said. "I don't know what's the matter with me. I used to love food, especially fatty, salty food. The worse it was for me, the more I loved it. There was this dance you did with your own figure, imagining men sizing you up all the time. Chocolate, French fries . . . now just mentioning them makes me *sss*ick. Sukie, help me. I keep forgetting why we came here. Tell me."

"To be together," Sukie reminded her, rather sternly. "To revisit the scene of our primes."

"Our prime-crimes," Jane said, with a flash of her punning old self. Sukie had imagined before turning old that quirks—bad traits and mannerisms—would fall away, once the need to make a sexual impression was removed; without the distraction of sex, a realer, more honest self would be revealed. But it is sex, it turned out, that engages us in society, and keeps us on our toes, and persuades us to retract our rough edges, so we can mix in. Without the sexual need to negotiate, there is little to curb neurotic crankiness. Jane was succumbing to hers.

"I remember Eastwick as a fun hick place," Jane complained, "but it's gotten homogenized, all *ss*moothed out— the curbs downtown all fancy granite, and the Old Stone Bank twice the size it was, like some big bland cancer gobbling up everything. And the younger people, the age we were when we were here—*ssso* tiresome, just from the look of them, toned-up young mothers driving their overweight boys in overweight SUVs to hockey practice twenty miles away, the young fathers castrated namby-pambies helping itty-bitty wifey with the housekeeping, spending all Saturday fussing around the lovely *home*. It's the Fifties all over again, without the Russians as an excuse. You wonder how they managed to fuck enough to make their precious children. They probably didn't—it's all *in vitro* now, and every birth is cesarean, so the doctors won't get sued. People go around mourning the death of God; it's the death of *ssin* that bothers me. Without *ss*in, people aren't people any more, they're just *ss*oul-less *sheep*."

"Oh, Jane, we've been here only for a week. To have fun, we've got to *try*. We should pretend Eastwick is a foreign capital we're visiting. What kind of things would we do?"

"We'd visit the cathedral and the palace. But who wants to go *ss*tare at the Unitarian church and that squat cinder-block Town Hall with its fake-rustic veneer of clinker bricks?"

"Don't be so negative! You wouldn't even go down to the beach the other night for the fireworks."

"Lexa agreed with me. Who wants to go mill around on the wet sand with a lot of beered-up riffraff?"

"Listen to you! With that attitude you'll never go anywhere. You'll just crouch indoors, complaining about riffraff. *We're* riffraff! America is riffraff—that's its beauty!"

Sulkily Jane tried to defend herself. "I thought the fireworks were lovely from up here, the three of us standing in the parking lot."

"They were hidden by the trees."

"Half-hidden. It made them look bigger—these giant jellyfish appearing and fading through the oaks, above the cypresses. It was like being invaded from space."

"Yes, except you kept complaining about the mosquitoes and made us come back inside to these stuffy rooms. You couldn't see a thing from our windows, just the shadows of the cypresses leaping up and fading back."

"They felt bigger than mosquitoes. They felt like sparks when you stand too close to the fire. Anyway, Lexa was bored, too. Fireworks go on too long. It's really a *ss*candal, like most government *ss*pending. The fireworks companies sell these little towns more than they can afford. So then they cut music and art from the school curriculum."

"You made us come inside before the climax. Fireworks have a plot, they mount up to a climax."

"We'd had enough."

"*I* hadn't had enough," Sukie said. "I missed the climax."

"We heard it. It was just a lot of noise. Bang-bang-bang-bang-BOOM. There. Now you've had your climax."

The conversation felt dangerously close to becoming a quarrel. Where was Lexa? They both needed her, for a stable triangle. After a silence, Sukie told Jane, "I bumped into an old lover downtown just now."

"Oh? Unlucky you. Mine are all dead, I hope."

"Tommy Gorton. I didn't know him at first—he had gotten fat and run-down, with a scruffy beard and ponytail to establish some kind of identity for himself as a local character. He had wrecked his hand hauling in cod, and has no real job, just a drudge of a wife to support him. But—you would have liked this—he hinted he was ready to sin. He said he hoped he'd see me again. He seemed such a boy when I, you know, had to do with him, but then in the car driving back I was doing the numbers—he was only eleven years younger than I! That doesn't seem much at all, at our age now. He looked so beautiful to me then, everything newly made and perfect. This fuzzy firm ass. Abs like a washboard."

Jane said sourly, "No wonder you write romances."

"I'm trying to get some momentum on one, now that we're more or less settled. All I need is an hour a day, right after breakfast, with the second cup of coffee; it pours right out."

"You don't think that's somewhat *ssss*elfish and boring of you? While Lexa and I do what? Tiptoe around and speak in whispers?"

"You don't need to, just don't come into my room."

"Have you looked at *my* room? It's like a prison cell. No—it's like a gas chamber."

"Widows need interests, Jane. What ever happened to you and your cello?"

"Oh, that. It never had the right timbre after that odious Doberman of mine chewed it up in one of his jealous fits. And then Nat's dreadful mother hated the sound of my practicing, though in that enormous house I don't see how she could hear it. She was deaf only when it *s*suited her."

"There are summer concerts around here. I see posters in the window of the Superette."

"I'm scared to go out," Jane suddenly confessed. "There's something unfriendly out there. The other side. I can feel it. We shouldn't have come back. Sukie, it's a terrible mistake!"

"Jane, this is so unworthy of you! You're imagining things." Sukie needed help, lest Jane's panic spread to her. She listened to the sound of a car on the gravel driveway below, thinking it might be Alexandra. She hoped so. Hostile space and time loomed around her. One of the sensations of being a widow was of the world being much too big—of her having misplaced whatever it was that would make it small enough to control.

"We need to get out," Sukie resumed, "and start *doing* things. There's a chamber-music concert Saturday night, in the auditorium in the new wing of the public library. The boy in the Superette was telling me the new wing ran a million dollars over budget."

The two women listened, hearing someone who must be Alexandra climb the stairs, her footsteps heavier and slower than they used to be. Her key scraped and fumbled at the door; she brought into the low-ceilinged room a pink face and hair damp and straggled from the breeze at the beach. Outdoor air ballooned from her broad body like the kelpy scent of a crashing wave. "It was lovely," she said. "I walked today to the right for a change, toward the public end. There's a kind of lagoon now, where there used to be just a slope of hard sand. Children can dabble in it without the mothers and babysitters worrying about a wave carrying them off." Sensing that the two others had been talking and had something to propose to her, she flung her weight in its flowing beach wrap down in a big plaid armchair and asked rhetorically, "*How* could I have spent so much of my life away from the ocean?"

"Di*ss*contentedly," Jane suggested.

Sukie said, "Jane and I have an idea."

"I can feel that," said Alexandra. "Good. This group needs ideas."

The new wing of the Eastwick Public Library was larger than the original, a nineteenth-century benefaction of lumpy brownstone that had sat with a certain touching self-importance at the center of a gentle dome of public green. The glass-and-concrete addition took up again as much space and had caused a new driveway and a generous parking lot to pave over swathes of grass where children and dogs used to play. The much-vaunted auditorium, with its lobby and an adjacent function room, extended beneath a main floor devoted, table after table, to computers where town idlers played video games and ingeniously searched for pornography. The section of children's books, once a modest nook of colorful slim volumes presumed to be transitional to adult reading, had greatly expanded, into tall cases of inch-thick walnut, as if to memorialize the end of reading for all but a few of the library's patrons. The concert-and-lecture hall, optimistically conceived to hold improving events almost every night, betrayed its subterranean condition with stifled acoustics that to spectators in the back corners gave tonight's concert a spectral, mimed aspect. The chamber group was divided between aspiring music majors in the nearby community college and elder adepts whose skills had plateaued at a level of complacent competence. Jane, whose own playing had once formed the fiery center, the furious inner resort, of her emotive life, listened with a seething impatience as the figures on the stage insistently sawed and swayed through Vivaldi with his sugary whine, Beethoven's surly tangle of near-dissonance, and a bit of Ravel like a wispy handkerchief disappearing up a wide-cuffed sleeve.

Then, after a brief intermission during which the narrow lobby loudly overflowed with all the exciting things that small-town people manage to find to say to one another, day after day, get-together after get-together, while only a sneaky remnant of former addicted multitudes ventured outdoors to pollute with cigarette smoke the night air above the drastically diminished green, one of Bach's great cat's cradles was essayed, an arrangement for strings from *Die Kunst der Fuge*, its themes crisscrossing and lifting a third and then a fifth between his giant ghostly fingers, hoary formulae like *e f e f, d e d e* brought to the last and highest paroxysm of the Baroque, the thrilling counterpoint snapped shut at last as the Lutheran fist, *ritardando*, emphatically closed. Jane had once played this fugue under Ray Neff's direction, and her left hand's fingers twitched on her knee in the familiar motions, though the calluses given the tips by pressing in earnest on the strings had over the years become vestigial.

Through her haze of irritation and nostalgia it slowly dawned on her that the person she had taken for a male first violinist, who counted the first measure audibly and with a silent lunge gave the downbeat—a stout, somewhat hunch-backed figure with steel-rimmed glasses and effeminate bangs, straw-dull hair cut short—was in fact a woman, in baggy black slacks, and not just any woman but one she knew, whose choppy dictatorial gestures and pedantic, metronomic nodding rang a disagreeable bell: it was Greta Neff, not only still alive but less changed by three decades than she had any right to be. Jane looked again at the little photocopied program they had been handed by a teen-aged girl at the door — a round-faced girl with a dewy pink complexion, who didn't look as though she should be wearing, as she was, several thumb rings and a tiny silver dumbbell piercing an eyebrow — and satisfied herself that Greta Neff's name was not listed. But there was a *G. Kaltenborn, violin.* Greta's German maiden name. Jane knew her story. She and Raymond Neff had met when he was in the Army and stationed in Stuttgart. Jane had heard the story in bed with Ray. Her heart, remembering Ray in bed, skipped a beat. Whatever had happened to him, Eastwick High's bandmaster and the leader of the plucky chamber-music group in which Jane had played cello? A fussy little man with a soft body and the high nasal voice of a small-town dominator, he had seemed effeminate but had fathered six children on Greta and had leftover sex drive enough to perform for a time as Jane's lover and, before that, as Alexandra's. It had been a minor episode for Alexandra but for Jane something more: with all his failings, including his horrible, laughable German wife, he knew his way around a woman's body. He had had a musical touch. People laughed at Ray, but under his hands and tongue there was bliss for Jane. And he was by no means as meagerly endowed as his shrewish voice suggested.

Her dark blood simmering, Jane went right up to Greta at the reception in the function room afterwards. Sukie and Alexandra, bewildered by her sudden purposeful animation, warily tagged after her into the heated little hubbub of townspeople voicing congratulations that were at bottom self-congratulations: classical music, Beethoven and Bach, right here in Eastwick! The crowd gave way before the trio of strangers, who were not strangers to everyone, and who had been preceded by rumors of their reappearance. "Greta Neff," Jane said in a voice that, after two hours of silent listening, came out as a croak. "Do you remember me?"

"Haoew," the other woman said, her first language peeping through the twisted diphthong, "coot I forget, Chane? I hurt you were all pack in taown, but I cootn't belief it." Her pale-lashed eyes, a dishwater blue behind the thick lenses of her steel-rimmed spectacles, had taken in Sukie and Alexandra, standing behind Jane like embarrassed bodyguards.

Sukie spoke up: "Greta, we were sorry to hear about Raymond."

What had there been to hear? Jane asked herself. Sukie had been out gathering news but not sharing all of it. Raymond must be dead. Just that past week Jane had joked about hoping all her old lovers were dead, but it was different to learn that one of them really was. Poor Ray, trying to bring culture to this backwater, where all people cared about was games and sex and the tax rates and the cod catch.

"Yes, vell," Greta said impatiently, "it was a mercy in the ent. He had pin suffering a lonk time. It was cancer," she explained, "of the powel."

"How terrible!" Alexandra exclaimed. Her worst fears were of cancer—your own cells turning evil, multiplying, blocking your organs with senseless scarlet cauliflowers of flesh, attacking even the intestines that had kept your excrement out of sight and smell, adding shame to pain, an artificial exterior bag to the rotting body. "Poor dear Ray." The "dear" must have sprung from those moments years and years ago when, new to radical marital discontent and to the radical sexual possibilities proclaimed by the youthful prophets of the Sixties, she had shared a furtive horizontality with Ray for some frightening moments, scarcely able to believe that this was really happening, this betrayal, this clumsy release, this renewal of primary energy. She and Ray were new to it and not expert and quickly gave each other up as more enduring affairs pushed their timid start aside. Soon, from Eastwick to the golden coast where the stars had long assumed the freer, more privileged life-styles of gods and goddesses, the American middle class gave up puritanism and stampeded into restless adventuring and mutual exploration. The spontaneously dropped "dear" fell strangely on the ears of these women, igniting among them, amid the communal hubbub, a flare of recognition that they were all of them widows, undefended women startled here into remembrance of a man, keepers of his flame, a rather ridiculous man but one heroically devoted to music and beauty where he found them, and one whose feats of local organization and promotion had won admiration from even Sukie, who had never seen Ray naked and spectacularly aroused. "It was a very impressive concert," Alexandra told Greta, in acknowledgment of this warmth surreptitiously kindled among them, and in polite cover-up of the tactless word "dear."

Greta, who had begun to turn away to greet other well-wishers, was arrested by this pleasantry, taking it literally in her single-track Teutonic style. "Dit you sink so? Chane, do you agree?"

Jane, who had endured the concert in a daze of hypercritical tension, looked her old enemy in the eye and said, purringly, with the two-edged courtesy of Boston gentry, "I took it as a *ccc*ivic experience—a lesson in democracy, the *ss*enior players bringing the babies along."

Greta blinked behind her glasses, uncertain how deeply this jabbed. In her slow, relentless way, she pronounced,

"You must haff youth. Usserweisse, a group dies." And with that she did turn away, leaving the pernicious trio to ponder whether or not this dark saying had been meant to apply to them. They had included a younger member in their own group once, and had killed her.

Except for Greta's, this Eastwick crowd contained no face familiar to Alexandra, though for a moment she thought she glimpsed old Franny Lovecraft on the far side of the room, blue-haired and shrunken, laying down the law to some unseen auditor, her head twitching with the motions of her tongue like a lightweight bell being rung by a ponderous clapper. But Franny had been old when Alexandra was not yet forty and still full of juice; by now the crone would be laid in her grave, her chirpy little body in its coffin as brittle and dry as a flower pressed in a Bible. Franny had courted Alexandra in a fashion, trying to enlist her in respectable local circles, stopping now and then in her old black Buick, with its grille like a harrow, pretending to be interested in her flower beds, inviting her to come to this or that Garden Club lecture or church supper with a fascinating speaker, a missionary for years in the South Seas, or even, at one importunate visit, to be a junior member of the Horse Trough Committee, the highest such honor the town could bestow on a woman—trying to keep Alexandra in touch, the bothersome old thing, with Eastwick's core of public decency, the hum of blameless activity sublimating the dark anarchic instincts an unattached divorcée might fall prey to. For Franny was a woman, and knew what women were, dirty and yearning and in need of being controlled. *Sweet old bores*, is how Alexandra had thought of Franny and her husband. What had been his name? It came to her: Horace. A fussy little sly man, driving his boat-size, well-preserved

Buick with a maddening care, especially when you were behind him trying to get a child to a dental appointment or baseball practice, and watering his weedless lawn on West Oak Street with the sly air and sideways twinkle of a man daydreaming. The Lovecrafts were absent from the concert, dissolved by time as if they had never existed, a pinch of pollen lost on the wind—they had been childless—and Alexandra might as well have been the same, for not one person came up to her or Sukie or Jane in the chattering gathering, as if a circle of taboo had been drawn around them. They huddled there holding their paper cups of saccharine raspberry punch, talking to one another.

"Well!" Jane said. "What did you make of that?"

"Greta?" Alexandra asked. "She tried. She wasn't as sinister as I remembered."

"You don't remember her very well," Jane said. "She was worse. Ray somehow intimidated her—her GI in shining armor, bringing her out of Hitler's nightmare Europe to the Land of Gold—and now nothing intimidates her. She's lethal."

"I thought she took your slap pretty well, about the young and the senile mixed in together in the chamber group."

"I never said *sss*enile," Jane said, "though that cellist several times in the *largo* had no idea where she was. She was off by a full measure."

Sukie spoke up. "I felt Greta was holding something back. Jane's right. She's surer of herself. She's never remarried—while we sank back into being housewives, she was consolidating her powers."

"Why, Sukie!" Alexandra exclaimed, startled, as when they were naked side by side in Darryl's hot tub, by how moving she found the pagan simplicity of this younger woman. Her sweet nipples had been rosy and erect amid the droplets of steam condensing on the organic Teflon of her skin. "Are you saying marriage makes a woman powerless?"

"It warps you," Sukie said. Her plump upper lip clamped onto the lower as a snail's broad foot clamps onto a leaf, the adhesion indicating that she found the topic distasteful and had nothing more to say upon it.

It was a signal to go; but as the three routed interlopers moved toward the double exit doors, someone in the crowd did approach them, hurrying to do so, and wryly smiling, as if to disavow the haste that implied a previous neglect. This person spoke with the rapid ease of a practiced speaker. "I see you're going," she said, "but I wanted to introduce myself. I'm Debbie Larcom, the parson, I guess you'd have to say, of the Unitarian Fellowship. It's lovely to see some fresh faces at these concerts; they're supposed to attract summer people but the same loyal regulars tend to show up. Just like church." She was a shapely small brunette with pleasingly precise features. Her straight nose held a pink bit of flaking sunburn. There was nothing clerical about her except a certain reserve in the long-sleeved gray dress whose hem came below her knees, here at the height of summer. But her abashed grin was endearing, and the intelligent complexity of her gray-green eyes. As if flashingly possessed by a male devil, Sukie entertained a vision of this gracious woman naked, that compact, precise body bared as as white as virtue itself, even as Sukie politely gave her own name and returned with her own grip the other's cool, narrow, sinewy hand.

"We could be regulars ourselves," Alexandra was telling Deborah Larcom. "We're here for the summer."

"We lived in Eastwick ages ago," Sukie said, a bit breathlessly. "We knew one of your predecessors, Brenda Parsley. She was the Unitarians' first woman minister."

"We were very proud of her," Jane drawled with Bostonian irony. In truth the three villainesses had ruthlessly bewitched Brenda, so that moths and bees came out of her mouth when she preached.

The young clergywoman's face, professionally alert and responsive, showed no special spark of recognition. "I've heard the name," she admitted, "but that was way back, in the Sixties or early Seventies."

"Exactly," Jane snapped. Alexandra could tell that Jane had taken one of her dislikes. And Alexandra jealously felt Sukie's arousal, burdening her fragile breathing.

"Water over the dam," Deborah Larcom lilted with an anxious gaiety. "Before I was even born." The triple dose of intense female scrutiny was tripping her into self-doubt; her impulsive spurt of welcome was running down. "Well, I just wanted to say hello. Needless to say, we'd be delighted to see you at the Fellowship some Sunday." There was that awkward moment, with clergypersons, when they've made their pitch and wait for a clue to what no external evidence declares, the status of God in the consciousness of another. "It's not just services," she gamely pursued in the face of their silence, "we do Tuesday suppers, singles welcome as well as families, and are planning an anti-Iraq rally for later in the summer."

Before their non-responsive silence became painfully prolonged, Alexandra said, "We really don't know exactly what our plans are."

"Come if you can," Debbie Larcom sang in relieved farewell, her duty done. With the middle fingers of both shapely quick hands she tucked her long and glossy dark-brown hair behind her ears—slightly cupped, like Sukie's—before, flashing one more appealing, wryly qualified smile, she whisked herself away, leaving behind like a whiff of perfume the contrast between a virtuous and elastic young woman and the three old ladies, gone brittle and dry in their corruption. Her appearance before them had been a chastisement; they had once been such as she, here in this very town.

Above the dark of the sleeping town a bulky woman hunched at her little battered drop-front desk on the third floor of her ill-kept house. Her shadow agitated the wall behind her, and the sagging ceiling. *They are here*, she wrote, gouging the lined yellow paper with her ballpoint. *All three of them, bold as you please.* She had often heard the phrase, in the mouths of these New Englanders, but hesitated. Shouldn't it be *bold as they please*? In her fury she ignored the nicety and wrote on, in her blocky, upright European hand, *They have taken quarters in the Lenox Seaview Apartments, which should make access easy for you where you know it so well. They showed no shame in coming to a concert the group founded by my dear husband was giving. The fat sympathetic one, the dark unsympathetic one, the sexy pretty one rendered nervous by being so. All old and shameless and useless, vermin under-foot. Kill them. Kill them as once they did your innocent sister kill.* This was probably faulty English grammar, but, possessed, she pushed on with her methodical upright handwriting: *I advise the dark one to be first—there is already in her aura an unhealthy, rotten look. You will know most better.* She pictured him, the radiant one, eternally young, his fair hair curly as in some painting from the Catholic religion of her youth. She added, in a more tentative hand, emotion imparting a tremor, *Come, stay with me. The house is big, a sad expense on Raymond's piffling school pension. The children are forever away. Come be my strength. Evil must not unpunished go. This is—is this the phrase?—your chance of gold.*

Nat Tinker's estate entailed a mare's nest of trusts and codicils to his will, and long-term bonds that to avoid fines and penalties shouldn't be cashed for years. His mother, still alive upstairs in the huge Brookline house, wasn't too senile to be obstructionist when you least expected it. At home in her own rooms Jane had a fax and e-mail but in these reduced conditions—like a summer camp but without canoeing lessons and ghost stories around the campfire— she had to receive and dispatch documents to the lawyers and bankers by mail. Express and registered mail involved going to the post office, and parking on Dock Street in summer was a much worse hassle than it used to be; when you did find a space it was blocks away and involved a long walk in the sickening sun. She didn't understand it, she used to be a great beachgoer, with her dark complexion taking a tan on the first day and needing no lotion thereafter, except on an all-day sail; but now the overhead sun hit her with a somehow radioactive force, so that she felt poisoned— nauseated and faint. She had taken to wearing broad- brimmed straw hats, but the small holes in the weave seemed to be pelting her face with a buckshot of photons. Her wrists, her knees in shorts, her elbows when she wore short sleeves all protruded into an insidious hail from the vibrantly blank blue sky. Even as self-consciously quaint and retro a downtown as Eastwick's surrounded Jane with debilitat- ing emanations: carbon monoxide from car exhaust, radon from the granite beneath the asphalt, electrons leaking from the taped-up neon tubing advertising Milwaukee beer at the Happy Hours Liquor Mart and the Rhode Island lottery at the Bay Superette, gamma rays from the little camera that took her picture when she used the ATM at the Old Stone

Bank, a mist of voltage falling from the drooping cables and condenser cans on the poles overhead. In front of the post office, three paces from the two flap-mouthed collection boxes, an especially sinister pole, splintered by the cleats of climbing troubleshooters and soaked in faded creosote, held a boxy gray transformer whose hum was deafening, once you stood and listened to it. One July mid-afternoon Jane was standing near it, hearkening to the hum, wondering if she might just faint right on the sparkling sidewalk, when something leaped across a gap and jabbed her in the side—what they call in boxing a kidney punch. "It quite took my breath away," she told Alexandra, once she was back in the rented condo. "It still tingles."

"Maybe we should complain to the selectmen, or the electric company," Alexandra said lazily. "It sounds like a short circuit." She had been lying stretched out on her queen-size bed, immobilized there while Jane and Sukie had been off in their respective cars. Sukie had taken the BMW in the direction of Exeter and the South County Museum; she was doing some research for her next romance, which was to deal with a ravishing plantation mistress and a black slave. Rhode Island had begun as Providence Plantations and supported a Southern-style economy and a large slave population well into the eighteenth century; there were still some barn ruins—tumbled walls of stones bigger than bales of hay—from that benighted, idyllic era.

"Wood doesn't conduct," Jane snapped. "That's why they use it for poles."

"Make a cup of tea," Alexandra suggested. Then she asked, overcoming her humiliating dependency, "Can I use your car for an hour? I really *must* go see Marcy and her boys. It's shocking—it's been two weeks since we first got here and she helped us settle in, and I've not managed to visit. We've talked on the phone about it, but then one of us, maybe me, wanders away. I just haven't got the energy to be a mother again."

"Energy," Jane said. "I can't remember what it was like to have any. The thought of opening up the microwave sickens me." There was an electric stove in the kitchen, but the widows, having done with catering to husbands, were averse to elaborate cooking and used the microwave oven to warm leftovers, thaw ice cream, and bring a cup of water to a simmer. In spite of her avowal, Jane went to the microwave with a mug of faucet water and opened the microwave door, that door of tinted thick glass through which food could be watched undergoing transformation—steaming, melting, spitting. A malevolent stench seemed to gust out at her; she may have imagined it—a chill as if she had opened a refrigerator and quickly shut the door on an odor of spoiled food. Another of her disagreeable sensations was that *she* was the closed container, and the spoiling was within. Her insides did not feel right, and hadn't since Nat had died. Up until his death, his complaining, ungrateful boyish ego had monopolized Jane's attention. There, she reflected, was the good that utterly selfish people do: they drive those around them into self-forgetfulness.

Alexandra loved whipping along in Nat's antique Jaguar with its top down. She could feel herself, in the eyes that watched her drive through town, flash by, an apparition of breezy womanhood, a kerchief snug beneath her chin. Tree branches and electric cables and house gables streamed overhead, and sunshine spattered on the windshield. Marcy lived out where Cocumscussoc Way became seedy, leaving the town center behind and trailing into a no-man's land of abandoned saltwater farms and derelict vegetable stands and failed riding schools and shuttered, overambitious restaurants. The mailbox, one of those new squat plastic ones molded in one piece with its post and therefore impervious to the roaming vandals who batter metal detachable ones, proclaimed in white stick-on letters THE LITTLE-FIELD'S. The ignorant apostrophe annoyed Alexandra. Howard had originally had his electrician's shop in the house, in a basement section next to a one-car garage, with its own door and a modest sign. But success bred of default—nobody wants to dirty his hands at a trade any more, while local gentrification ups the demand for services—had given him an office on the upper reach of Dock Street, an answering service, and a young assistant from one of those Central American countries where the poor are still eager to work. Alexandra did not see many signs of prosperity in their scruffy yard, with its scattered toys and drum-shaped aboveground pool, or in the peeling exterior of their split-level ranch, a stranded-looking left-over from the Levittown era.

Marcy came to the front door, in sluggish response to its three-note chime. She looked her age, which was close to that of the house. Kissed, her cheek seemed clammy. Alexandra said to her, "Darling, you *don't* make a plural name by adding an apostrophe 's.' That forms a possessive."

Marcy was slow to understand; her wits had thickened along with her legs. "Oh. The mailbox. Howard did the lettering, with a little kit, and when I saw it it was too late to change. Does it matter?"

"I don't know why it annoys me so. Like people saying they could care less, when they *don't* care, and that somebody graduated Brown, when they graduated *from* Brown."

"Language changes, Mother. It's a growing, living thing."

"Growing in all the wrong directions, it seems to me. In the direction of dumber and dumber." Only her children, especially this oldest one, made her sound like such a scold. "How *are* the boys?" she asked, to change the subject, before realizing that "dumber and dumber" would have appeared to serve as the transition, as in fact the phrase had. "Is little Howard still enjoying the computer game?"

"He says the blood looks too fake and there aren't enough what they call 'ho's being butchered. I know, it's deplorable, but they all go through this phase. He hates, by the way, being called 'little Howard.' "

" 'Howard Junior' to me seems even worse. Your father and I didn't agree on everything, as you know, but we *did* agree not to saddle any male child with being a junior, as if his identity is preëmpted from the start." Her words echoing in her ears, she said to Marcy, "Forgive me, dear. I don't know what gets into me when I talk this way."

"Guilt," Marcy answered readily. "You feel guilty toward me for my having to act the mother to my three siblings when you skipped out on us emotionally." Her face, bare of any makeup, had an aggressively waxy pallor; her hair didn't even look washed, let alone tinted, and *why* didn't she do something about that translucent wart on the side of her nose? Didn't Rhode Island have any plastic surgeons? New Mexico crawled with them. The child kept on unleashing her grievances: "I used to *pray* you'd stay home instead of going over to that man's awful place. I'd be awake until one or two in the morning until I heard you stagger in. That house used to seem so vulnerable, out there all by itself on Orchard Road. Owls would whistle right outside the windows. I'd keep hearing creaking footsteps."

"*Well,*" Alexandra said, her face hot as she looked around her. The living room bespoke a gauche prosperity, with its white shag carpet and a huge flat black television screen facing a pair of bulbous fake-leather, buff-colored armchairs, lopsided, creased, and stained from hard use by two male adolescents. "This house I dare say holds no such sinister mysteries. Congratulations."

"And then," Marcy continued, not bothering to hide her trembling lips, her watery eyes, "you say snobby mean things like that to me to defend yourself against criticisms of *you* you're afraid I might make. Talk about preëmptive."

"Thank God, so to speak, for daughters that double as amateur psychoanalysts. Linda drawls out over the phone what an uptight Yankee I am. If the North had lost the war like we did, she says, we'd all be less achievement-oriented. We'd be able to taste the sugar in the whiskey sour. God knows who feeds her these sayings; I hope not her husband. But I *am* sorry about the owls. I was learning how to be a witch, and they only offered night courses."

"You joke, Mother, but I *am* interested in psychology, and've been thinking of going into counselling, when the boys are a little older. The trouble is, Howie and I—"

"*Must* you call him 'Howie'?"

"—he and I are so set on moving to Venice when the boys are in college or maybe even when and if Howie Junior goes to boarding school—"

"Venice, Florida, I assume you're talking about. You'll have to learn Italian for the other one."

"—that there's no sense in getting the license in Rhode Island when I'd be practicing in Florida."

"Such a depressing state, Florida. Alligators and old people. And they keep it so flat, so people can get about pushing walkers."

"Howie loves to fish." Seeing that her mother would not interrupt this wifely assertion, Marcy smoothed the lap of her shorts, in which she had, evidently, been tending the fenced garden out back, where the Littlefields grew easy, surface vegetables. Her bare knees were dirty, which made her seem all the more touchingly a child, chunky and thick-legged and stubborn and yet winsome. "Mother, I haven't offered you anything. Some coffee. Or tea? I don't know what your diet is these days."

"Diet, you're right, I should be on one, but no, thank you. It's before four, too late for the one and too early for the other. I'm the poor mouse of the three of us over there, so I can get out only when one of the others doesn't want her car. I'm not complaining; it puts me in my place."

"Have you enjoyed being back, so far?"

"Yes, I have, oddly, though all the few people still alive that we knew seem to bear grudges. I'm amazed at how green and wet everything is. Being back here reminds me how I felt when after my mother died my father sent me east to Connecticut College for Women, everything so lush and old. I won't stay forever, dear, I won't hold you up. I'll just sit and chat with you for five minutes. Where are the boys?"

"I *told* you, Mother, when we talked over the phone. The boys are at camp for three weeks. In Maine."

"My goodness—you and Howard do throw your money around! Do the boys like camp?"

"Roger a*dored it*. He went last year and next year will qualify for white-watering and rock-climbing. He could get killed! Howie Junior is a little timid still—he needs to have his big brother there."

"He'll be fine. Eric was the same with Ben. Now he's the adventurous one. The kid-brother complex—the kid brothers turn out tough as nails. Did you know that a saguaro cactus needs to have what they call a nurse tree, a palo verde usually, so this tiny thing—this little tiny pin cushion, you can hardly see them at first—can live and grow in the shade?"

Marcy was looking at her meltingly, and said with tears returned to her eyes, "Oh, Mother, it's so nice to hear you talk this way!"

"What way? It's the way I always talk."

"About Nature!"

"Don't go teary on me, please. I have a practical question, for you to ask Howard. Could standing near a telephone pole give a person a shock? A sensation of being punched in the side?"

Marcy straightened up in the armchair she had chosen, her eyes drying. *This generation*, Alexandra thought. They grew up watching us rebel against our pious upbringings and in reaction have reverted to all the old sentimentalities, family and home and such other tyrannies. "Why, no," Marcy said, "I wouldn't think so. Everybody would be suing towns and companies if it did."

"It happened to one of my friends, she just told me."

"I'll ask Howard, but as I say I doubt it. He does say that electricity is a funny devil—it surprises you sometimes."

"My friend isn't the most trustworthy—she's full of strange sensations these days. You know her—Jane. She approached you about the rental. You called her a game old gal. Jane learned her witch lessons rather too well, I'm sometimes afraid."

"Mother, I don't find that joke very funny. What men used to do to those poor women was horrible. And they did it to thousands."

"Who's joking? Girls your age just can't realize how few opportunities there were for women when I was young. Our job was to make babies and buy American consumer goods. If we fell off the marriage bandwagon, there was nothing much left for us but to ride a broomstick and cook up spells. Don't look so shocked, it was *power*. Everybody needs power. Otherwise the world eats you up."

"What about children? Isn't having them and loving them power enough for most women?"

" 'In sorrow thou shalt bring forth children,' " Alexandra quoted, the quotation being fresh in her memory, " 'and thy desire shall be to thy husband, and he shall rule over thee.' Isn't that utterly disgusting?"

"Not to me, so much," Marcy admitted. "There's truth to it." She set her feet in their dirty gardening sneakers solidly on the already soiled white carpet (why do these children buy white carpet and then not take care of it?) and stood up on her thick legs. Why are children so disappointing? They take your genes and run them right into the ground. Marcy asked pathetically, "Would you like to help me weed?"

"Do I look dressed for it? That bad? Darling, it's a lovely invitation, but at my age once you bend down there's no guarantee you'll get back up."

The child acknowledged that this overture was another failure, swinging her heavy red hands in a hopeless way. "I used to love it when you'd get into our garden on Orchard Road, with the zinnias and tomato plants. You seemed more my mother then."

"More than other times? It's strange, my dear, but part of your assignment as a parent is to forget you are one. You're no good to your children if you're just a homemaking ninny who doesn't give them any room to grow in. You mentioned Nature. It's a funny devil, as Howard says of electricity. I used to think I loved it, but now that it's chewing me to death, I realize I hate it and fear it. In Canada I had the experience of there being too much Nature, and only at the end did I get on top of it. I had a religious experience, I think. But the trouble with such experiences is that the other thing, the other side, whatever it is, the place you get to, isn't very *clear*—it just *is*, for a minute. Then it's over. Gone."

While pronouncing all this she had slowly pushed her creaky body up from the fat easy chair she had taken, with its faint sour tang of young malehood, and straightened up to confront her daughter. Alexandra was two inches taller, thirty pounds heavier, and twenty-three years older.

Marcy, looking alarmed, asked her, "How is it doing the chewing?"

She meant her mother's death, which she couldn't face even to the extent of phrasing it unambiguously. Alexandra smiled at the sad fact of mattering without any trying on her part, just existing as a shield, an intervening layer, between her child and the grave. "Oh," she said, with an unfeigned diffidence, "the usual aches and pains and a sense of growing incoherence. And there are spells of the incontinence problem they keep advertising on television—before television and indoor plumbing, I suppose, people just dribbled. Really, Nature asks women's insides to do too much. On the other hand, since being east my skin is much less dry and itchy. I'm terrified of cancer, of course, but my doctors tell me it's all in my mind. Keep it there, I tell them. For seventy-four, I'm doing well. Don't you worry, honey. My Grandma Sorensen lived to be eighty-eight. The last time I saw her she was up on her own roof, having crawled out a dormer window to hammer down the chimney flashing."

"Ever since Howie's mother passed," Marcy said in her worried, nagging way, "you're the boys' only grandmother. You're very important to them. *Do* come see them when they're back from camp in August. They want to love you."

"Oh, dear," Alexandra said, pleased nevertheless. "I'm not

sure at my age I can stand up to too much love. I'm not used to it."

"I—"

"Don't say it. Same here."

"I'll have you to dinner when the boys are back. Why not bring the others?"

"They'd like that. Eastwick hasn't been as welcoming as they expected. A little family fun might keep us out of mischief."

Sukie spotted Tommy Gorton, in a gray sweatshirt, at the far end of Dock Street, and he had spotted her a minute before; day after day they had been hoping for the other to appear. The first, purely accidental encounter had been under a postcard-clear sky, but today, by mid-morning, a glowering cloud mass had slanted in from the northeast, and they needed to find shelter as the first drops of rain began to dot the sidewalk. Nemo's Diner seemed a safe place; it had not yet been sold to Dunkin' Donuts. A long aluminum box with rounded corners and a broad red stripe along its sides, the diner in thirty years had gone from being a casual relic of Fifties modern to being a self-consciously retro curiosity, a souvenir of younger days for old-timers while trendier places like the Bakery Coffee Nook and the fish restaurant, the Friendly Grouper, located out on the rebuilt dock, attracted the arrivistes in town. Nemo's still had a counter and wooden booths, with little vanilla-colored jukeboxes that, for a quarter, would still play golden oldies by Frankie Laine and Patti Page and Fats Domino and the Chantelles and (the latest hits) the Beatles. Customers rarely spared the quarter; the booths at the back tended to be taken over by the old-timers, who treasured silence and nursed mugs of coffee and old political grievances that could still be warmed, in trios and quartets, into loud indignation. Sukie and Tom, after one glance at the filled back booths, gravitated in unison toward the little round tables up in front, near the picture window that overlooked Dock Street. Raindrops flecked the big pane and accumulated into rivulets that staggered and then streamed downward. It had been to one of these tables, Sukie remembered, that she had brought Jennifer Gabriel one bitter winter day not many days after the girl's father had committed suicide, having murdered her mother in a drunken rage. Against the cold, Sukie remembered, the orphan wore a dirty parka patched with rectangles of iron-on vinyl, and a long purple scarf of an unsuitably loose-woven wool. Rebecca, the slatternly Antiguan with an awry spine, must have been behind the counter then, but the black woman had long ago disappeared from the town.

Sukie glanced across the tabletop, its varnish worn away over the years by repeated place settings, to look again at Tommy's bad hand, but he had already hidden it in his lap, while signalling with the good hand for the waitress. Where wicked Rebecca used to appear, now a round-faced girl with broad silver rings on both thumbs was summoned. Sukie remembered her from somewhere. Where? The concert, handing out programs. Could she be a Neff granddaughter? It was unsettling to think that the town had been taken over by grandchildren, and her own generation had sunk into a subsurface of DNA.

"Two coffees," Sukie told the girl. "Right, Tom?" As always with him, she found herself in charge. He bleakly nodded, gazing into his lap. "And, oh yes," Sukie suddenly said, remembering, "an order of johnnycakes. We'll split it."

"Johnnycakes?" the girl asked, blushing as if she were being teased.

"You know," Sukie told her. "You have to know—they're a Rhode Island specialty. Balls of baked dough, all crumbly and buttery. Delicious."

The girl's puzzled blush persisted. "We have bagels, and croissants"—every consonant pronounced—"and I'll look if any doughnuts are still left in the case."

"No," Sukie said, convinced that this thin-skinned, thick-headed girl was a Neff descendant. "Never mind. They're not the same. I'll keep my figure." She added this last sentence to be pleasant, but the girl blushed more deeply, imagining an allusion to her own full, succulent figure.

"Things never are," Tommy said, rather sulkily, when the girl was gone. "The same."

Sukie felt he was trying to tell her something disagreeable, and she went defensive in turn. "This is news you think you're telling me?"

"Well," he allowed, "you seemed to come back as if everything would be still here waiting for you."

"I never thought that. And a lot of it still is. This town could use a makeover."

Slumped back in his fragile bentwood chair, he shrugged. "It gets it, bit by bit. New folks move in. Young folks, with their own ideas. The Bronze Barrel—you know, on the road over to Coddington Junction—"

"I *know* where it is. Though we didn't use to go there much. We were more into private parties."

"—it's become what they call a sports bar. They have three big screens playing different sports events every hour of the day and night they're open. I don't see how anybody can stand the ruckus, but the young people all take to it. They have to have the noise. And where your old newspaper used to be, you probably noticed, there's a health center now. Exercise machines and so on."

"Yes, I looked in the windows and there were all these people on treadmills staring back at me. With headphones on, like a row of zombies. It was frightening."

Tommy informed her, slouching as if his information served as a poor substitute for what he really wanted to say, "The old presses and Linotypes had to sit on a reinforced cement floor, so the conversion was easy enough. They moved the equipment right in, in one night. People don't use it in summers the way they do in winter. You should see it then. Old ladies, too, hugging and puffing away. Everybody these days wants to live forever."

Old ladies, too. Was he trying to warn her off—to put her in her place? Let him. Let him have his precious Eastwick, summer, winter, fall, and spring. "Do people," she asked, "miss having the *Word*? We used to flatter ourselves it gave the town more of an identity, even a weekly, where people could see their names in print."

"Well," Tom said, wincing as if words were painful, "print doesn't mean to people what it used to, it may be. A considerable number get what news they need off the Internet. They don't need much. Sports, celebrities. For self-advertisement there's all this blogging. It's amazing to me anybody has the time to read such crap, but I guess they do. Some woman pretty new in town tried to get up a Xeroxed local newsletter when the syndicate that had bought up the *Word* closed it down, but people didn't take to it enough for it to pay. Also, you know, pardon my getting personal, what happened concerning the *Word* when you were still around spooked people a little—gave it a bad name."

How personally was she to take this? "Well, la-di-da," she said, a response that was both combative and lame.

The round-faced waitress, with her cruelly pierced eyebrow, brought the coffees, served in tall Starbucks-style brown mugs instead of the old-fashioned thick china, with handles and saucers, that Sukie remembered in Nemo's. "Is that girl a Neff?" she asked Tommy when the waitress had retreated.

He shook his head curtly. "A Jessup. Remember Mavis, used to run the Yapping Fox?"

"She doesn't look anything like Mavis."

"Well—they say Hank before their divorce got around." He tried to take a sip of his coffee, but it was too hot. He set it down with a grimace, wiping his lips, half-lost in his beard, with his paper napkin.

"Tommy," she asked him, "are you uncomfortable?"

"Well, since you mention it, it's not entirely comfortable, sitting here next to this plate-glass window with my wife working at the bank in the next block. People in Eastwick still talk—that hasn't changed."

"But I'm an old lady. Surely Jean wouldn't mind."

Uncomfortably he shifted his weight in the fragile bent-wood black-shellacked chair. "She knows about you and me. I told her before we got married. I figured I should tell her the works. You weren't my only, you know."

"Of course not. You were a very attractive young man. And you knew it, thanks in part to me. As you say, people talk. Ex-lovers talk. They don't mean to betray the old one; they just want to come clean with the new one. It's recycling. It's even an inverted form of loyalty, I suppose. Talking keeps it alive—the former romance."

Tommy perceived the challenge: to render a reckoning. He lowered his voice, so the two had to sit forward and lean toward each other above the little round table. "You gave me your all, in a certain line. I've never seen the beat of it. But Jean's my meal ticket. Without her, I'm on welfare."

That he was risking his meal ticket was an idea, Sukie

judged, exciting to his vanity—he was back out at sea, hauling in nets that might break with their live weight. "If you say so," Sukie said softly back. "You have to eat. But just now, seeing you way up in the next block, I felt we'd been looking for each other. I was sure of it."

"Sure," he said, his voice a bit louder, as if the other townspeople around them were welcome to hear. "Why not? You were a luxury, the deluxe platter, served up for no reason. I was an ignorant local yokel, and you, my God, you used to look smashing, parading up and down Dock Street in those suede-colored outfits with your orange hair and a bright scarf at your throat. I used to see you and think, *In a couple of hours, a couple of days, I'm going to be tugging that skirt down and undoing her bra snaps and fucking her right up to her ribs.*"

"*Shh.*" She had to touch his hand on the tabletop to quiet him, and it was the wrong hand, the bad hand, the ruined hand, which he had unthinkingly brought up from his lap. He quickly pulled it back out of sight. The early-lunch people were drifting into Nemo's, glancing their way, so she leaned her face closer to his with a growing urgency, her damp hair falling forward. "That's what I wanted to hear," she whispered. "What I meant to you. Was I just a silly piece of ass, an older woman who had no sense and no shame? Did you despise me even as we screwed? Some men do, you know, and still women open themselves to them, we're that desperate. How desperate did I seem to you? How ugly?"

"Why, not at all," he said, with instant clear-eyed conviction. His hushed voice grew husky with sincerity: "You were beautiful. *And* desperate. You seemed like somebody searching, and I was where you were searching that summer. And not just me; I had heard about you and Toby Bergman. It didn't matter."

"Toby," Sukie repeated, as if she had never heard the name before. "He was nothing, compared with you, Tommy."

His coffee was cool enough to drink now; he took rapid gulps, finishing up. "You don't have to say that. Look. It's all biology. We were both in our biological primes. You were— what?—thirty-three. It takes women years to get into sex. Guys are turned on at fifteen. You see it all the time now on television news, these schoolteacher women in their thirties who fall in love with a teen-age student. Everybody's horrified—the kid's parents, the school board, the sheriff's office, the whole community. Outraged. But it's biology. You and I were *there*, as they say, for each other."

As Tom swiftly, gulpingly talked, too knowingly, Sukie resented being generalized into an instance of a widespread phenomenon. As he had relaxed into a lecture, he had smiled, and let his missing tooth show. It occurred to her that the stinginess of his smiles was an attempt to conceal his dental embarrassment. She told him, not caring if she was overheard since she knew now that this encounter would not be repeated, "To me, Tommy, you were like something coming out of the fog, with your shoulder tasting of salt. Women get foggy, they have to, it's too upsetting otherwise. It's too tragic—the parting part of it, the way it gets over, whether you stay together or not. The intensity, I mean. You were gentle, is what I wanted to say. Thank you. Men don't have to be, especially young men, to whom it's all just come true— the dirty joke isn't a joke. Women want it. They really want it. You didn't take advantage and get sadistic, even though you could have. I would have let you. You were sweet."

"Hey," Tommy said, ready to stand up, impatient to put distance between them. "I was just human. An easy lay is an easy lay. And you blew, too. That was an extra, back then."

Her eyes teared up as if she had been slapped. When he

said "You blew" in that casual hard-hearted way his pale lips from within his nest of facial hair leaped in her vision like that circled portion of a documentary film doctored to focus attention on an overlookable detail: the human mouth, versatile and perverse. "You go," she said, putting on a casual smile in case any of the old-timers in the back booths glanced their way. "I'll stay and pay. Be nice to Jean. I know you will."

As if this had been a threat, Tommy darted a frightened look down at her from his regained height; the protruding bulk of his middle-aged belly swelled his dirty sweatshirt. He smoothed his unkempt mustache back from the dent in the middle of his upper lip and a look she had forgotten, a spoiled boyish pout, came over his face as he tried to decide if there was anything more to say. He decided there wasn't and left her there staring out the picture window, which had become semi-opaque as the morning's rain settled in. She saw his ponytail hurry by in the smear.

"Well, I was just dumped," she told Alexandra, who was sitting in her favorite chair in the condo, the one comfortable one, a broad plaid recliner, puzzling over a segment of last Sunday's *New York Times*. This was Tuesday. The *Times* was a slow, filling meal.

"Dumped?"

"Given the gate. Put out to pasture. I ran into Tommy Gorton, the gorgeous young harbormaster I knew toward the end of when we lived here. He reminded me rather firmly that he has a wife he's very dependent on. And scared of, I gathered."

Alexandra, who had been enjoying her solitude luxuriating in the sound of New England rain drumming on the roof, put down the Travel section to give her disturbed friend her full attention. "Did you need to be reminded? You expected something different?"

"Well . . . not really. But I thought *he* might. I intended to point out to him that at my age there was of course no question of resuming our relationship."

"Darling, how sweet of you to think even that that might need to be said."

"He wanted me, Lexa. I could feel it when we were a block away from each other and his face was just a little pale dot above this blur of a beard. You know how you *know*. The psychic electricity, it flew between us. But then, in Nemo's, he became very unmagical—a big sad maimed lummox whose life had amounted to nothing. I had to coax even the littlest compliment out of him."

"I'm sure," Alexandra said, sighing with ostentatious patience, as if dealing with a child full of questions. "It was a long time ago, sweetheart. He wanted you, if it would make him twenty-two again."

"You know," Sukie said, "we can change these people."

"Oh? How?"

"The way we used to. Erect the cone of power." Her upper lip, plump as if bruised, flattened slightly against the lower in a kind of smirk, daring Alexandra to contradict her.

"Oh, my. Do we still have what it takes for that? Do we want anything badly enough?"

"We can want for others. And for Jane. Where *is* Jane?"

"Off at the doctor's, she told me."

"What doctor? My God, she found one in the Yellow Pages?"

"No. She looked up Doc Paterson in the White Pages, and he was still there. He's still practicing."

"That's incredible," Sukie said. "He *has* to be dead."

"Why? He wasn't that much older than we were. People just make doctors older in their minds, because they need to believe in them." Henry L. Paterson, "Doc Pat" to the town, had been a plump bald man with hands that seemed inflated, they were so broad and soft, so cleanly scrubbed. He was a pre-pharm practitioner, whose folding black bag held mostly sugar pills. He healed with a bland smile of patient under-standing and a dulcet laying-on of those hands. If no healing resulted, he prescribed stoic resignation.

"He shouldn't be still practicing," Sukie pronounced, declaring her relative youth in her immunity to Doc Pat's passive magic. "If Jenny Gabriel had had a decent up-to-date doctor, she'd be alive and wouldn't be weighing on all our consciences."

"He can refer Jane if needs be. He has a son, a surgeon in Providence."

"I remember the son, a pudgy brat I suspected of getting his rocks off looking through our files."

"He's not a brat now. He's a guy who takes your life in his hands."

"It's incredible." Sukie flounced, shaking the raindrops from her hair and kicking her damp shoes toward the sofa. "It makes you realize that all the people we've gone through life trusting, doctors and policemen and stock analysts, don't know any more than we do."

"That seems an unjustified conclusion."

"I mean, they're just grown-up children."

"You seem indignant, *chérie*. How else would you do it?"

"I don't know," Sukie admitted. "Maybe robots," she suggested. "They're getting more and more sophisticated."

Alexandra didn't deign to answer, but picked up the Travel section of the *Times* again. In Arizona, she was reading, an Indian tribe that felt neglected because the section of the

Grand Canyon they controlled wasn't visited as much as the white man's section was going to build a U-shaped "sky-walk" out over the edge. It had a glass floor and would give you a one-hundred-forty-foot walk for seventy-five dollars. If you could stand it, you could look straight down, nearly a mile down to the canyon floor. Alexandra would like to go try it when she got home. She was sure it would terrify her, even though looking out the little plastic window in the airplane for some reason didn't. Reading about the skywalk, and looking out her window here at the sullen wet day, with its sooty purplish wisps travelling sideways across a backdrop of dirty-white rolls of nimbus cloud, made her miss the West—its dryness, its bisque color, like a landscape all of pottery. She wanted to say some of this to Sukie, but the other widow, having kicked off her shoes, had gone into the next room barefoot and was sitting at her tiny table with her HP laptop. Her fingers made a pattering sound very like rain on the roof as she raced along, rarely stopping or even hesitating, through one of her romance novels, perhaps a new episode based on her recent heartbreak. The hurrying, scrabbling noise of her keyboarding coated the air of the room with a furtive film of panic; it persisted even after the sound of the rain overhead entered a lull.

When Jane, finally, preceded by the grinding of her Jaguar tires on the gravel drive below, and the dragging scuffle of her footsteps climbing the uncarpeted concrete stairs of the Lenox Mansion Seaview Apartments, came in through the door, she looked as if she had seen a ghost. Her face was as gray as the day, her once-black hair showed white roots, and her body looked shrunken, as if, already petite, she had been photocopied at a reduced size. She had taken a hit.

"How was Doc Pat?" Alexandra asked her, in a casual voice meant to minimize any dramatics.

Jane opened her mouth to answer but waited until Sukie had stopped her tapping in the next room. Then she dramatically told the other two, "The *sss*illy man doesn't know what's wrong with me. He listened to my heart and breathing and looked into my ears and the backs of my eyes and it all seemed normal to him."

"Well, that sounds *good*," Sukie said, still eyeing the glowing small word-processor screen, where some ghostly action had been taking place. Her hand sneaked up from her lap and tapped out a quick correction.

Alexandra decreed, "That's lovely, Jane. You must be very relieved." In fact, she was, in that buried quadrant of our beings that relishes others' bad news, disappointed. Jane had been looking awful, and behaving so self-centeredly.

"I mentioned my abdominal sensations and he wants me to have an X-ray with his son, up in Providence," Jane said, looking around. "Is there any coffee left, or did you two pigs drink it all?"

"I never touch it after noon," Sukie said.

"I need it black," Jane said. "Black, black. Maybe with a little Jack Daniel's*ss*, after what I've been through."

"Are the X-rays looking for cancer?" Alexandra dared ask, even though she hated even to pronounce the word. Your own body cells, out of control, little machines going berserk.

"I suppose," Jane answered, "but not only. He said everybody over sixty should be checked for, what was the phrase, an abdominal aortic aneurysm. Something when he tapped my tummy with the stethoscope in his ears made him listen twice."

"Isn't it funny," Sukie said, coming into their main room, returning from the cave of make-believe, "that doctors still do that? Tap and listen. It seems so primitive. An internist I had in Stamford was always copping a feel."

"Good cop, bad cop," Jane said.

"Ha ha. Then when I'd look at him," Sukie persisted, making a pained mouth, "he'd put on this solemn righteous face as though he hadn't touched a thing. Doctors—*really*. I do hope we get national health service and put them all out of work."

"X-rays scare me," said Alexandra. "They say they add up in your body."

"They do, I don't doubt it," Jane concurred. "But that's not why I need a drink. A bizarre thing just happened to me. You both remember where Doc Pat's office is, on Vane Street, a block back from Oak?"

"Sure," Alexandra said. "When Oz and I moved here, I remember Vane Street had the town's few surviving Dutch elms. They had green boxes attached to them, like invalids on oxygen." Guiltily she glanced at Sukie, remembering that this was the direction in which Sukie's emphysematous lungs would be taking her.

But Sukie hadn't apparently noticed anything personal in the simile. "They cast such a nice soft feathery shade," she remembered aloud. "When they finally died the town replaced them with those dismal Norway maples, with those big dull leaves the light can't get through. At the time the story was Herbie Prinz and Ed Arsenault's nursery had cut a deal."

"*Any*way," Jane said, determined not to yield the stage, "I was leaving Doc Pat's office, walking to where I had parked the Jag up at the corner of Dock, and there in the thick shadows, the rain had just about stopped, the trees were dripping, the shape of this man came toward me and just as we passed he said, 'Hello, Jane!' "

She paused for effect, having deepened her voice to a man's.

"What's so bizarre about that?" Sukie asked. "He recognized you—they recognize me downtown all the time."

"I'm not you. Nobody knows me except my old music students."

"What did he look like?" Alexandra asked.

"Young," Jane slowly answered, having closed her eyes. "I mean, at least younger than me. I wasn't looking at him, thinking about the X-ray and wondering what Doc Pat thought he'd noticed with the *ss*tethoscope. Until this man spoke my name in this horrifying way I wasn't paying any attention. I saw this shape coming toward me and must have moved over on the sidewalk so we wouldn't bump." She closed her eyes again. "Tallish, and a little heavy— filled-out, more, not obese—and, I don't know, *sss*ilvery, somehow."

"Silvery?" Sukie echoed in surprise.

"That isn't quite the word, but *ss*mooth, with a sheen like a sort of statue, and—what's that word?—androgynous."

"Androgynous!" Alexandra exclaimed. She was not always able to restrain an impulse to tease Jane; if we all took ourselves so intensely, the world would be at constant war. "My goodness, Jane, it sounds as if you got quite a good look."

"I tried to reconstruct, after he had passed me. It went *right through me*, the way he said 'Hello, Jane!' in this fake actor's voice."

"An androgynous fake actor's voice," Alexandra mocked, deadpan.

"All right, laugh if you want to," Jane said, her lips tightened as if to spit, "but you'll *really* laugh at the next thing I tell you." She paused again, demanding they look at her, her intense little face yellow-gray, almost a mummy's, under its tiara of white hair-roots.

"Spit it out, Jane Pain," Sukie said as the silence stretched uncomfortably. She thought of her laptop in the other room, its screen still flipped up, its little toothpick cursor pulsing beside her last word.

"When I turned my head to look after him, I felt a shock."

"A shock?" Alexandra asked. "Like the one up by the telephone pole at the post office?"

"Not that bad. That one nearly knocked me over. This one was smaller, almost a tease. There have been others, too, at least one or two a day, but I know you both already think I'm being a nuisance, so I haven't been saying anything."

"We don't think you're being a nuisance at all," Alexandra protested. "You're just naturally high-strung."

"Absolutely," Sukie agreed. Lest her participation seem too detached, she asked, "Did he remind you of anyone you knew?"

"Ye*ss*," Jane hissed, glad to have been asked. "Somebody. Dimly. But I can't think who."

"Why not?" Alexandra asked, rather lazily. Really, Jane could be tiresome. All these mysteries and shadows— the silvery flicker of a half-recognized visage, the big drops of absorbed rain released one by one from the dense maple leaves in the midday gloom. So New England, so *Scarlet Letter*.

"It's as if a *ss*pell is hiding him. When I try to think who, I get *ss*cared."

The other two, long consecrated to evil and its callous self-absorption, chose not to press Jane and give her the satisfaction of being coaxed.

Sukie did muse aloud, "I wonder where he came from. Nobody just goes walking along Vane. It's too far from the shops."

Jane brightened. "I think I know where," she said. She needed no coaxing. "After the shock—it felt like a sarcastic nudge in my gut—I didn't dare look around again for a minute, but, getting back in my car, parked up at the corner, I did look back, and the man had disappeared! I drove down Dock to Oak and then up to the Union Church and back to Vane and he was nowhere to be seen! It fit with my sense, somehow, the way he was walking, that he belonged to the neighborhood. As you say, why would anybody be walking? It's all private homes up there."

"What was he wearing?" Sukie asked, joining in, a bit breathlessly.

"White pants, like painter pants," Jane promptly responded. "And a pale T-shirt with some lettering on it I didn't have time to read."

"He sounds like a kid."

"He *was* a kid," Jane said. "Grown old."

Alexandra tried to clarify: "And he disappeared into thin air."

"Into the *neigh*borhood," Jane insisted. "Think. You know how the backyards on the lower side of Vane abut those on the upper side of Oak. And who lives on Oak, about the middle of the first block, in that mansard-roof Victorian that needs paint and has that crappy-looking outside staircase for the apartments she's had to put in upstairs?" She paused, luxuriating in the attention boring in upon her from the other two. She answered herself: "Greta Neff!"

"Greta Neff," said Sukie.

"*Yess!* She hangs on there, in that drafty decrepit barn Ray never should have bought in the first place, it was *way* beyond his means, I told him so at the time and I remember him telling me grandiosely he needed it because he had six children and he wanted each to be able to practice his or her instrument without distracting the others. Greta hangs on there out of spite. It's an unpainted eyesore, dragging the neighborhood down with it; it's ruining Oak Street property values; everybody *ssays sso*." Jane was working herself up into a trance, a frenzy. "Oh, God," she cried. "When he walked by me, nearer than I am to either of you, I went *cold*. The way he said it—'Hello, Jane!'—was as good as him saying, 'I'm going to *get* you!' Cold just rolled off of him, on this hot day. I *ssswear* it!"

"Oh, dear." Alexandra waited in case there was any more outburst, then told Jane, "Sukie and I were saying, before you came in, that we should see if we can still erect the cone of power."

"Oh, ye*ss*—*any*thing." Jane's face reddened and underwent a contortion that became sobbing, the gasps of sobbing from a soul too parched to produce tears. Between gasps she produced words: "All these years—with Nat and his dreadful mother—I tried so hard—I've kept it so buttoned up—but I was the one—who was hardest on Jenny—who wanted her dead most—for no reason, for that a*ss*hole Van Horne—and now she's come back. That was my feeling—there under those trees. Not her exactly—but somebody just like her—with that same awful glow, of somebody—too perfect. I hated that little weasel for that—being so perfect, so good and innocent, that hateful *ss*mugness good people have."

Alexandra and Sukie exchanged glances. Jane had to make dramatics of everything. She had to be the star, even if a dark star.

Sukie that same July had sneaked off some Sunday mornings to the Unitarian Fellowship services. She knew the building—a pretty little Greek Revival with a shallow Doric-columned porch, on Cocumscussoc Way off of Elm,

beyond Oak, put up by nineteenth-century Congregational-
ists but gone under to the Unitarians in the 1840s. She knew
it from the Johnson-Nixon years, when she was a reporter
for the Eastwick *Word* and bedevilled Ed Parsley and then
his officious wife, Brenda, occupied the pulpit, in that
tumultuous period of protest and counterculture, of public
and private riot. The present days were tamer, just as Debbie Larcom was a tamer, less tormented person than the
unfortunate Parsleys. Sukie found her brain nagged by the
image of this perfectly formed clergywoman. When Debbie
officiated, it was with a strict, sober sweetness, enunciating
each hollow phrase as if it were a crystal chalice brimming
with meaning; when she preached, it was with utter natural-
ness and clarity, taking Jesus and Buddha as equivalent
embodiments of goodness, citing Doctor Schweitzer and
Mohandas Gandhi and Mother Teresa and Martin Luther
King as manifestations of the divine in human form. To
illustrate her points, she drew upon her own life—that of a
normal upper-middle-class girl from Mount Hebron, outside of Baltimore, her mind full of the usual vanities, until
a call (there was no less old-fashioned way to put it, she
explained with a flutter of her shapely hands) broke in, a call
to be less selfish and vain. The call could not have come at a
less convenient time, for its recipient had married and borne
two children, both still in diapers; but faith and determination and a saint of a husband helped her through.

Sukie's lower lip trembled; the story seemed her own, with
some minor differences—lower-middle instead of upper-
middle, upstate New York instead of suburban Maryland,
witchcraft instead of Unitarianism, a vindictively contested
divorce rather than a supportive spouse. But the thrust was
the same, of a woman winning through to a career and self-
respect against the stacked odds in a patriarchal world.

Though Deborah Larcom made a show of turning her head toward different sections of the congregation, Sukie knew she was preaching to *her;* when the other woman's eyes paused, in their restless sweep, at Sukie's place in a pew, her thick black eyelashes flared, her irises sent sparks.

The next Sunday, the minister preached about selves. She took as her text Matthew 16:25, gender-corrected to "For whosoever will save his or her life shall lose it, and whosoever will lose his or her life for my sake shall find it." Deborah Larcom began, "We live in a very self-conscious age. There is a magazine called *Self.* There is a book called *Our Bodies, Our Selves.* We want to find our *selves*, and to be true to our selves. My *Webster's New Collegiate Dictionary* holds two full columns of compound words, beginning with 'self-abandonment' and 'self-abuse' through 'self-interest' and 'self-reliance' and 'self-satisfaction' down to 'self-willed' and 'self-winding.' So—what *is* this self, this precious entity each individual uniquely possesses, be he or she a twin or triplet or a baby just extracted from its mother's womb?"

Sukie, sitting at the back of the church, thought of her own children, the three she had with Monty, and little Bob, whom Lennie had fathered to authenticate her second marriage, infants pulled from her pelvis slimy and blue and breathless with astonishment. A warm sword of shame went through her innards as she realized that she had raised them too casually and, now that they were long safely grown up, communicated with them rarely. The small lithe woman in the pulpit, in a white surplice and gold tippet and cream-colored turtleneck, would never be an irritable and diffident mother; she was too *good*—goodness radiated from her like the sparkle surrounding a candy bar in a commercial on Saturday-morning television. On another Sunday, in a demonstration of Unitarianism's wide embrace, a mentally and physically defective teen-aged parishioner had recited the concluding words of blessing; he held an arm crooked against his chest and dragged one foot coming to the forefront and spoke in a rolling hollow voice eerily detached from his face; in a kind of paroxysm he began to shake uncontrollably, and Reverend Larcom, though distinctly smaller than he, put an arm around him to quell his shaking. Both called out in unison, "Go, and love one another!" Not only Sukie but the women on either side of her in the pew dabbed at the sides of their noses.

"Buddha says," Debbie was saying today, " 'Forget the self and its craving, its craving for attention, for praise, for love, for worldly goods, for recreational vehicles and flattering clothes.' My husband and I used to own a Hummer, so we could take it up mountain trails, though we almost never got to any mountains. When I think of the time I used to spend posing in front of dress-shop mirrors, trying to decide— perky, but *too* perky for my age, or too staid for my age?— bringing things home and then sending them back, I blush in embarrassment. Buddha says, 'Forget self-aggrandizement, self-deception, self-importance, self-regard. Our goal is non-self, *anatman.*' The selflessness of Nirvana is the Buddhist's goal, the release from exertion and pain, from selfishness. Non-attachment, *atrishna*, is the path out of *dukhka*, suffering, and *samsara*, the endless cycle of incarnations. And what does Jesus say? Jesus says, 'Forget the law. Let the dead bury the dead. Forsake your families. Give all that you have to the poor. Possess no treasure, for where your treasure is, there will your heart be. No one who puts a hand to the plow and looks back is fit for the Kingdom of God. Consider the lilies: they toil not, neither do they spin.' Jesus and Buddha, *and* Brahma and Allah, say 'Empty yourselves out.' For only when we have given up everything—our fine cars, our spic-and-span homes, our well-dressed children and their excellent grades in school, which do such credit to us, and our memberships, our sexual conquests, our bank balances, everything that we permit to define our *selves*—when we have given all that up, or it has been torn from us, is our self then gone? Has it disappeared, leaving only emptiness? No: the self turns out—and here is the miracle—to be still there, transformed. A new self emerges from the utter emptiness. Ladies and gentlemen, boys and girls, we *bloom!*" She flung wide her arms in their loose white sleeves; her hair surrounded her tipped-back head like a black halo, an electricity having entered the high space of the nave with her sudden gesture. "We are free," she confided in a dramatically lowered voice to the sparse crowd of congregants in the summer-torpid sanctuary, "free in self-forgetfulness. The world *pours* into the vacuum, the world of others, the beauty and power of Nature, of all that is not our *selves*. The self-forgetful self is no more empty than was the universe in the instant before the unimaginable Singularity that has produced a billion billion stars with all their planets. In that instant the empty universe was full, full of potential; so with us, if we but relax into the serene vast Other that surrounds the pinched, fearful, jealous, murderous self. Infinite energy and infinite peace await us at the boundary of our selves, if we can but reach that too-well-defended frontier and trust ourselves to pass over, to let go, to surrender ourselves to that divine otherness that passeth all human understanding. *Shantih, shantih, shantih.* Amen."

Sukie, sitting in the back, hastened to leave. Other Sundays, she had sneaked away during the last hymn, but today she wanted to be greeted by the minister, to be touched by her. As she rose she saw Greta Neff, her pasty profile and stocky mannish form, standing up in one of the front pews, with some companions, adult children or roomers. A heavy white-haired man was with them. In the Unitarian narthex, decorated with two drab potted palms and a bulletin board tacked full of notices and pleas for virtuous causes, Sukie grasped again, as some weeks ago, the younger woman's sinewy cool hand; being clad in a loose clerical gown brought the Reverend Mrs. Larcom closer to the nakedness that had flashed into Sukie's mind on that first occasion.

"That was wonderful," she said. "I love hearing you." She felt dazed after an hour of focusing on the figure in the pulpit, her white gown and smile, her black hair and brows winking in overlapping afterimages.

"Thank you," Deborah Larcom said, still a touch tense and self-absorbed from the effort of the service. Her lovely, intelligent eyes darted toward the next in line. Since Sukie in her bewitched daze didn't move, the minister briskly added, in a joking voice, "So bring your two friends next time."

Sukie laughed, one incredulous syllable. "They'd be shocked to know I'm here. It's just that . . ." She trailed off, having begun to try to explain why she *was* here. Under her gown, under her clergy shirt and bra, this young woman's breasts would be as firm and smooth as her diction, as round as the orbs of her gray-green irises, the nipples as tender a pink as the little bits of sunburn on her straight small nose, on the exquisite cartilage of her narrow nostril wings. "I wonder whether sometime . . ."

"Yes?" With a touch of impatience, as the line behind Sukie was bunching up.

"I could visit you."

All business: "Of course. Call the fellowship secretary, Mrs. Neff, for an appointment. Until Labor Day the office is on summer hours, every weekday nine to noon." She gave one last, uncertain look into Sukie's face, trying to puzzle out her need.

Two children, a boy and a girl about five and seven, had come up behind their mother in her ecclesiastical gown. The little boy shyly took Deborah Larcom's idle, left hand; the girl, more understanding and respectful of her mother's role, stood patiently at her side. Her features were less precise than Deborah's, blurred by the father's—that saint's—coarser genes. This woman was claimed. Sukie was being a nuisance. It was her turn to say, "Thank you." She moved out the high double doors, onto the columned porch, down the worn wide wooden steps, blushing, spurned, vowing never to return.

The three accursed women agreed to attempt resurrection of their supernatural skills on the day when Jane's tell-all X-ray was scheduled. Her anxiety about it might have otherwise projected a dark spot on the transparent cone of power. Propitiously, this day was Lammas, the second of August and the first of the three harvest celebrations on which a sabbat was most appropriate. The moon, Alexandra saw on the kitchen calendar from Perley Realty, would be three days on the waning side of full, which did not strike her as unlucky although, in the event, it proved to be so. It fell to her to prepare the arrangements. The other two deferred to what they insisted were her profounder powers—her deeper reach into Nature and the mysteries of the Goddess. "I'll set it up," she promised them, "only if we agree this will be a hundred percent white magic. I don't consider our presence in Eastwick to have been a success so far. In July it was mostly discordant; people don't know what to make of us and they're hostile. I'd like August to be a month of harmony, of healing. Years ago we grabbed what we wanted from the town and then left. Now we've returned to give something back."

Sukie protested: "I think I gave plenty back. I made some discontented husbands less so, and brought a little style to this dowdy boondocks."

"Not to sound *s*self-centered," Jane said crossly, "but I had imagined the focus of the cone would be *my* healing, not Eastwick's. I feel terrible most of the time—headachy, nauseated and dizzy when I stand up suddenly, with a sort of gnawing under my breastbone." She put her fingers there, between her skimpy breasts. "I don't mention these things all the time because I know you both think I'm being a terrible drag. I'm *sss*orry, but if I don't feel better soon I'll have to go back to Brookline and get some decent medical attention. Doc Pat is a good example of why hospitals have compulsory retirement. He's *s*senile. It's been cute to be with the two of you, but I must get real help."

"Don't go before the X-ray," Alexandra begged her. "Go that far at least with Doc Pat."

"I *dread* it," Jane blurted. "It *has* to upset your insides, to have those rays beamed through them. The air has all these rays and particles in it, we all know that, but I can *feel* them. Radio, radon, neutrinos, now dark energy, that's the latest they've discovered. They say it's pushing the universe apart faster and faster, till soon there won't be anything, just a kind of super-thin gruel, cooling down to absolute zero. All the nice harmless things people used to believe in—ghosts, goblins, fairies, unicorns—and now these horrible forces are all we have instead. They don't *care* about us, they don't even know we're *here*."

"Jane," Alexandra told her, with maternal firmness, "you

must calm down. You must get yourself in better alignment or the cone will shatter as soon as you step into it."

"I'll go with her up to Providence for the X-ray," Sukie volunteered. Jane had become so estranged from them that she could be discussed in her presence in the third person. "I'll get her some ice cream on the way back."

"I'll have this place ready," Alexandra promised, aware of a gnawing within her, too, a worry that her faith, so long untested, would be insufficient, and the cone would not materialize.

The merchants of Eastwick yearned to make it a tourist trap, and several shops along Dock Street stocked aromatic candles the size and shape of Sterno cans, and crystals like transparent rock candies, and bracelets of cheap metal bearing the hammered impress of sigils and runes. At the formerly Armenian hardware store, Alexandra bought a putty knife, with the requisite black handle, that could do for a ceremonial athame, and one of those two-sided travel mirrors on a folding wire stand, to serve as a window into the astral world. Back in the condo, as the shadows of August's noticeably shorter days gathered in the corners like cobwebs, Alexandra, who in her prime took pride in her physical strength, pulled the coffee table and the plaid recliner and, one end at a time, the sofa back from the center of the living room. The furniture's feet left deep dents in the carpet. She vacuumed the exposed carpet, a burgundy color that when they first entered these rented rooms greeted them with what seemed a pleasantly earthy ground note; it invisibly absorbed dirt, not just red-wine stains but beach sand and bits of grit carried on shoe soles, dead flies, live dust mites, shed skin, negative energy, fingernail clippings, and the tiny screws that hold spectacle frames together. Such particles faintly rattled and tingled in the vacuum cleaner's hose and aluminum extender tube.

When the ceremony was over, she would vacuum up the magic circle she now drew on the carpet with a line of detergent granules of Cascade, straight from the spout of the box. She drew four-fifths of a circle the size of a queen-size bed, or of a fairy ring of mushrooms found in a forest. She had bought five aromatic candles—rose, peach, raspberry, lavender, and aqua in color, and spaced them evenly around the circle she had drawn, forming the ghost of a pentacle. A cheap broom, its shaft a rod of plastic instead of wood— honest wood whose grain recollects the annual cycle of growth—had been provided in the closet of the suite's back room along with a defective vacuum cleaner and a rickety ironing board. Alexandra placed this broom as a chord on the arc of the vacant fifth segment, making a symbolic door into the circle, for initiates only.

In the center there must be an altar. For this Alexandra laid on the wine-colored carpet an oak breadboard that had come with the kitchen, and on top of that an old brass brazier, beautifully weathered and charred, that she had spotted in a roadside flea market on the back road to Old Wick. She collected cushions from all the rooms, arranged them in three comfy heaps within the circle, and waited.

Jane and Sukie were late. It was nearing six. Alexandra nibbled at the crackers and cheese—pumpkin-colored Gouda and moon-white Münster—that she had driven all the way, in Nat Tinker's antique Jaguar, to the Stop & Shop to buy, along with some ready-made chicken curry and chopped broccoli salad for them to eat afterwards, if they weren't too exhausted or transported to eat. Sabbats classically occurred at midnight, but, with so many young Wiccans in the workforce filling nine-to-five jobs, that tradition had been adjusted, and surely didn't apply to women over a certain age. For wine, Alexandra had chosen Carlo Rossi Chianti in a two-liter screw-top glass jug, to be poured into mock-copper chalices, encrusted with embossed and painted jewels, which she had spotted on a back shelf of one of the town's candle shops. They were made of foil-covered paper and weighed almost nothing in her fingers. Her hands, she thought as she toyed with an empty chalice, had held up pretty well under time's battering. A little plumpness helps keep the skin taut as we get older. Jane's hands, she had noticed, were repulsively emaciated and veined, their arthritic joints shiny with painful swelling, and even Sukie's—dear Sukie, who carried herself as if still a contender in the lists of love—looked ropey in a decent light. She decided that uncorking the Chianti and sampling some might ease her wait. The Goddess wouldn't mind. Alexandra cut herself another small slice of the Münster.

She had worked so hard, making everything shipshape for their ritual, that by the time the other two returned, not much before seven, gabbling and giggling over their shared adventures, Alexandra found herself vexed. "You might have at least called," she said.

"They kept telling us it would be only ten more minutes," Sukie explained, scarcely repentant. "And neither of us could remember our phone number here!" She and Jane laughed all the harder together, realizing there was nothing much to laugh at; the joke was all in their attitude and in Alexandra's annoyance. By way of apology, Sukie exclaimed, "Oh, how cute everything looks! Lexa, you've been so dutiful!"

"Yes," she answered simply, sternly.

Jane would not be rebuked. "They were *ss*tupidly inefficient," she said, of the radiological staff in the Providence hospital. "Doc Pat's *s*son looks just like he does, only six inches taller, and with no panache at all. Really. Nat used to say nobody with brains goes into medicine any more—there's too much easy money to be made in finance, all the good minds go to business school. And even the ice-cream place we stopped at on Route One—they didn't have multicolored jimmies, just the brown kind, that looks like mouse turds."

"Stop saying that!" Sukie cried. "I couldn't get it out of my mind, licking my cone!" And they both broke down into hilarity again. Looking back, they wondered if it wasn't laughing this way that broke something inside Jane; she had laughed so little lately.

"The cone of caca," she said, laughing.

Alexandra was offended, but determined not to give the other two any more pleasure by showing it. They set her up as a mother-figure so they could be naughty children. "I'm not sure," she did say, stiffly, "we're in any mood to generate a unified elevation of energy."

"Put on my elevation shoes," Jane said. "Beam me up, *S*scottie."

Alexandra asked, "Did you two have anything to drink on the way back from Kingston?"

"Kingston-size martinis," Jane said.

"Just one margarita each," Sukie confessed, "at that sports bar that used to be the Bronze Barrel. Remember Fidel and his margaritas? And his marinated capybara balls? Darryl would wolf them down."

"He was a capybara cat," Jane said. "Uh-oh. Lexa's getting cross."

Jane looked like such a waif saying this, such a withered

little old-lady waif, with her hair undyed for a month and showing an inch of snowy roots, that Alexandra relented, asking her, "Did it hurt? You were afraid it would."

"The X-ray? Of course not. Though they make such a pretentious fuss about it, running into their little lead-lined safe rooms and throwing the switch while you stand there without even a bra and take the full blast. They're electrocutioners. All these doctors—they watch us die, and expect to get paid for it."

"Mammograms are the worst," Sukie contributed. "The way the nurses stretch your tits this way and that against this icy glass. They only hire sadistic bull dykes."

"And after all that," Jane continued, "when I asked what the X-rays showed they said Doc Pat's son had gone home and would read them and be in touch with his father. Anyway, it's all foolish—whoever heard of an aneurysm on your abdominal aorta? The whole process left me a griping pain in my solar plexus. In my dolor hexus."

"You poor dear," said Alexandra, reassuming her role as mistress of the ceremony. "Should we have something to eat before we begin? There's cheese, Gouda and Münster, and those nice seaweed-flavored rice crackers the Japanese make that I found in that tiny gourmet section they have now at the Stop and Shop. And there's chicken curry and broccoli salad if you're starving, but I don't think we should try to raise the cone of power on full stomachs. Everything about us should be *clean*. We should all take showers. Jane, you use yours, and Sukie and I will share."

"Suppose *I* want to share with Sukie," Jane said with a dark look. "Or with you."

"We'll share the cone of power, that's enough," Alexandra stated, testing her authority. "Don't give us a hard time,

Jane. You're overexcited from being the center of so much attention. We need to hurry. The moon is a waning one. We have to be at a hundred percent to draw it down."

"How shall we dress afterwards?" Sukie asked. "I brought nothing black, and nothing with big sleeves."

"In nothing," Lexa decreed. She had had more Chianti than she had realized. "We'll go sky-clad. Like I said, we must give a hundred percent."

"I *can't*," Jane announced. The refusal stretched the tendons of her throat; they stood out alarmingly. "I've become an old bag. So have you two. Ancient bag-hags. I *won't*."

"Speak for yourself, Jane," Sukie said haughtily. "Do some exercises if you don't like your body. Yoga, qi gong. Just twenty minutes a day does wonders. It tightens you up all over."

"It's the spirit that matters," Alexandra assured her. "To me, you're beautiful. I see through the physical envelope."

"Then why do you want to take a shower with Sukie?"

"I said we'd share, not both get in together. We need space, Jane, to release your chakra energy. Being sky-clad releases us. It unties the *aiguillette* of inhibition intrinsic to Western man. Our healing powers, self-healing and other-healing, need to be *free*; they need to be cleansed of such impurities as jealousy. Come, dear. Take my hand. Put it on your belly with mine. Can you feel it? I can feel your pain kicking. There. And there. It wants out. Let it out, darling. Let your self be free. Fre*ee*," Alexandra repeated. "Kuh-*leeen*."

Skin and water, warmth and flesh, the widows submitted to the cleansing—Jane wearing a plastic shower cap that made her look, if anybody had been with her to see, like a

Victorian maid; Sukie with her long cedar-colored hair bundled and pinned and held by hand as best she could out of
the torrent; Alexandra alone fearless of getting her head wet,
thrusting it into the thick of the forceful element, her
clutching fingers working up an oozy lather on her scalp and
then letting it be belted and drummed upon by the scalding
liquid rods. Playfully Sukie, not yet towelled dry, sensed the
rapture of her sister in witchery through the steamed-up
shower door and re-entered the stall, giggling and getting all
wet again, the other body not unwelcoming, the bulbous
nubs and bulges of the two of them rubbing and bumping,
beslimed with soap, their skin feeling to their shut eyes as if
shining and burnished. Then Sukie, all rosy in her buttocks
and heated face, fled the other's wet caresses out the glass
door, and Alexandra followed at her more stately pace, bowing into her vigorous towelling, already from her scrubbed
scalp to the thin-skinned tops of her feet tingling with the
power the three beldames were about to put on.

In their summer quarters' big room, on the freshly vacuumed burgundy carpet, they gathered self-consciously, their
nakedness an airy shared sensation. The hair on their fore-
arms stood erect as if electrified; their eyes helplessly fed on
the wrinkles, the warts and scars, the keratoses and liver
spots, the slack muscles and patches of crêpey skin crinkled
like smooth water touched by a breath of wind, the varicose
veins and arthritic deformations with which time had overlaid their old beauty. This beauty from Nature's standpoint
had been serviceable, merely — enough to attract a member
of the opposite sex for insemination. That achieved, they
had naturally, like the females of many species, regarded
their mates as disgusting leftovers, fellow-dupes of procre-
ative madness. Their eyes — gun-metal gray, tortoiseshell

brown, gold-flecked hazel—could not stop moving in unaccustomed survey of one another, with minute ocular motions
that twitched their lips into ironic, reflective smiles.

"Well, the invitation said, Come as you are," Jane broke
the silence by saying.

"I think we've done pretty well, considering," Alexandra
responded.

"*You* have," Jane accused. "Fat smoothes everything out."

"It's the ass, isn't it?" Sukie said thoughtfully, trying to
look behind her and down. "Luckily," she decided, "you
can't see it. And the tits. The damn things droop." She
cupped her hands around her own and lifted them an inch or
two, to where they had been thirty years ago. When her
hands came away you could see that her nipples were erect.
Sweetnips.

"To me, you both look gorgeous," Alexandra loyally main-
tained. "Not exactly Botticelli any more, but not Grüne-
wald, either."

"Shouldn't we be getting going with this?" asked Sukie, of
all people to be uncomfortable in her skin. "Lexa, tell me
again what to do. What the point is."

"Healing, sweetness. Healing whatever is wrong with
Jane, and undoing whatever wrong we did here."

"*What* wrong?" Jane asked angrily. "Who are you, if I may
ask, to say what was wrong and what was right? None of us
liked Felicia, but none of us told Clyde to hammer her to
death with a poker, either."

Alexandra answered, "She was spitting feathers and pins
that we had put into her mouth. By way of the cookie jar,
remember?"

"Who *sssays sso*? They both died that night, with nobody
else there."

"The police," Sukie intervened. "They found the pins and

feathers on the floor, next to the body. They didn't know how they got there, but I did. As a reporter, I saw them. The things were still wet with spit."

"Who says it was *her s*spit?" Jane argued. "They didn't have DNA testing then."

"There was still a pin and a feather in her mouth," Sukie said. "A guy I knew on the force then told me. I don't suppose either of you remember him—Ronnie Kazmierczak, the brother of the boy killed in Vietnam they renamed Landing Square after. He didn't stay a cop long. He said his job was mainly to keep the have-nots from robbing the haves; he became a hippie and moved to Alaska. He used to write me a little. He said he didn't mind the cold, he'd stopped feeling it. He never came back."

"Boo hoo," Jane said. "I suppose we're to blame for *that*, too. Even if Clyde was annoyed by her *s*spitting feathers, most men wouldn't have beaten their wives' heads in because of it."

"It was the way she talked all the time that he minded," Sukie said.

Alexandra begged, "For Heaven's sake, let's forget Clyde and Felicia! It was Jenny we definitely killed. In your kitchen, Jane. We made a wax doll—"

"*You* made it," Jane interrupted.

"I made it with you advising and with elements you had gathered. We all stuck pins in it and said the words. The evil words. She was dead by the end of the summer."

"More boo hoo. She died of cancer of the ovaries, metastasized. She was riddled with it, it had been in her for years."

"Please," Alexandra involuntarily breathed. The thought, the image of intimate cells gone wild, took the wind out of her.

"It happens to people all the time," Jane went relentlessly

on. "Our spell might have had nothing to do with it. It might have been somebody else's *s*spell. Brenda Parsley and Greta and Rose Hallybread—they were just as witchy. There was a lot of malevolence in town in those years."

"A lot of woman power," Sukie agreed, seeing that Alexandra had been stricken into silence, lost in fears and qualms.

"*Wait!*" Jane cried, having seen something in space. "All this talk, it just came to me. The man who said hello to me on Vane Street, outside of Doc Pat's, who we thought might be staying with Greta Neff a few steps away on Oak. I know who he was. He was Chris*s*topher Gabriel. Jenny's brother. Remember what a handsome boy he was? Darryl whisked him off to New York and they disappeared. It was *him.*"

"It was *he*," Alexandra corrected. She had recovered her focus and was impatient to get the ritual of healing, of undoing evil, under way. Jane was being obstructionist and negative-minded as always.

"Why is he *here*?" Jane asked. "Why is he *back*?"

"Only *you* think he's back," Sukie pointed out. "Only you saw him, or think you did, on that dark street, in the rain." But in the Unitarian church, come to think of it, in the front pews, Greta had been with at least one full-size man, a stranger, an accomplice. Greta had enlisted Deborah Larcom's beautiful goodness in the murderous conspiracy.

"But I *did*," Jane was insisting. "That was him. He. Older, fatter, faggier, but *him*. Beautiful little Christopher. His curly angelic silvery hair. *He's* the one doing it to me."

"Doing *what*?" Sukie asked. "Jane, please." Like Alexandra, she was exasperated now with Jane's egocentric distraction from the business at hand. She had catered to her all day to Providence and back and was hungry, and they shouldn't eat until after the ritual.

"*Killing* me!" Jane answered. "The shocks! The way my stomach hurts all the time! Not my stomach exactly, but in the vicinity, like something is rubbing thin. Right under *here*." She touched her breastbone, between her deflated little breasts; in her nakedness the gesture repulsively roused an image of the lightless world within her—the purplish organs asymmetrically interlocked, the slippery black interior suffused with blood being endlessly pumped around. No, not endlessly. We all have ends. The heart beats time. Time beats us.

"That's interesting, Jane," Alexandra rather loftily interposed. "We can look into it, beginning with Greta, though I must say dealing with her is *not* my idea of a pleasant time. But—"

"And not just *me*," Jane continued in her agitation. "Don't think, you two, you're just by*ss*tanders. He must be after you as well. He blames us all for his sister's death, he's come after all of us. Darryl must have shared some of his powers with him, and now he's come after us. He's *out* there. I can *feel* it."

"Please, baby," Alexandra urged. "If everything you feel is true, all the more reason, then, to erect the cone of power. We'll do *white* magic. We'll petition the Goddess on your behalf. We'll tell her we're sorry about Jenny."

"It's too late," Jane said. "I'm not *s*sorry."

Alexandra appealed to Sukie: "What do *you* think?"

"I think we should do whatever idiotic thing you've set up for, so we can *eat*. All I've had since noon was an ice-cream cone with the wrong kind of jimmies on it."

"I'd love a martini," Jane said. "It's a real craving. Easy on the vermouth, Lexa, thank you very much." When Alexandra was slow to move, Jane said impatiently, "Never mind, Lazybones. I'll make it myself."

"Well, I would hope so," Alexandra told her. "I'm not sure there is any vermouth."

"*Ss*crew the vermouth, then. I need to put some clothes on or have the heat turned up."

Sukie in her hunger had discovered the cheese and crackers; her lips sparkled with salt and crumbs. Her big teeth curved slightly outward, giving her plump mouth its provocative, subtly thrusting shape. To Alexandra she pronounced, "The Münster is delicious. The Gouda seems dry. Where did you get it? You said the Stop and Shop? There's a better place for cheese in Jamestown."

She was spilling crumbs into the magic circle; her bare feet unconsciously nudged the carefully drawn line of Cascade. Sukie's ankles, though still slender, bore little spider veins, like purple threads in a pair of white socks.

"*Please,*" Alexandra said, exasperated nearly to tears by her little coven's unruliness. "Let's come to order. The Goddess hates confusion. She hates bad housekeeping."

"She does housekeeping?" Sukie asked.

"I'm in too much agony for this," Jane announced, coming from the kitchen. "I *did* find the vermouth, Lexa, right where I thought it was. But somebody'd been drinking it. Who? Or do we have alcoholic mice?" She sipped and made an acid face.

Alexandra ignored her, explaining, "Before we ask anything of the Goddess, we must enter the circle. The broom is the portal. I'll move it aside. But before we enter, we must circle it on the outside, deosil."

"Deosil?" Sukie asked. "What's deosil?"

"How can you have forgotten, baby? Clockwise. The good direction. To do evil, you circle widdershins, counterclockwise."

"All this formalism," Sukie complained. "It seems to me we used to do it all *naturally*—being witchy was just a stage of life, like menopause."

"It was what came be*fore* menopause," Jane said. "*Just* before, before we gave up. Oh, that beautiful *sang de menstruës*. Who would ever think we'd mi*ss* it? The cramps I'm having right now are worse. There's no egg involved, to egg us on."

"You need ease. We all need ease," Alexandra told them in a voice pitched to be lulling, her mother-voice. And the other two did not protest when she led them around the circle, three times deosil. The night outside was black enough to make the windows mirrors in which their pale wobbling bodies were reflected. Unsteady illumination came from underneath, from the tinted squat candles on the floor, placed on the five points of an invisible pentacle. Fearful, as she bent over, of releasing a gust of rectal smell, Alexandra moved aside the plastic-handled broom, and entered the opened circle. Sukie followed, then Jane. Their three shadows noiselessly wheeled on the low ceiling, overlapping, enlarging, multiplying in the fivefold candlelight. They stood there, close enough to seem—if some goggle-eyed spectral presence were looking in the window—one flesh.

Jane gracelessly, hoarsely broke the silence: "What's that old breadboard doing in the middle?"

"It's the altar," Alexandra explained, her voice pointedly soft, befitting a mystery. "I found it in the kitchen, under the sink, with the tea trays."

"And the bronze bowl?" Sukie asked, trying to achieve the same low, respectful pitch.

"Brass. From a flea market in Old Wick. The little bell came from another—somebody's dinner bell when everybody over in Newport had maids and butlers. These chalices"—she passed out two—"I bought right on Dock Street. Eastwick is oddly well equipped for the Craft."

"The Craft," Sukie said. "I haven't heard it called that for years." She fiddled the chalice, lighter in weight than a bird, in her slender hand. "It's tinfoil," she said with mild surprise.

"Hold it still, please. I'm pouring." Alexandra, with a reach that gave her a whiff of her own armpit, produced from outside the circle the heavy glass jug of Carlo Rossi Chianti.

"What rotgut," Jane said, but held out her chalice nevertheless, for her share, on top of the Martini and the Margarita. In the shuddering dim light the red wine looked black. The three forsaken souls held out their faux chalices—the fragile gilded cardboard, the jewels that were mere blobs of paint—and touched them in mid-air.

"To us," Alexandra said.

"To us."

"Yesss. To uss."

Sukie wiped a mist of wine from the fine hairs on her upper lip, and contemplated the arcane arrangement assembled on the carpet. Her voice came out patronizing yet sympathetic: "Lexa, sweetheart, you've worked so hard to get us in touch with the Goddess."

Jane wisecracked, "Doesn't she have a cell phone yet?" Her blasphemy grated on the others, a symptom of her unhealth.

"Her num-ber is un-list-ed," said Sukie, in the voice of an automated electronic menu. No one laughed.

The solemn black windows—thermopane Andersens, on cranks that when new worked like charms but that over time had accumulated dirt and rust and become balky and stiff—rebuked the prattle with their silence. The windows witnessed the shadowy witcheries in the room like a row of square-shouldered widows in speechless mourning.

"And the deck of cards?" Sukie asked, her voice, the lightest and youngest of the three, straining under the weight of the powers about to be invoked. "Are we going to play Old Maid?"

Again, there was no responsive laughter. The universe holds vast volumes of nothingness, yet these colossal gaps between the stars are cumbersome doors that can be opened, admitting sudden winds and the groans of sluggishly awakening presences. "A tarot deck," Alexandra explained. "I bought it downtown. Let's sit." Her voice had become level, gentle, casually firm. "Is everybody comfy on their cushions? Is there enough space for all our legs?" In truth it was awkward, at first, to arrange themselves, in the bed-size space, without feet and hands getting in another body's way, and without exposing, by putting their knees up or spread apart, their nether parts, hairy and odorous and for many Christian centuries unspeakable.

Alexandra picked up the little silver bell, a tinkling remnant of a bygone class system, and as if to summon servants lightly shook it. The questioning peal glimmered outward from their circle, in wider and wider circles.

"Do we still remember," Alexandra gently asked, "the names of Her retinue?" She began the litany: "Aurai, Hanlii, Thamcii, Tilinos, Athamas, Zianor, Auonail."

Jane took it up with the vehemence of a sufferer tormented into sacrilege: "Tzabaoth, Messsiach, Emanuel, Elchim, Eibor, Yod, He, Vou, He! I'm amazed I still remember!"

Sukie began haltingly: "It's been so long. Astachoth, Adonai, Agla—there are those three 'a's—then On, El, Tetragammaton, Shema, Ariston, Anaphaxeton . . . surely that's enough retinue for Her, Lexa."

Silence. The black windows. The little fluttering candle flames dug down into the drums of colored wax, bringing up a sickly perfume that concealed and forgave whatever odors drifted from between the unholy wantons' legs, their nests of once thick and springy curls turned gauzy and gray, pubic clocks ticking unseen, decade after decade, in their underpants.

"Goddess, are You there?" Alexandra asked the silence in an elevated voice. She tinkled the small bell, and after some seconds softly asked the other two, "Do you feel a vibration?"

"Not really," Sukie admitted.

Jane, hopeful for herself, ventured, "I'm not sure."

"We mustn't hurry Her." Alexandra, so daintily it sounded like an apology, rang the bell again, and then once more.

"I definitely feel it. Her," Jane said greedily. "I have this gushing warm sensation that everything will be all right. I'm in Her arms!"

"Good," Alexandra crooned, nursing her along. "Good." She closed her eyes, to better receive the sensations of alignment. It was like on a radio, the station between two other stations: faint music, melody, straining through the static. "Inside each of us," she intoned, "there are obstacles and inhibitions that tie us down, that prevent us from being free. Goddess, untie these *aiguillettes*."

Silence. A car's tires crunched the gravel in the parking lot below. Whose? Some revenant's, from prior time.

"So what now?" Sukie asked with asperity. "How long do we have to wait, and for what?"

Why was Sukie the source of discord, of doubt? Alexandra guessed that she was jealous of the Goddess. She still wanted to be a goddess herself.

"Shut up," Jane told Sukie. "Let Her talk."

"Our wedding rings," Alexandra was inspired to say. "She doesn't think we should still be wearing them. They come between us and Her. Between us and astral reality. Can you get yours off?"

"My God, yes," Sukie said. "It keeps falling off of its own when I wash my hands and rattling into the bathroom sink. It wants to go down the drain."

Her own, Alexandra discovered, was the most reluctant to let go; it was embedded in the fat of her finger. But, painfully, she worked it past the first knuckle, its bunched creases blanching under the pressure. The ring had left a white dent in her finger, like a tiny tree being girdled.

"Let's put them on the altar," she commanded. "With our left hands, the hands that wore them."

Three sinister hands reached out, placing the rings so they were tangent, each to the two others—Sukie's thick band of gold engraved inside *Forever* by a jeweller in Greenwich; Jane's thinner ring like a link in the long chain of Nat Tinker's ancestors; and Alexandra's own, middle-size and the longest worn, slipped onto her third finger in the bald daylight of a sandstone chapel whose clear glass windows had contained a view of crumpled dry Western mountains. Slipping the ring on her finger, Jim Farlander's nicotine-stained fingers had trembled, either with bachelor-party hangover or simple nervousness. The ring was hers to wear but the shackle of marriage his to bear. She felt his skittishness in the touch of his hand and recited her concluding vows like a ranch-hand lovingly calming a shying horse. Her eyes warmed at the memory, and perhaps her near-tears were the Goddess's gifts. "There," she pronounced aloud. "We are free. Whatever *aiguillettes* bind our hearts have been untied. Let Your healing power enter into us unobstructed. We are Yours purely." She addressed the other two worshippers:

"My thought was this. We should undo our bad deeds by committing a good deed."

"Bad, good," Sukie said scornfully. "The context is what matters. What's good one day is bad the next. All's fair in love and war."

"Oh, don't," Jane whimpered. "We're trying to make me better. We're fighting Chrisstopher's evil."

Sukie was studying her own hand, held out before her. "I like it without the ring. Naked. I do love naked."

"It's scary for me, to have mine off," Alexandra confessed. A wedding ring, she thought, is an *aiguillette*—it ties us down, but holds us in.

"Lexa, what's next? Tell us what to do," Jane begged. She was regressing, her voice pulled backwards into childishness.

Alexandra took the tarot deck and spread the cards on the carpet face-up, in their four archaic suits—Cups, Coins, Wands, and Swords—plus the twenty-two tarots, forming the major arcana. They were gaudy little gateways into an alternative realm. "You pick one," she instructed Sukie and Jane, "that reminds you of someone needy you know—someone in trouble. Concentrate on it under the cone of power, and when you feel you've made the transfer to the astral plane, burn it."

"Burn it?"

Alexandra held up the folder of paper matches that had been sitting on the altar, the same with which she had lit the aromatic candles that flickeringly dispensed their smoky perfume. "I tried to get cards without too much coating. I'll go first." She looked over the scattered array and selected a court card, the Queen of Cups, who in her empty expression could have been Veronica Marino O'Brien, the queenliness borrowed from her mother. Alexandra bowed her head and projected onto the glazed small surface her inner simulacrum, limned in neuronal connections, of the person its image conjured up. To the Goddess she offered the prayer *Let her be fruitful. Untie her tubes. Let her claim her heritage, the fecundity of her parents, Gina and dear Joe.* Alexandra felt she had been heard, the Goddess bending low out of the stars, her long hair streaming like a comet's tail. The suppliant held the card by one corner and held a match under the opposite corner and when it reluctantly caught fire let it fall into the brass bowl, where it burned blue with a green rim to the flame, the chemical-coated card curling upon itself, a single rectangular ash shattering in the end like gossamer pottery. She had watched the process of oxidization so intently that her brow and throat and collar area had sympathetically broken into a sweat; the circle she had drawn had become the base of a cone of power like a bison-skin tepee overheated by a cooking fire of mesquite twigs at its center.

"Me next," Sukie said, "though I'm not a hundred percent into this." She picked the Page of Coins, a youth with a conceited profile. She showed it to the other two malefactresses and shut her eyes to hurl her wish, her desire, through the flimsy pasteboard to her maimed former lover, Thomas Gorton. *Heal,* she commanded within herself. *Perform the impossible, as You do with each birth, each falling in love.* She felt the Goddess within her, the power of sex and generation, a ribbon of DNA tweaked in Africa and snaking forward into a teeming future, cells knitting from microscopic knots into upright men and women intact and beautiful in every ligament and vein. She held the match; the flame sluggishly took; the purple fire widened its way up the card like invading hordes in an animated map of human history, consuming with black blistering the conceited profile. Sukie let the intact ash fall into the brazier, where it writhed and audibly crinkled at the last turn of its own molecular transformation. The fingers of her left hand stung, having held on too long. Looking up from the stinging, she saw that a bluish haze had gathered on the ceiling. She wondered how sensitive the condo's smoke alarm was, and prayed to the Goddess to suppress it.

"Now you, Jane. Your turn," Alexandra instructed, in the nurturing voice of the mother witch, Nature's agent, though she was unsure that Jane had any capacity for good deeds in her. "Take a card."

Jane's withered hand reached and seemed to touch the trump card called Diabolo. It showed a skeleton gracefully posing, ankles crossed, with a long bow and arrow the size of a spear. Jane's hovering hand jerked back, and she emitted a strangled noise that sucked the gaze of the two others to her face; it looked congested and rapt. Beneath the mannish dark eyebrows, her eyes flicked to first one, then the other of her companions. Her expression seemed indignant. Then her eyes rolled back in their sockets. Her open mouth turned black with overflowing blood.

"Baby!" Alexandra cried, suddenly loving her, yearning to undo whatever had gone wrong.

"My God," Sukie said. The Goddess had evaporated. The moon burning outside the windows leaned its near-full orb toward the unseen sun. Both women in their nakedness struggled to embrace and right the body of the third; Jane had gone limp as a drained wineskin even as she convulsed in spurts of writhing resistance to whatever was possessing her.

"Shit. It hurt*ss*," the stricken widow whispered. Blood spilled with her words down her chin, while Alexandra leaped up in a lightning-flash of shaky bare flesh to seize the telephone and punch in a number that was not unlisted, 911.

iii. *Guilt Assuaged*

THE WOMAN at the other end of the line assured Alexandra that the Emergency Medical Technicians knew just where the Lenox Mansion Seaview Apartments were—"Off the beach road, up there hidden on the left," the dispatcher stated, dropping into chattiness. Yet an agonizing fifteen minutes passed before the ambulance siren sounded, first in the distance and then enormously close, its cry cut short in a screech of brakes and the crackle of driveway gravel. At first, in those minutes, Sukie chafed Jane's cooling hands while Alexandra tried, with humiliating incompetence and revulsion, to breathe life into Jane's wet, slack mouth and to thump action back into her heart. Her maneuvers felt ungainly and panicky and futile, even as she tried to remember, from episodes of idly watched hospital dramas on television years ago, what else she might do to keep Jane from slipping deeper down into the chasm that had abruptly opened beneath them. There was still, it seemed to her, a subterranean stream gurgling in Alexandra's ear when she pressed it to her friend's scrawny breast. Jane's eyes had closed and her body no longer resisted its invisible tormentor.

The first high wave of the crisis had washed away the women's awareness that they were in the condition of Eve, but then as with the couple in the Garden they knew, and were afraid. "They're on the way?" Sukie asked, her face stretched so smooth by panic that she looked to Alexandra young, a near-girl again. "My God, Lexa, we must get dressed! We must dress Jane! Where did she put her clothes?"

"She showered on her own, they must be in her room." A great thickness of circumstance clogged Alexandra's brain; the faster her heart beat, the slower she seemed to move, her knees and hands jutting into view like the camera operator's in an inept video. She had to push herself to enter Jane's little windowless room, which already had a crypt's stillness. Black slacks and a tan jersey, with underwear on top, were primly folded on her narrow single bed. Her shoes, simple severe Boston-style low heels, were tidily toed in under the bed. How innocent and defenseless they suddenly seemed, useless! The other two renters had stuck her back here as if she were a maiden aunt, or a troublesome child, in this room where sunshine entered only through a clouded plastic skylight. By sharp electric illumination Alexandra caught sight of herself in the big mirror on the back of Jane's door, her arms holding Jane's clothes, her shoulders and lower body bare. Her mouth shocked her by being smeared with bright red: Jane's blood, from the moments when she had tried to lend her her breath.

Dressing the unresisting body brought back the unpleasant sensations of dressing a child—the sulky refusal of limbs to bend the right way, the little surges of obstinate dead weight. Sukie, tugging and pushing with her, said, "Remember the girdles they still made us wear in the Fifties? With the snaps for long stockings? Wasn't that barbaric?"

"Atrocious," Alexandra agreed. "Your hips got stinking hot."

"Thank God for pantyhose."

"Thank the Goddess, I would think."

"Boy, after this, keep that Goddess away from me."

As they together tugged up the slacks, Alexandra asked, "Would you have guessed Jane would wear such low-slung underpants? Lace-edged yet."

"She had that funny little husband to keep interested. It took a lot to arouse him, Jane told me."

"And me."

"And, then, it's so hard to throw underwear away. You think, Oh, it'll go through the wash once more, what the hell."

As they lifted Jane up to do the bra and jersey, Alexandra timorously asked, "Does she feel warm enough to you?"

"Well," Sukie responded, "I don't notice blood pooling in the fingertips. That's often a clue, in murder mysteries."

"Could you reach me the portable shaving mirror from the altar? I'll hold it in front of her mouth."

"Oh, *please*, Lexa. What can we do in any case but what we are doing? Make her presentable."

"I know, I know. Damn it, I *know* there's something else we could be doing, if we were doctors or better witches."

"If we were better witches this wouldn't have happened at all," Sukie said. Fetching the mirror, she hesitated at the entrance to the magic circle, then scrupulously moved the broom, or besom, aside, rather than step over it as if its magic were null. Held to Jane's mouth, the mirror, meant a few minutes ago to serve as a window into the other world, sent magnified reflections of Jane's features skidding; Alexandra's hand shook, but even so the mirror caught bits of mist, of life-breath.

"What do you think it was?" Sukie mused. "She just sort of exploded."

"She kept blaming electricity," Alexandra recalled. "There. How does she look?"

The third woman's body lay stretched on the carpet with a strangely bridal air, having been dressed by others. A corner of her lips tucked in as when she had made a pun she was pleased with. Her hands were crossed on her chest; they looked too large and veiny for so petite a woman.

"Wedding rings," Alexandra remembered. "Get them."

As she obeyed, Sukie said, "We better pick up all this stuff before the paramedics get here."

"Don't call it 'stuff.' Call it 'tools.' Or 'energy channellers.' "

"And vacuum up the circle on the carpet."

"Our magic circle," Alexandra said, "short-circuited."

"You sound like Jane. This is all too terrible. I can't believe it's happened." Sukie squatted down, her thighs fattening, her breasts lightly swinging, to put Jane's wedding ring back on the unfeeling hand.

"The left hand," Alexandra reminded her.

"Of course, sweetie. The one with the calluses."

Alexandra's ring was no less reluctant to squeeze past her second knuckle on the way on than it had been on the way off. "We must get dressed ourselves," she said.

"I keep forgetting I'm naked. Isn't that crazy?"

"You look darling." Alexandra guiltily gazed down at their unconscious partner in sin. She felt a need for some kind of ceremony. "We love you, Jane," she called, over a widening gulf.

Sukie repeated, "We love you, Jane. Hang in there."

And the two of them hastened to retrieve their clothes and neaten their hair and, in Alexandra's case, wash her face and apply fresh lipstick. The siren of rescue was heard a mile away, halfway up the beach road where the old apple orchard had blossomed and borne fruit before being turned into tract houses, and grew louder approaching the causeway, and wound its whooping bleat around the mansion before braking on the gravel below the windows. Sukie hastily gathered up the cards, the bell, the mirror, the candles, the breadboard, and the brass bowl holding the flaky ashes of the two fiery invasions of the astral plane; she carried these things all into the kitchen and slammed cabinet doors while Alexandra pushed a roaring Electrolux over the sacred ring. The Cascade pellets rattled in the extender wand and pelted in the flexible hose, windblown into a netherworld populated by dust mites.

The downstairs doorbell rasped. Sukie buzzed the visitors in. The stairs shook with a thunder of footsteps; the EMT team rushed through the open door, in their lime-green scrubs. There were three of them, two men and a woman, all younger than any of the widows' children. The man with the most equipment attached to him said breathlessly, "We had a hard time finding this place. Nobody in town wanted to tell us."

The woman, who carried the least equipment, wrinkled her nose, smelling the sweet candle smoke and noticing the freshly vacuumed swaths on the carpet. But the emergency lay stretched out before them; within ten minutes they took Jane away on a stretcher, still alive, they promised, but swaddled to her chin in a silver thermal blanket and hooked up to colorless drips that fed into both her wrists.

She died in the Westwick Hospital that night, or, rather,

early the next morning, when the waning moon, like a wafer being dunked, was surrendering its glow to dawn's first tea-colored tinge. Her abdominal aorta had burst and there was no repairing the rupture. Blood had swamped her insides. Doc Pat was to have read the X-rays next morning, and his son in Providence had been going to propose a preëmptive operation, which for a woman her age, with her recent history of uncertain health, carried significant hazards. No one, the medical establishment assured her two stricken friends, was at fault. As deaths go, Jane's had been quick and easy—among friends, not painless but the pain lasting only a few seconds before her consciousness closed down.

Of these three, Jane had been the only witch to truly fly, and in death she lifted the other two out of Eastwick. After a mere month the town had re-exerted the spell that had mired the unfortunate trio decades before—the curious sense that at the town's borders meaningful reality ceased. Their plans, discussed by phone and e-mail all spring, to use Eastwick as a springboard for improving trips elsewhere—up to Providence and its museums, down the coast to New London, over to Newport—had proved too ambitious. Beneath the seductive sun of daily habit, of meals and errands and the threefold pursuit of various threads of local interest, inertia had set in.

Now, with Jane's death and the social arrangements it compelled, the outer world pounced, exhilarating and confusing the two survivors with its color and variety. Brookline, that seceded civic entity fastened to Commonwealth Avenue like a big tick sucking vitality from Boston's body politic, was, between Beacon Street and Route 9, all curving streets and multi-million-dollar homes of brick and stucco set on small, earnestly green lush lawns overloaded with manicured shrubs and select trees. The Tinker house had a deeper front yard than most, and a higher, darker profile, crowned by a dormered third story with a turret as empty as a church belfry.

Sukie had already met the mistress of this mansion, but Alexandra was unprepared for the shock of magic imparted, with a gleam of mischief, by a century's longevity. Death had apparently chosen to overlook this woman—evidence, Alexandra conjectured, remembering the trip she and Jane had taken together, that the Egyptian hope of eternally prolonged *ankh* had a possible practical basis. The remarkably old lady was the size of a thirteen-year-old, or a carefully packed mummy. She met them in her entrance hall, at the foot of a great wide walnut staircase that diminished upward into a gloom of darkening wallpaper. She had descended to her daughter-in-law's funeral party by means of a cage elevator whose shaft was installed beside the staircase and rose through its turns like a staff through the snakes of Mercury's caduceus; since its spindly frame offered no substantial obstacle to the eye, Mrs. Tinker's descent, that of a veritable *dea ex machina*, was observed with wonder by the mourners gathered on the terrazzo first floor. As gently as if entrusting to Alexandra's broad hand the delicate treasure of a stuffed extinct bird, she laid four dry fingers in the younger old woman's palm, which was moist in the humid heat of early August in the East.

"So you're Alexandra," Mrs. Tinker said in a creaky, rustling, but distinctly articulated voice. "Jane adored you." The creases in her cheeks were so deep they suggested streaks of warpaint on the face of an Indian brave; her face overall was the parched yellow-brown that cheap books turn at the edges of each page, without being directly touched by sunlight. Her lower eyelids had sagged, exposing the palest of pinks on their inner sides.

Adored me? Alexandra asked herself. Could it be true, when her own adoration tended toward Sukie, and both she and Sukie were slightly repelled by Jane's livid aura of rage and doom? "We loved *her*," Alexandra said, speaking softly, as if the slightest gust of air would shatter the apparition before her. Even the black folds of Mrs. Tinker's silk mourning outfit looked perilously brittle.

"I'm so glad, then," she brought out in her husk of a voice, "she was with the two of you when her end came."

Her end—no euphemism here, no talk of "passing," and yet no terror, no noisy modern nihilism. The phrase made death seem comfortable and limpid and natural, the fruit of year upon year, decade upon decade, its fall finally met with a vanished era's stoic upper-class manners. Detecting Alexandra's interest in the topic, Mrs. Tinker told her, "We must all come to the end." Yet she said this with the lightness of one to whom it did not apply, and with a smile of startling elasticity in the mummified brown face—a stretch that tugged her scored cheeks with a darting, almost girlish tension. Her lips were no ruddier than the skin around them, but fleshier. She had been a beauty, Alexandra suddenly saw.

As suddenly, she confessed to the ancient woman, "I haven't quite assimilated that yet. I'm not sure Jane had, either. Her last look at me—do you want to know?"

"Yes. Of course. One must always know whatever there is to know."

"—seemed indignant."

"Jane was vexed," Mrs. Tinker pronounced. "And in a hurry. Like a metronome. Have you ever tried to play a musical instrument to a metronome?"

"No," Alexandra said, nervously, for she felt more guests

behind her, coming in at the great front door. "I'm a musical dunce. I always envied Jane her talent."

"She was a metronome set too fast for my son's and my taste," the old woman resumed, blinking away the other's interjection. "We had set a *largo* pace in this household, and I fear it chafed my daughter-in-law's patience. And here is the lovely Suzanne," she continued, turning just the small amount needed to change the angle of her attention, like a calibrated figure on a clock. Sukie had joined them, bringing her warmth and curiosity and determination to be noticed. "Hello again, my dear. What a sadness, since last we welcomed you to this house."

She is one of us, Alexandra saw. *A heartless sharp-eyed witch. She is small and incisive and witty and wicked, like Jane. Men marry their mothers.* Nat had married his mother, and of course the two women had hated being duplicated in the same house. The entire spiritual architecture of their household—the two women as mutually repellent as the like poles of two magnets, and suspended between them the little son-husband, taking shelter in his antiques, his clubs, his feckless good works—was bared to Alexandra in an instant of closing her eyes; she felt the tension still in the air, in the weight borne by the slanting, polish-soaked dark woodwork.

Sukie, too, was experiencing second sight: she blurted to the widow Tinker, "I can't believe Jane is really gone. I expect her to pop up at any second."

"And spoil my party," the old lady rasped, giving another of her unexpectedly wide-lipped smiles; the girl she had once been shone through, from deep in the last century.

The party was assembling, milling about awkwardly in the shadowy high hall. Jane's mother-in-law turned and introduced Alexandra and Sukie to a bulky middle-aged man with a sloping back to his head, which was heavily thrust forward, like an American buffalo's, and a gaunt woman wearing a desperate amount of makeup. "I'm sure you remember Jane's wonderful children," Mrs. Tinker said and, with a senile lack of ceremony, turned away.

Thus confronted, Alexandra apologized to the two. "I didn't recognize you. It's been so long. You're all grown up."

"And then some," the fat-necked man said without smiling. "We remember you, though."

Of course. A fat boy and a skinny girl. They had been obtrusively present in Jane's ranch house, running in and out of the kitchen begging for attention and for dinner, the night the three women had concocted Jenny's fatal spell. Exploring their liberated powers, they had had little patience with their children. They had felt that stupid women since Eve had been docile, loving mothers—perhaps not Eve, considering how Abel and Cain turned out. At any rate, motherhood had been thoroughly tried, in sorrow and out of it, and it hadn't been enough.

There was a tense, resentful silence, which Sukie tried to fill, dredging up these children's names with her reporter's trained memory. "Roscoe and Mary Grace, right? And there were two others, younger or older, I forget which."

"Younger," said the sullenly staring hulk, in his double-breasted black suit. It was he, Sukie realized, who was the Internet bridge player, his huge head thrust forward toward the four-sided computer screen, the dummy imaged for all to see. "We were four. The four little Smarts." Unexpectedly, his lips flicked back in a mirthless smile, revealing small, stained teeth.

"Everybody had four children back then," Sukie gamely offered.

Alexandra asked, "Your father. Sam Smart. Is he still alive?"

"No" was the monosyllabic answer.

The gaunt woman, her eyelids loaded with turquoise tint, decided to join in. "Dad died," she explained, exposing her own teeth; they were long and unnaturally straight.

"I'm so sorry," Alexandra said.

"He and Mom are together again now," the man said.

"Really? How will Mr. Tinker like that arrangement?"

Roscoe's impressive brow lowered in her direction. "It's all explained in the Bible." His face was doleful and gray.

"Is it really? I must look up the passage." Alexandra revised her opinion; it wasn't that Jane had been neglectful, it was that her children, fat or skinny, were odious.

Sukie politely intervened. "The other two. Are they here, too?"

"No," came the reluctant answer. "Jed's in Hawaii. Nora married a Frenchman and they can't be reached in August. They're skin-diving and doing dope in Mozambique."

"How extraordinary the world is!" Sukie desperately exclaimed. "Everything coming closer. We're widows now, and we love travelling. Your mother travelled with us."

"Roscoe hates travelling," his sister said. "He gets claustrophobia in the airplane and then agoraphobia when it lands."

"You think about it too much," Sukie advised him, as pert as a maiden facing up to the Minotaur. "Take two drinks at the airport bar and you'll wake up wherever you're going."

The conversation was mercifully cut short by the sharp thump, three times, of the ancient hostess's cane on the foyer floor. With one paper-brown hand bunched on the cane's handle and the other clinging to the bent arm of a broad-backed African-American in a driver's uniform, Mrs. Tinker led the assembled mourners out into the sticky white sunshine. A line of cars glared and sparkled blindingly in the driveway, stretching from the porte cochere back to the curb and out along the street. The mourning mother-in-law was settled into the lead Cadillac, behind black windows; next came the two dreary children and their spouses, who for this family observance had demurely donned cloaks of invisibility. Sukie and Alexandra followed far down the line, in Lennie Mitchell's navy-blue BMW. Nat Tinker's pet Jaguar had been swiftly reclaimed, along with Jane's pathetic leavings of clothes and toiletries, as part of her estate.

In the privacy of the car, Sukie urgently announced, "I *saw* him."

"Saw who?"

"*Him*. The man Jane saw on Vane Street, outside Doc Pat's."

"Really?"

"Really. He looks just like she said, like an angel gone a little heavy and seedy. He was at the back of the crowd in the foyer, coming out of the other room as we shuffled out. I saw him just for a second, but he stood out. He wasn't wearing the proper sober kind of clothes."

The church was not far away in the twisting, tree-shaded streets—a modestly posh structure, half-timbered in requisite Episcopal style, of iron-tinged fieldstone. This was a memorial, not a burial, service. Jane's body, that flat-chested round-assed little body that had tempted Sam Smart and Raymond Neff and Arthur Hallybread and Nat Tinker into coitus, was a canister of ashes now, no more than would fill a saucepan: all those bones and tendons and bodily fluids, that agile tongue and insistent sibilant voice and the glittering wet light of her tortoiseshell-brown eyes reduced to gray powder and calcite chips and already slipped into a small square hole in Mount Auburn Cemetery two miles away across the Charles. This had been her world, and her two companions in bygone mischief listened as a Jane they had scarcely known was exposed to public view.

The pair of adult children present read aloud excerpts from letters Jane had written to Samuel Smart when he was in the Army waiting to be shipped to Korea—a different Jane, more kittenish and collegiate than the one Sukie and Alexandra had met in Eastwick, by which time Sam Smart had become a comic memory, a pinch of the dead past sprinkled into the conversation for piquancy. She missed him, the letters declared, she prayed for his safe return, she lived in hopes of bearing his children, knowing they would be beautiful and precious.

Then, striking a balance between the husbands, a tall, square-shouldered, ostentatiously lean gentleman in a blazer and close haircut stiffly climbed up into the pulpit. He spoke at first with a diffident hesitancy that made the congregation nervously shift in their pews. Then, warming as he adjusted to the height and sacrosanct strangeness of the pulpit, he assumed the sonorous ease of a well-practiced toastmaster; he leaned out toward his audience and confidentially shared his impression of how his old friend Nat Tinker, whom he had known since they had been shy, puny first-graders together at Browne & Nichols School, and with whom in the years since he had golfed and sailed and shot quail in South Carolina and elk in Alaska and sat on many worthy boards—how dear old Nat had bloomed, had "come out of himself" once married to the late, "far-from-plain" Jane. He had never, he asserted, while his lean, white-capped head tilted this way and that like a hungry gull's, seen such a transformation as had overtaken his beloved friend upon his marriage, on the far side of forty—when he should have been, by all actuarial charts, beyond redemption—his marriage to this "ineffable soulmate," dear departed Jane.

"Not even on the occasion," he amplified, "of his getting a hole-in-one at the twelfth at the Country Club—a short but testing, as I need not explain to many of this congregation, par-three on a platform green from an elevated tee— did Nat radiate the satisfaction and, can I say, the primal joy which his bride mysteriously inspired in him." *What an old chauvinist pig this fancy talker is*, Alexandra was thinking. There was nothing mysterious: Jane knew how to be dirty, and men need dirty, especially class-bound cases of delayed development and excess propriety like poor little Nat Tinker, pussy-whipped by a mother who even now didn't deign to die. The eulogist archly suggested as much: "Jane rescued him, it seems not too much to say, from his cherished antiques; she brought into his life of bachelor connoisseurship and conscientious altruism a beautiful object—a 'piece,' as they say in the trade—he could touch without fear of its breaking." Shock muffled the responsive tittering from the pews; old-fashioned decorum regained some of its lost force in an Episcopal church—the Gothic arches and crockets in sombre dark woodwork, the Gospel illustrations in leaded stained glass, the brass cross suspended overhead like a giant draftsman's tool, a pattern of rectitude. The Yankee eulogist winced, swallowing his disappointment at his jest's miscarrying. He hurried on: "Jane brought to the marriage an ease with Boston ways, an impudent wit, a dazzling smile, and a wicked sense of humor—her puns!—that swept into the well-stocked chambers of my old friend's staid life like a gust of April air when in the days of our youth the maids would energetically throw open the windows for spring cleaning." He reared back in the pulpit, tucking back his shoulders, to gauge the reaction to *this* sally. It fascinated Alexandra to see how the courtly oldster, with his long beak and crest of fresh-cut white hair, preened on the fact of his own continuing survival as he gaily danced on the edge of gossip and scandal. In a gentler tone, confidingly leaning into a patent untruth, he told the congregation, "The harmony and affection instantly kindled between Jane and her mother-in-law was beautiful to behold and to feel in their shared home, as within a castle doubly secured by the rule of two magnificent queens." He bowed his head to the front pew. "We all unite in sympathy, Iona, with you in your recent double loss—a beloved only son and a daughter-in-law who came to be loved as a daughter—knowing that in your century of gracing this Earth you have acquired strength and wisdom enough to sustain not only your own soul in this needful hour but that of your kin as well. Bless you, my dear treasured friend."

Iona Tinker, whose antique first name Alexandra had not heard before, sat unflinching in the front pew, rigidly enduring this stately tirade, in her weeds of faded, brittle silk, beside Jane's two neglected children and their self-effacing spouses and a few youthful samples of the third generation and even some restless infants from the fourth. The tribe continues, though its individual members fall.

And as to Jane, their wicked witchy Jane, the more she was extolled, the more absent she seemed—a little square hole in the church's atmosphere, suspended above their heads like the rectilinear cross. The ideally unnoticed suspension wires stretching from its arms to the dark-stained ceiling beams caught accidental bits of light like the brief streaks of shooting stars. The suave eulogist reluctantly wound up, searching in vain for the perfect word to close Jane's case. He had not liked her, it was clear to Alexandra. Nobody here had. She was of their sort and yet not, and that was worse than being a raw outsider, anxious to conform, easy to excuse. Only other witches could have liked Jane, in their collusion of rebellion against the oppressions of respectability. And the eulogist had failed to mention the one passion that had lifted her into selflessness—her music, her cello, the pain in her left, fingering hand.

With relief the congregation fell back into the Book of Common Prayer. The voices rose in petition, a monotonously growling beast snapping up each morsel of the martyred Cranmer's phrasing. The Prayers of the People were led by Roscoe's pale, frail wife, hitherto invisible. Her reedy voice bored in with the insistence of a weevil's jaws: "Lord, who consoled Martha and Mary in their distress; draw nearer to us who mourn for Jane, and dry the tears of those who weep."

"Hear us, Lord."

"You wept at the grave of Lazarus your friend; comfort us in our sorrow."

"Hear us, Lord."

"You raised the dead to life; give to our sister Jane eternal life."

"Hear us, Lord."

"You promised Paradise to the thief who repented; bring our sister Jane to the joys of Heaven."

"Hear us, Lord."

Alexandra's eyes burned and watered as her tongue and throat joined in the huge, futile chorus. Jane was gone; she, Alexandra, would be next. Already, from the remote provinces of her body, her numb feet and the disused interior of her womb, bulletins foretelling her death kept arriving; fits of dizziness and nausea signalled that her organic fabric was rubbing thin; the wall between inner and outer had become permeable. Tears broke down her face.

At her side, Sukie asked in a whisper, "What does going

'from strength to strength' mean? 'In the life of perfect service'?"

Sukie had never had a churchgoing husband; both Monty Rougemont and Lennie Mitchell had been modern men, dapper scoffers at otherworldly consolations. Whereas Alexandra's Oswald Spofford had been dutifully devout, serving on church councils and bribing the children to go to Sunday school, and Jim Farlander had some supernatural inklings left over from his days as a peyote-smoking hippie. "It's about the levels of Heaven," she answered, as the first line of the concluding hymn, "Morning Is Breaking," surged on all sides in the uplifted voices of elder Brookline. "Life goes on," she quickly continued to explain. "Change goes on. Heaven is not static. It's a place where things continue to happen, like Earth."

At the service's conclusion, as they filed out, Sukie asked, like an annoying child, "What does it mean, 'The peace that passeth human understanding'?"

"Obviously, dear, it means it's beyond understanding. Use your head, for Heaven's sake." Was this to be their new relationship, mother and querulous child? Embarrassment over her tears for Jane, which Sukie must have noticed, had shortened Alexandra's temper.

"There's a reception afterwards, in the parish house," the younger, rebuked woman said. "Do you want to go to it?"

"No. Do you?"

"Yes," Sukie said.

"Why? Haven't you had enough of this scene?"

"No." She tried to explain: "Churches interest me. They're so fantastic. And suppose the silver man comes?"

"Silver man?"

"That Jane saw, outside Doc Pat's."

"Sweetie, please don't go crazy on me." Yet Alexandra allowed Sukie to follow the drift of the crowd, not down the aisle to the narthex but through a double swinging door to one side of the chancel, down a linoleum-floored hall past the choir-robing room and some ministerial offices, on into the parish hall, already a sociable hubbub. There were more people than had been privileged to gather at the Tinker mansion. Mrs. Tinker, closely tended by the dapper paid minion whose snotty telephone voice offended Alexandra years ago, formed a reception line with Roscoe Smart and his skeletal sister Mary Grace. Again, Alexandra thrilled to the touch of the old lady's warm brown hand, the four fingers laid parallel into her palm like pretzel sticks. Beyond, a long table covered with a white cloth held plates of cookies and watercress and pimiento-spread sandwiches from which the bread crust had been trimmed, and a crystal bowl filled with a punch the chemical color of lemon Jell-O. The parish hall extended, in subdued form, the ecclesiastical mode of the church itself: dark-stained beams crisscrossed overhead, creating triangular cobweb sites.

Alexandra felt Sukie stiffen at her side. The younger widow drew closer to say, "He's here, too."

"Who? Where?"

"Don't turn your head. Just casually slide your eyes to your left, to about two o'clock."

"I see him, I guess. He looks out of place, and nobody is talking to him. Who is he?"

"Lexa, it's obvious. Like Jane said. It's Chris Gabriel."

"Who? Oh. The brother. I can hardly remember what he looked like."

"He was never with us," said Sukie, whispering with a conspiratorial urgency to which Alexandra, older and weighted down with the glossed-over horror of Jane's eternal absence, found it difficult to respond. "He never used the hot tub, or danced to Darryl's music, or even ate with us."

"Those lovely fiery meals of Fidel's," Alexandra musingly recalled. "Hot tamales, and enchiladas, and that salsa that made your eyes water."

"He was a lazy late adolescent then," Sukie went on. Her breathing was affected by a draft from this door that had excitingly opened, showing deep stairs down into the past. "Not so much insolent as bored, reading magazines and watching *Laugh-In* in another room. Now he's *here*. The nerve. I'm going to talk to him."

"Oh, *don't*," Alexandra instinctively said. "Let's let it alone." This ill-fated attempt to relive what was gone, to dig up its mostly imaginary magic—wouldn't they both be better off just taking the little bit that was left of their lives, their widow's mite, and retiring with it to their corners of Connecticut and New Mexico?

But Sukie had already aimed herself toward the intruder, dodging around knots of Tinker acquaintances to stand in his presence. The boy, as she still thought of him, had grown taller, or else she had slightly shrunk, her bones eroding as well as her lungs. She tipped her face up toward his like a sunbather determined to catch the day's last rays. "Don't I know you?" she asked.

"It's possible," he said. His voice had the hollow ring of a man who has found for his life's rationale no deeper basis than his own attractiveness, rather than any self-forgetful passion or profession. In this he reminded her of Darryl Van Horne, in the same way that this parish hall echoed the showy architecture of a church.

"You're Christopher Gabriel."

"Actually, Mrs. Rougemont, I use my stage name now— Christopher Grant."

"How nice. After Cary, or Ulysses S.?"

"Neither. A long first name goes better with a monosyllable, and I got sick of people saying 'Blow, Gabriel, blow.' "

"My name isn't Rougemont, either—not for over thirty years. I married a man called Lennie Mitchell."

"What happened to him?"

"He died, Christopher."

"People do. Hey, I'm sorry about your friend Jane, by the way."

She took in a gulp of breath to say, "I don't think you are. In fact, I think you killed her."

He blinked—his eyelashes were as pale as his curly, silvery hair—but otherwise registered no reaction. "How would I have done that?"

"I don't exactly know. But she felt it. Some kind of a spell. She kept getting shocks."

He smiled, without cracking the glaze of his studied, self-congratulatory diffidence. "How curious," he said. His lips had a pouting, bee-stung quality more appropriate to a pampered female. The sky-pure blue of his eyes was clouded by their being deep-set and a bit close together, under silvery-blond eyebrows beginning to grow bushy and tangled in the way of middle-aged men. He would be about Tommy Gorton's age—no, a bit younger. He had nothing of Tommy's inflamed, sun-battered complexion. Rather, he had a pristine indoor pallor, as of one whose plunge into life had still to be taken. He had retained the smooth imperviousness, the untouchable hostility, of youth. He could not resist showing off, volunteering, "Mr. Van Horne, before he pulled one of his disappearing acts, taught me some spooky stuff about electricity. But you'd never get the cops to listen. As far as they're concerned, your old pal died of natural causes. So will you. So will I."

It was as if there were, Sukie felt, a long icicle within him which came over into her body, thrilling her, steeling her, instilling in her the recklessness of a war to the death. "Will I be next?" An onlooker among the mourners, seeing her eager smile and rapt expression, and the flirtatious angle at which she held her unnaturally red head, would have imagined her excitement to be amorous.

Chris hesitated, and lowered his eyelids as if in shame. "No," he said. "The fat one will be next. Of the three of you, you were nicest to me. You talked to me sometimes, instead of just rushing into Darryl's party mode. And you were nice to my sister. You used to take her to Nemo's for coffee."

"I'm not sure I was nicer, I'm just more extroverted than Alexandra. It was my habit, from being a reporter, to talk to people."

"You were *nicer*," he said stubbornly. He was still a young man in the way his conversation didn't branch, didn't send out probes and amusing side shoots, but stuck to the same few thoughts, the same limited asexual agenda. He couldn't have lived with Darryl, that ramshackle magus of jubilant digression, very long.

"Tell me about you and Darryl," Sukie commanded, in her perky, shameless interviewer's manner, with a grin that exposed her prominent front teeth up to the gums. "Where did you both go, after Eastwick?"

"New York, where else? He had a place up on the West Side, a block from the river. Kind of crummy. I thought at least he'd be on the East Side. Most of the art he had in the Eastwick house wasn't even his, he had it on trial."

"What did you *do* all day?"

Christopher Gabriel shrugged and reluctantly moved his bee-stung lips. "Oh, you know. Chilled out. Smoked dope. He was out a lot. He had a lot of creepy friends. I hung around the apartment at first, scared to go out, watching TV. Then I got the idea from watching the soaps of being an actor. I had turned eighteen, and back then that was old enough to handle liquor, so I got jobs waitering and with catering services so I could pay for acting school."

"You poor thing. You did this without Darryl's help?"

"He put me on to a few guys. But they just mostly wanted me to hustle. Nobody knew about AIDS yet, but I didn't want to be a hustler. I could see that was the way straight down. Darryl's way of loving somebody was to see them go to Hell. He had a lot of ideas about acting and would spiel on about the demonic side of it, all this theory, but I stuck pretty much to my own plan. The acting school I went to was very practical—hold your head like this, project from the diaphragm. Once I began to get jobs he'd try to hit me up to help with the rent. I moved out finally. He was a leech."

"Where is he now?"

"Who knows? All over the map. We lost touch."

"So you've been hexing us all on your own?"

Christopher knew he was being led on; his lips did not want to move at all. "Who says I'm hexing you?"

"You did. Just now."

"Well, maybe so."

"Well, congratulations."

"Darryl showed me the general approach on electromagnetism, but I did some refining on my own. He was full of ideas, but not so hot at seeing things through."

"Tell me," Sukie teased, "the antidote. How to reverse it."

"Come on. I wouldn't give you that, even if there was one. There isn't one. It's like life. One-way." He was looking around now, guiltily, like a boy getting bored and restless in the grip of an inquisitive adult. For immature people, Sukie thought, it's a kind of magic not to tell about themselves. Like savages and being photographed. Anything you let out, the world will use against you.

"Why do you hate us so?" she asked. "All these years later."

She had side-stepped, to make him look her in the eye; sky-blue rays shot from his deep sockets, from beneath eyebrows beginning to be shaggy. The hair of his head, curly soft blond as she remembered it, had become thick stiff waves dyed platinum. "There was nobody for me," he brought out, in a voice at last with emotion in it, "like Jenny. From when I was a baby on. She was nine years older than me. She was a perfect person. Once our parents began to fight and get estranged, she was my mother." His bee-stung lips trembled.

"She died, Chris," Sukie said, "like you said, a natural death. What makes you think we had anything to do with it?"

"I know you did," he said stubbornly, looking away from her ardent gaze. "There are ways to direct Nature. The currents of it."

The mourners around them were beginning to drift away, toward the exits and the liberating out-of-doors. Alexandra came up to Sukie, blurting, "I've just been entangled with the most im*pos*sible man, that pompous snob who eulogized Jane, if that's what you call it. He was telling me all about his and the Tinkers' joint ancestry; he was Nat's second cousin, and the old lady's step-nephew, as if that would turn me on. He had the crust to invite me out to dinner, having just shit all over Jane with his innuendo, but I told him we had to get back to Rhode Island. Don't we?"

She had not seen, or had chosen to ignore, the silvery man standing there. When Sukie turned back to him to make introductions, and to make the conversation a three-cornered inquisition, he was not there; he had melted away.

On the drive south to Eastwick—Route 9 to 128, 128 to 95, 95 through Providence to Route One and the western shore of Narragansett Bay—Sukie described her conversation with Christopher Gabriel, omitting only his announcement that the next victim was "the fat one." But Alexandra seemed to sense it, and the gap in Sukie's story hung between them as one roadway slid into the next, concrete into asphalt and back.

"Electromagnetism?" she did ask.

"He said Darryl showed him some stuff about it, through which I guess he was giving Jane those shocks she complained about. But to be realistic it wasn't those that killed her; it was her aneurysm."

"A spell utilizes a tendency the body already has," Alexandra suggested.

"He did say something about taking Nature and altering the current of it."

Alexandra said to herself as much as to Sukie, "I know what in my body he'd use."

Sukie didn't want to know, but had out of courtesy to ask, "What, honey?"

"Cancer. My fear of it. Fear of something makes it happen. Like when a person afraid of heights walks a narrow plank he tenses up so much he makes a misstep and falls off. Your body is cooking up cancer cells all the time. With so many cells, some are bound to go bad, but our defenses—antibodies and macrophages—surround them and eat them up, for a while. Then the body gets tired of fighting, and the cancer gets ahead. You try to stop thinking about it, but you can't—your whole system bubbling up with these evil cells. Skin cancer. Breast cancer. Liver cancer, brain cancer. Cancer of the eyeball, of the lower lip if you're a pipe smoker. It can happen anywhere. The whole thing is like an enormous computer: one bit, one microscopic transistor, goes offline and takes the whole computer with it. Tumors have the ability to create their own veins and arteries, to commandeer more and more blood!"

Sukie felt Alexandra's monologue growing under her, a monstrous damp growth penetrating the orifices she sat on. "Lexa, *please*," she said. "You're venting. You're talking yourself into hysteria."

"Hysteria," the other lightly mocked. "You sound like a man, putting women down because we have wombs. The most horrible thing about cancer is how much like having a baby it is, growing inside you whether you like it or not. Remember how it felt—throwing up, needing so desperately to sleep? The baby's body was fighting with ours for nutrients. The baby was a parasite, just like a cancer."

Sukie was silent, absorbing this ugly parallel. "I'm wondering," she said, "if you shouldn't go back to New Mexico, to be safe from us. Us Easterners." The idea was beginning to grow inside her of saving Alexandra, even at the cost of sacrificing herself.

Alexandra laughed, showing her reckless side. "I'm not going to let some queer kid scare me away. We've paid two months' rent, and I let some old friends from Denver have my place for August. They love the opera in Santa Fe."

"He's not a kid," Sukie objected. "And I'm not sure how queer he is, or was. What I do know is that he has it in for us, and wants to kill us. He told me himself."

"Let him try. Men have had it in for women since time began, and we're still around. You could say he's right, we shouldn't have done that to his sister. All Jenny did was marry the man who asked her. That's all that most of us do." She fell silent while Sukie concentrated on getting off 95 and heading south. "Anyway," she resumed, "I can't leave Eastwick until I've made things better with Marcy. When I'm with her I turn into a supercilious nag. She accuses me of not caring enough about her and the children. She's right. I'm selfish. I cared more about those little clay bubbies I used to make than I did about my own flesh-and-blood children. The bubbies were *mine;* the babies were something Oz and Nature made me have. Right from the beginning, nursing the helpless little dear things, the flesh-and-blood babies, I felt taken advantage of. *Used.* I didn't *want* to be somebody else's milk wagon."

"You're too hard on yourself," Sukie said, closing her lips on the assertion in that adorable way she had, as if something delicious was dissolving in her mouth. "I watched you being a mother. You were quite loving. Giving your sandy children a hug at the beach and so on. Much better than Jane."

"That's one of the reasons I liked Jane—she was so bad she made me feel good about myself. She hated those kids of hers. You saw why—the two that showed up today."

"I thought they were very touching, really. They were repulsive, but unlike the two younger ones they *did* at least show up and go through the motions. Burying your mother: what a strange obligation. Society expects us to do it; we don't know exactly why, but the undertakers and clergypersons see us through it. We can't wrap our minds around what happens to us—these milestones. Weddings and funerals. Graduations and divorces. Endings. Ceremonies get us through. They're like blindfolds for people being shot by a firing squad."

Even Sukie, Alexandra thought, *is aging*. She studied the younger woman's profile as she drove the car; when she squinted at the road ahead, a fan of curving wrinkles reached back into the hairline above her ears. Her eyes had grown permanent lilac-tinted welts below them, and her teeth when she grinned revealed tiny dark gaps where her gums had receded from her eye-tooth crowns. Still, Alexandra loved her enough to touch her slender hand, bearing on its back not only freckles but blotchy liver spots as it rested lightly on the steering wheel. "What about you?" she asked. "Wouldn't you like to leave Eastwick and go back to Stamford? Jane's death casts a pall, doesn't it? To a Westerner like me, Eastwick is a kind of lark, but to you it's more of the same, just farther up the coast."

"No," Sukie said, grimacing into the blinding splash the sun, lowering in the west, threw onto the dirty windshield. "We'll both stay. I have nothing at home except Lennie's suits hanging in the closet. I haven't had the heart to take them to the Salvation Army. I'm thinking of eventually moving to New York. It's stupid for a single woman to be suburban. What would Jane want? She'd want us to stay. She'd say, *Ssscrew that sssilly Chriss. He always was a brat.*"

In the moment of mimicry Jane's voice had entered Sukie's mouth with an illusion of channelling that made both women snicker in alarm. Sukie's hand on the wheel flipped over to caress Alexandra's—a gesture of comfort confessing how vulnerable, how helpless in their bravado, the two damned souls were. Sukie said, "I didn't realize you had rented the house in Taos. Are you that hard up for money?"

"Jim left enough, but not much more. Everything costs more than it used to. Even clay."

Soon Sukie turned the BMW off Route One onto 1A. They passed through Coddington Junction and then picturesque Old Wick, a collection of Federalist houses clustered, as if to seek protection from their inexorable deterioration, around a rambling crossroads inn under brave new management, sporting fresh white paint, croquet wickets and lawn chairs on the lawn, and a grouted signboard promising in golden letters FINE DINING; then came Eastwick, and outer Orchard Road, and the crasser commercial note of the Stop & Shop in its struggling mall, a scatter of unappealing stores—picture frames, videos, health foods—inadequate to the vast, presumptuous imposition of asphalt on acres of land that can never grow sweet corn, potatoes, or strawberries again. The Unitarian church, with its squat octagonal tower topped by a copper weathervane of a cantering horse and top-hatted rider, appeared on the left, and on the right glimpses of saltwater—a luminous bile color—flickered between the trees, beyond the breakwater's rusty boulders. The backyards of Oak Street materialized, with their swing sets and beached dories. The blue marble horse trough lay ahead, sporting its tiny forest. Alexandra's weary heart quickened among the familiar shop fronts and clapboarded houses from earlier centuries; she had lived here, fully lived, with children and a husband and lovers and friends, although the plod of duties and errands and monthly bills to pay had in part concealed from her the bliss of those departed days. Here, now, the long daylight of June and July was giving way to August's gradual closing-down. It was after seven o'clock, dinnertime, and already the lamps behind the house windows seemed to burn from deeper within, more intensely. Long shadows crossed Dock Street from curb to curb. A more determined summertime mood animated the teen-agers in their scanty pale clothes; they clustered and chattered along the stretch of storefronts, under the spindly trees wound with white Christmas lights,

a little more loudly, more defiantly, squeezing the last allot-
ments of fun from the strengthening dusk. Along Oak and
Vane Streets, older citizens and visitors moved singly or in
couples with a deliberate, self-conscious leisure on the dark
Victorian lawns and the sidewalks, whose daytime pattern of
shade was, when the streetlamps came on, abruptly recast
into electric fragments and patches whose webby pattern of
leaf and branch trembled and swayed in the evening breeze
rising off the water.

"What do we need?" Sukie asked, having swerved into a
lucky parking spot near the Superette.

"Milk?" Alexandra answered. "Cranberry juice. Yogurt?"
It seemed they had been away such a long time, burying Jane
in Boston's precincts, that everything perishable in their
refrigerator would have spoiled. They dreaded returning to
the condo, just two of them.

"How about a frozen pizza to warm up in the microwave?"
Receiving no answer, Sukie decided, "I'll go in and see if I
get any inspiration." She slid out of the BMW and slammed
its expensive-sounding door. She loved displaying herself on
Dock Street.

Alexandra let her go into the Superette alone, feeling safer
sitting in the car, letting the downtown bustle flow over
her. The shop lights, fluorescent and neon, played eerily on
the teen-age faces flashing by—Eastwick's children, flaunt-
ing their growing power, ignoring the old woman sitting in
a parked car, vying for attention from their peers with
female shrieks and boisterous boyish jokes, testing freedom's
depths, licking and brandishing ice-cream cones from the
Ben & Jerry's that had replaced, in the row of merchants,
LaRue's Barbershop. *Little do they know,* Alexandra thought,
what lies ahead of them. Sex, entrapment, weariness, death.
She wished Sukie would stop parading her charms (her

orange hair with its sheen, her big curved teeth with their shine) in the garishly bright interior of the Superette and come drive them, the lonely two of them, down the beach road, the same road, minus about ten seaview McMansions, that, thirty years younger, she used to speed down in her pumpkin-colored Subaru to the beach or, her heart racing in tune with the engine, to the Lenox mansion, in the days when Darryl Van Horne lived there and every night was a party night whose opportunities might crack open the jammed combination-lock of her life.

Eastwick, like partly pretty towns all over New England, in attempting to attract tourists and keep residents entertained, crammed manufactured festivities into August, as if to make up for the month's lack of any festal holidays. The dropping of the two atomic bombs and the consequent end of World War II had never quite earned red numbers on the calendar. Instead, there were heavily promoted tours of the abandoned woolen mills, equipped as museums, amid the ranks of stilled machinery, with exhibit cases and enlarged photographs of the industrial past. In former farming communities, there were early harvest suppers and agricultural fairs, though the numbers of contenders for the Biggest Squash or Sleekest Hog dwindled every year, along with the entrants in the sheep-shearing contest and the mule pull. In once-Puritan settlements, first-period—pre-1725—houses were thrown open for a paid tour, and local spinsters and crones donned long skirts, lace-trimmed aprons, and linen caps to act as docents in their own antique homes. Antique fairs, book fairs, art fairs filled village greens with hopeful stalls and a friendly shuffle of bargain-hunters, trampling underfoot grass already flattened and brown. In

Eastwick, there were days of boat races, in a range of classes from manfully rowed double dories to wheel-steered yachts under full sail. On shore, to console children and land-lubbers, a merry little travelling carnival had been set up in the piece of land owned by the Congregational, now the Union, Church; the church trustees had acquired the land for expanded facilities that were never built. It was challenge enough, every five years, to give the grandiose existing edifice a coat of white paint and, every twenty, to repair its rotting steeple, battens, and sills.

There was no keeping Sukie away from bustle and bright lights, though Alexandra had returned from Jane's memorial service averse to both. The appliances in the condo, as she walked past them, gave her, if not a distinct shock, a tingling unease that reached deep into the depressed circuits of her being. Standing next to the telephone pole in front of the post office one day on Dock Street, trying to remember what errands, other than mailing a birthday card and small check to her Seattle grandson, had brought her downtown—such lapses of short-term memory were more and more frequent, alarming her with the sudden blanks in her mind, obliterating what a half-hour ago had been glaringly obvious and absurdly banal—she had been nearly knocked flat by an unseen spark that scooped out all the muscles on that side of her. Though none of the several people around, intent on their own errands, noticed the phenomenon, it penetrated her like a shouted insult, and left her infected with the nausea of a sudden swerve. The mundane sunny scene around her—glaring sidewalk, fleshy people in summer shorts casting squat self-important shadows, wilting zinnias in beds next to the concrete post-office steps, the American flag hanging limp on its pole overhead—seemed abruptly distasteful, like a rich dessert being offered up for breakfast.

This distaste stayed with her the rest of the day. She was shaken. Her appetite had already been declining. When food was set before her, her body had trouble remembering what purpose it served. Her saliva glands were phasing out.

At the carnival, the false excitement—the shrieks from the Whirlabout, as the circular cages at the end of their long tilting arms flung the willing captives this way and that; the more sedate frights occasioned by the spasmodic rotation of the Ferris wheel, stopping at the bottom to change passengers while all the other seats swung, springing panicky cries from those hoisted topmost into the cool night—pressed on her, dazed her, chewed and nibbled to nothing the still core that had always before confidently welcomed surprise and fresh sensation. She felt local eyes flicking toward her with suspicion; people sensed her estrangement now or recalled her evil reputation from decades ago.

Sukie chided her: "Get *with* it, Gorgeous. This is meant to be fun."

"Fun. I wonder if I'm not beyond fun."

"Don't *say* that. Look at all the happy children."

"They look ghastly to me. They shouldn't be up so late, and they know it." Children were burying their faces in paper cones of cotton candy, and trying to open their mouths wide enough to bite through the thick glaze of candy apples. Grown-ups were barking at them, urging them to take some death-defying ride, to take a gamble on some cruelly rigged game of ring toss, denying them the safety and silence of their own beds, bewitching them with ridiculous hopes of something happening if they stayed up late enough. Alexandra used to feel that way, in this very town, but that was ages ago. Another person, some other woman, with a sounder stomach and more buoyant attitude, had partaken of nocturnal expectations.

"Look!" Sukie exclaimed. "There's Chris Gabriel!"

"Quick! Let's hide."

"Why? There's no hiding now. You yourself said, 'Screw him.' "

"Did I say that? It was you, being Jane."

The apparition, in white painter pants and a T-shirt bearing a slogan, came toward them, beckoned by Sukie. He looked young in the carnival lights, his face angelically smooth, his lips plump and pouty, his curly platinum hair thinning only in the back and in two gleaming swaths at his temples, framing a widow's peak from which a single trained lock hung limp. He suggested a taller James Dean, if Dean had lived into middle age. With that movie star's slant half-smile, he asked, "How's it going, ladies?" Though his waist had thickened over the years and his face had coarsened, his voice was light and lazy, like that of the teen-ager they dimly remembered. The lettering on his T-shirt said in two lines, the first green and the second black, BURN CORN, NOT OIL. His presence had an odd reflective quality, it seemed to Alexandra, as if from an opaque coating of vaporized mercury. It was hard for her to see in him a purpose as earthy as seriously intending her death. Yet the rumor of it gave them a sort of erotic connection, a potential for affectionate teasing which Sukie short-circuited with an anxious, jealous voice.

"We're doing quite well," she answered, tucking her hair behind her ears and tilting back her face to look him in the eye.

"Great," he said, slightly startled by her engaged tone.

"What are you doing here?" Sukie went on. "Are you still staying with that odious Greta Neff?"

"Yeah. Kind of."

Meaning, Alexandra supposed, that Greta was only "kind

of" odious. She spoke up, in a gentler tone: "Mr. Grant, are you staying in Eastwick for the rest of the summer?"

The young-old man, this lean boy turned flabby avenger, gazed upon her through irises of an electric pallor, rimmed in a darker blue. She saw that he could indeed do her serious harm, the way an innocent creature like a bear might, or a machine in operation, or a law of blind Nature. "I have some business I want to finish," he said, mildly enough. "It may take a while."

"You don't seem," she said, hoping to smile away how shaken his deadly, soulless gaze had left her, "to be getting out into the sun much. By August here, you should have a tan."

"I use a number-forty-five sunblock," he told her. "You should, too. Skin cancer is no joke."

"At my age," Alexandra said, quite gaily, considering how she hated this topic, "it almost is, there are so many worse kinds."

He got serious with her, assuming a professional air. "For television work, they give you the amount of tan they want. Directors hate it if you show up sunburned on Monday. It doesn't cover. If you want a tan, buy it in a bottle, they tell you, especially the actresses. In porn shoots, out in the Valley, the feeling was that bikini shadows on the actresses would get the viewer thinking about what they looked like in bathing suits, who they had gone to the beach with, what they had in the lunch hamper, what normal women they were, all of which tends to kill the fantasy."

Sukie cut in, her voice edgy. "And not enrich the fantasy? Make the girl realer?" *She shouldn't keep trying to protect me*, Alexandra thought. *I can protect myself, if I think it's worth doing.*

Christopher seemed dubious. "The guys who watch this

stuff on video are pretty simple. They don't want a ton of reality."

"Do you know a lot of porn actresses?" asked Sukie.

"A couple. They're nicer and more average than you'd think. A lot of them are into yoga. It's slimming, and uplifts their spiritual side. It helps them relax between sessions. Everybody says how hard it is for men doing porn—*un*hard, I should say—but it's not a piece of cake for women, either. Those hot lights, all these jaded grips and assistants watching. The women who get ahead in the business are those who don't let their boredom dominate them."

Alexandra asked him, flirting to keep down her terror—for the eternity of death had come out from behind the wan bustle and inane scratchy music of the fair to confront her with its endless leaden reality—"Is this one of the kinds of acting you've done?"

His sullied skyey gaze, as he turned it upon her again, seemed gentler this time, contemplating her like a deed already done, achieved in his mind. "Maybe," he said. "If it was, I wasn't very good at it. You got to like pussy a *lot*. And the jobs that weren't fly-by-night, done in a motel room with a handheld videocam, are out on the West Coast, like I said, in the Valley. I didn't want to leave New York. You get brainless if you do."

With one of her little gasps, catching at Alexandra's heart, Sukie asked, "You don't like women *at all*?"

"I said a *lot*. To do porn you either like them a lot or hate them. Hate isn't bad, for the purpose. They're the stars, you're the meat. I didn't feel strongly either way. The directors have told me that's my limitation. I'm not talking just porn now. I'm talking acting in general. All the women are so narcissistic and pushy, compared with my sister."

"She was lovely," Sukie said quickly.

"So bright and sweet," Alexandra agreed. "That was so unfortunate, what happened to her."

"Yeah," he said, a little stunned by so much agreement.

"Listen," Sukie said. "Chris. Why don't you come by for a drink sometime?" Now Alexandra was stunned. Sukie hurried on, "I bet you'd love seeing what they've done to the Lenox place, inside. Love it," she qualified, "or hate it."

"I don't know," he began.

"We'll lay in champagne. It'll be like the old days, with Darryl."

"I don't drink," he said. "Hangovers aren't worth it for me. They get into your skin tone. You begin to look slack."

"Then come for *tea!*" Sukie cried, becoming, in Alexandra's view, something of an embarrassment, her voice gone strangely small and high, as if she were shrinking back into a girl inside her elderly body. "We'll make some wonderful herbal teas, won't we, Alexandra?"

"If you say so," she said, the intractable fact of death still stuck at the back of her throat.

"Next Tuesday," Sukie pursued. "Tea for three, at four. Four-thirty. You know where we are, don't you? Second floor, the entrance at the parking lot out behind."

"Yeah, but," Chris began.

"No buts," Sukie insisted. "Be honest—it's very boring over there at Greta Neff's, isn't it? How much sauerkraut can you eat?"

"O.K.," he said to Sukie, giving in in the graceless limp way of a teen-ager. His gaze returned once more to Alexandra. "You know," he told her, "in a set-up like this"—he gestured to include the Whirlabout, the inflatable funhouse, the merry-go-round with its electric calliope and burden of groggy children, the naked colored bulbs strung from stall to stall—"taken apart and dragged to the next town and slapped back together by a bunch of rummies and drug addicts, there's a lot of loose connections. Have you felt any shocks yet?"

"A few small ones," Alexandra admitted. "I try to ignore them."

"There you are," he said, and forced a grin from those frozen pretty-boy lips, and repeated his sweeping gesture, expansive yet clumsy in a manner that brought back to the two women the spectre of his vanished mentor, Darryl Van Horne. "Electrons," he said. "They're everywhere. They're *existence*."

"Tell us about it Tuesday," Sukie said. "We're making a scene." The crowd was thinning, revealing sorely trodden grass—a flat salad of footprints in the garish electric light. The back of Christopher's T-shirt, they saw as he walked away into the melancholy last hour of the carnival, was lettered, in two lines, one green and one black, ELECT AL, DUMP W. It was an old T-shirt.

The two women huddled some moments, consulting, beside the cotton-candy stand. Above a streaked plastic tub a lanky mechanical arm kept twirling into being paper cones of spun sugar for which there were no more customers. The children had at last been taken home to bed; only bored high-school students remained, and grease-stained workmen furtively beginning to pack up. Alexandra asked Sukie, "What possessed you?"

"Well, why not? Get him close up, look him over. It's our only chance." She spoke in her reporter's voice, incisive yet dismissive, and her pursed mouth looked smug.

"He wants to murder us."

"I know. So he says. It could be just hot air, and Jane was a coincidence."

"I really should tell you, dearie, that I found you *very* irritating, the way you kept making up to him. You were much too cozy. What's *up* with you?"

Sukie's hazel eyes innocently widened; the reflected carnival lights swam in microcosm among the gold specks within her irises. She avowed, "Nothing but your best interests, darling."

"Mrs. Rougemont!"

This may have been the second time the voice had called out, but Sukie had been walking along Dock Street brooding upon the possibility of virtue and self-sacrifice (can there be such things? or is it all hypocrisy, self-serving in disguise?) and holding in her mind's eye the image of Debbie Larcom, her compact, precise white body inside the plain gray dress like a pale flame swathed in smoke.

Annoyed at being interrupted, she turned, expecting to see Tommy Gorton, overweight and borderline disreputable, bearing down upon her with hippie-length hair and unkempt beard, his missing tooth and maimed hand. But his beard and hair had been trimmed, and his bearing had become more erect. She caught a whiff of the arrogant youth she had known, in love with her but beyond that with his own beauty, which she had revealed to him.

"Tom," she said, with a carefully measured warmth. "How nice. How *are* you?"

He couldn't contain his good news; his red face was bursting with it. "Look," he said, and held up his poor wrecked hand. A few fingers of it slowly wriggled. "I have movement in it! There's some feeling."

"Why, that's lovely!" she said, taken aback. "What does your doctor say?"

"She says it's a miracle. She says to keep exercising it."

Sukie was distracted by the unexpected pronoun—but of course; many doctors now were women, including her own in Stamford. In the Middle Ages men had wrested the healing arts from witches, and now they were giving them back, since, as Nat Tinker had observed, the real money was no longer in medicine. Her own doctor, though taller and older, had the same smiling calm as Debbie Larcom, a self-contained ardor, as if the practice of virtue provided a sensual reward, like suckling a baby. Women were at last inheriting the world, leaving men to sink ever more abjectly into their fantasies of violence and domination.

Sukie said, "I'm so happy for you, Tommy." But her heart had long moved on from hopes of happiness with Tommy Gorton; he was, like the rather desperately beckoning shops on Dock Street and the glitter of saltwater sliding seawards at their backs, a remnant of past adventures, dear to her primarily because she had survived them, her basic bright pure self unscarred. "When did this start to happen?" she asked, to be polite, since Tommy clearly wanted much to be made of this development.

"That's the thing. About two weeks ago. I was sitting at home, watching some idiot celebrity game show on the boob tube while Jean was finishing up in the kitchen, when my hand began to tingle. It brought me right out of the chair; I hadn't felt anything in it for twenty-some years. Then, that night, there was this ferocious itching. It kept me from sleeping, but I didn't give a fuck. Something was *happening*. In the morning, I stared at it and thought I could make the fingers move, a little. And it seemed to me the alignment of the bones was better—more normal. And that's been the story every day since; every day, a little better. Yeah, there's pain. But it's a pain going somewhere. Already I can hold a fork with it. Look." He made a pinching motion, with his still-repulsive, purplish lumpy hand. Sukie was embarrassed by this interview, in the middle of a busy morning on Dock Street; but she had the impression that the passersby were deliberately ignoring them, having each heard Tommy tell his story before.

"The thing of it is," he was saying to Sukie, fixing her wandering gaze with his eyes, their whites reddened by age and drink and self-pity, "it had to be you. You and those others did something."

"What could we have done?" she asked. Images came to her from the far-off time when Jane was still alive—the three of them sky-clad at the summoning of the Goddess that Alexandra had arranged, in the circle of Cascade granules that formed the base of the cone of power; the tarot cards reluctantly turning to ash in the brass bowl; her choice of the Page of Coins, a simple-minded, conceited, beautiful yokel, and for lack of a better idea hastily asking Her to perform the impossible, a minute before Jane's mouth filled with blood and she whispered, "Shit. It *hurts*." Sukie stammered, semi-retracting: "Of course, I felt terrible it had happened to you, but—"

"I know you can't talk about it," Tommy said. "It's dark stuff. But—I hang around the fire station and hear the latest scuttlebutt—the paramedics who responded said the place had a funny smell to it, and the rug had just been vacuumed, and the victim's underpants were put on backwards. When I put two and two together, I damn near cried. In fact, I *did* cry. You were always so great to me."

"It was selfish pleasure, Tommy. You were beautiful."

Rather horribly, he took a step closer to her, there in broad daylight, dropping his voice so that no one passing would hear. "I still could be. After your doing this for me, forget what I said about Jean. She'll understand. And if she doesn't, she can stuff it. She's a cold bitch. She says everything I want in bed is against her religion."

He was offering himself, and his effrontery touched her, but even with two hands—and how complete could the healing be, bought with one tacky tarot card?—he was old news. She'd rather go down on Debbie Larcom, the black triangle where her white thighs joined. "No, Tommy, don't even say any more. We did our thing ages ago. It was a different time, a time for a lot of things. Now is a different time. I'm an old lady."

"You're still a knockout. I bet you're still—what did we used to call it?—crazy."

Somehow this allusion insulted her. Perhaps she was looking for an insult. "Not crazy enough to keep talking to you smack in the middle of town," she said. "Good-bye, Tommy. You and your lady doctor, take care of that hand."

Rebuffed, he shrank in her sight as if she had swooped into the air and were looking down from the height of a flagpole at this pathetic balding fisherman abandoned on a sidewalk bright with foreshortened summer people in skimpy play clothes.

Sukie and Alexandra were both so nervous getting ready for having Chris Gabriel to tea that they kept crossing paths in the condo, bumping into each other more than once. "Are you going to accuse him?" Alexandra asked, after one near-miss in the tiny kitchen, Sukie carrying a plate of carefully arranged Pepperidge Farm cookies, lemon-flavor and gingerbread men in artful alternation, and Alexandra moving in the other direction with a little Japanese bowl of dip, chopped mussels and crabmeat in mayonnaise, to be served with seaweed-flavored rice crackers available only in the under-patronized gourmet section of the Stop & Shop.

"I already did," Sukie replied. "After Jane's memorial service. He didn't deny it. He just didn't say how." She had suppressed Chris's telling her that "the fat one" was next; in suppressing this during the car ride home, she had begun to build a structure of thoughts and intentions hidden from her sister witch, as she had once hidden her masturbation and her determination to leave home from her parents, back in that stuffy brick semi-detached house in the little city like a dull-red nail at the end of a Finger Lake in west-central New York State. Holding back a growing part of herself made her parents seem contemptibly stupid, and though she could never allow herself to feel superior to Alexandra, it was true that, as her visions of virtue and self-sacrifice developed, the older witch seemed increasingly sleepy, absent-minded, and passive. She was like a big white grub paralyzed by a spider's sting. She was being eaten alive from within by tiny hatching spider babies.

"Don't ask how," Alexandra told her. "I can't bear to think of it. If we can visualize the method, we'll start doing it to ourselves."

This thought sounded bizarre enough to prompt Sukie to ask, "How *are* you, anyway?"

"Tired," Alexandra confessed.

"Don't you sleep?"

"I can hardly keep awake. Except at night. I get a few solid hours, and then am bolt awake. The peepers are so noisy, down by the pond. What do they find to say to each other all night? The moon overexcites them. It's so bright lately, the birds start chirping at three. I get up and look out the window and there it is, high above the trees, like some horrible white eye filling a peephole. All the world trying to sleep, and it's shining on and on, idiotically. It shows how little we matter."

"The moon is almost new now. Remember how it was just beginning to wane when we—"

"Let's not talk about it, please," Alexandra begged.

"—when we prayed to the Goddess," Sukie insisted on finishing, as if the Goddess had been Alexandra's own, unfortunate idea.

"What a bitch She turned out to be," the older woman admitted. "We'll never know what Jane's prayer was, that she got such an answer."

"Mine got an answer," Sukie confided. "I saw Tommy Gorton downtown last week, and his awful hand seems to be healing. He has feeling in it, and some motion. I don't know how much better it can get, but he was so full of beans about it he offered to fuck me."

"Really! Why didn't you tell me this before? It's thrilling!"

She had kept it to herself, Sukie supposed, because she had woven it into her private visions. The sorceresses still had hallucinatory powers of some sort. Sukie didn't want to remind Alexandra of her weakness for younger males, which might reveal her shadowy intention, her secret dream. She had a vision of an ideal young male, Actaeon or Hyacinthus, baring to the moon his pure naked chest, with its lovely, purely ornamental nipples. "I don't know," she answered evasively. "I didn't want to jinx it, and Tommy seemed so hopeful. I'm afraid the miracle won't go any further, like so many of them." Numbed, as if ever so slightly drunk, by her mythic vision, she moved to a window overlooking the parking lot and changed the subject: "I worry that the tide will be too high for Chris to get across the causeway."

"Chris, is it? Darling, the bank raised the causeway. Nobody would buy a condo they can't get to."

"There've been all these floods in the papers. Global warming, don't you hate it?" By pressing her cheek against the glass she can see the far corner of the causeway. Yes, steel-blue floodwaters appear to have covered it, but out-spreading ripples, making the marsh grass sway, suggest that a car has just passed.

"What did you say when Tom offered to fuck you?"

"I said 'no dice,' of course." Sukie regretted having let this other woman any distance whatsoever into her privacy; it embarrassed her that they had been sky-clad together a few weeks ago.

"Do you miss sex?" Alexandra abruptly asked from the sofa, where she had set herself, half-reclining like a Roman at a feast, before the carefully arranged hors d'oeuvres. "I find I don't. All that mess. Between me and Jim, it had got-ten pretty perfunctory, though, bless his sweet soul, he tried to make it still interesting for me."

"Me neither," Sukie lied.

Both of them started from their poses when the buzzer from the lobby at the base of the stairwell rasped. It was an unduly loud rasp, rude as a burglar alarm, but they had never learned how to moderate it; the bank, their landlord, cashed their checks, but dialing its number never uncovered a per-son, just a recording that offered a number of routes to an eventual non-responsive silence. The footsteps coming up the stairs were so bounding and youthful that it was another shock when the door opened on a city-soft, androgynous, middle-aged man, breathing hard.

"Sorry, sorry," he panted.

"You're not late," Sukie reassured him, though by Alexan-dra's wristwatch he plainly was.

"The causeway had water on it, the way it always used to," he continued, getting his breath back, "and I had to decide if I dared push through. I didn't want to drown that rattle-trap Honda of Greta's she let me borrow."

"That poor car must be on its last legs," Sukie said.

"All the more reason to be tender with it," he said, affecting a tone of gallantry, crossing to Alexandra as if moving through a stage direction, handing her a can of Planters salted cashews. "A hostess present."

"Hostess*es*," Sukie jealously hissed.

"Of course. Hostess*es*."

Alexandra asked from the sofa, "Did Greta know you're coming here?"

"She did. She does. And if I'm not back in two hours, she said she'll call the police. The dear girl feared I might come to harm." He had exchanged, momentarily, the surly, laconic bad manners of adolescence for a stagier diction left over, no doubt, from his stints in afternoon soaps, with their airless studio acoustics and meticulously groomed versions of everyday costume. He had donned for this occasion white, brass-studded jeans, L.L. Bean boat moccasins, a Listerine-blue T-shirt saying *Mets* in an ornate script, and a yellow cashmere V-neck sweater draped around his shoulders, the sleeves lightly knotted at his throat. He looked around him and, reverting to boyishness, exclaimed, "Weird! This used to be just space, where Darryl had his high loud-speakers in the big hot-tub room, with the skylight that rolled back to show the stars."

Sukie said, "You can still see some of the hardware, in what was Jane's room. They just painted it the same color as the walls."

Mentioning Jane changed the tone of the occasion. Sukie stopped herself from chattering on, her lips ajar as if stuck on a thought, and Christopher looked down at the wine-colored carpet and actually blushed.

"Tea," Alexandra reminded them, seeing that she was in charge of these two children. "Christopher: regular tea with caffeine—we have Lipton and English Breakfast—or herbal? We have chamomile, Sweet Dreams, or Good Earth green tea, with lemongrass."

He said, "I don't do herbal, thanks—too funky—and I can't take caffeine after two in the afternoon. Even a nibble of chocolate keeps me up all night."

"So much for tea, then," Alexandra concluded.

"What else have you got to drink?" Christopher asked.

"Wine?" Sukie's voice sounded shy, tentative. "It's been opened, but has a screw-top."

"What color?" he asked Sukie.

"Red. Chianti."

"What brand?"

"Something Californian. Carlo Rossi."

"Oh boy. Giant economy size."

"Alexandra picked it out."

"You ladies don't exactly pamper yourselves, do you?"

Alexandra intervened, speaking to Sukie as if this man weren't here. "Why are you knocking yourself out for this brat? We said tea; tea is what I'm going to have. He can have a glass of water if he's so fussy."

"A spot of Scotch with the water would be even nicer," Christopher conceded, in the more carrying voice he must use on television.

When has he last acted? Alexandra asked herself. *This is a pathetic has-been, or never-has-been.* Yet here he was, a guest of sorts. His announced intention to kill them had created an intimacy.

"I'll look for some," Sukie said, servilely.

While she was heard opening drawers and closet doors in Jane's windowless back room, politeness compelled Alexandra to make small talk: "We don't drink much any more. I know we used to, when you knew us before."

"It was horrible," he petulantly told her, "listening to the bunch of you, getting sillier and louder and then starting to shriek. The shrieking, the horrible laughter. How could I sleep?"

"I'm sorry—thinking about you wasn't on our agenda. But now, no, drinking can be a trap for widows. We're trying to prolong our lives."

"Good luck," he said, giving her a theatrical sidelong glance—as if in a zoom-lens close-up, while the background organ music lifts and shudders to emphasize a portent.

Sukie triumphantly, looking flushed and overeager and adorable, brought back a pint bottle of Dewar's Scotch. "Found it! That sneaky Jane, it's almost all drunk! She never offered any to us!"

In a mutter of terse inquiries—"Ice? Water? How much? That enough?"—Sukie with a heavy hand concocted two Scotches-on-the-rocks, while Alexandra stubbornly, disapprovingly poured herself tea. She had decided on Sweet Dreams, wondering what it would taste of. It tasted of nothing. It tasted of water too hot to drink.

"Have a cookie," she urged Christopher, holding out the carefully arranged plate.

"Please. Carbos and sugar. I should lose ten pounds even so."

"I think a flat stomach on a man is repulsive, past a certain age," Sukie said. "In Stamford you see all these exercise-conscious guys who think they have to look trim in business suits, and after a certain age they begin to look preserved, like mummies. They haven't let the male body do its natural evolution."

Alexandra, irritated by Sukie's anxious-to-please chatter, addressed Christopher: "You were going to tell us about electrons."

The topic lit him up; the man shed his stagy inertia and made jerky, excited gestures to go with his exposition. As he talked, he more and more resembled Darryl Van Horne—the explosive, ill-coördinated gestures, the tumbling words, the yearning for a theory that would let him master the universe, wresting it from the Creator's hands. "They're *amazing*," he said. "They're *every*thing, just about. Take a current of one ampere—guess the number of electrons flowing past a given point in one second. One measly second. Come on—guess."

"A hundred," Alexandra said truculently.

"Ten thousand," said Sukie, trying harder to play the game.

"Hold on to your hats, ladies—six-point-two-four-two-oh to the eighteenth power—that is, over *six quintillion*! In a cubic inch of copper, there are one-point-three-eight-five to the twenty-fourth—that is, one and a third, more or less, *sep*tillion. Now take hydrogen, the simplest atom, one proton and one electron, in perfect balance, though the electron is only one-thousand-eight-hundred-thirty-seventh as heavy. But boy, are they strong! Their negative electrostatic force would instantly tear apart any piece of copper big enough to be seen, if it weren't for the equal positive charge of the proton in the atom." His hands, plump and unmuscular but more human—skin and wrinkles and hair—than Darryl Van Horne's had been, enacted in air the violent tearing motion. "How about that? That crummy old brass bowl on the table there wouldn't last a nanosecond without its protons and neutrons. Neither would we. That's what I'm saying. We're all full of electrons, chock-a-block full. We're dynamite, potentially."

Sukie and Alexandra had been so forcefully struck by his demonic resemblance to Darryl Van Horne that they had hardly heard what he said. Quintillions, septillions, super-super-zillions—what did such numbers mean, when there was only one of each of them? One life, one soul, one go.

"The proton happens, electrostatically," Christopher went on, wiping with his thumb and middle finger some saliva from the corners of his lips, "to attract an electron *exactly* as much as electrons repel each other. *Exactly*. Otherwise, there would be no universe. Not a particle, not a shred of matter, just a chaotic high-energy seethe—the Big Bang needn't have bothered to happen. God could have just kept sitting on His hands. What it adds up to is, if there's an excess of electrons in a body, or of protons, they need to go elsewhere, and there's an electric *charge*. If there's less electrons than there should be, there's a positive charge. If it's protons, there's a negative. In air, the readjustment is called a spark; when you're one of the bodies, there's a shock. Not a pleasant feeling, I hear. Over time it does things to you. You run on electricity; your brain runs on it, your heart, your muscle responses. All matter consists of electrons and atomic nuclei—protons and neutrons, made up of up and down quarks. Neutrinos, yes, they exist, but just barely, and muons and tau particles even less so—they're unstable. That's all, folks. Electrons are everywhere—currents and potential currents are everywhere. So, if you get my drift, it takes very little to nudge the currents one way or another."

He looked at them expectantly. "It's like love," Sukie suddenly announced. "A force that permeates the universe."

"She's such a romantic," Alexandra apologized.

Christopher frowned, the flow of his discourse impeded by these female interventions. "Love's something else. It doesn't exist the way electrons do. It doesn't exist independent of our animal behavior, with the sex drive."

"You loved your sister, Jenny," Sukie pointed out.

It seemed to Alexandra that he blushed, as when Jane had been mentioned and he looked bashfully down at the carpet the color of wine. "I was dependent on her," he said. "We had lousy parents."

"Your father was a sweet man. So naïve. So needy."

"Sukie." Alexandra's tone rebuked the younger woman for sentimentally displaying her intimate knowledge of a lover, Christopher's father, unhappily driven to his death. "Let him finish. About electrons," Alexandra said.

"I don't want to tell you too much," their guest said. He sipped his Scotch. "Darryl—Mr. Van Horne—"

"We know who you mean, Mr. Grant," said Alexandra, with a touch of asperity. She could see the Scotch affecting the man's manner, increasing his confidence, his arrogance, his lazy male ease. They had only promised him tea, tea that she alone was drinking, even though it had no taste and was rapidly turning tepid.

Christopher's eyebrows, coarser than the silvery-blond pencil-lines of his teen years, bobbed up and down snobbishly. His plump lips crinkled as if to express, to a phantom other male presence in the room, his painfully felt superiority to their female company. He continued, "So, given the ubiquity and practically infinite number of electrons, they are not hard to play with. You don't even need wires to contain electromagnetic fields; Maxwell theorized as early as 1864 that the field around a displacement current is as valid and measurable as the ones around a wire, and Hertz and his oscillator in the 1880s measured the speed and length of the waves. The speed was the same as the speed of light, which showed that they were a form of light, or vice versa. The length, well, as even you probably know, where the waves were long enough, not just millimeters between crests but meters and *kilo*meters, you get radio waves; you get the wireless telegraph and radio, you get radar and television. *Now*," he went on emphatically, seeing the women about to raise questions or change the subject, "our old friend Darryl Van Horne was fascinated by Maxwell's central intellectual maneuver of considering electricity an incompressible fluid, which is a fantastic premise. It cannot be. But the equations worked out on this imaginary basis fitted perfectly the actualities of electromagnetic fields. This looping out of reality into fantasy"—he used his hands, in the wide way Darryl did, to render the trajectory—"and back again fascinated him. Another thing that seemed hopeful to him was the spookiness of quantum theory. The wave particle duality, the uncertainty principle, and the co-dependent polarization of two entangled particles, electrons or photons, so that measuring the spin of one ensures that the spin of the other will be complementary, instantly, even if they are light-years apart, raising the delicious possibility of teleportation transcending the speed of light—to Darryl these illogical apparent facts were like rough seams left on the underside of the fabric of, pardon the expression, Creation. They were gaps God couldn't cover. They could be exploited just as the defects of human perception and intuition could be exploited for the illusions of stage magic. But the magic would be real, just as wireless electricity is real. The quantum reality of particulate entanglement over a distance could be extended to the supra-particulate world as well. A cathode-ray oscilloscope, for example, can project a beam of electrons by means of horizontal and vertical metal deflecting plates. It can make a fluorescent material glow; it can also saturate a substance, including that of a human being, with excess electrons, giving it a negative charge, so it goes around like a wire with the insulation rubbed off."

Both women broke in with irrelevancies, as he knew they would. Sukie exclaimed, "Cathode, Cathar! The heresy at the root of romantic love! You're still talking about love!"

And Alexandra: "That's what you did to Jane somehow! And now to us!"

Christopher blushed. "Not at all," he lied. To Alexandra he said, "There are technical difficulties I won't take your time explaining. Mr. Van Horne ran into them and wandered away, the way he did. He had so many ideas he could never see any of them through. And he kept moving, from one borrowed apartment to another, so he was always leaving equipment behind. That's why I broke with him, eventually—I needed stability. I was getting calls from producers, I was in my early twenties and what they call telegenic, I couldn't show up on the set after a night of his lousy carousing. He was always inviting people in—useless people, street people, vicious hangers-on and total phonies. When I'd complain, he'd say, 'They have souls,' as if that made it worthwhile. A lot I cared if they did or didn't. I just wanted some regular meals and the same bed to sleep in every night. He was restless. He wanted to go everywhere, the more outlandish the better—Albania, Uzbekistan, Zimbabwe, Fiji. Sudan. Iraq. He loved the names; he was good at learning languages, a smattering. The numbers, 'yes' and 'no.' China—he loved the idea of China. 'A billion and a quarter souls!' he'd say. 'On the verge of all the evils of capitalism, and not a god left to protect them!' "

"We all went there," Sukie told him. "It was fun, but still very innocent. Darryl will be bored silly."

"When we knew him," Alexandra pointed out, "he was so bored that *we* amused him. And then even the Neffs and the Hallybreads amused him."

"He had no discrimination," Christopher complained, looking down into his glass, empty but for two half-melted ice cubes. "Is there any more Scotch?"

"I'll give you the rest," Sukie said, selflessly pouring. "I'll switch to wine."

"So will I," Alexandra said. "Herbal tea is a delusion."

Christopher cocked an eye at this. "How's your appetite these days?"

"Not good," she admitted. "I feel a little queasy, especially in the morning and night. Are you doing it to me?"

He pulled at his drink before answering, thoughtfully licking his wet lips. "You're doing it to yourself," he said. "You feel guilty about my sister."

"And about my daughter, too," she agreed. "The one who lives right here in Eastwick. She never got away, poor thing. She got stuck here, looking for whatever it was I didn't give her."

"Attention," he proposed. "And rules to live by."

"Oh, *please*," Sukie protested. "Let's not be morbid. I'm getting hungry. There's no more seaweed crackers for the dip. I'll bring some from the kitchen. Stale Ritz will have to do." She left the room.

"People give themselves cancer," Christopher solemnly told Alexandra.

"I know," Alexandra said. "Out of guilt or stress."

"It's a proven physiological mechanism," he pontificated.

"Think of what Darryl would do if he were here!" Sukie called from the kitchen. "He'd play the piano!"

"We don't have a piano," said Alexandra. "We don't even have a record player." The very expression dated her, she realized.

"We have a radio," Sukie called. "For the weather, and the dreary news." She returned, bringing in her toothy bright smile and a rearranged platter. "Try WCTD," she directed. "Ninety-six-point-nine FM. They do jazz classics toward dinnertime."

It is curious, Alexandra reflected as the party changed gear, how much harder women work, when there are two of them, to please and flatter a man—even this man, a poor specimen by most standards, an overweight poof trying to wreak vengeance on elderly women on behalf of an insipid little sister long dead. *Long dead:* Jenny was a hollow husk, in her coffin in the new section of Cocumscussoc Cemetery, and a pale sly thing ever dimmer in Alexandra's memory: sly, shy, a bride of eternal night. For less than a second, like the quick opening of the circular leaves of a giant camera, or of the retractable ceiling that used to be up here, Alexandra looked into the depths of her own death, the pure everlasting nothingness of it. Then, mercifully, the shutter sucked shut again, tight as an anus. She was still in this brightly lit room.

Sukie had found WCTD, the signal from Ashaway strong enough to infuse the tinny small radio, whose primary service to the temporary tenants of the condo was to tell the time in large red numbers to anyone who, awakened by urinary pressure or the stirrings of a guilty conscience, shuffled bewildered through the living room in the hours after midnight. The music, smudged with static, tumbled out—the deep-voiced stride piano, the soaring clarinet, the rousing cornet, the drums romping through the insistent brass beat of the high-hat cymbal, each instrument, with a courtesy from an older era, taking its solo turn and then sinking back, to a spatter of applause, into the ensemble's jubilant restatement of the tune. *Yes, yes, yes,* the massed instruments kept chanting, until the last bar thudded to its end.

"Remember Darryl and his 'A Nightingale Sang in Berkeley Square Boogie'?" Sukie said in the moment's silence. "He was awful but could be so wonderful."

The radio spoke, not with the youthful voice of a university student but with the growl of an elderly jazz aficionado, a professor or janitor allowed to play disk jockey for a few evening hours. He gave the provenance (New Orleans, 1923, or Chicago, 1929, or Manhattan, 1935) and the band and soloists (King Oliver, Louis Armstrong, Benny Goodman) with a mournful gravity befitting a beautiful but bygone mode.

Christopher asked, "How did people ever dance to this stuff?"

"You Lindied," Sukie answered. "You jitterbugged. Shall I show you how?"

"No, thanks."

But another classic disk—"now, folks, for a change of pace, a honey-smooth swing number that topped the charts back in 1940, the great Glenn Miller's 'In the Mood'!"—was placed on the turntable twenty miles away, on the Connecticut line, and, by the miracle of electromagnetic waves, crackled irresistibly out of the tiny brown radio in Eastwick. Sukie stood close to the plaid recliner where the Gabriel boy sprawled, trying to ignore her.

"This way," she said, shifting her weight invitingly from foot to foot. "Watch what I do. Sidestep with the left foot, one-two, and then step in place with the right foot, three-four, toes and heel, and then swing the left behind the right, quick, and step in place with the right, and do it all again. *Dig* it. *Feel* it. Hear those trombones! In the *mood!* Do-dee-

*dah*duh! In the *mood!* Do-dee-*da*da!" Sukie stood there, shimmying and snapping her fingers opposite a nonexistent partner. Embarrassed for her, Christopher at last, as if hoisted by an invisible magnetic force, stood, and let her take his one hand and put the other behind her back in fox-trot position. "*Yes,*" she said, when he began stiffly to imitate her weight-shifts. "Don't be afraid of stepping on my feet, I won't let you. When I give your hand a little squeeze, push me away, and then let me come back to you. Remember, two beats on one foot, then quick with the left foot behind. Wonderful! You're *get*ting it!"

Alexandra was numbed by too much Nature—the spectacle of a stiff man being captured by an animated, flexible older woman. Sukie was having a high old time, perspiring freely in the low-ceilinged room; Christopher was being led, not altogether against his inclinations, into a realm full of pitfalls, on the very area of burgundy carpet where Jane's plea to the Goddess, whatever it had been, had been answered by a burst of blood.

The record stopped. "There you have it, guys and gals," the gravelly old voice said, " 'In the Mood,' with that fantastic ending. The tune was originally a twelve-bar blues composed by Joe Garland and Andy Razaf. The main theme previously appeared under the title 'Tar Paper Stomp,' credited to trumpeter and bandleader Wingy Manone. One story goes that after the Miller recording became a big hit, Manone was paid off not to sue. Rocker Jerry Lee Lewis did a later, non-big-band version, and those of you with rabbit ears can hear a few phrases from the intro in the background of the coda of the Beatles' 'All You Need Is Love.' " The disc jockey, Alexandra decided, was no janitor; he sounded more and more professorial. "And now another sentimental treat," he growled, "a platter to bring tears to the rheumy eyes of those of us over a certain age—Bunny Berigan, who played in the Miller band as well as for Paul Whiteman, the Dorseys, Benny Goodman, and his own short-lived aggregation—Rowland Bernard Berigan, born in Hilbert, Wisconsin, and dead at thirty-three in New York City, of cirrhosis of the liver, favoring us with his singing voice as well as his moody, stuttering trumpet work, doing his signature rendering of 'I Can't Get Started,' melody by the great Vernon Duke, lyrics by the ditto Ira Gershwin, recorded in 1937. Listen up, all you out there."

The song began at a languid tempo that could only be slow-danced to, close. "Enough," Sukie decided, after trying in vain to budge Christopher into a few paired steps. They parted, both of them pink-faced and moist. Christopher's *Mets* T-shirt bore sweat-stains in the center of his chest and in two wing-shapes at the back, where his shoulder blades made contact with the cloth.

Sukie, slightly panting, presumed on their new relationship and said to him, "Tell us about New York. Would I like to live there?"

"No," he told her. "What they get for rentals now is ridiculous."

"My husband didn't leave me poor. The city was always expensive."

"It's worse now. Arabs. All the rich Arabs and South Americans are buying up apartments in case their countries blow up. The U.S. is everybody's escape hatch."

Alexandra broke into this tête-à-tête, saying to Christopher, "Didn't Greta Neff want you back in two hours? You can make it, assuming the causeway has dried out."

"Oh, Lexa," Sukie reproached. "Christopher is telling us things. He's getting to like us." She poured some red wine from the glass jug into his empty Scotch glass, and turned down the clock-radio, which was still rustling with immortal jazz. The red numbers said 8:47 when he finally left. His thanks and farewell were those of a portly, deep-voiced gentleman, but his pale-blue eyes had the glaze of a befuddled youth.

"I didn't think he told us a thing," Alexandra complained to Sukie when his car had crackled away over the gravel on the lot below. "You and he seemed to be greatly amusing each other, but the evening didn't do much for *me*. It came to me for a hideous instant in the middle of it all that he wants me *dead*, and you're giving him jitterbug lessons and the last of Jane's Scotch."

"He needed them; he's been repressed by his gay theatrical crowd. They have all these impossible hopes of being rich and famous and live hand to mouth in cold-water flats, the poor dears."

"Poor dears—he's out there pumping us full of electrons somehow."

"Or so he thinks. I'm not sure he has much more to tell, actually. He's just parroting Darryl's ideas without fully understanding them."

"If they're understandable. I'm not sure I understand *you* any more. You get very engaged around this little monster."

"He's not that little."

"He is in my sense of him. The kid brother Darryl kidnapped. And now he's come back determined to kill us, like one of these high-school kids who decide it would be fun to do a Columbine."

"Us? Me, too?"

"Why not? You were there. There were three of us. You were furious with Jenny, too."

Sukie considered, with an adorably petulant plump-lipped moue. "It was all so long ago, it's hard to believe we did it."

"That's what these pederast priests must think, while the church is being sued into bankruptcy. But they get hauled into court. Justice is done. Sukie, I'll tell you frankly: down deep I'm terrified."

"Don't be terrified, Gorgeous. We still have magic, don't we?"

Alexandra looked down at her hands. They resembled two fat lizards. Their backs were roughened and mottled by sun damage—days at the beach, days in the garden, days riding in the desert, her hands holding the reins, days walking Cinder in the high ranch country. Her nails were cracked with dryness; arthritis had taken and twisted some joints so the knobby fingers pointed in slightly different directions. These were the hands of a stranger, someone she wouldn't regret leaving behind. "*You* may," she told Sukie. "I think my magic's about used up. Just the thought of casting a spell nauseates me."

"Mother, you look thin! Is anything the matter?"

"Don't I look better thinner?" Alexandra realized this was not the thing to say. Her sickly appearance had been reflected as a flash of dismay on her daughter's face. *We look alike*, it occurred to her—on the heavy side, faces a bit too broad to be exactly beautiful. Marcy even had the little cleft at the tip of her nose, though less decisively. The child had inherited her father's indecisiveness—Oswald Spofford's pathetic desire to be accepted by others, to be one of the blameless sheep. Most people, she tried to tell him, weren't worth being accepted by. Better snub them before they snub you. Be one of the wolves.

Looking into a mirror, she could have flattered herself— turning her head to smooth out the tension lines, lowering her chin to hide the throat wattles that had become, as the fat beneath her skin ebbed, more prominent—but there was no eluding her oldest child's stricken gaze.

August, with its steamy spells and its little green knobs bunched ever thicker on the fruit trees and its fully ripened insect population biting and stinging and eating leaves to lace, was winding down. Alexandra was fulfilling her promise to Marcy to come to dinner when her grandsons Roger and Howard Junior were home from camp. *Bring your friends*, Marcy had said, but the boys had come home two weeks after Jane had died, and since then Sukie had developed a mysterious attachment in the town that took more and more of her time. It was never clear when she would be eating with Alexandra, or if the BMW would be available for Alexandra to borrow for her own meager errands—walks on the beach when the afternoon sun was too low to burn her skin, visits to the sleepy Eastwick library for books by the Western authors (Cormac McCarthy, Barbara Kingsolver) favored by her reading circle in Taos, visits to the Stop & Shop for meat and fresh vegetables to make a decent meal if she had, for once, persuaded Sukie to have dinner in the condo with her. Sukie had acquired in relation to Alexandra the casual arrogance of the relatively rich, flippantly heedless and distractedly breathless with the unexplained importance of her private arrangements. The three women had begun their summer vacation together full of intentions to explore this little state, to keep track of summer concerts and plays around Narragansett Bay, to go on excursions to the famed opulent "cottages" of Newport, or to take the summer steamer ferry from Galilee to Block Island, or to incorporate a pleasant roadside luncheon into a visit to Gilbert Stuart's birthplace or—remembered from their witchy days—the touchingly modest, gloomily pastoral so-called Smith's Castle, a relic of the fabled plantation past. But when Jane became sick and died, such idle jaunts, for the two survivors, became implausible. Alexandra felt herself joining the Eastwick natives in their daze of stuckness— stuck with almost nothing to do, but the days nevertheless passing with an accelerating speed, eating up her lazy life as the insects ate the summer's leaves. Once, when she complained to Sukie of her elusiveness, the redhead—whose own face in self-forgetful moments seemed to shrivel into itself, suddenly smaller, as if crinkling and withering in an unseen fire—snapped at Alexandra, "Can't you see, you dope? I'm trying to save your life!"

Alexandra's life felt so insubstantial and precarious to her that she did not press the other for an explanation but silently turned away, a rejected lover hoping with silence to wound in turn.

Tonight something suddenly came up—a call on Sukie's cell phone and a return call, both unexplained—that Sukie needed the BMW for, so she dropped Alexandra off at the Littlefields' on its seedy stretch of Cocumscussoc Way, peremptorily telling her to apologize on her behalf and to have one of "them" drive her home to the condo. When, considerably embarrassed, Alexandra phoned her daughter to say that Sukie was at the last minute unable to accept the Littlefields' hospitality, Marcy said firmly, "Good. Better. We'll have you all to ourselves."

The boys pried themselves up out of the well-worn, food-stained armchairs, gave their grandmother limp hugs, and let her try to kiss them. Roger turned his face in sharp aversion, but little Howard, the sunnier and younger of the two, held still for a peck on the cheek. Roger had conspicuously grown, along his father's stringy lines, and seemed to have a shadow on his upper lip, a faint dark echo of the excessive brown hair drooping from his scalp and covering his ears. "How old are you now?" Alexandra asked him.

He looked at her with some surprise. "Thirteen," he answered.

Marcy intervened. "He just had his first birthday as a teenager."

Alexandra felt a cold stab of guilt. "Oh, dear—when? I fear I missed it."

"You did," Roger told her calmly. His eyes, a surprisingly dark brown, were nearly at the level of hers.

Marcy said, in a tender, forgiving tone, "The day before yesterday, Mother."

"I'm appalled at myself. I quite forgot that anything at all wonderful happened in August."

"That's O.K., Grandma," the boy gallantly allowed, confronted with the discomfiting sight of an adult in the wrong.

"Now, you mustn't let me go," Alexandra pleaded, taking up the feeble role, that of a coy penitent, left to her, "without whispering in my ear what you'd like for a present." The boy's expression didn't show a spark, so she thought to add, "Perhaps you'd prefer, rather than think of a present, a little gift of cash. Though, really, little is what it would be."

Her sense of what a dollar, or ten dollars, would buy, had frozen somewhere in the Sixties, while standards of expenditure had risen, and billionaires had replaced millionaires as epitomes of good fortune. "You think about it," she concluded, a bit sharply, and turned to the younger grandson. Howard Junior was fairer and more finely tuned than his brother, and at nine years old his round face, with its gappy front teeth, showed a properly cheerful avidity. Alexandra tried to remember back to when she had the energy to want something wholeheartedly. She had wanted white figure skates like Sonja Henie's when she was six, and when she was twelve she had wanted to get her ears pierced and fitted with rhinestone studs in the jewelry department of the Denver Dry Goods Company, and when she was seventeen she had wanted a bronze-colored taffeta strapless dress to wear to the junior prom and her father's permission (her mother was dead by then) to stay out until two with her date, the school's rangy second-string quarterback. Decades later her desires had settled on the magic word "out"—she had desperately wanted out of her marriage to Oz, dear obliging, well-intentioned Oz, though what her reasons were had become a fading puzzle, a revulsion less against this particular average man, perhaps, than against the deadly limits of a woman's life.

"How did you like camp?" she asked the smaller boy.

The older one answered for him: "It was O.K.," he said, dragging the syllables to imply that it hadn't been. A sullen puzzled shadow passed across his face as if cast by his floppy overabundance of dark-brown hair.

"It was *great*," Howard Junior piped up; the gaps between his teeth seemed a kind of reverse sparkle in his sunny face. "A boy in my tent broke his arm falling off the monkey swing!"

"Tell Granny what all you learned at camp," Marcy prompted.

"How to feather your paddle when you canoe," the smaller boy brightly supplied.

"To braid gimp," his brother said. "It was *stu*pid. The counsellors were stupid. They were these teen-agers who just wanted to make out with each other in the woods."

"And now you're a teen-ager yourself," Alexandra reminded him—a reminder that was not, on second thought, very helpful or grandmotherly. Alas, it was her métier to make mischief, even with her humorless daughter tensely listening.

But Marcy was not in her most disapproving mood, and her husband's returning from a day's work lightened the atmosphere within the split-level ranch house, with its awkward mix of shabbiness and newness, soiled white carpet and oversize hi-def television. There's something about a man. Howard was the same lanky, loose-jointed type as Jim Farlander, confident with his hands; Alexandra and her daughter had a kindred taste in mates. In his clean gray workshirt and trousers, he brought to the household its center of gravity. He ruffled Howard Junior's summer-blond hair as the boy embraced his father's legs, and held up a flat palm for his older son to high-five; he startled Marcy with a kiss warmer, Alexandra saw, than she had expected, and even flirted with his mother-in-law, having touched her cheek with his and squeezed her waist at the same time. "You look great, Grandma," he told her, having scarcely looked.

"Don't lie to me," Alexandra said. "When I showed up at the door, your wife looked horrified. I'm old, Howard." *Time treats men so gently*, she thought; he could have belonged to either of them, mother or daughter.

"How's those electric shocks coming?"

"I still get them, but they may be my imagination. They aren't the worst thing in my life."

"Oh? What is?"

He paused in his circuit of the domestic bases, having glanced toward the jocular evening-news team on the big flat plasma screen, and stooped to scratch the head of the family familiar, an overweight golden retriever thumping its heavy tail against a chair leg. "The worst thing," he prompted. He had an unusually wide and flexible mouth for a man, and a prominent nose that looked tweaked sideways, as in a drawing slightly out of perspective. When he smiled in anticipation of her answer, his ragged teeth encouraged exposure of her own imperfections.

"It's hard to put words to," she told him and his listening family. "A feeling of discouragement. A sense," she clarified, "that the cells of my body are getting impatient with me. They're bored with housing my spirit."

"Mother!" Marcy cried, in what seemed genuine alarm. "Do you have any pain? Have you seen a local doctor?"

"Jane saw Doc Pat a few weeks ago, and I think it helped kill her. She was the one getting shocked when I asked for your opinion; now I'm the one."

Marcy, more alert than usual, asked, "What about Mrs. Rougemont, whatever her name is now? How's *her* health?"

"Mitchell. Fair. She hasn't reached my stage of aging yet. She's younger, by six years. And always was more proactive. You know me, darling—I've always been afraid of"—she couldn't bring herself to name the disease—"Nature. The way it kills you when things inside get just a *little* bit off. Don't mind me—I'm an old lady. I should be getting used to dying, it's very immature not to. But, please, let's not discuss this any more in front of the boys. Right, boys?"

Roger smiled, with a lopsided tug of his lips like his father's smile, but the effect was not reassuring. "It's like the song says, Grandma," he said. "Life sucks, and then you die. Kurt Cobain wasn't afraid to die. He wanted to do it. It's no big deal, the way they do it now. These bombers in Iraq, they commit suicide all the time." Like the talking head on the too-wide, too-vivid screen, he was just giving the news.

"Hush, baby," Marcy said.

"Yes," Alexandra agreed. "I've sometimes wondered if there aren't so many people in the world now—I can't tell

you how many billions, it used to be two when I was a girl—
so many people now that young people, more sensitive and
less selfish than I can ever be, haven't taken up a kind of
global death-wish. Not just school shootings and these
Islamic martyrs, it's the drug overdoses and car fatalities in
the papers every day, teen-agers driving themselves at ninety
miles an hour into trees, and then their friends and neigh-
bors telling the television camera what beautiful cheerful
perfectly normal girls and boys they were."

"Mother, please. Don't encourage him. Even as one of
your jokes."

"Who's joking? Forgive me, dear. I know how you feel; I
didn't want to see my parents die, either. You don't even have
to like them. Their death makes your own life mean less.
They've stopped watching."

Little Howard Junior, following the conversation above
his head with round blue eyes, blurted, "We all like you,
Grandma."

"Thank you, Howard. And I like *you*."

The older Howard said, paternally levelling with her,
"There's other doctors in town than Doc Pat, Alexandra. He
keeps his shingle out just to feed patients up to his son in
Providence. A bright young doc from Sloan-Kettering in
New York City has opened up two doors down from me on
Dock Street, beyond the P.O. He's young—up on all the latest bells and whistles. But he told me he doesn't want to
spend his whole life scraping by in the Big Apple, paying
triple taxes and those tremendous rents. Small-town life—
the green space, nobody locking their doors at night—suits
him just fine. A fine little family, too. Two girls, cute as buttons. He wants to keep them in the public schools until the
ninth grade and the hormones kick in. He'd be somebody

for you to see. I could put in a word and get you an appointment before Labor Day."

Marcy intervened: "Howie, I think Mother needs *less* Eastwick, not more. She and her friends thought returning here would make them younger, but of course it hasn't. Is that unfair to say, Mother? You're disappointed. The magic you thought would happen hasn't. Am I being too psychological?"

That pink wart on the side of her nose, Alexandra thought. *Why doesn't she have it removed? Warts become cancerous.* A month ago, she would have been dismissive of her daughter's attempt at analysis, but today she felt worn down and only said, submissively, "No, it's not unfair to say. I'm not sure it's true. I don't know exactly why we came. Perhaps it was to face what we did here. To make it right, or less wrong, before we—"

"Die!" little Howard piped up, showing his gappy teeth in a gleeful grin. He must be a joy to his teachers.

"Howard!" Marcy scolded. She called her child Howard and her husband Howie.

But in the child's saying the unsayable Alexandra saw that right here, in front of her, was one answer to death—her genes living on. The tussle of family life, the clumsy accommodations and forgivingness of it, the comedy of membership in a club that has to take you in at the moment of birth. As they shuffled to seat themselves around the table, moving into the warmth of the meal that Marcy—dear, lumpy, modest Marcy—had prepared, Alexandra pictured levels and layers of inheritance and affinity invisibly ramifying, cards dealt out to absent and dead and yet-to-be-born players. Everybody gets a hand. They seated themselves, husband Howard and mother Marcy at opposite ends of the dining table and the grandmother facing the boys from the sides like a third child, with a child's potential for misbehavior. The chair beside hers had been left there, though the place setting for Sukie had been taken away.

The table, a rather heavy-footed old mahogany, seemed faintly but profoundly familiar. Had it come from the Denver household, as part of Alexandra's inheritance, and been left with Marcy when her mother abandoned Eastwick for the West? Alexandra couldn't quite tell, with an embroidered tablecloth covering it, and a healthy, calorie-light meal being served upon it: chicken with bow-tie pasta in a thin sour-cream sauce, broccoli with raisins and diced carrots, and a zucchini-rich salad from their own garden. She thought of her other children—Linda a willowy imitation Southern belle in Atlanta, Ben bullish and Republican in Montclair, and Eric, her baby, a graying hippie making do in Seattle at a murky intersection of music and electronics, managing a store called Good Vibes. Eric had repaid his being her favorite by becoming most like her, cultivating a slight talent within a bohemian enclave located where America thinned out into Never-Never land. He had pacified his brain with drugs while she had been wantonly seeking self-fulfillment in witchcraft. Nature, behind her back, in spite of her, had been bringing to ripeness her true self-fulfillment, her offspring and their offspring, those who amid the globe's billions owed her their being, as she owed them her genetic perpetuation. Families were stupid, but less stupid and selfish than individuals. Still, in the midst of her kin, she missed the friend, the peer in wickedness and unconventionality, who was to have been seated beside her.

. . .

"Do you like this?"

"I do," he said, his sometimes boyish voice under some tension.

"Can you tell it's a woman and not another man doing it?"

"Not really. Sort of."

"Is it a bad difference?"

She couldn't tell from his silence if he was concentrating on what to answer or letting his mind drift somewhere else. She hoped not the latter, though in fact it is a familiar female problem, your attention wandering just as the other person is getting interested. What you think about gets so interesting it drops your body and its sensations away. She was having no such problem now; her attention was fully engaged by the intellectual, psychological-somatic problem before her, there in the motel darkness dimly lit by the moon, which had been new and now was swelling toward full again. Outside, in the salt air, they had noticed the moon before opening the door to their numbered room there in the decaying motel beyond the shuttered-up pizza shack, its tipped oval face hanging sad and stark above the pillar of its reflection in the still Bay, beyond the crescent of pallor where East Beach, two miles from the broad public section in the view from the Lenox mansion, became pebbly and narrow. Earlier in this tryst, before it became so interesting to her, she had knelt on the bed and tugged back the rough curtain, as coarse as burlap, and peeked. Shadows of young people could be made out against the moonlit stripes of the shallow breakers cresting. Young, heedless voices could be heard, rising above the rhythmic whisper of crests collapsing, when the curtain closed. Its weave was coarse enough to let through pinpricks of the radiant air outside, from which they were as sealed off as if underground. She had begun by kissing, even sucking, his beautiful, purely ornamental male nipples, with their tickly haloes of hair. The sensations had made him laugh, but they were not funny to her.

"No," he said, after thought. "Not bad. Nice. Your perfume reminds me of my mother's." Her head had slipped to the base of his torso; a sweet fragrance had floated across his chest to his nose. "Maybe it's just your shampoo. She didn't use perfume, at least by the time I knew her. It wasn't natural, she thought it wasted the environment."

"Don't think about your mother. It distracts you."

"You can tell."

"Oh, yes. *It* tells me."

"Do you want me to come?"

"I wouldn't mind. But I don't want to waste it. If you do, can you come again?"

"How soon? How long do we have?"

"We both should get back, eventually."

"Does she—?"

"Care? Yes. She loves me. Not like this, but loves me. And I her."

"Did you ever—?"

"Touch? Yes. We may have brought each other off once in a while."

"You don't remember?"

"We were high. And sleepy from the hot tub. It was like we were all mixed up with each other."

"I should have come out and joined you."

"You were too young. It would have made it entirely different."

Both realized they were drifting away, and they concentrated for a minute. "Can you—?"

"What? Ask me."

"Get down a little farther?"

"My God! I'll gag."

"Get down as far as the freckle."

"What freckle?"

"I thought you were nearsighted. *That* freckle." His indicating finger seemed the nose of a fish, nudging a stalk of coral.

"How did you get a freckle there?"

"Sunbathing. On Long Island."

"And the guys you were with could do the freckle without gagging?"

He was silent, offended at her invasion of his privacy. She watched to see if he would wilt and begin to tilt. He did not. She flicked with her tongue, enjoying the perversity, competing with all those guys from the beaches of youth.

He read her mind, there in the filtered moonlight. "Is that how you think of your own lovers, as a mob of 'guys'? There weren't that many. There's a jealousy factor, and you had to be careful, once AIDS was out in the open. I'm HIV negative, you should know. I got the rep of being chicken. But Darryl set the example. He was very careful, that way."

"I know. With us, too. He didn't like losing control."

"And you do."

"I'm not afraid of it. It's like dreaming. You can come out the other side, still being you. Hey. You're ready. Yummy. Let me drink at the fountain of youth." She tightened all over, knees and feet together, going into a purposeful crouch there on the dank bed.

"No," he said again, in his deeper, more theatrical voice, touching the top of her head. The broad white parting; the soft mussed abundance dyed the orange-amber tint that had been its true color, more subtly. "If you do me," he explained, "I'm not sure I can do you."

"Too gynecological, huh?"

"It's not like I've never been with a woman before, but—"

"I know. We feel it, too. Disgust."

"Not disgust, please. It's just *strange*, until I'm more used to it."

"You want to get used? Are you saying you want to fuck me?"

He hesitated. A declaration was coming. "I want to be *with* you. Since you've decided you want to be with me, I don't know exactly why."

"Why? I'm crazy about younger men."

"I'm not younger."

"Than me you are."

"Yeah, but—"

"I *like* your fat belly. It's silky and wobbly, like a puppy's. I don't want you fucking Greta Neff."

"Please. Don't be grotesque. She's such a dyke."

"What's grotesque? It's all grotesque, if you look at it in a certain light. We have other things going for us; we just have to work this part of it through. You want to fuck me in the ass? So I'll be like another boy?"

"It wouldn't be. And actually, I was usually the catcher."

"Oh." She had to think that through. "I see. And I'm not equipped to pitch. Poor me. But I can buy one. One of those things. A dildo. You'll have to help me strap it on."

"Listen. Why don't we just lie here in each other's arms and talk? And cuddle. Don't women like cuddling?"

"They like everything except being ignored." She lifted her face to look into his, across the bulge and fuzz of his abdomen. "I'm game for whatever you want. I like the idea of me having a penis. At last. But I wonder if it wouldn't be healthier for *you*, for our relationship, for you to get used to being the other thing. A pitcher."

"You're probably right." His mouth felt dry, parched by the new prospects dawning, here in this underground.

"Couldn't you imagine me as another boy? I did think to bring Vaseline."

This dried his throat further, the cold blood of it. "You know," he warned, "even with it, it sometimes hurts."

"I do know. I've been there, with some of the guys. And I had no idea how big you were."

"I'm sorry. It's something you can't help."

"Don't say things like that, Chris. You're the pitcher now. Say things like 'There it is, baby, all of it. Take it to the hilt, you cunt. I'm going to *womb* you, you bitch.' But that's with the vagina, and I won't inflict that on you yet."

"I'd be happy with just your mouth. You have a nice mouth. And your hand."

She laughed, wickedly, and flicked his engorged glans with her grainy tongue, keeping her eyes rolled upward toward his face. He could see the half-moons of her eye-whites in the light coming through the rough curtain. "You would, would you?" she teased.

"Tell me," he said, beginning to act the pitcher, "about these guys you let butt-fuck you."

"Don't be jealous," she continued to tease. "One of them was my first husband. Monty. Montgomery Rougemont. He was latent, I can see now that I've lived more. He despised women. If they acted at all uppity, he called them butch. It turns out he was the one who was butch. He tried to sell it to me as a handy method of contraception. It didn't do a thing for me but sting the next time I took a shit."

"About my size. Darryl—"

"Let's not bring Darryl into this, honey. Aren't we having a nice time, just the two of us?"

"Yes, but he—"

"Let's concentrate on *us*. Do you want to see my vagina? Have you ever looked at one?"

"Of course."

"Why 'of course'? Many men haven't. Straight men. They're scared to. It's the Medusa's head, that turns them to stone. Uh-oh. You're losing your stoniness. I guess you're not ready to think about vaginas yet."

"No. I am. I'll *get* ready. But—"

"I know, darling. I know."

She said nothing then, her lovely mouth otherwise engaged, until he came, all over her face. She had gagged, and moved him outside her lips, rubbing his spurting glans across her cheeks and chin. He had wanted to cry out, sitting up as if jolted by electricity as the spurts, the deep throbs rooted in his asshole, continued, but he didn't know what name to call her. "Mrs. Rougemont" was the name he had always known her by. God, she was antique, but here they were. Her face gleamed with his jism in the spotty light of the motel room, there on the far end of East Beach, within sound of the sea. The rhythmic relentless shushing returned to their ears. She laid her head on his pillow and seemed to want to be kissed. Well, why not? It was his jism. Having got rid of it, there was an aftermath of sorrow in which he needed to be alone; but there was no getting rid of her. "Call me Sukie," she said, having read his mind. "I sucked your cock."

"You sure did. Thanks. Wow." His voice came out boyish. He kissed her shiny face; already the stuff was drying. Her hair where it had strayed onto her face was sticky and stiffening.

"Was I as good as a man?"

"Better." But there had been a strength, of tongue and ruthless iron finger-grip, that he had missed.

She snuggled deeper into the pillow, not bothering to wash her face, looking at him with one eye. "Tell me about New York. I've never lived there, you'll have to teach me. Lennie loved suburbia, and we went into the city less and less. You must know lots of special private places. Art galleries, off-Broadway shows. Clubs on the far West Side. I still love to dance."

"Places change. What's in one year is out the next."

She read his mind and asked, "Am I too old to dance with? I'm not even seventy yet. Are you afraid I'll embarrass you in front of your gay friends? Why? They can understand. Nobody is young forever, and every artist needs a patron. I think we'll look fine together. I don't look my age, everybody says. And tonight: I won't ask if you love me, but didn't you love *it*?"

"I did. You give great head."

"And won't you love living in New York in the nice big apartment you'll help me choose? Not one of those roachy basements you're used to, sharing with a bunch of creeps."

"Sure," he agreed. "Great."

"Next time," she said, with drowsy confidence, "it'll be my turn to have the orgasm."

In all those years of his being her lover, Alexandra had never been in Joe's house. It stood in a section of Eastwick seldom included in her rounds back then, the so-called Polish section, though there were more Portuguese and Italian offspring of immigrants than Poles—tightly packed narrow houses well away from the water, five or six blocks beyond Kazmierczak Square, which the Yankees and summer people still called Landing Square, though the town meeting thirty years ago had passed by a fair majority the official vote renaming it for a fallen Vietnam soldier from this neighborhood. A big red-brick Catholic church, blank-faced but for a double door and some shallow tall pilasters worked into the expanse of brick, lifted its green copper cross above the rows of asphalt-shingled rooftops. Joe's was one of the better houses, narrow but stretching back into an acre where he had, in the Italian style, laid out a pair of vegetable gardens and built between them a fieldstone arch leading to a half-dozen fruit trees—apple, pear, peach, plum—that he called his orchard. Alexandra remembered driving by, a lovelorn divorcée, and stealthily glancing in and coveting the devotion Joe's big backyard showed, especially in April, when his trees broke into blossom. She saw his touch everywhere. A grape arbor flourished along the side of the house, the eastern side; it got the morning sun, and the vine leaves gave a cooling shelter to his outdoor table and chairs in the afternoons and early evenings. He had brought a Mediterranean temper to harsh American conditions. As soon as Alexandra had begun to let Joe fuck her, the plants in her own garden, especially the tomatoes and rhubarb, perked up; he had a green thumb, or something similar.

Parking the car at a curb crowded with old Detroit models, venturing up the concrete steps Joe's hands had poured and his feet so often climbed, she felt her heart thump and flutter in her chest like a moth flinging itself against a hot light. She had lost so much weight Marcy was alarmed, but Doc Pat, quite shinily bald and nearly blind in one eye, assured her that there was nothing wrong with her but the ineluctable course of Nature. That was the advantage of a senile doctor; he discovered nothing that would demand action from him. The electric shocks had seemed to be letting up lately, mysteriously, but her memory lapses were worse—she felt she was sleepwalking from morning to evening, and was often surprised by where she found herself. At night, settling to really sleep, she had pains in her fingers and cramps in her feet and, throughout her body, a sour backwash of dread, as if everything she ate was asking, *Why bother?* She woke up anxious around four, and dragged through the day. Constipation alternated with diarrhea, and there were pains above the back of her neck as if her skull were softening. Her feet felt like lumps, even without shoes on, so that her contact with the earth lacked precision, and she now and then dizzily lurched. Floaters nagged her vision as tinnitus nagged her hearing. Lying in bed or sitting inert in a chair, she resented the repetitive business of life — rising, pissing, eating, answering the telephone — after seven decades and more wherein these duties had been lightened by a vague expectation of some wonderful eventuality. Now expectations had become a nuisance, and indifference gave her an inverted courage; otherwise she would never have dared ring Gina Marino's front doorbell.

The widow opened the front door and peered through the screen door warily, an unmistakably hostile dark, squat shadow. "What you want?"

"Actually, Gina, I've come to see Veronica. Is she home?"

"Always home. I tell her, get out of the house, but she stay inside. Thirty-nine, and like a child hiding. Mike is giving up — he stay forever at the Barrel."

"I thought the Bronze Barrel had become something else — what they call a sports bar."

"Whatever they call it, idea the same — drink to forget." The shadow of her head tilted behind the aluminum mesh, as her hand lifted toward the handle of the screen door. "You have business with Veronica?"

"I have something to ask her. It will take less than a minute, but I didn't want to ask it over the phone, it was too personal. If you don't want me in your home, Gina, perhaps Veronica could come visit me, over at the Lenox Mansion Apartments, at the end of the beach road. I'll be there another week."

"How she get way down there? All day Mike has the car. Come in, then. We're none of us getting younger." She had to fumble at a hook-and-eye as well as the handle, and the screen door creaked, for want of a man's lubricating attention. "Ronnie!" Gina called, hardly raising her voice, as if the house had so long held her and her daughter that signals between them flew through the wood.

And Veronica did answer, in a sullen timid voice, from upstairs. "What, Mama?"

"Somebody to see you." Gina eyed Alexandra and nodded. "Go up," she said.

Alexandra pushed herself, her unfeeling feet, up the steep carpeted stairs. Penetrating the house and its secrets was startlingly easy, like an unplanned seduction. The house had a smell she couldn't quite place, stale yet warm—the odor under sofa cushions, along with hairpins and stray coins, the secluded staleness sweetened by whiffs of life, of cleaning fluid and of garlic bread baking in the oven. Joe had brought the odor with him into her house, a trustworthy smell, most vivid on a winter day—the children all at school, black-capped chickadees flickering at the feeder, Orchard Road bright with the previous day's snow, icicles beginning to drip from the eaves, her own skin tingling and rosy from the bath she had taken in anticipation of his visit. He would park his truck behind the house and come in through the sun porch and shrug off his bulky parka, worn grimy in spots, and let it fall on her braided rag rug, and drop after it his jaunty little bog hat with the narrow brim; the sour-sweet male scent of him would gush from his grubby green wool work sweater and the neck of his shirt collar and the old-fashioned sleeve-less undershirt that exposed his frothy armpits as in nothing but her blue bathrobe she hurled herself into his embrace.

The stairs attained a landing and a papered hallway that went in one direction toward the front of the house, where she guessed Joe had slept with Gina, and the other way to the back, where Veronica lived childless with Mike O'Brien. She came into the hall to greet her visitor: "Mrs. Spofford!"

"Farlander," Alexandra told her, smiling to think how true the name was here in Eastwick. "I was Spofford when you were a little girl, but that was a long time ago. Where shall we talk?"

"In here, I guess," the younger woman said, standing aside, unsmiling but not unfriendly. She was taller and thinner than Gina, with Joe's Roman nose and his liverish shadows under the eyes, features unfortunately homely on her female face. Like Marcy, she seemed to have been brought up in the world without sufficient instruction in fundamental graces, so that every motion had to be thought through. Awkwardly she admitted Alexandra into what did the O'Briens for a living room. The room's closed doors pre-sumably opened into a bedroom and a bathroom. An iron-ing board had been set up, a basket of laundry fresh from the dryer beside it. The singeing scent of the patient process seemed to arise from the depths of Alexandra's childhood; her heart cozy and damp with love, she would watch her own mother iron—testing the iron's hot bottom with a licked finger, poking its hissing nose into the corners around a man's shirt collar, demonstrating to her girl child a precious fraction of the domestic expertise that made a home.

"Those stairs," Alexandra said. "I feel weak." Even had Veronica waved her toward a chair, which she didn't, Alexandra would have remained standing. She felt herself for the first time a violator of Joe's domestic arrangements. He had always come to her; she had received him into her home and her body; the rest of his life was his business. " I'm leaving Eastwick soon, and I have a simple question to ask," she said. "Simple and personal."

Veronica stared with something of her mother's foreign opacity, though her eyes were lighter. "Ask it," she said.

"Have you missed your period this month?"

The words sank in. The woman's tired eyes widened. "My God," she said. "You *are* a witch. I thought it was just something people said."

Alexandra blushed in satisfaction, the first time in days she had felt her blood move. "I tried it, for a while," she admitted. "Before my second marriage. Do I gather that your answer is yes?"

"*Yes*. I haven't told anybody, not even Mike. Not even Mama. I'm so frightened I'm imagining it, or that I just skipped the curse this one time. I'm afraid I'll lose it. I'm too *old* to have a baby."

"You're a year short of forty," Alexandra told her. "That's not old for a woman any more. Why would you lose it? Think of all the women in the history of the world who couldn't lose it, though they desperately prayed to. Nature doesn't want us to lose babies. It wants us to hang in there. Do you smoke or drink?"

"No. A glass of wine now and then, to keep Mike company."

"No more wine. Let Mike keep *you* company. I assume he keeps you enough company to be the father."

Veronica only slowly understood. Then *she* blushed "Oh, yes. He still wants me, when he's had a few. How could it be anybody else?"

"Well, there are ways, but never mind. I see they don't apply to you. Would you and he want a boy or a girl?"

"I suppose a boy, but we'd be incredibly grateful for either."

"I had two of each," Alexandra said, speaking out of a depth of experience she seldom drew upon. "Girls are easier for the first fifteen years, but after that boys are. Girls get secretive. Boys get less bumptious. My guess is you'll have a boy. Here's a way to tell the sex, once you're out of the first trimester: Tie your wedding ring to a length of thread and have your husband hold it suspended over your belly. If it swings in a circle, it'll be a girl. If it swings back and forth, it'll be a boy."

Veronica laughed, an unaccustomed violent sound that embarrassed her. She covered her mouth with her hand and then took the hand, reddened by housework, away. "Why are you doing this for me?" she asked.

"Nature's doing it; there's no proof I did anything. There never is. Maybe I made a wish. Offered up a little prayer." Alexandra hesitated before making the next confession: "Your mother asked me to."

"My mother? But what did she say? When?"

"She didn't say. She implied. In front of the Stop and Shop early last month."

"But *why*?"

"Why did she ask, or why did I oblige?"

"Both."

Again, Alexandra hesitated. "I owed her one, as people say. She knew it. I knew she knew it. I'm so happy for you, that it worked out. But don't give me the credit. Give Mike the credit. Give the Virgin Mary the credit, if she's still your goddess."

Veronica's lips parted, her eyelids flared, but she did not admit the witch to this part of her.

"I should go," Alexandra said. "Your mother must be wondering."

Veronica was flustered by the need to be polite, to be grateful, yet not absurd. "You said you're leaving town?"

The coastal light lasted a few minutes less each afternoon. Pumpkins were ripening in the fields at the end of their writhing vines. The moon was throwing shadows. "Before Labor Day. I began with two roommates; one died, and the other is looking for an apartment in New York."

"Is that sad for you? You said you felt weak."

"It's sad, but that's life, or Nature, or growth, or death, or something. The weakness may be all in my imagination. Unlike your baby."

Veronica began to laugh again, and checked herself; her lips sealed shut a lovely smile, bashful but proud, adorably smug, like Joe's after he had fucked Alexandra and gotten his clothes back on and escaped out her door to the brightness of Orchard Road, wet with snow melt and the friction of traffic. Veronica awkwardly felt her guest deserved a little more conversation. "How has it been for you?" she asked. "Being back in Eastwick this summer?"

"It was . . . useful," Alexandra decided. "It confirmed my suspicion that I belong elsewhere. There was less here than I remembered."

"I guess those of us who never left already know that. But isn't that true of all places?"

"Yes. It's in *us*. How we look at things. A certain place, a time of life—they seem magical. Mostly looking back."

Veronica half-turned, back toward her ironing, back toward a life less lonely now by one more family member, a dependent adoring friend her body was creating.

Alexandra said, in a voice firm enough to halt the other woman's turning away, "I know it's time for me to go. I know you're dying to rush downstairs and tell your mother. But something occurred to me. You were married the same year your father died, yes?"

"That's right. Nineteen ninety-nine."

"I knew him, you know."

The innocent woman blinked. "I guess I knew."

The wicked old witch could not stop herself from bringing Joe into it, giving herself the satisfaction of conjuring him up, at this great distance, in his vanished force, a force that had moved her, and that she had welcomed, without enough valuing it in the greedy haste of those days, into herself, into the dark side of herself, the fertile, natural side, where her IUD had been inserted to annul Joe's seed. She needed to bring Joe up onto her tongue, in exchange for the favor she had done this aging girl. "I think," she told Veronica, "if Joe had lived a year or two longer—if he had been around to give his blessing to you and Mike—you would have gotten pregnant right away. He had a green thumb." She gave the mother-to-be a kiss on her cheek, and turned to negotiate on infirm feet the steep downward stairs.

Georgiana du Pelletier luxuriantly stretched her pale and curvaceously rounded arms outward as if to seize the transparent air of this fine Caribbean morning. Her exquisitely shaped lips, rosy without any application of lip paint [ck anachr. early 19th cent.?], stretched in a dainty feline yawn, exposing a coquettishly arched tongue the same vital tint as her lips, whose corners turned upward in a smile that deepened with remembered pleasure the piquant twin dents of her dimples and brought a light blush to her fair but sun-kissed [cut?] cheeks.

Her eyes—sky-blue, with a shadow of the deep marine blue where the coral shoal drops off—strove to focus on the present and its many claims. Yet her outstretched hand, each finger finely tapered, came into inadvertent contact with gauzy mosquito netting, triggering in her mind a different texture—oilier, swarthier, underlaid with powerful musculature—that she had caressed on the far shore of last night's sea of dreams.

Sukie considered writing, "She had dug her meticulously buffed and shaped fingernails ecstatically deep into Hercule's broad, heaving back," then admonished herself that a proper romance never dwells on sexual details, lest it slip over into pornography and lose its targeted demographic of dreamy, dissatisfied women. Specifics might scare off female readers. Women know the facts but don't like them spelled out. On the ledge outside Sukie's apartment window, filthy pigeons cooed and preened and bobbed their little beady-eyed heads. They mated in an angry flurry of feathers and stiffened spread wings that was alarming to observe close up, twenty stories in the air. The avenue far below, a river of reflected sun glitter and misty car exhaust, squawked and bleated with frustrated traffic. It was September, and the great city still held a summery languor and heat.

The songs of tropical birds—the demure chirping of the busy little yellow birds [ck correct name], the raucous cries of the paired, great-beaked lapas—sifted through the bedroom louvers. The field slaves, up since dawn, were moaning rhythmic folk songs in their musical patois, out in the white hectares of sea-island cotton. Nearer to hand, her female house slaves were exchanging murmurs of gossip as they hung up wash in the drying yard—gossip very possibly concerning the affairs of heart of their comely mistress. Georgiana's late husband, the dashing and ruthless planter

Pierre du Pelletier, had, as if in premonition of his apparent death by shipwreck en route to Jamaica, admonished his bride that, were she by any Heaven-sent misfortune to become a widow, she must run the plantation with an iron, unflinching hand. Though slender of flesh and delicate of bone, she had ridden herd on the two hundred enslaved blacks with a cool efficiency that had astonished the white foreman, Irish-born Jerome "Blaggart" Maloney—he of unkempt raven locks and sneering crimson lips and green eyes that followed her figure with a baffled would-be pos-sessiveness that sometimes sent a shiver up and down Geor-giana's straight yet pliant spine [run-on sent.?]. Profits had swelled under her punctilious yet humane management. She had forbidden use of the lash, and the ponderous iron manacles that chafed the very skin from anguished ankles were left to rust in the empty disciplinary dungeons and oubliettes. The slaves gratefully flourished. They would become insolent and rebellious, Blaggart Maloney warned, and their uprising would bathe their island in such blood as had bathed Santo Domingo. In mockery she had tapped her folded fan on the tip of his pock-marked nose. Until that dire day, she had spiritedly informed him, her word was law. Even the burros with their long-lashed soulful eyes and the paper-colored humped Brahma cattle imported from Cey-lon [ck] seemed to know and to rejoice that a woman was in charge.

The bleached-teak double doors to her coffer-ceilinged *chambre à coucher* were gently pushed open, and Hercule, the young underbutler, entered in the absurd yet charming fern-green costume of a male domestic—tightly fitted knee-length breeches, lapel-less [lapel-free?] high-collared coat with white piping and claw-hammer tail, gold-buttoned vest with white cambric neckcloth, the elegant whole resolving to, where a European servant would have worn narrow black pumps and clocked silk stockings, ebony bare calves and broad bare feet, the more silently (Geor-giana playfully reflected) to pad across the subtly creaking

floors of precious purpleheart wood from the cloud-capped
forests of northern Brazil. Silently, but for the whisper of
foot-sole on wood that she had to hold her breath to hear,
Hercule came to her bed and lay across her lightly blanketed lap, tingling with its secret need to urinate [omit?], an
ample bed-tray holding, like a lush Dutch still life, a poly-
chrome breakfast of

Though the romance formula did not admit of sexual
specifics, it did permit and even encourage detailed accounts
of food. Yet Sukie had never been much of a cook. This had
been something of a pity, since both Monty and Lennie had
had images of themselves as worldly men who knew how to
live well, and they would have appreciated a wife whose
gourmet cooking relieved them of the expense of resorting
to restaurants, with their pomp of coat and necktie, pretentious and inattentive waiters, and generous, undeserved tips.
For romance readers, food description took the place of
explicit sex, and it strained Sukie's imagination. The tip of
her tongue poked from between her lovely lips as if to attract
gustatory inspiration with a stubby pink antenna.

guava juice in a champagne flute, thin slices of humming-
bird breast served on coin-size fritters of pounded maize, a
fresh-caught butterfly fish filleted and poached in its black-
striped skin. On a side dish, strips of banana were sliced lon-
gitudinally and soaked in honey as palely dark as a varnished
violin. There was no way to eat them but to pick them up
and then suck her fingers clean one by one. Two miniature
croissants, called by slaves *les cornes du diable*, waited to be
broken and spread with unctuous mango butter the orange
of a hurricane sunset. A chased silver pot, the surface of its
round-bottomed body and rod of a handle alike thick with
stylized vegetation, had descended down the du Pelletier
line from the time of the Sun King and now in Hercule's
steady grip poured, into Georgiana's expectant cup of

eggshell-thin Sèvres porcelain, coffee enriched by the addition of crumbs of raw cane sugar to the consistency of tar. Only now, after three scalding sips, could her eyes open to take in the majestic presence of her graceful, opaque black servitor.

He had held her in his arms last night. He had penetrated her to her very soul. Yet there was a strangeness to him, as he lowered his lids to keep from spilling a drop of her refill. Nothing in his face, not so much as a twitching nerve, acknowledged last night's raptures, her total bestowal of herself. What did she know of his thoughts? He was of another race, from another continent, which might be another planet. Their bodies spoke the language of love across a great gulf of taboo. Even as her loins tightened around the convulsive expulsion of his seminal essence [cut?], the thought welled up in her, *He wants to kill me.* He could slay her in the garish morning of a slave rebellion without a moment's hesitation, though the night before he had availed himself of her tenderness and had lavished kisses of hand and tongue upon her dulcet alabaster epidermis. In his eyes, did her skin glare with the hideous pallor of a disease to be wiped from the face of the earth? Even now, the deference with which he served her might be a murderous irony. His dark presence in her white room was as alien as metal in flesh.

Georgiana suppressed these disquieting thoughts. Shifting her legs under the pinioning bed-tray, she made the china and silver crowded upon it chuckle. As Hercule bent low above her to remove the laden encumbrance, she was assailed by his masculine aroma, and dared ask aloud, "Did you enjoy last night, *mon bel esclave?*"

She felt him stiffen; the contents of the bed-tray momentarily chattered. Birdsong and unintelligible gossip filtered through the louvers, then stopped, as if at the approach of a predator. Hercule's shaved round skull, and the smooth pillar of arteries and tapering neck muscles that supported it, loomed close above her. "Don't know what you mean, missy," he said, his eyes brimming with fear. His irises were as black as his coffee; the whites of his eyes had the yellow bloodshot tinge peculiar to his tropical race. She felt the gulf between them as suddenly impossible to cross. He murmured, "Mistah Blaggart, he watchin'."

Sukie stopped her typing—keyboarding, they called it now—in a daze of suspended disbelief. Her eyes burned from focusing on the screen, without blinking. *Blink more*, her ophthalmologist had told her. The sounds of the Upper East Side, transmuted into the background noise of a treacherous Caribbean island, reasserted themselves as what they were—the auditory detritus on the dirty floor of a desperately crowded metropolis. Subconsciously, while cooking up an erotically charged breakfast on an island where the slaves are bound to revolt, she had heard the elevator door open and close on this floor. She waited to hear Christopher's key in the lock, and his slithering stealthy footsteps in the front hall.

"It's me," he called out, as little boys do back from school or play. His soundless feet, cushioned in the most expensive of new New Balances, passed through the living room and halted at the threshold of the tiny room, a maid's room originally, where she had established her writing equipment. On Sukie's imaginary island of Santa Magdalena, it was morning; here in reality it was late afternoon, the hour when skyscraper shadows swamped the streets and commuters filled the sidewalks like termites fleeing a burning building. The fire was over in New Jersey, a red sun at the western end of the cross-streets. It was the Manhattan hour to change gears, to start thinking about the restaurant to eat out in or else to face the kitchen and a refrigerator low on leftovers. Yet Christopher appeared in her doorway with a matinal radiance, that of a messenger from another world, with such hopeful news for her as Magdalene received at the disturbed cave, or as Mary, at the other end of a divine life, had received as she was reading in virginal solitude. *Fear not*, Christopher seemed to be saying. *Chill out.*

"How's it going?" he asked, leaning against one side of the doorframe. He had lost some weight. Returning to the city, no longer spoiled by Greta Neff's Germanic cooking, he had put himself on an exercise regimen, and had taken on, in self-defense against excessive restaurant portions and Sukie's refusal to cook, shopping and kitchen duties himself, along slimming lines of fish and brown rice and fresh vegetables *al dente*. He also had taken to doing housework, making the washing machine and the vacuum cleaner roar into life while Sukie was trying to concentrate. She had acquired, in a sense, a wife.

"O.K.," she answered. "It's trash, I guess, but when I'm into it it seems something else. Truth, maybe. Where have you been all afternoon?"

"Oh . . . you know. Checked in with Max—he has a couple feelers out for me, in sitcoms in development. Worked out at the club for an hour, with weights and the StairMaster. Walked along the river as far as Ninety-sixth. Saw some guys I used to know and we sat on a bench and talked. They were saying there's going to be skyscrapers going up in Queens, besides the green one that says Citi. We decided we liked Queens the way it is, low and dingy, so real working people can afford to live there, instead of the phonies and rich foreigners in Manhattan."

He was telling her too much; he was hiding something. Usually he responded, "Oh . . . nowhere special," or, if her question had concerned where he was going, the curt word "Out," sometimes adding, "For some air," or even, "I don't know how you stand it, cooping yourself up all day."

Max was his agent, by whose agency any acting work would arrive. Christopher was at an awkward age, still a bit young-looking for roles as a father or a business heavy, yet far too old and plump for the kind of romantic role that, now and then, twenty-five years ago, he had filled for the cameras. After viewing some of his old tapes, Sukie had asked him how he had liked doing kissing scenes. He had answered that he didn't mind; most sex was acting anyway. And this had made her think. She had always considered herself a sexual enthusiast, a fool for a pretty cock, able to rise out of herself in the act, the acts as they unfolded first in the dusty plush interior of pre-war family sedans that her dates had borrowed for the evening, or on the sofas and carpets and beds of furtively utilized homes in that fingernail of an upstate city, and then, as she aged, legally rented hotel rooms and vacation cottages. Not that it was always easy for even the freest and healthiest woman to get with it. Sex was an art and could be like the earliest, those cave paintings of bison and furry elk and spindly-legged antelope in ochre paint on oozing walls, the depicted beasts scored by the scratches of actual flint spear-tips inflicting wounds meant to be magically transferred to the actual hunt, becoming real kills. The paintings were not as easy to reach as art books made them seem: the cave painter had to wriggle through a series of tight and anfractuous passageways, slippery and stifling, before dropping down into the utmost secret chamber, where he could attack, or create, the potent images. So sex and its climax were reached; thinking back upon the contortions and humiliations exacted from her over the years, Sukie wondered, if this had been acting, who had been the audience? The answer was herself, herself the stage and the performer as well as the audience. Her sex with Christopher—and it was not always she who initiated it—

was a charade but knowingly so, enacted sometimes with cross-dressing costumes and comical plastic gadgets, against perhaps the deep grain of their given natures but stealing strength from perversity, from a sensation of trespass and a mechanical persistence that substituted for youth's senti- mental excitement and illusion of discovery a cool knowing- ness itself exciting.

A machine needs adjustments, and these can be fine enough to be called tender. As a whole their cohabitation needed tact—from him to avoid making her feel her age, and from her to avoid comment on his poverty, his pathetic financial dependence. They were both adepts at duplicity. Among the world's journeyers, they travelled light. Unlike heterosexual men fully weighted with the social imperatives of jealous rage and possessive bullying, he would never harm her physically. Side by side, they attended concerts and plays, movies and museums, as freshly attentive as children to the concoctions that go by the name of Culture. They both enjoyed shopping and followed, at a distance, turns of fashion. He was, it turned out, sincerely a Mets fan, and she found she liked, their first month in town, sitting in a great bowl of shouting people on a sunny September day, as passenger jets glinted overhead on the descent path to La Guardia. She loved, after so many suburban years, riding the subway, the unobstructed speed and the economy and racial mingling of it; she regretted that she had come to it so late that admission required a paper ticket rather than a substan- tial metal token.

Nevertheless, for all their light-heartedly companionable moments and undemanding mutual tolerance, their charade of marriage wore to Sukie a hellish aspect, not a hell of fire but the one of ice. Apartment buildings were stacked stories high with cubes of ice, and she and Christopher Grant were one more frozen unit of phonies and foreigners. They were zombies; there was a rotten-egg smell of damnation. Sukie had settled for less than perfect, and this, in her romantic imagination, was a sin. There was punishment—revolt and conflagration—ahead for their island. But not yet. Georgiana and Hercule will come through. They will wind up in each other's arms forever; that was the kind of book she was writing.

Halloween, more or less

Dear old Gorgeous—

I've been *bad* about writing, I know, I know, but I bought a new computer so I could submit this new novel I'm working on on a single disk, that's the way the penny-pinching publishers expect it now. It's a laptop to carry with me if Chris and I do any travelling, and Microsoft has put a lot of clever new deviltry into the program, so instead of a mouse you have one of those infuriating little mouse substitutes, a square of magic metal in the middle of the keyboard bigger than a match folder but smaller than a pack of cigarettes (I still miss smoking, especially when at parties and when I'm writing, though it's been years since my emphysema was diagnosed in stern enough terms so that my choice seemed to quit or die) that you stroke with your finger though just the merest touch sends the arrow on the screen skidding right into some icon or other that changes the typeface or goes triple column or turns everything a hideous color you can't figure out how to change back. Really I want to cry and smash the damn machine some days, I'm too old for all the technology it takes to do anything these days, even drive a car. I've traded in the BMW for a more compact and environmentally sensitive Toyota hybrid so I can get around the city and not have it stolen—who would steal a hybrid?—and its dashboard is like some stealth bomber, all little cutesy international pictures and code words. I can't figure out what it wants from me. I can't even change the FM radio station without getting some blabbermouth sports talk show, guys phoning in to shout at a host who shouts right back, on AM, full of static from all the wires in this wired town. Electricity—who needs it? Chris says electricity is a misnomer, strictly speaking there isn't any, there are electrons but electricity is a lazy catchall term. There are just particles with charges, and some without. Also, New York is a lot more distracting than Stamford, I suppose that's why young people keep flocking here though they have to live in packing cases under the bridges practically, and Chris is always at me to go to this and that meaningless event with him, like art happenings where the woman keeps cutting herself in the arms and touching her own pussy. Monty and Lennie had the virtue of leaving me alone once in a while so I could daydream but then they had *jobs*. Funny, isn't it, how the merest detail of these dead husbands becomes precious? I thought both of their jobs were bullshit at the time. Selling people stuff they don't really need—that's all capitalism has come to. That, and using up irreplaceable natural resources while Africa starves.

But by now the Mets have stopped playing—Chris is a baseball freak, who would have thought it?—and the perfect fall weather must be arrived in Taos, and your health will be blooming again. You needed to gain weight, dear heart. I've never seen you look so peakèd as when we finished up with the condo. (Sorry to stick you with so many of the last-minute details; the bank was a real stinker not to give us our deposit back until the ceiling was repainted, I never noticed any smoke stains, it was kind of yellowy anyway.)

You had your bodily complaints, but then we all do. Women's bladders get moody, for another thing. Sometimes not a drop though you know you have to go, and other times you laugh or sneeze and there go the underpants. It's all on television, if you watch the news and peg yourself as a pathetic ancient. *Moi*, my skin is sun-allergic, my lungs are

too smooth inside, my gums recede to the point of peri-
odontia. You were simply *depressed*, is my diagnosis. Maybe
about Jane's death—she was a pill, a bitter one, but ours to
swallow—and maybe just about you being the oldest of us
three, and our leader always: the big sister, who is supposed
to be wise—the oldest and the most magical, even though
Jane *could* fly, a bit, like a flying squirrel. But I think what
the Goddess did to Jane that time made you (*you*, Lexa)
wonder if it wasn't all nonsense. OK, maybe it is. I live now
in the national headquarters of nonsense distribution and
don't let it get to me. I take life as it comes, day by day. If
you look straight up, past all the new construction (these
fucking double-parked Dumpsters *every*where!) there's still
a slice of blue sky. Somewhere in all this there has to be a
reason for existence, there's so much of it. I mean, all that
exists, the billions of light-years' worth of it.

I wormed out of Chris how he was giving us shocks, I say
us though he was saving me for last, I guess. It was based on
Darryl's experiments and what was left of his equipment. In
quantum theory, which isn't so much a theory as a kind of
helpless description of the crazy way things really *are*, it's
been proved time and again—if you split a particle, a photon, say, one half will have clockwise spin and the other
counterclockwise, and when you measure the spin of one,
even if they've travelled a long way from each other, and it
spins clockwise, the other will be counterclockwise even
though *there's no way they could have communicated.* This is
called cooperation between separated systems. It's one of
the many ghostly things about particles; they're not only
particles but waves at the same time, and a single photon
passing through two slots makes interference patterns with
itself, and electrons and their antimatter mates, positrons,
appear out of nothingness all the time in space, though only
for a billionth of a trillionth of a second, roughly. Honestly.
That's how scientists think the universe got started—some
antimatter forgot to cancel out matter. Or some virtual
particle slipped over into being non-virtual. Darryl's idea,

when he was still hoping to be a great inventor and make a
lot of money, which he needed for his travels and extrava-
gant life-style—he had hoped to sell it to the U.S. Army
but it really would kill only one person at a time, and
slowly at that—was to combine this cooperation-between-
separated-systems principle with electrons. It was like the
sympathetic magic we used to do. One of the things about
witchcraft was that it only worked for people around you,
people you *knew*, in the village. For electron transfer at a
distance you needed the victim to be fairly close, in the same
small town at least. Even lightning can't jump more than a
mile or two. And you had to have something with the person's electronic essence rubbed off. The reason you walk
across a room and get a shock when you touch a doorknob
is that the friction of your shoes has taken electrons from
the carpet and the excess is attracted to the protons in the
doorknob. You feel the charge coming *into* you when in fact
it is leaving. The way your slip used to cling to your butt
when women still wore slips—you remembered how infuriating that was, though it didn't make a spark like brushing
your hair in the dark does. Those were excess electrons
seeking what they call electrostatic equilibrium.

Now—I know, this is exhausting me too—the strange
(creepy even, but then he *was* creepy, but *so* funny) thing
about Darryl is that he had kept from the old tennis-and-
hot-tub days up at the Lenox mansion bits of our clothing
that we had been too stoned or relaxed or guilty to remember to take with us when we'd at last go home to those poor
saintly deserted children of ours. Tennis shorts and shirts,
peds, sweatbands, hair bands, combs, underpants and bras
even, left I guess in the changing room or on the edge of the
hot tub, and he kept them along with other souvenirs of
other souls he'd tried to captivate, and when Christopher
figured out whose things they were and when Greta Neff,
who had been very sympathetic to him when he became an
orphan (unlike us, I guess), tipped him off that at long last
we'd come back to Eastwick, he dug up this electron gun

Darryl had in his lab (they're almost a dime a dozen, every television set has one, it produces the little dot that moves across the cathode-ray screen, from the back of the cathode-ray tube, shot out by thermionic emission and passed through a hole in the anode—I just looked this up, I've never been one of these writers so lazy she gets some lackey to do research for her) and would blast Jane's and then your little unmentionables, the sweat on them dried for thirty years, *shoot* them full of electrons and, by extension, in a version of cooperation between separated systems, *you*. The excess of charge would build up in your body and not only generate shocks but mess up your insides and your general morale. It was diabolical. Chris was really angry about his sister. The method wasn't precise, but then the quantum world isn't either, it's all probabilities, nothing exactly exists, everything's a ghost until it's measured, and then the measuring instrument is somehow so intrusive it makes the next measurement impossible. Anyway. Don't worry about a thing, old love. Christopher swears Darryl's electron gun is broken—it began to go haywire after popping Jane's aneurysm—and he has no idea how to repair it and can't afford to pay a repairman. Money between us is sort of a touchy business, but that's another topic.

The city as I say is a constant pain and hassle and yet looking back at Eastwick it had its negative side too. (Tommy Gorton sent me some clippings from the cheap Xeroxed sheet that is no substitute for the *Word* and they *did* sell Nemo's, finally, but Dunkin' Donuts has promised to preserve some of its historical features in their renovation. And the Unitarians put off their anti-Iraq rally until after Labor Day and it pretty much fizzled anyway, there's not the fury Vietnam aroused, volunteer soldiers and National Guard call-ups are doing the dying and people are more worried about the economy.) But I began to tell you: one night after roaming around with Christopher—I know, I abandoned you those last ten days or so but I was fighting to save your life, seducing a man with a very weak voltage for the fair sex and a cold-hearted murderer to boot—he had to get back to the Neffs', Greta was always pulling a huge poisonous sulk after twigging that he was seeing me, and all alone in that section between Hemlock and Vane—I was trying to get back to where the BMW was parked on upper Dock Street—I stepped into the most awful darkness, like stepping into a bottomless puddle, I can't describe it, up near the land next to the Union Church, that used to be Congregational and before that the Puritan meetinghouse with these three-hour sermons and nothing but dying coals in footwarmers to keep you from freezing. There were no streetlights or houselights on, though I was near a house, that of somebody I didn't know—and how many houses, when you think about it, in Eastwick *did* belong to people we didn't know, though we *thought* we knew everybody—and I was in this antique darkness, just a pocket of it left over from the forest when the forest was everywhere and people would go to bed in these miserable villages terrified of Indians when the sun went down. Suddenly I couldn't see anything, just the shapes of trees and bushes—tall ones, arborvitae probably—against the slightly paler sky, no stars in it, no moon, and me utterly lost and blind just a few blocks from the Superette pouring light onto the sidewalk and the late sailboats motoring back into the harbor and the drop-out kids hanging out noisily at the Ben & Jerry's where the barbershop used to be. I could hear the traffic swishing but was as alone as in a desert, it was like being locked into a closet as a child, which is something I can remember my Neanderthal parents threatening to do but I don't think they ever actually *did*. I felt then how lightly civilization sits on this continent. There is this darkness waiting to sweep in again.

Chris morbidly liked to visit the graves of Jenny and his parents out in the new section of the Cocumscussoc Cemetery, and there in daylight you could see how the granite markers had aged, darkened with mold and lichen so the names and dates were hard to read. But a lot were recent graves, the edges of the markers still sharp, people I used to know those years in Eastwick, rotting in their long boxes underground but still alive in my head, bright cartoons in my mind down to the way an individual person squinted or laughed or said certain things, their live expressions still in me as if my brain were another sort of cemetery, a floating cemetery, all sparks that will glimmer out like fireflies, like the little volunteer daisies you see on the graves. That was terrifying in another, sunlit kind of way.

But let's not be terrified, you and I. We're survivors. So is Chris. He's been in the apartment and out and in again while I've been writing this. I've checked a few of the technical terms with him, not that you would care. Among the things he's taught me is the amazing reason we see *anything* is that the shell of zipping-around electrons around every atomic nucleus bounces photons back into our eyes. And that electrons are always looking for a gap to fill so it *is* like love as you all poked fun of me for saying. He says to say hi to you and tell you he's sorry if you have any lasting discomfort, he was crazy to blame witchcraft for anything real.

Mucho amor (everybody speaks Spanish here),

"Sukie" was scrawled in red, with that inflated twitchiness of twenty-first-century people unaccustomed to wielding a pen. Beneath it she had written a 212-area telephone number, and an East Side address. Alexandra had skimmed the dense pages of computer type and set the letter down on the glass table, glass that in its horizontal reflection imaged the vertical panes that held her view of tawny, grassy land, high dry prairie from the same dull but beloved Western palette as her spacious living room's adornments—clay pots, Navajo, Zuni, Isleta Pueblo, and less heavy, less spiritually decorated pots by Jim Farlander, displaying his tactful hands as they caressed spinning clay. Small Navajo rugs played little brother to the bigger one nailed to the adobe wall away from the sun. Chairs covered in leather and deep sofas covered in fabric duplicated the same color or lack of it as the cattle country outside.

Alexandra had returned to absence: the absence of massy green Eastern foliage, and, as vivid each morning as a cock's crow, Jim's. She had somehow thought that his absence would repair itself—a wound that would heal, a plant that would rejuvenate. But no, with that tight-lipped manly consistency she had loved, he stayed away, and granted her a silence in which her thoughts could revolve as they would.

There was much to do. His shop, which could afford to languish during the hot months, had to be reopened, and stocked. She must return to the potter's wheel, offering up her own, more tentative Farlander pots. And she could return to sculpting her little bubbies, her little feminist fetishes, and not have to compete with a husband for space in the kiln. Business had accumulated in her absence, though she had paid her cleaning woman, Maria Graywolf, to check on her house and forward bills and letters that looked important. Among the communications that did not look, to Maria's far-sighted, Native American sense of priority, important enough to forward were a number of notices of meetings of the Mabel Dodge Luhan Property advisory board, several tax bills now woefully overdue, a letter from Ward Linklater bemoaning her absence and inviting her to dinner as soon as she returned and ominously advising her in a postscript that neither one of them was getting any younger. Another came from a gallery owner in Santa Fe who wanted to talk to her about a retrospective exhibit of Jim Farlander's "neo-Native" ceramics—she didn't like that "neo-Native," but maybe it was like "post-modern." She would be pleased to see Jim honored, she responded.

She liked having her very own vehicle to drive again,

though the hard-used Ford pickup needed transmission work. It was good to be surrounded again by bright yellow-on-red license plates saying LAND OF ENCHANTMENT, rather than Rhode Island's cool blue-on-white OCEAN STATE. Her resuscitated telephone rang with demands and invitations from her Taos crowd of grousing, hard-drinking artists. Alexandra felt better, more herself. The possibly cancerous unease in her body, the faint seesawing nausea, subsided. Her lack of appetite vanished with her first dip of hot salsa with a dry tortilla, and her first Mexican meal of quesadillas, black beans, and rice. Her feet seemed less numb, though she still stumbled on uneven ground, and struggled to get up from her sofa. She was an old lady, all right; there was no dodging that. Death was around the corner, along with Ward Linklater demanding to share dinner. But back in the West she didn't feel old. She felt like one of those burstingly white thunderheads that don't collapse into rain no matter how high they climb above the mountains. Her old black Lab, Cinder, had survived the two months in a kennel, and he and she resumed their walks in the tawny high country, dog and woman alike hobbled by arthritis and tender feet.

What perfidious delusions, you might say, these Godfor-saken women permit themselves! Forgiving themselves the unforgivable, shedding guilt as casually as when younger they shed their clothes. One of them forming with her dirty hands plump small idols of clay, the other forming a brittle liaison with one of the Devil's own party, the third gone to a warranted doom, her last utterance obscene. The Lord keeps strict accounts; He knows to the penny the debts death calls in. There is no revision of the last accounting— *no* reconstitution, *no* revisiting, *no* assuagement. There is at best for the non-elect blessed oblivion, which ends desire and fear and their tormenting agitation. We thanked Heaven to see the unholy wantons flee our abiding seaside hamlet the second time.

Absorbed in the daily happiness of a real life resumed, Alexandra left Sukie's letter unanswered for months. Christmas season had been coolly sunny and crammed with visiting grandchildren and adult children; all four of them, Marcy, Ben, Linda, and even Eric, had managed to come, in shifts. Marcy, using e-mail and her big-sister prerogatives, had organized it. Alexandra resisted so much conventional attention. Was she really so near to dying, that they all insisted on gathering? She had no Christmas tree but had set up a Peruvian crèche of clay dolls amid her windowsill display of miniature cacti. It fascinated the younger of her grandchildren, who kept pricking their fingers. One of them, Linda's baby, little Beauregard, dropped and broke the baby Jesus lying in His manger of painted clay. The toddler sobbed in terror, conscious of having committed a blasphemy, until Alexandra, employing the deft touch developed in sculpting bubbies, painstakingly glued the several fragments back together. "Better than new," she assured the wide-eyed child.

Afterwards, as the new year unfolded around her, Sukie's letter nagged the lonely matriarch. There had been cheer in it, a reaching out, widow to widow. She could picture her friend's pert and avid face, its faded freckles and the plump upper lip that gave her expression in rare repose a tentative, bruised vulnerability.

One bleak January day, with a dusting of overnight snow on the oleander and the prickly pear outside her picture window, and with the fresh fall radiant on the Sangre de Cristo Range far in the east, she impulsively telephoned the number that Sukie had penned in red. The distant instrument rang so often that she expected the answering machine to pick up; but the voice was suddenly Sukie's. It said, "Hello?" Alexandra knew from just the chastened, hollow tone of this one word that Christopher had left her; he had melted back into his half-world, the half he had inherited from Darryl Van Horne. "Lexa?" the wary voice asked, with witchy intuition.

"*Well*," Alexandra answered, pleased. "Where shall we go together this year?"

JOHN UPDIKE was born in 1932, in Shillington, Pennsylvania. He graduated from Harvard College in 1954, and spent a year in Oxford, England, at the Ruskin School of Drawing and Fine Art. From 1955 to 1957 he was a member of the staff of *The New Yorker*. His novels have won the Pulitzer Prize, the National Book Award, the American Book Award, the National Book Critics Circle Award, the Rosenthal Award, and the Howells Medal. In 2007 he received the Gold Medal for Fiction from the American Academy of Arts and Letters. John Updike died in January 2009.